Cop

Cover design © 2016 by Resplendent Media

No part of this book may be reproduced in any form or by any electronic or mechanical means, including information storage and retrieval systems, without written permission from the author, except for the use of brief quotations in a book review.

This book is a work of fiction. Names, Characters, places, and incidents are either the product of the author's imagination or are used fictitiously, and any resemblance to actual persons, living or dead, events, or locales is entirely coincidental.

The following story contains mature themes, strong language and sexual situations. It is intended for mature readers.

All characters are 18+ years of age and all sexual acts are consensual.

Table of Contents

Introduction 3
Chapter 1 5
Chapter 2 7
Chapter 3 10
Chapter 4 14
Chapter 5 19
Chapter 6 21
Chapter 7 30
Chapter 8 38
Chapter 9 42
Chapter 10 45
Chapter 11 50
Chapter 12 54
Chapter 13 58
Chapter 14 62
Chapter 15 67
Chapter 16 71
Chapter 17 75
Chapter 18 85
Chapter 19 97
Chapter 20 103
Chapter 21 107
Chapter 22 111
Chapter 23 116
Chapter 24 120
Chapter 25 125
Chapter 26 129

Chapter 27 134

Chapter 28 139

Chapter 29 144

Chapter 30 146

Chapter 31 149

Chapter 32 156

Chapter 33 161

Chapter 34 166

Chapter 35 174

Chapter 36 178

Chapter 37 185

Chapter 38 193

Chapter 39 199

Chapter 40 207

Chapter 41 215

Chapter 42 222

Chapter 43 227

Chapter 44 232

Chapter 45 239

Chapter 46 245

Chapter 47 251

Chapter 48 257

Chapter 49 266

Chapter 50 271

Chapter 51 277

Chapter 52 281

Chapter 53 286

Also By Lauren Landish 293

Introduction

Don't forget to check out <u>Ambition</u>, Book 2 in the Mr. Dark series!

Sophie

Medical student Sophie White is working two jobs to pay for her college tuition. But when she meets the handsome, dark and mysterious Mark, she is thrust into a world that she never knew existed.

Mark

A man of confidence, Mark exudes a quiet power and seductiveness, but who he is and how he acquired his wealth remains a mystery. When he meets the lovely Sophie White, he is smitten, and despite every fiber in his body telling him not to, he brings her into his dark world.

* * *

Sophie

Mark turned to me, his eyes smoldering and powerful. "Sophie, if you want me to leave, all you have to do is ask. I can walk out that door, and Tuesday we'll have a very nice, very polite date."

"Or?"

"Or I can stay."

Mark's words were accompanied by a promise of something in his eyes, something I'd never felt before. Sensual, and utterly satisfying, his eyes said to me that if I let him stay, my life would never be the same again. Still, my hand reached for the doorknob, resting on it for a moment before falling away to hang by my side. I turned and walked towards him, putting my arms around his neck. It was so different than the kiss in the parking lot. Without my high heels on, he almost towered over me, looking down into my eyes. "You know, we never did finish that dance."

Chapter 1
Part 1 - Sophie

"Come on Sophie, you've been cooped up in your apartment for weeks now."

The needling voice in my ear belonged to Tabby Williams, my best friend. A relentless man chaser, she lived by the motto YOLO. Five foot five, a hundred and fifteen pounds, with auburn red hair and blue eyes, she could pretty much seduce any man she wanted.

How the two of us became friends is a mystery that really had a lot to do with luck more than anything else. Coming into a new city from high school, the two of us had been put together in the freshman dorms by pure random assignment of the computer. I had been sitting at my desk, trying to set up my computer when Tabby walked in, two jocks already following her, carrying some of her bags.

There should have been no reason for the two of us to hit it off as friends, but we did. When my 'freshman fifteen' ballooned into my 'freshman forty-five,' it was Tabby who not only made sure that the idiots around campus didn't give me any crap, but also helped me work my way back down.

"It's all my fault anyway," she told me over and over again during my sophomore and junior years, "I'm the one who kept ordering the bargain double large pizzas and then only eating three slices."

You can see how it went. By the end of junior year, we were officially known among our social group as *The Odd Couple*, and did everything together. It was Tabby who convinced me to get a tattoo on my shoulder during senior year, and it was I who convinced Tabby not to just jump into marriage with Ted Bickerstaff, the frat boy she'd been dating who saw her more for her tight ass and perky tits than the young woman I called my friend.

"You came to college to get your MA, not your M-R-S," I told her. When Ted got caught cheating on his senior thesis and kicked out, she thanked me by taking me to the Bahamas for Spring Vacation.

Unfortunately, graduation caused us to drift apart some. Tabby went immediately to work on her MBA, while I had to pick up two jobs, one as an unpaid intern in a local emergency room as a way to get my foot in the door with the local healthcare providers, and another tending bar at a local Irish tavern. I didn't blame Tabby, while she didn't talk to her folks that often, they were able to pay for it. Mine couldn't. But over the past two years, we'd gone from seeing each other every day to maybe three or four times a month.

Tonight was one of my few nights off, and I had originally planned to spend it doing some long overlooked cleaning of my apartment, and then crash. I had an early double shift at the ER the next morning running files, doing admin stuff, and avoiding Dr. Green staring at my ass. He's a creepy bastard, plain and simple. When Tabby called at six thirty, I knew my plans were going out the window.

"Tabby, I've got a seven in the morning start down at the ER tomorrow," I said to her, trying to get out of it, not that it ever worked. "Seriously, can't we put this off until Saturday?"

"Are you kidding? DJ Manik is only in town through tonight. He's one of the best, and I was able to score tickets for three of us. So I invited you and Kelly. You know you two had fun the last time we went out together. Besides, name the last time you had a Saturday night off. You're either slinging drinks down at the tavern, or down in the ER treating the same idiots you would have been serving any other night."

"I know, but you know what's going to happen. You're going to get drunk, Kelly's going to get picked up by at least two men, and possibly go home with both, and where does that leave me? Catching a cab home after midnight and maybe putting you to bed? You've got a strange idea of what I like to do on a Wednesday night."

Chapter 2
Sophie

Three hours later, I could hear my words running through my head. After picking me up, and then spending twenty minutes harassing me to change into something sexier, Tabby, Kelly and I went to the club. I had to admit, though, the DJ was pretty good. I'm not normally into remixed hip-hop, but this guy was good, putting enough house beats into it that I thought it was pretty damn decent.

Still, as soon as we were in, both girls had drinks in their hands and men orbiting them like they had gravity wells or something. As the third wheel, I soon found myself alone at the bar, while Tabby and Kelly worked the dance floor. I looked on enviously as they had two super hot guys each, teasing and grinding until I was sure the guys were about ready to blow a load in their pants. The night was going exactly as I thought it'd go.

Sighing, I took my club soda and headed upstairs. The music was a bit quieter up there, and I could at least think for a moment. Looking down on the dance floor, I considered my options. It was kind of like those old *Tom & Jerry* cartoons I watched as a kid, when the devil would pop up on one shoulder while the angel popped up on the other. On one hand, I could go down to the floor and get myself my own guy. I mean, I'm nowhere near as hot as Tabby, but I considered myself at least average.

By now, I'd lost most of the weight Tabby had helped me put on in my early college days. At five foot seven, one hundred and forty-nine pounds, green eyes and brown hair, I had gotten myself into a little better shape, and I'm sure I could find myself a guy to dance with down there. Still, I knew my stomach still had a bit of a pouch, but with the outfit I was wearing, it wasn't going to show. That was my first option, and perhaps the most fun.

The second option was the smarter one. Enjoy my drink, make sure that Tabby and Kelly were set for the night, maybe sit and enjoy the music for a few, and then head on home. It was a smart idea. I mean, I was in my last year of my Master's degree, and could look forward to becoming a physician's assistant within six months. I'd been volunteering in the ER to work on getting a reputation on top of my internship, and hopefully getting a letter of recommendation. Showing up with a hangover and sleep deprived was not the best way to do it.

I was still deciding which option to take when I saw him for the first time.

The funny part was, he didn't look all that out of the ordinary. He was about six feet tall, maybe a hundred and seventy or eighty pounds, dirty blonde hair, and was wearing a black silk shirt with what looked like designer jeans. What caught my attention though was the way he carried himself. The only thing I can think of to describe it is that he looked like a lion on one of those Animal Planet documentaries, relaxing amidst a savannah of prey. He exuded confidence, but not in that cocky way that I saw a lot of the posers in the club try and pretend to be. He didn't need to puff out his chest, and I didn't see him wearing any bling at all.

What caught my eye the most about him was that he was looking at me. I checked both left and right before I knew, but he was looking at me, that was for sure. He nodded to me and smiled, making his way through the crowd with lithe grace to approach me. "What's your name?"

It wasn't the most original opening line that a man has ever used on me, but there was something in his eyes that said *I don't need a come on, you're going to want to talk to me*. It was true, honestly. I wanted to talk with this man.

"My name's Sophie," I told him, giving him what I hoped was my best smile. "What's yours?"

"Mark," he said, offering his hand. I shook, and was pleased by what I felt. There was a restrained strength in his grip. I could tell he knew he could crush my hand, but he didn't feel the need to. He held my hand for a moment before letting go. "So you're a nurse."

His comment took me off guard. How in the hell did he know that? "Close, but not quite," I replied, shaken. "I'm in school to become a physician's assistant. How'd you know that?"

"Your thumb and the tip of your forefinger is callused, like someone who has done a lot of injections or carried a knife. You could have been a chef, but your hands aren't built like a chef's. Also, your hands are really heavily lotioned. The only jobs I know that need that are either manual laborers who work with greasy tools, or medical professionals who are constantly washing your hands with chemical filled junk. I didn't say doctor because you're too young."

I was impressed. "Wow. Can you tell me what sort of hand cream I use, too?"

"Aveeno Oat Complex Cream," he replied with a grin. "The almost total lack of odor and no greasiness at all gives it away. It's a good choice, by the way. I like to use Nivea with CoQ10 myself in winter."

I couldn't help by laugh. He was dead on. "Wow, you're pretty observant. Just what do you do with all that observation skill?"

Mark smiled, and there was a hint of danger in his smile. More than ever, he reminded me of a predator, and I wondered for a moment if I was his prey. "I'm a freelance troubleshooter," he told me. "My clients contact me whenever there's an issue that they can't take care of themselves. I go out and make sure their businesses are protected, and that they aren't going to have any problems."

"Interesting," I replied, smiling. Suddenly, a thought came to my head. "Listen, would you like to dance?"

Mark chuckled and shook his head. "Not really. I came down here tonight thinking it was R&B night, not dance-house. But, I needed to blow off some steam, so I stuck around. Glad I did, really."

Chapter 3
Mark

I'd seen Sophie long before she saw me. I had come to the club about two hours earlier to meet with a business associate of mine who owned a partial stake in the club. In return for his investment, the club gave him a good place to conduct business where the police would find it hard to set up wiretaps or surveillance. After the meeting, I found three women who wanted to have some fun, typical club girls, but nothing too shabby. It actually was a pretty good club.

She carried herself like a woman who was still a bit unsure of her own attractiveness. Five-seven before her three-inch heels, with a nice figure, but she hid it with a looseness to her blouse that was supposed to be sexy, but actually disguised the curves of her body. I had almost dismissed her from my mind when I saw her peel off from her two girlfriends to come upstairs. Most of the third wheels I've seen in this club either end up getting themselves shitfaced, or just turn into some fratboy's slampig, neither of which I find sexy in the least.

This girl, though, she looked like she had her head pretty well screwed on, other than her self-image. She wasn't downing alcohol for false courage, and she wasn't clinging to anybody who'd give her attention. I decided she was worth my time, and a hell of a lot more interesting than Tammy, Sunny, and whatever the other girl's name was.

"All right you three, go have some fun or something. I've got something to do," I said, disentangling them from my arms. What's-her-name had been pressing her newly enhanced breasts into my side and gave me a pout. I rolled my eyes and looked at her. "Baby, you head downstairs and you'll have all the cock you want in about two minutes looking the way you do."

I hadn't meant it as a compliment, she was a dumb slut, but she took it that way anyway and smiled. She pulled a business card of all things out of the edge of her bra and handed it to me. "Call me some time, sugar?"

I glanced at it, and noted that her name was Rachel, and she was a legal secretary. I momentarily wondered if she was sucking her attorney boss' cock or not. Then again, maybe her boss was a woman and she could have been munching rug. Either way, she didn't look or act smart enough to be worthwhile to any business outside of a strip club. "Sure baby," I said, pretending to tuck the card into my pocket while secretly palming it. No way was I going to call her. "But go have fun for now."

Before the three could say anything, I disappeared into the crowd, working my way around in a large circle. The upper floor of the club is laid out in a large ring shape, with three staircases leading to the main floor. The VIP rooms are along the back wall, closest to my business associate's office, and I made my way past them where the five bodyguards gave me a respectful berth. I kept my eyes on the tall woman and worked around until I was ready for her to notice me. My impression of her increased when she noticed me more quickly than I'd anticipated.

After introducing myself, we fell into easy conversation. Sophie was smart and funny, although I quickly could tell that she was overly self-conscious about her appearance. Looking at the way she constantly did her best to twist her waist or hide her stomach, I assumed she was one of those girls who had lost a lot of weight, probably within the past three or four years. In any case, she was, in my opinion, sexy as hell.

"Listen, would you like to dance?" she asked me all of a sudden, biting her lip, not in that intentional *I'm trying to be sexy* way, but instead as an unconscious expression of her want for me, and her own self-doubt.

I hadn't come to dance, especially not to the music that was playing tonight, so I tried my best to decline politely.

"Oh," she said, only slightly dejected. She wanted to continue on with our conversation, but she didn't know what to do next. We were in a club, after all.

I decided to take her out of her misery. "I don't particularly like this music. How about we get a VIP room, where we can control what we listen to? It'll be quieter."

Sophie gave me a sideways glance. "You must think I'm the sort of girl who does things in clubs often."

I threw back my head and laughed, honestly amused. "Sophie, that was the farthest thing from my mind. I just wanted to talk more and get to know you. Besides, like Chris Rock said, there's no sex in the champagne room."

Sophie returned my laughter, her tension now broken. I could tell by the way she carried herself that she wanted me, but she also wasn't the type of girl who slept with a man on the first night. "Okay. First, let me check on my friends. I don't need a guilt trip from them if they're looking for me."

"That's fine. I'm going to get something from the bar. Would you like something?"

Sophie

I thought about Mark's offer for a moment, then smiled. "One drink only, but nothing strong. I have an early shift at the ER tomorrow and I can't afford to be hung over."

I had expected Mark to be resistant to the idea. Most men, when they offer me a drink, are looking for one thing. Most of them are upset when they realize that I'm not an easy lay. Mark took it in stride, his confident smile growing. I seemed to have gone up a notch in his eyes. "That's fine. How about a special mimosa?"

I don't know if Mark was lucky or just really observant, but he picked the one drink that I enjoy most. "What's so special about them?"

"I know it's going to sound weird, but the bar here has a special mimosa that mixes the orange juice part with another blend of juices. I like it, it has a bit more oomph to it taste wise than a normal mimosa."

I thought about it and nodded. "Sounds great. Meet you by the bar in a few minutes?"

Mark nodded and stood up, offering me his hand. When he helped me to my feet, I could feel his hand resting on my upper arm, his slightly callused hands sending tingles through my skin. His dark eyes looked into mine, and I could feel my heart speeding up another notch. "I'll have your drink ready," he said calmly.

Instead of escorting me to the stairs, he turned and almost melted into the crowd, leaving me to make my own way down to the floor. As I walked, I thought about him. I'm not the sort of woman who sleeps with a guy on the first meeting, but there was something about Mark that made me want to open up to him, to beg him to take me back to his place. It was an unfamiliar feeling, but admittedly, it felt perversely amazing.

It didn't take me long to find Tabby and Kelly. They were at one of the tables surrounding the dance floor with two guys. "Hey ladies, how's it going?"

"Ah, we're doing greaaat!" Tabby said, giving me a drunken giggle. She was already at least tipsy, if not fully drunk. "This is..... what's your name again?"

"John," the beefcake next to her said. He was a bit older than Tabby and me, probably getting close to thirty. He was fit, and I could tell he had money. Still, there was something about him that didn't do it for me, and I was confident that even a drunk Tabby could handle him. "How you doin?"

Jesus, he sounded like a stereotypical refugee from the Jersey Shore. How'd he get to our town?

"Tabby, can I talk for a second?"

"Sure," she giggled, wiggling out of the booth. I had to give John credit, he didn't look too worried about it, although the way his eyes were fixed on Tabby's ass was something I didn't appreciate. Once we were a few feet away, she looked at me. "What's up?"

Tabby's lack of drunken slur in her voice made me do a momentary double take. "You doing okay?" I asked, looking into her eyes.

"I'm fine," she said, leaning in. "I'm just planning on cockteasing this guy for a while. Decent dancer, but not good enough for me."

I smiled and looked her over again. "Okay. So you're just acting a bit with him. Look.... I kind of met a guy upstairs. You good on getting home by yourself if you need to?"

Tabby smiled and squeezed my hands in glee. "Good. It's been too long for you. Go have some fun, and I hope it works out for you."

I was touched by the fact that not only did Tabby care enough about me to encourage me to have some fun, but also respected me enough to trust my judgment. "Thanks, Tabs. You and Kelly take care of yourselves. Stay safe."

"You know me, babe. Have fun."

I left Tabby, who twirled and giggled again in her *drunken* state, her red hair whipping around to go back to the table. I found Mark by the bar, a special mimosa in his hand. "Here you are," he said. "My drink will be delivered up to the room in a few minutes. Shall we?"

I could barely control my breathing as I walked up the stairs to the second floor, and I could feel Mark's eyes look me over, especially my legs. I'm proud of them, they're well toned, but this time, I felt nervous. He was a very sexy man with a silent confidence that I found seductive, and my mind kept thinking about him and his hands running over my legs, cupping my ass. I shook my head, trying to clear my thoughts before goosebumps broke out on my skin.

Chapter 4
Mark

The VIP room I got was the smallest in the club, which was fine by me. I don't roll with a posse or have an entourage. The bodyguard, a big guy named Jerome that I knew was effective for his size rather than his skill, gave me a respectful nod as I came to the door. "Sir."

"Jerome. I have a drink order coming up. It's the only interruption I would like for a while."

"Of course. You'll have privacy."

I led Sophie into the VIP Room, closing the door behind us. The thick insulation cut off the house music, and I took a deep breath of relief. I detest house music. "So what would you like to listen to?" I asked, as I let the silence wash over me in an awesome wave. "The sound system in here is connected to an online database. I think they once told me it has over a million songs available."

With her student budget outfit comprising of a wine-red satin top, only semi-tight black skirt and forty dollar heels, I would have expected either pop or hip-hop. "Does it have Hans Zimmer?"

Her request pleased me. While Zimmer is no Beethoven, he's one of the best modern composers today in my estimation. Williams is the master of the brass, but Zimmer's got him beat in percussion and strings. "I'm sure I can find something," I said, keying the touchpad and searching. Finding what I wanted, I tapped in the request for random selections, and soon could hear my personal favorite come muted over the speakers. "What do you think?"

"*Time*," Sophie replied, taking a sip of her mimosa. "Nice. I've used his work on *Crimson Tide* and Nolan's Batman movies for cardio workouts myself, but this is a pretty good one too."

I sat down next to her, and for the next hour, we discussed music and art of all things. It was nice, an amazing change of pace from the normal conversations I have in my line of work, or the typical conversations I have with women. I didn't once have to discuss just where I got my shirts from, or how expensive the watch I had on was.

As we talked, I was more and more impressed by Sophie. She kept herself to only two mimosas, sipping the drink carefully and not letting herself get drunk at all.

I didn't tell her that the whole time I was sipping flat ginger ale, a modification of an old trick that I picked up from reading *Batman* as a little boy. With a drop of orange food coloring added, it looks just like aged scotch. By the time the last song drifted away, I knew that I wanted to see her again.

"You know, if you don't mind, I think I would like that dance now," I said, setting my empty glass aside and standing up. The VIP room had a small open area in the front. I'm sure it's been used for plenty of dancing of a different type than what I was wanting, "Would you?"

"I'd enjoy that," Sophie said, letting me pull her to her feet. She wasn't swaying at all, which was a good sign to me. She had handled the alcohol well. "What did you have in mind?"

Instead of answering, I tapped my request into the controller. The lights dimmed slightly, and slow saxophone filled the air. "Slow dancing should always be done to jazz," I told her, pulling Sophie in tight. My hands found the swell of her hips, resting lightly on the generous curve there. There's a saying that I agree with, even though I deride most people who use it. Real women *do* have curves, and Sophie's were wonderful. Pulling her in tight, her breasts pressed against my chest, I could feel both of us breathing heavier, our eyes locked on each other as the slow jazz morphed, acquiring a heavy undercurrent of bass that brought us closer and closer together. I could feel Sophie's nipples harden against my chest, and my cock was aching inside my jeans, when she pulled back, suddenly shy.

"I'm sorry...." she said, her hand resting on the swell of one beautiful breast. "I forgot. I can't. I have early work in the morning."

I was just about to reply when my cell phone, which I keep only for work, rang. I stifled a curse and pulled it out of my back pocket, flipping open the old fashioned looking phone. Despite outward appearances, it has all of the security technology you can get. It pays to be secure in my profession. "Yes?"

Sophie

I couldn't believe what I'd just told him. I regretted what I'd said the moment it left my lips. Could I be any more of a geek? I don't know what came over me, the man was obviously into me, and I most certainly was into him. I guess I just got scared on where we were headed.

Mark listened on the phone for less than a minute before sighing and nodding. "Fine. I'll take care of it tonight. Yes, I'll call you when it's done."

He slammed shut his phone and looked over at me. I could still see the impressive swell of his cock in his jeans and my body was still thrumming with arousal. Still, I could read it on his face. "Work?"

"The danger of being a freelancer," he said with a small smirk. "On the other hand, I can set my own vacations."

"I understand. Well, I should go anyway. It's a long cab ride back over to the North Side."

Mark shook his head and grinned. "You won't have to. The client that called me, they're located on the North Side. I can give you a ride if you want. I promise, I'll be a total gentleman."

I looked at him and considered his offer. Again, the angel and the devil were sitting on my shoulders, both of them talking in my ear. *You should really go home and take a long cold shower, get ready for work tomorrow*, the angel said. *If you like him, you could get his phone number and set up a real date. If he's actually interested in you, he'd be willing to do that.*

Yeah, and if you do that, you can spend another couple of months with no sex except your fingers and the dildo you keep in the nightstand, the devil replied in my other ear. *And for fuck's sake, you're on the pill, even though its been ages since you've seen any action. Do you remember how he felt? He's fucking ripped, and that cock you felt pressed against you, honey . . .*

I could hear the devil give a little cheer of victory before whispering a final piece of advice. *Just keep Harpgirl over there quiet, and get his phone number too. If he's halfway as good as we think, you're going to want to call him up again.*

My decision made, I focused back on Mark, who was giving me a perplexed look. "Sorry, just thinking," I said with a sheepish grin. "Okay, I'd love a ride home. You know where King Street and Graham Avenue meet?"

"Yes, there's a few apartments in that area. Not a great area, but I've seen worse."

There was no condescension in his voice, just a simple statement of fact. It was actually kind of cool to hear it, a lot of guys gave me a look like I was a hood rat when they found out where I lived. "Vista Garden Apartments."

"All right. Let's go then."

When we left the VIP room, Mark slipped the attendant outside a folded up bill.

"Thanks for the service J," he said quietly, before leading me out. I felt a big boost to my ego when I saw Tabby and Kelly, both still playing with their boy toys, catch sight of us. Tabby did a double take before clapping and giving me a big thumbs up from across the club. "I see your friends approve."

I glanced over at Mark, who was grinning confidently and looking at me with a look in his eyes that bordered on cocky. He turned his grin to Tabby and returned the thumbs up, causing my bubbly friend to burst out in laughter. Over the loud club music, I couldn't tell what she said to Kelly, but I trusted Tabs. She'd had my back for a long time. If I was leaving the club with a handsome guy, Tabby would be cheering me on.

Walking through the parking lot, I was surprised at first when I felt Mark take my hand as we walked. "I enjoyed our talk and our dance," Mark said. "I'd like to do it again sometime."

Whoa. Was this vision of masculinity really asking me out on a date? "I'd like that," I finally said. "Give me your phone number?"

"I've got a card in the car," he said, reaching into his pocket and thumbing his security tab. I was only partially surprised when an electric blue Mercedes responded.

"Wow, nice wheels. What is it?" I asked, looking at the gull-wing doors. "I've never seen a Mercedes like this."

"GT-S, all electric drive," Mark replied, opening the door and helping me into the low-slung passenger seat. I know I gave him a very nice look at my legs getting in there, but I didn't mind at all. "I'm into being green."

And spending it, I whispered to myself after he closed the door and came around, checking out the interior. All leather seats, a Bose sound system, and enough of those little touches that said this car was easily in the six-figure price range. Whoever Mark was, he had money. I waited until he settled into the driver's seat before saying anything. "I have to say, it's an impressive car."

"Thanks. Cars are one of the only things I like to splurge on," he said, turning on the engine.

The ride back to my apartment was surreal. Other than the wind flowing over the vehicle, it's almost totally silent. "Wow, you could be a ninja in this thing," I commented when we were about halfway to my home. "I'd never hear you coming."

Mark nodded and I could hear him chuckling under his breath. "I enjoy it that way," he said. "What about you, what do you drive?"

I laughed and looked over at him. "You'd laugh if I told you."

"Oh, come on. You know if you don't, I'm going to spend five minutes in your parking lot guessing what it is until you tell me one way or another."

The North Side isn't exactly Hell's Kitchen New York, but it's not the sort of place a guy just hangs out in a Mercedes sports coupe either. I didn't want Mark to have any problems, so I gave in. "Fine. I drive an old Honda Civic. I mean, the thing's so old they still have that old badge on the back, the one that looks like it says CVCC instead of Civic?"

"I know what you mean. I'm not afraid to note my first car was one of those too," Mark said. He glanced at me out of the corner of his eyes and smirked. "What, you thought I was born with money? When you get to know me well enough, you'll find all sorts of surprises."

The comment touched me. Maybe he really did want to see me again and wasn't just giving me a line back in the parking lot.

Chapter 5
Mark

The Vista Garden Apartments weren't the worst apartments I'd ever been to. My work takes me to worse places sometimes, although I didn't exactly like hanging out in locales like this. I spotted Sophie's Civic almost immediately, and noted that it was parked in the slot for apartment 212. I filed it away, along with the fact that her car had a parking sticker for not only the local university, but the university hospital. Her story about being a student wasn't bullshit.

"I'm sorry that our dance got cut off," I told her after stopping the car. "I know it's a bit sudden, but are you busy Sunday night?"

"Yeah," she told me sadly. "I'm doing a night shift at the ER. But I'm free Tuesday."

"Tuesday it is. I'll pick you up here, seven o'clock Tuesday."

Being the gentleman I am, I went around and opened the door for her, helping her out of my Mercedes before pulling her in for a kiss. Her lips were just as soft as I had hoped, and her body molded itself nicely against me. She was a bit shy at first, but when my tongue probed at her lips, she opened herself willingly, until she was clutching against me. I was tempted to delay my work for the night, but knew that I couldn't. Instead, I broke our kiss regretfully and looked into her eyes. "It was wonderful meeting you, Sophie. Can I ask, what's your last name?"

"Sophie White," she said, biting her lip again in that unconscious sexy way she had. "What about you?"

"Mark Snow," I said, both of us chuckling at the similar nature of our last names. I thought about giving her one of my five different aliases, but I decided against it. "It was a pleasure to meet you, Sophie White."

I headed back to my car before remembering that I promised Sophie my card. Reaching into the slot in between the cell phone holder and my stereo, I grabbed the slim metal case that I kept my cards in. I flipped it open and considered which of my different cards to hand her. Finally, for reasons I still don't fully understand, I handed her my professional card, the one that read "Mark Snow, troubleshooter," along with my cell phone number. I had never given it out to a regular person before.

"Here, just in case you thought I wasn't telling you the truth earlier," I joked, handing her my card. "Call me when you get off work tomorrow?"

Sophie's smile was worth the niggling little voice in my head that was telling me I should have given her one of my aliases. As I drove away into the night, I only hoped my appointment in the North Side wouldn't take me too long.

* * *

Mark

I had bought my Mercedes not for the performance, although it was a great car, but, like Sophie said, for its ability to be totally silent when I wanted it to be. Driving slowly, I crept up until I was about two hundred yards away from my destination before I pulled over and waited. It's one of the advantages of an electric car. I can sit in idle mode in total silence and very few people will notice me.

I have a very hard and fast rule in my line of work, one I've adopted personally. I always make sure the problem is present before I go in and do anything. Too many operators in my profession just go in there regardless of the mess they make. I prefer to prevent future problems for me and my employers, and for that reason, I was highly sought after.

It took me almost thirty minutes to verify that the problem was there, and that I wouldn't be creating a scene or causing more mess by going in. Fine. I reached under the passenger seat of my car and took out my tools.

Time to go to work.

Chapter 6
Sophie

I barely was aware of walking up the steps to my apartment, or going inside and locking the door behind me. When I got to my living room, I flopped down on the couch, trying to find something to watch on TV to wind down. But my mind was still whirling with the feel of Mark's lips on mine, and his strong arms pulling me into him. The confident feel of his kiss was different than any other first kiss I'd ever had, and my body betrayed my morals. I'd never slept with a guy on the first meeting, but I wanted him so badly it literally hurt. If he asked to come in, I'd have most definitely said yes.

"I gotta get a shower," I said to myself, pushing myself up off the couch. "For fuck's sake, I have work in the morning."

Taking off my clothes, I had to literally peel my panties away from my body they were so soaked. The scent of my arousal smacked me in the face, and I moaned, wishing there was something I could do about it. The way my body was feeling, however, I knew that anything I did would be empty. It's kind of like when you know you want a real drink, but all you have around is Diet Dr. Pepper. It's just not good enough.

The cool water of the shower cascaded over my shoulders and hair, which at first helped with my arousal, but when my already tight nipples got bathed in the water, the painful pleasure had me gasping, my head leaning against the tile of the shower, silently begging for something to help release the pressure inside me. I could feel the warm wetness dripping down the insides of my thighs, and knew that if my hands went anywhere near my waist, I'd be masturbating like crazy within seconds. The thing is, if I did, I'd be left frustrated and unsatisfied.

Taking deep, shuddering breaths, I quickly washed the areas that I could without increasing my arousal, and at least getting the sweat washed off of my arms, legs and shoulders. Finally, I did what almost every other time calmed me down. I massaged shampoo into my long hair, an herbal blend that I always use whenever I need inner peace. It takes a long time to wash my hair because it's so thick, so by the time I finished, I thought I might have myself under control.

At least, I thought I was under control, until I got out of the shower. The first sign to me that things weren't as calm as I had hoped was when my nipples tightened again as I pulled my terrycloth robe on. Fireworks sparkled in front of my eyes when the cotton scraped over my breasts, and I had to lean on my sink while I tried to regain control.

"Fuck this," I groaned, looking up into the mirror. The woman who looked back at me was desperate with lust and needed sex, regardless of if it was good or not. "I guess I'm going through a few batteries tonight."

I was heading back to my bedroom, my mind filled with thoughts of Mark's body and my vibrator trying to blend themselves, when a knock came at the door. I stopped and considered ignoring the knock, when it came again. Glancing at the clock on the wall, I could see it was almost eleven thirty.

Tabby, you better be out of cash and smashed out of your mind, I muttered to myself as I headed for the door. *Because if you just came to see if I went home with Mark or not.....*

My quiet monolog cut short when I opened the door, and I saw Mark standing, leaning against the door frame. "Sorry, did I interrupt you?"

I stood there like an idiot for at least five seconds, until Mark's face broke out in a bit of a cocky grin. "I guess I did. How was your shower?"

Looking down at myself, I realized I was still wearing my robe. "Uh.... nice," I stammered, sounding like an idiot. "How did you figure out my apartment?"

Mark chuckled. "How about you let me in your apartment, and I'll tell you?"

I stepped back, the angel of my morals falling silent as Mark's handsome smile melted any resistance I might have had. "Um... sure. Come on in."

I watched as he calmly made his way across my living room and stood in the middle, looking around. "It's nice. A lot of little touches that elevate the place."

"Thanks, I think," I said, closing the door. "But you haven't answered my question."

"Pretty simple, really. You said you had an old Honda, and an old Honda is parked in slot two twelve. I figured it was a pretty safe bet."

I had to admit what he said made sense. "Note to self, don't tell guys I just met about my crappy car," I joked, trying to clear my head. It was hard to do with him standing there. He was even more handsome in the light of my living room than he had been in the muted lights of the club. "But Mark, this is highly irregular."

Mark turned to me, his eyes smoldering and powerful. "Sophie, if you want me to leave, all you have to do is ask. I can walk out that door, and Tuesday we'll have a very nice, very polite date."

"Or?"

"Or I can stay."

Mark's words were accompanied by a promise of something in his eyes, something I'd never felt before. Erotic, sensual, and utterly satisfying, his eyes said to me that if I let him stay, my life would never be the same again. Still, my hand reached for the doorknob, resting on it for a moment before falling away to hang by my side. I turned and walked towards him, putting my arms around his neck. It was so different than the kiss in the parking lot. Without my high heels on, he almost towered over me, looking down into my eyes. "You know, we never did finish that dance."

With liquid grace and restrained strength, Mark pulled me into a dance, both of us moving sensuously and slowly to unheard music. I should have felt stupid. I mean, there I was, in my old terrycloth bathrobe, slow dancing in my living room to no music at all. I should have felt like the world's cheesiest idiot.

Instead, all I was aware of was Mark's eyes, and the feel of his hands on my waist, and the fact that under my robe I was still as naked as the day I was born. I know my breasts were straining against the old cotton, and with each heartbeat I could feel myself growing hotter and hotter.

"You're going to have to ask for it," Mark said, guiding me around until I was leaning against the wall. "So what do you want me to do?"

"Kiss me," I whispered, my mouth suddenly dry. "I want you to kiss me again."

"And?"

I could see the challenge in his eyes, and the smirk on his face. I should have been slapping his face. I should have been calling him a perverted asshole. Instead, I opened my mouth and said the truth. "I want to have sex with you."

His chuckle sent ripples down my spine. "How clinical. Are you going to ask me to put my penis inside your vagina now? Tell me what you really want, Sophie White."

"Fuck me," I said, a plaintive note in my voice I had never heard before. "I want you to fuck me."

Mark pulled me away from the wall, almost sweeping me off my feet as he half carried, half pushed me over to the couch. We fell onto the old sofa in a tangle of arms and legs, Mark somehow turning us in midair so that I landed mostly on top of him. His lips found mine again, demanding and possessive, and I submitted to him willingly. I could feel him pressed against my thigh, and my pussy quivered at the thought of his hard cock penetrating me, filling me up.

I almost screamed when Mark's left hand slipped inside my robe, cupping my right breast and kneading the soft skin. I'm proud of my breasts, which are a rightful D cup, even after losing weight. Mark knew just what he was doing, rubbing his thumb over my nipple until it stood up like a pink gumdrop on my skin, sending jolts of pleasure through my body. "Marrrrkkk," I could hear myself moaning as he left my lips to explore the curve of my neck, his lips sucking and nipping at my skin. It had been far too long since I felt a man on me like he was, and none of the previous ones measured up to Mark. "I need you."

Mark

I could hear the want in her voice. Inside my head, a war was raging. Part of me wanted to be tender, to be romantic and polite. But I had heard it in her voice, and in her eyes. Sophie had been with enough Mr. Nice Guys to fill her dance ticket for a while. She needed a Bad Ass. She wanted me to take charge, to dominate her. I wasn't sure if it was because of prior relationships that went wrong. Or maybe she was a natural submissive, I hadn't made up my mind yet. Either way, me being a nice guy wasn't going to give either of us what we wanted. So I let part of my work personality creep in, not that it was hard after just completing an assignment.

"You're being very demanding," I growled, pushing her up and off of me. The fact that my push took the robe off her shoulders and let it hang from the belt around her waist was an unexpected bonus. Her breasts were perfect, the sort that hung round and full, slightly sloping to mouthwatering pinkish red nipples. It took all my concentration not to just feast upon her breasts hanging there so close to my face. Instead, I tore my eyes away and grinned at her. "If you want something, you need to use the magic word."

I scrambled back and stood up from the couch, my cock straining painfully at my jeans. Fixing a smirk on my face, I reached down and stroked her face, brushing some of her lustrous hair out of her eyes. "On your knees."

Sophie blinked once, then blushed, climbing off the couch and onto the carpet in front of me, kneeling at my feet. The tug of her knees pulled her robe the rest of the way off, revealing her entire body to me. She was even more beautiful nude than she was in her sexy club wear, and my cock pushed at my jeans to the point I swore the zipper was going to burst. She looked up at me with her large, beautiful eyes, her face still slightly pink, and put her hands together on her lap. "Please...."

"You want my cock?" I asked, unbuttoning my shirt with my left hand while stroking her face with my right.

"Yes, Mark. I want your cock," Sophie said, bringing her hand up to rub the bulge in my jeans. She ran her hand all the way from my balls to the tip, her eyes growing wider with every inch she found. "It's huge."

I shrugged. "You can handle it," I said, letting my shirt fall from my shoulders and to the floor. Sophie moaned softly, and started working on my belt, which she unbuckled quickly before freeing my cock. Her soft hand wrapped around me, and I remembered talking about hand lotion with her in the club, causing me to smile. God bless Aveeno for sure.

Sophie smiled and ran her tongue over her lips, caught up in the moment, looking up at me as if she was waiting for permission.

I nodded, moving over and sitting on the couch, my legs spread. Sophie reached out with her tongue, licking me slowly around the head of my cock while her hand slowly pumped my shaft. I groaned softly, enjoying the wonderful tingle her tongue caused, the tip of her tongue going down to trace the veins of my cock. She was amazing, finding all of those secret little places that left me oozing precum, close to the edge. "Stop," I commanded, barely controlling my voice.

Sophie sat back, and I regretted the strictness in my voice. She wanted me to control her, not hurt her feelings. I sat forward and pulled her up, giving her a tender kiss. "I said stop because I want you to do something that no other woman has ever been able to do," I said, stretching the truth just a bit. Other women had, but never one with a naturally endowed body. "I want you to wrap those beautiful tits of yours around my cock until you need me inside you."

The grin that spread over her face was worth the temptation. I knew that as wonderful as she felt, any more stimulation would leave me dangerously close to coming even before she did. Still, I couldn't help but give a small gasp when she lifted her breasts and swallowed my cock between them, almost totally disappearing between the soft mounds. Working her hands up and down, Sophie stroked my cock with her breasts, her tongue flicking out to taste my precum every time the tip emerged. It was heaven, plain and simple. Still, I kept the slightly cocky grin on my face, and hummed my pleasure.

Sophie

A part of me thought that Mark was being playful with his arrogance as I worked and licked his cock, but I really didn't care. I wanted him, and I had to have him. His precum was salty and sweet on my lips, and I could barely contain myself as I kept working my breasts up and down. Finally, I couldn't take it anymore, and I looked up at him with my needy eyes. "Fuck me."

He stood up and pulled me to my feet a bit roughly, pulling me over to the edge of the couch and pushing me over the arm.

I could feel the juices dripping down the inside of my thighs, my ass and pussy exposed to him. He stood behind me, the tip of his cock barely brushing against my hamstrings, teasing me with what I needed so badly. I sobbed in need and frustration as he dragged the thick length up my left ass cheek before letting it slide down the right, then actually taking it in his hand and slapping it up against my clit. "Go ahead and beg, Sophie. I know you want to."

Swallowing the sobs of need, I looked back over my shoulder, tears filling my eyes, and begged. "Mark, please. Fuck me, make me yours."

Mark

My heart almost wavered when I saw Sophie's eyes brimming with tears before she begged. Still, I went with my gut, and promised myself that I would give her the climax of her life after I heard her beg, as a reward and a thank you. Keeping my eyes fixed on hers, I slid my cock inside, working it in and out in slow, short thrusts.

I'd never felt a pussy like hers before. I've read about finding that supposed perfect fit, I mean, I'm a guy. I've heard it described as everything from warm apple pie, to velvet gloves, to slippery vacuums. I don't know what the hell a slippery vacuum is, but I can say that being inside Sophie was a paradise. The pressure of her muscles against my cock was perfect, lighting up every nerve in my body and causing my heart to literally skip a beat. "Damn," I whispered half under my breath.

"It's been a while, sorry," Sophie said in apology, not understanding my meaning. Instead of correcting her, I pulled back, pushing in again and again until I felt something that was a rarity, the trimmed hair at the base of my cock settle against her ass. Few women could take my cock without complaint, and here I was with a beautiful, voluptuous woman bent over for me, not only *not* complaining, but moaning in a lustful release, pushing back against me.

I started thrusting, long smooth strokes that I knew I could sustain a while. While on the outside I kept up the cocky persona, inside my mind I was feeling a tectonic shift in my heart and soul. In my line of work, it doesn't pay to get close to anyone. It's too dangerous, for both of us. You could be taken away from each other at a moment's notice. But regardless, I could feel myself shifting on the inside, wanting to please her more and more, and I knew she was working her way inside me, even if she didn't realize it. It scared me, and it thrilled me.

Sophie

The first tickle of Mark's pubic hair against me left me breathless. When he started thrusting, his thick cock pistoning in and out of me, I was left senseless, waves of bliss cascading through me. Each slap of his hips against me was a sharp reminder to breathe, or else I would have suffocated having forgotten how to.

Mark's cock penetrated me deeply, deeper than any man had ever done before. My fingers curled into tight balls on the sofa, my breasts pressed against the cushion, and I groaned loudly, not caring if my neighbors, a nosy old lady named Francine and a Hispanic couple, the Mendozas, heard me. "More, please. Give me more."

Mark responded by speeding up, his cock filling me faster and faster. I almost lost it when I felt him start to circle his hips as he thrust, his cock almost twirling inside me with every hammering penetration, touching me in different ways each time, lighting up my body. I could see stars, and was on the verge of blacking out, when a thought roared into my brain, dragging me back to consciousness.

If I was role-playing as submissive to Mark, then I couldn't come first. Not without his permission. Instead, I mustered every bit of strength I had and pushed back harder, squeezing my body around him, trying to please this sexy man who was giving me the fuck of my life. The least I could do was try and give as good as I was getting.

I don't know if what I was doing had any effect, but it sent explosions off in my body. I pushed and grunted, my sexual side consuming me as his perfect cock pounded me relentlessly, his hips punishing my ass cheeks. My orgasm was rushing up on me, but I held on grimly, gritting my teeth to please Mark, giving him everything I had.

Still, it wasn't enough. I couldn't hold back any longer, and clamped down as hard as I could, lust and pleasure and regret choking my voice. "Mark, I'm going to come," I gasped, "I'm....."

I was going to say *I'm sorry*, but my throat closed up, and my body exploded in climax. I was glad Mark had me bent over the couch, because I lowered my face to the cushions and screamed my joy and pleasure, every nerve in me feeling the pleasure of his cock. Suddenly, I could feel him tense and his cock swell as he began to erupt and satisfy me completely. Relief and accomplishment filled my heart and soul, and I knew that my initial prediction had been right, letting him in was going to change me forever.

* * *

Mark

After our climax, I carried Sophie to her bedroom, laying her carefully on her bed. She only had a queen sized bed, a bit small for me, but I wanted to stay with her. Instead, I stood up, intending to go out to the sofa, maybe get my things and go, when her voice stopped me in my tracks. "Mark," she whispered, her voice close to breaking again into tears, "don't leave. Stay."

I looked over my shoulder at her, realizing my error. How many times had she been *pumped and dumped*, as an associate of mine tended to say? She said she was no easy lay, and I believed her, but I've known plenty of women who weren't easy, but still got walked out on as soon as the guy got his rocks off. I regret to say I've done it myself more than once.

But not with Sophie. I couldn't, not after what she did for me, did to me. Instead, I turned back to her, and knelt next to her bed. "I'm not going anywhere," I whispered, kissing her on the forehead. "I just want to get my cell phone, set my alarm. You've got work in the morning, remember? And I need to get up early too."

She looked at me with those trusting dark eyes of hers and nodded. "Okay."

I walked out of the bedroom and to the living room, scooping up my clothes as I went. My jeans were in a puddle at the edge of the couch where they had worked off my hips while Sophie was bent over the arm rest. The cell phone was in my back pocket, and I could see the flash that said I had a text message waiting for me. I hadn't felt the vibrations with Sophie's distracting presence. I flipped it open, and nodded to myself.

Congratulations on another successful assignment, the text said. *Have another ready. Will call tomorrow afternoon.*

I closed the message box and turned on my alarm, setting it for five thirty. Five hours of sleep. I can operate on that, I've operated on less. Going back into the bedroom, I found Sophie already lightly snoring, her fist tucked under her chin while she lay on her side. I snuggled in behind her and pulled her tight against me. She moaned incoherently, and laid her hand on my arm. "Goodnight," I whispered into her hair, giving it a kiss. "Sweet dreams."

Chapter 7
Sophie

I was downing my second Redbull of the morning when I walked into the emergency room at the University Hospital that Thursday morning. "Morning everyone," I said, stifling a yawn as I put my thumb on the time clock reader. It scanned my print and beeped, noting my time of clock-in. "How is everything?"

Brad and Cassandra, two of my co-workers who were at the desk, glanced up, Cassandra giving me a concerned look. "You okay Sophie? You look like you're going on two hours of sleep."

"More than that," I replied, "but not too much more." After Mark put me to bed the night before, we were supposed to have about five hours or so to get sleep. Instead, I woke up at three in the morning with an intense need to pee. I guess it had something to do with the alcohol the night before, it does that to me sometimes.

Afterward, I couldn't get comfortable again. I didn't blame Mark, my bed is pretty small, but I was used to lying in the exact middle, and kind of sprawling out all over the place. Instead, we had to press our bodies together in order to fit both of us on the bed, which was the cause of the whole problem. I'm sure that was a new experience for him. From appearances, he was very well off.

Regardless of the wonderful sex the night before, feeling Mark's body against me in bed soon had me aroused, and despite my best efforts, I couldn't fall asleep no matter what I did.

My wiggling and squirming woke Mark up, his chuckle turning into a moan as my ass moved around against his rapidly stiffening cock. Of course, one thing led to another, and we had a second round of wonderful sex before I could drop off for more sleep, only to be awoken by the alarm seemingly minutes after closing my eyes. So, my five hours of sleep ended up being about three and a half, broken up into two parts.

"Well, keep on your toes," Brad commented without lifting his eyes from his computer screen. He was responsible for a lot of the record keeping, especially with the insurance providers. When I first started volunteering at the ER, I wondered why he kept a bottle of eye drops next to his keyboard all the time. After helping him out one shift, I stopped wondering. I had glowing letters dancing in front of my eyes the whole rest of my night. How Brad put up with it, I didn't fathom to guess. "Doc

Green is coming in today at noon."

I rolled my eyes. "Green. Well, I guess I could expect it. But why noon? He's normally on morning shift."

"He was in late last night," Cassandra said, a grin on her face. "He was supposed to be out of here at midnight and back in for first shift today."

"So what happened?" I asked, finishing off the last of my energy drink and tossing the empty can into the recycle bin. "I've heard he could pull a shift like that no problem at all."

"The problem is, ten minutes after his shift was technically over, and he was finishing up his paperwork, the ambulance brought in a bleeder," Brad interjected. "From your part of town, even. A loan shark for the Russians, Karl Vaslov. Apparently he was sitting in his living room last night watching *The Daily Show* or something when somebody kicked in his door and attacked. He came in with a laundry list of internal injuries, along with his tongue being cut out. He was pretty much DOA, but wasn't clinically dead yet, so Green had to spend another three hours working on him. Vaslov finally coded out at three thirty this morning, and Green got out of here about four thirty."

"Huh. Well, I guess I'll take the small favors created by the death of a criminal," I replied, wiping my eyes. I caught one piece of crusty eye gunk that I'd missed earlier, the scratchy little bit scraping my cheekbone as I worked it out. "I'm only on until two today, and I've got a shift at the Shamrock this evening. Any chance to get work done without Green around is good for me."

One of the attending physicians, Dr. Morrison, dropped off a chart with a laugh. "Face it, Sophie, if it wasn't for Green, work here would be very boring for you."

I half yawned, half laughed and pulled on my short jacket that showed I was a volunteer assistant on top of my scrubs. "True, Doctor. But I think I'd rather have boring shifts than entertaining ones."

Morrison nodded and grabbed the next chart in the line off the wall. "That's fine. Okay, let's see, I've got you down for health clinic duty starting at ten, but until then stick close. You've been working on your sutures a lot lately I noticed, I might just let you try them out on a real human today."

I liked Morrison. He was in his mid-forties and ugly as sin, but a nice guy. He had even had me over to his house along with a bunch of the other volunteers and med students the summer before for a barbecue, and I was able to spend three hours hanging out with his teenage daughter, who thankfully looked nothing at all like her father. "Thanks, Doc. I promise, I won't sew my fingers to anyone's scalp today."

Morrison nodded. "Better not, or else I'm just going to leave them there. Come on, Mrs. Wong in exam two isn't going to like waiting much longer."

The first three hours of my shift went well, and at ten, I headed over to the community health clinic. A partnership with a local charity, it was a huge tax write-off for both the hospital and the corporation behind the charity. The clinic provided low-cost community health care for the local area, and often gave away services to those who couldn't pay for them.

While noble in nature, the reality was I spent a lot of my time wiping stuffy noses and trying to explain to woefully unprepared, uneducated and uninterested parents that feeding your child real food from the supermarket instead of fast food and convenience store stuff would go a long way towards some of the problems they kept bringing their kids in for.

Their kids didn't need pills for their cold, they needed fresh oranges. Their anemic child would be a lot better off with some spinach or kale with their dinner instead of coming in for shots. Sadly, most of my lectures got nasty looks from parents, and not a week went by without someone loudly stating that I had a lot of nerve trying to tell her how to raise her children.

But today was vaccination day, so I got to give my right thumb a good workout. As I was sticking dose after dose of measles vaccine into little kids' backsides, I reflected that at least the clinic didn't have to deal with the affluent parents some of the private doctors did. I don't think I could have dealt with any soccer moms whipping out blog posts from anti-vax websites and trying to trip me up with 'facts' from Jenny McCarthy. We didn't get that sort of parent in the clinic. I suppose it was just trading one type of headache parent for another.

After two hours, the clinic closed down for lunch, and I headed back over to the ER after a ten-minute break where I exchanged a few text messages with Mark. I planned on taking my lunch after my shift was over, so I wanted to see if I could tag along with Dr. Morrison on any more cases. Instead, almost as soon as I waved to Cassandra, I heard the voice I was not looking forward to in the least. "Well well, back from baby butt duty, Pure-D?"

I hated Dr. Green's nickname for me. He's a good doctor, a clinical genius in a lot of ways, and one of the best in the entire state at what the ER docs jokingly called "meatball surgery," stabilizing patients and keeping them alive long enough for the other surgeons to take over.

I'd seen him take a teenage gunshot victim and in the middle of the ER, crack her sternum open, pinching the woman's pulmonary vein closed by hand while applying what amounted to super glue to hold it closed before she bled out. The girl ended up with a seven-inch scar that I'm sure would make her want to wear high necked shirts for the rest of her life, but she was at least alive.

Still, Dr. Green was an asshole with a juvenile sense of humor. My second shift in the ER, after mistakenly leaving my bra behind in one of the staff changing rooms, he had settled on my nickname. Dredging the back alleys of his mind, he tied in my bra size with my last name, and then some old movie or another he watched where a character uses the phrase "Pure-D white." And so my nickname was born. Since then, I've never taken off any of my underwear in the staff changing rooms.

At least I wasn't Dr. Green's only target of harassment. Almost every intern, volunteer, or doctor who couldn't threaten his position as an ER institution had something about them he could comment on. His list of complaints in HR was a mile long, and the one time I had gone up to talk to them, the woman who took my complaint just nodded. "Let me give you some advice," she told me after reading over my carefully handwritten form. "Glen Green is never going to get himself fired from this hospital unless you can find pictures of him with his dick out around the underage candy stripers. He's too damn good, and he's happy down there in the ER. The administration deals with him because he's pulled more miracles out of his ass in the past two years than most doctors do in an entire career. So they put up with him, and he knows he's never going to be promoted past head attending physician of the ER."

"It's still not right," I said, sighing. "This isn't some stupid medical TV show. What's next, he walks around limping with a cane and popping drugs, whacking people in the gut or back of the knee whenever he feels like it?"

The HR woman snorted and balled up my report. Before I could say anything, she tossed it in the trash. "I just saved your career, Miss White. Dr. Green is a total jackass, yes. But if this goes in his file, he's going to make your life a living hell until you complete your PA studies, and then he's going to torpedo your chances anywhere within a three state radius by slipping a very unflattering note into your student files right before you graduate. I've seen him do it before. So keep your head down, put up with his shit, and tell yourself that in about two years you can be done with him."

So I put up with it, Pure-D and all. "Clinic duty was fine, Dr. Green," I replied in my best professional voice. "I just wanted to get some more observations and work done around here until the end of my shift in two hours."

"So you can go get a bunch of micks drunk and give the evening shift work to do," Green replied, grabbing another chart and tossing it to me after glancing it over. "There, go pull your weight. Even a student could handle this one."

I didn't even reply, catching the chart on the fly and turning around. It was easier that way.

* * *

Mark

After Sophie left for work, I headed back to my apartment in the Park District to change clothes. As I drove, I found myself thinking about her, a small smile on my face. Besides being smart, she was more beautiful than she realized, with long brown hair and green eyes that grew darker when she was aroused. And the sex......

Distracted by the memories of the night before, I almost hit the truck in front of me, slamming on the brakes on my Mercedes just in time. The racing wheels reacted quickly, and I stopped just a few inches from the rear end of an F-150, the driver even opening his door to stick his head out and check there was nothing wrong. "My fault," I said, sticking my head out the window. "Gathering wool."

"Be careful, man!" the driver yelled back, slamming his door and stomping on his accelerator when the light turned green. I just let him go, he wasn't worth my trouble. Still, I drove the rest of the way back to my apartment carefully, parking inside the covered garage before taking the elevator up to the eighteenth floor. It wasn't the penthouse, but my condominium overlooking the Park was nice, and most of my neighbors worked in businesses far different from mine.

The guy above me was a venture capitalist, while the woman down the hall was a local television personality, who'd held a two person "welcoming party" in my condo with me about two days after I moved in. We barely spoke to each other now. After about the fourth time I turned her down for a repeat performance, she finally got the message. She wasn't angry or anything about it, although I could tell she was a bit peeved that I wasn't more star struck. Still, she had a steady stream of bed partners when she wanted them, and I had the same. She just wasn't my type.

After changing my clothes, I got ready for my morning routine. First, I monitored all of my investments, making sure there had been no major market changes that required my immediate attention. I didn't want to keep doing my job forever, you know, so I always took at least thirty percent of my freelancer fees and invested it, with a good mix of different investment vehicles. I could've retired a long time ago, but even when you're rich, you want more. Besides, I'm not so sure my employers would allow me to just walk away.

I decided to skip my typical thirty minutes of specialized cardiovascular work, but kept to my weight training and martial arts practice. I've set up a room of my condominium just for that, as keeping my body in peak condition is important for my line of work. As the sweat flowed from my pores, I could feel the stress flowing out of my mind as the tension built in my muscles, letting me think.

About halfway through my heavy bag work, I fell into that state that the Buddhists call *zen*, a kind of half-trance where my body just reacted, and my conscious mind could be somewhere else. That sort of stillness, even while moving, is the answer to the riddle *the more you seek it, the harder it is to find it.*

As my hands flew against the bag, I pondered the past twenty-four hours. Why had I chosen Sophie? I went to the club that night on business only, and planned on teasing the club girls just to give myself a good cover for being there. My original plan was to bring one of them to a hotel for a good romp in the sheets, maybe two if the mood struck me, nothing more, until I saw Sophie.

I certainly hadn't planned on having an hour long conversation about music and art with her in a VIP room, nor did I plan on giving her a ride home, returning back to her place after completing the night's work, and I *definitely* didn't plan to have some of the best sex of my life not just once, but twice. To top it off, Sophie was now the one person outside the very limited circle of my employers who had my personal cell phone number.

I still hadn't formulated any conclusions about Sophie, other than I wanted to see her again, and sooner than waiting until the following Tuesday. Unfortunately, I had neglected to get her cell phone number, and had to wait for her to call me at some point to get in touch with her. Regretting my oversight, I went into my kitchen to put together my post workout meal when my cell phone rang. It was a text message from Sophie.

I'm getting off work at about 2, it read. *You want to come by the University ER and get some late lunch before I start work again this evening?*

I checked my schedule quickly, and saw I had nothing except an expected phone call from a client. *I'd be happy to. Mind if I come down on the RIST instead of taking my car?*

No problem, the reply came after just a few minutes. *Looking forward to it. See you soon.*

I chugged the rest of my protein shake and jumped in the shower, quickly shaving and changing into my normal casual *blend-in* clothes, jeans and a t-shirt, along with some Nikes. Grabbing my phone and wallet, I clipped my keys to the inside of my front pocket and headed out the door.

There's a bus stop right outside my condo building, and I was able to catch a bus down to the terminal quickly. From there, I used the city's light rail system (Rapid Intercity Service Train, or RIST) to get within just a few blocks of the hospital. The sun was out, the sky was beautiful, and I actually felt like whistling as I walked the short distance to the hospital ER.

What I saw when I walked in the automatic doors caused my blood to boil. It took all my self-control to keep a calm demeanor as I watched Sophie get blisteringly yelled at by some asshole doctor. "What the hell do you think you were doing, you stupid jackass?"

Sophie was practically in tears as the doctor, who looked like he was about forty, continued to berate her about what I quickly figured out was nothing important. Instead, it seemed he just wanted to harass her and get the perverse pleasure of trying to make her cry. "If you think you can act with such total lack of thought and become a PA, you are sadly....."

I couldn't take it any longer. Working surreptitiously, I made sure my face was covered from the security cameras, and made my way outside to a fire alarm, pulling it and walking around a parked ambulance before going inside calmly. The braying alarm caused everything to stop in the ER, as the source of the alarm was tracked down. A quick check found my pulled alarm, but with no damage. I knew the security guards wouldn't investigate too strictly.

My little trick did have the desired effect, however, as the doctor broke off to check on patients while the rest of the staff started taking the steps needed for a patient evacuation. Sophie was kept busy for the ten minutes it took the security guards to check the alarm source and call it off, but she was done by two fifteen. I figured it was better than being cursed out for what would have probably been about the same amount of time.

When Sophie came out of the staff room, her frown disappeared when she saw me. "Hey, Mark!"

"Hey beautiful," I said, accepting the hug she gave me. "How was your day?"

"Oh, nothing out of the ordinary," she said, taking my hand and walking with me out towards the parking lot. I noticed a few of the staff members giving us quizzical looks, but they didn't say anything. "Although that alarm at the end was a bit unexpected. The ER doesn't get prank pulls like that usually until the night shift."

I grinned and looked over at her. "I figured it was a good way to get you out of being yelled at."

Sophie stopped in the parking lot and looked at me, her jaw dropping for a moment before a smile broke out on her face. "Oh, you sneaky devil!" she laughed, giving my arm a quick hug. "That was perfect! But won't you get caught?"

"Nah," I replied easily. "I saw the security camera when I approached, and noticed that with the way the ambulance was parked in the bay, the pull was totally covered. There's no way they could have gotten a clear image of me, even if your security guards decide to investigate." I pulled her in tight and kissed her gently, her lips warm and welcome against me. "Besides, I think it was worth it. Who was that guy anyway?"

Sophie shrugged and waved it off. "Dr. Green, he's the senior attending physician. He's an asshole to a lot of people."

I let the subject drop, but remembered the name and the face, filing it away for later. "So, what would you like to do before you start your paid work? I'm not too familiar with what's in the area."

Sophie thought for a second and then grinned. "You like Thai food?"

Chapter 8
Sophie

I took Mark to a little hole in the wall Thai restaurant about halfway in between the hospital and the Gold Shamrock, the Irish tavern I worked at. For a guy who had looked so at home behind the wheel of his electric sports car the night before, it was great to see him also relax in the shotgun seat of my beater Civic. "I see you spent your money wisely," he joked, tapping the stereo. It is an impressive sound system, though I rarely use it. "How much did it run?"

"I don't know," I said as I turned the corner out of the parking lot of the hospital. "I bought this thing used. The stereo came with it. The guy who sold it was an old man, who said his grandson had used the car before he joined the Marines. So I don't think he knew just how good the sound system was. But, since my MP3 player pretty much sucks in terms of battery charge, I don't play it often in here. I save it for when I go to the gym."

"Where do you go?" Mark asked, "And please don't tell me you go to Planet Fitness."

"I said I go to the gym, not to waste my money," I replied with a snort. "I'm still a university student, so I have full access to the facilities they have. What about you?"

"Mostly on my own," Mark replied, "But I do have a membership at Downtown Sports. Maybe we can go together sometime?"

I smiled and looked over at him. "You don't want to see me sweaty and in workout clothes."

Mark's smoldering look in reply sent little butterflies through my stomach, and I had to tear my eyes away from him to look at the road. "I've seen you in less than that, and I think every bit of it is beautiful," he said, his words causing me to shiver and smile at the same time. "And I can't wait to see it all again."

I didn't really have an answer, so I just smiled. Of course I wanted to have sex with him again, but I wasn't exactly used to being in this kind of situation.

Soon we were at the restaurant anyway. I glanced over at Mark, grinning sheepishly. "I'm sure it's not as glamorous as what you're used to, but it's good, and the owner is really from Thailand."

The restaurant was pretty quiet when we came in, since we showed up in that dead zone between lunch and dinner. Still, the hostess was polite, and we were soon seated at an orange booth covered in a blue plastic tablecloth, drinking iced tea from large plastic glasses. "I know the decoration looks pretty plain," I said, "it raised my doubts too. But, apparently the shop used to be a pizza place fifteen years ago, and when the owner bought it, he just kept the decor. It caught on with the university and hospital people, and he's been going ever since."

"It reminds me of the small town I grew up in," Mark said, and for the first time, I could hear a faint Southern accent in his voice. I guessed he hid it pretty well unless he wanted it to come out.

"Whole town had only nine thousand people in it, most of them country folks. We had only four different types of restaurants in the whole town. You could have Southern, fast food, your large chain family restaurant, a Greek place that doubled as our Italian place, and a single Chinese restaurant, converted over from a Dairy Queen. Good Chinese food, although they kept getting shut down by the health department, so take that for what it's worth."

I laughed and sipped my tea, a nice herbal peppermint blend the owner developed himself. "So how'd you end up in the big city?" I asked, trying to imagine Mark growing up in a small Southern town. He must have been the high school quarterback or something, he was such a great athlete. "Football scholarship?"

"Hmmm?" he replied, surprised. "Not at all. My family moved here when my mother died. I was twelve, and my father thought that he could make it better in the city than in South Carolina. So, just as I was getting ready for high school, he took me with him to Boston, where he had a new job lined up. I had to learn a lot, and quickly."

"I bet," I said, thinking of a country white kid from the South landing in a Boston high school. Even the private school kids would try and tear him apart. "Must have been better when you went to college."

Mark gave me that confident smile of his, with the right corner of his mouth quirked up as if I had said something funny. "I've never been to college," he said quietly, causing my mouth to drop open. "Everything I learned after high school I picked up either through reading or through my work. It's not exactly a classical education, but I've been able to make it work so far."

I blinked, shaking my head before finally finding my voice. "Mark, how do you do it?"

"What?" he asked, his smile growing.

"You keep surprising me," I said, pausing while our plates of Thai noodles were dropped off. "I recommend the peanut sauce. Anyway, you keep surprising me. Last night while we talked, you struck me as someone who's highly intelligent, but yet you haven't been to college. You tell me Boston, and I would not be surprised at all if you had then told me you graduated from BC or even Harvard. I had taken you for someone with at least an MBA, or maybe a military officer who got out and turned your skills to the business world."

It was the first time I'd ever seen Mark actually look bashful, and it was adorable. I felt my heart lurch in my chest, and I had to remind myself that I'd only known him for less than twenty-four hours. Still, something stirred within me, and it was more than just my libido.

"Thank you," he said sincerely, looking me in the eyes. He reached across the table, taking my hand again, and I could feel the spark of electricity jump between us. It was different than just the attraction we'd shared in the club or in my apartment. I was seeing him for the man, and not just the sexy body. It felt good. "But don't make me out to be more than I am. I'm still just a country boy from South Carolina who works as a freelancer."

"You seem like a lot more than that to me," I said honestly. "Not too many men would have figured out the perfect solution to my issue with Dr. Green today. Half of them would have charged in and gotten me in trouble with Green later, and the other half would have stood there impotently while doing nothing."

Our conversation continued as we lazily worked our way through the spicy food, downing it all with the large glasses of herbal iced tea.

I told him about my weight gain at the beginning of my undergrad years, and how Tabby had helped support me through getting it off. He told me he had to thank her whenever they first met for dragging me out of the apartment and to the club the night before. He also told me that he was glad I had sent him the text message during a quick break I had, since he felt like an idiot for not getting my cell phone number before I left that morning.

"I don't want to sound creepy or anything, but I really didn't know if I could have waited until next Tuesday to hear from you again."

"Considering I couldn't even wait twelve hours, I don't think it's strange at all," I said. Just then, Mark's cell phone rang, and he gave me an apologetic look. "Go ahead, I'm sure it's important."

"It is," he said before taking out his phone. "The only people who have this number are my work clients...... and you. Excuse me."

He slid out of the booth, heading outside to take his call while I considered his words. I was interrupted when the waitress, a pretty young mixed Thai and black girl who was in high school and helped out at her father's restaurants after classes, dropped off the check. "Here you are. I hope you two had a good meal."

"It was great as always, Helen," I said, using the girl's American name. She had a Thai name too, but I kept forgetting it. "And it was a great meal."

Helen walked back behind the counter to do some of her homework, and I looked out at Mark, who closed his phone and came back inside. "Everything okay?" I asked, picking up the check.

Mark grinned and took my wrist in a feather light yet strong grip, and pulled the check from my hands with two fingers. "Now, how would I feel as a Southern gentleman if I didn't pay on our first date?" he said with a smile. I could feel the blush all the way to the roots of my hair, and he stroked my cheek with the back of the first two fingers on his right hand. "Don't be shy, even if it is massively cute. And don't think this is a knock on your student status and income level. Tell you what, I'll make sure to get us reservations at Le Blanc for our next one, just to make us even."

I laughed at his joke, since Le Blanc is infamous for being the most expensive restaurant in the city. "Do that, and I'll have to move out of my apartment to pay for it," I said. "Then where would I stay?"

"Don't know," he replied, before leaning in to whisper in my ear. "I think I have an idea, though."

His hand came around to my lower back, pulling me in close to him, and he cupped the back of my head before kissing me. His lips caressed mine, and I threw my arms around his back, clinging to him while our kiss grew hotter and more passionate, only stopping when Helen discreetly tapped the register bell behind us. Mark pulled back with a soft chuckle, and I took a few moments to catch my breath before also laughing. "I'd never be able to bring you by the tavern," I joked. "I'd never get any work done."

"Well, I'm sure some day the bloom will be off this romance, and we'll be able to at least go a couple of hours without kissing or trying to take each other's clothes off," Mark said, holding the bill and stepping back. "But for now, let's pay this and get out of here. We've both got work to do tonight."

Chapter 9
Mark

I watched Sophie drive away from the parking lot of the strip mall where the Thai restaurant was located before heading down the street. I could have called for a cab, but I didn't want my movements to be tracked. Instead, I headed to my business meeting at a local boxing club in the Warehouse District, by foot as it was only a few miles away.

The walk was good, it helped me think about my work. Besides, even with my reputation, there was no way I'd bring my Mercedes anywhere near the Warehouse District. If Sophie thought her North Side apartment was in a bad neighborhood, she'd never spent any serious time in the Warehouse District. It was the sort of neighborhood where you didn't show any signs of wealth unless you wanted to be robbed, and you made sure to wear very specific neutral colors.

Arriving at the Warehouse District, I thought of the strange skills I'd picked up over the years. I found the boxing gym and went inside, taking a moment to watch the mid-afternoon crowd of boxers training. They were a unique group, most of them journeymen who were trying to sharpen up before their next paycheck taking an asswhipping from some prospect, or perhaps dreaming of getting that attention-grabbing knockout.

The place was anything but glamorous, with old bags hanging from the rafters wrapped in layer after layer of duct tape, to the point that you couldn't tell if the bag was really intact any longer, or if the guy was just punching a giant column of tape. It made Mickey's gym from the *Rocky* movies look shiny and well maintained, but it still put out some of the best boxers and MMA fighters in the area.

My client was the reason why. He was sitting on one of the benches that surrounded the fenced octagon cage in the corner. A great trainer, he was also an astute businessman, who knew both the good and the bad side of how to work contracts and fights in a sport where, if you dug hard enough, you tended to find lots of Sicilian names in positions of power, although there were also lots of Russians, Latinos, and others in certain areas.

"Hey Greg," I said, sitting down on the bench next to him. "How can I help you out today?"

"Nothing too serious," Greg replied, his eyes never leaving the cage. "Kid up there has a fight coming up in a month. His opponent is pretty dangerous, and the odds right now are not in our favor."

"Okay, so you want a scouting report on him?" I asked jokingly. "Thought you guys swapped tapes nowadays."

"Not a typical scouting report," Greg replied. "Instead, I was thinking maybe you could pay his gym a visit, and.... *verify* a rumor I've heard that his opponent has a bad left knee. Nothing too serious, especially with the magnitude of this fight, but something that might make him a step slow on his takedowns, and a bit more vulnerable to low kicks."

"That sort of info would be very helpful to a trainer, especially if his fighter has a pretty good kick," I said. "What's the pay?"

"Not a lot," Greg admitted. "Say, ten percent of our winnings on the action, and of course you can put your own money in if you want."

I shook my head. "Greg, you know I don't gamble like that. You know I normally handle more high profile stuff than this, but I'll be happy to give this guy a visit. You got his information?"

"Of course," Greg said, reaching inside his shorts and pulling out an envelope. "It's on this SD card. Also a small gift, thanks in advance."

I felt the envelope, and felt both the data card and what was most likely a prepaid credit card, one of the methods of payment I preferred. "Mind if I take care of it this weekend? I can give you a call Monday if you like."

"Probably better to do it tomorrow, I've heard this guy doesn't like to do gym work on weekends," Greg replied. "But Monday is great. Like I said, this fight has some serious implications. There's going to be guys from Vegas at the fight, and they've been giving us a few calls. If my boy up there can get an impressive win, he's got his ticket to the big leagues all ready to go. So, thanks man. Say, you want to get some work in? Just take it easy on the kid, he's no match for you."

I chuckled and stood up. "No thanks, Greg. You know my style doesn't match up well in the cage." Greg nodded his head in agreement, then offered his hand to shake. We shook hands, and I was on my way.

* * *

Mark

Heading towards the nearest RIST station, I made a snap decision, and took the University train instead of the Park train. Getting off, I headed back to the hospital, checking the ER. Dr. Green was still on duty I saw, although he looked like he was getting ready to leave. I melted into the background, and shadowed Green as he left to head to the parking lot. When he got into his car, I noted the license plate, and watched as he drove away in a cut-rate Lexus.

    I pulled my phone from my pocket and dialed a number from memory. "Hey, Luka? Yes, it's the Snowman. Listen, can you do me a favor and run a license plate for me? I'll text it to you. Yes, yes, I know you owe me one, and this makes us even. Just need his address. Text it when you get it. Thanks."

Chapter 10
Sophie

After our late lunch date, I didn't see Mark until the original day we had planned, Tuesday. Friday was packed with classes, while Saturday I worked a double shift at the tavern, and Sunday a double shift at the hospital. Monday Mark said he was busy with work all day, so I used the day to rest and just go to my morning class.

Sunday was the strangest shift I had ever done at the hospital. I had been dreading the shift, knowing it was sixteen hours with at least eight of them being with Dr. Green. Boy was I in for a shock when I came in.

First of all, Dr. Green was wearing an eyepatch when I came in, one of those temporary ones that we give out to patients who have had an eye injury. "What happened?" I asked Brad, who was manning the front desk.

Brad shook his head. "He says he walked into a door frame and smacked his eye a good one, but everyone knows he's full of it," Brad whispered, both of us taking glances to make sure Dr. Green wasn't nearby. He was safely across the ER in one of the exam areas, so Brad continued.

"He came in Friday night late, and they did X-rays on his head. If he ran into a door, he must have been doing it at a full on sprint, because he's cracked the hell out of his orbital bone. I think half the reason he has the eyepatch on is so that he doesn't freak out the patients with a swollen shut black eye."

"Jesus," I whispered, taking a closer look. On the edges of the bandage holding the eyepatch on his face, I could see some of the telltale yellowing of a fading bruise. "Any guesses as to what happened?"

"None at all," Brad replied. "He won't talk about it with anyone."

Our conversation ended, but for the rest of the day Green did everything he could to avoid me, passing me off to one of the other attending physicians, something he had never done before. When my duties required that I talk with him, he was almost painfully polite, never once using any foul language, nicknames, or even derisive tones. Instead, it was always "Miss White," and then passing me back off to the other doctors as quickly as he could.

Even the nurses and other staff noticed Green's odd behavior. "What the hell did you do to him, use your Jedi mind tricks or something?" Gary, one of the male nurses, asked about halfway through the shift. "I've never seen him act this way, and

I've been here almost as long as he has."

"I didn't do anything," I said, a little weirded out myself. "Seriously, I've been going to class and working at the Shamrock the past three days."

"Well, whatever you did, keep it up," Gary said, as he and I helped a patient into a wheelchair for going upstairs. "He's been nicer to everyone this shift, and even the patients are complaining less. Aren't you, Mr. Teague?"

"Go blow yourself," the patient, an old alcoholic who was in at least three times a month, usually with something connected to his kidneys or liver, snapped. "Fuckin' hospital people and your damn tests. Just stick me with the same damned IV you gave me last time and let me relax in peace!"

"Now Mr. Teague, you know I can't do that," Gary joked, giving me a wink. While Gary didn't often work with the patients, he had the uncanny ability to let almost any harassment or bad treatment from the patients just roll off of him. It had earned him perhaps the only semi-respectful nickname Green ever gave anyone, Duck. As in, water off a duck's back. "Pushing you upstairs for scans makes my life worth living."

By Tuesday, the mystery had gotten deeper, leaving the entire ER buzzing with rumor. Claiming a personal matter, Dr. Green took a sudden leave of absence with the hospital and got out of town, not telling anyone where. As I waited inside my apartment for Mark to pick me up for our date, I just set aside the whole thing, and thought about Mark.

Even though I hadn't seen him since the previous Thursday afternoon, we talked every day over the phone, or sent text messages to each other. We'd spent an hour on Sunday morning just talking, most of the time on speakerphone as we both went about our breakfast routines, just talking about the best places to get pizza in town. It was great, and the more we talked, the more I realized that not only did I like Mark, I was starting to fall for him. It scared me, honestly, but thrilled me at the same time.

I was tapping my foot on the carpet, dressed in my second best dress, a blue sleeveless one piece that stopped just above my knees. I could make it double as a cocktail dress if I wanted to by adding some accessories, but tonight I wanted it more casual, so I left them off. I was just checking my earrings for the fourth time when the doorbell rang. I checked my peephole and saw Mark standing out on the narrow concrete walkway. He was dressed up just a bit, in black chinos paired with a red long sleeved shirt that hid his impressive physique. Still, he looked devastatingly masculine, and my heart sped up just a bit.

"Just a second," I called through the door, turning to the small mirror next to my coat rack to check my appearance. I couldn't tell if I looked good or not, but at least my makeup didn't make me look like a clown in my opinion, so I opened the door. "Hey."

Mark's immediate response was both funny and touching. He said nothing, just looking at me with his funny little smile, his eyes going up and down my body while I stood there, fidgeting just a bit. "What?"

"You look beautiful," he answered, "and I wanted to take a moment to remind myself of that. Seriously, you look amazing in that dress. Shall we?"

We had decided on a classic date, going out to a movie. In our phone calls and text messages, we found that we both enjoyed the classic movie theater experience, and agreed to go to a recent blockbuster neither of us had seen yet.

"We'll probably throw out half of this," I said as I took a handful to munch on, "but it's just part of the tradition. Big popcorn, big drinks."

"And both of us doing extra cardio tomorrow," Mark whispered. "But you're right, it's a huge part of tradition. When I was a kid, I sometimes replaced the popcorn with candy, though. Two big movie theater sized Reese's Cups, or maybe the Reese's Pieces."

"Me too," I giggled, taking a sip of my soda. "Except mine was Junior Mints or Mounds. Now, though, no way. Maybe I'm just growing up, but all that sugar just doesn't do it for me anymore."

The movie started, and we both were soon engaged in the action on screen, enjoying the pretty mindless plot. You knew within twenty minutes who the love interest was, the problem and the solution. Still, it was an enjoyable movie, made even better when Mark put his arm around my shoulder and lifted the armrest between us. Snuggling against his strong chest, we balanced touches and bodily contact with watching the movie, until the end credits rolled, when my body was humming.

"Great movie," Mark said, his hand still resting on my shoulder, rubbing in slow, soft circles. "You ready to go?"

"Not really," I said, reaching up and kissing him. Our tongues met, a moan coming from deep in my chest as his hand brushed against my breast. His fingers molded against the curve, and we soon found ourselves making out like a pair of high school students, until a polite cough behind us interrupted us.

"Sorry guys, but I need to clean up," the staff member said, holding up his trash bag and broom. I felt myself blushing, but Mark just nodded calmly and helped me to my feet, his hand resting casually on my lower back. He handed the staff our half eaten tub of popcorn and led me out of the movie theater, acting for all the world like he owned the entire cinema complex.

Outside, we chatted about the movie for a bit as we walked across the parking lot, and Mark held the door of his Mercedes open for me. Coming around to the driver's side, he settled in before looking at me. "Back to my place?"

I could hear the question in his voice. If I said no, he'd accept it, while at the same time if I said yes, I'd be in for another experience I'd never forget. The decision was an easy one. "Your place it is."

* * *

Mark

It took a while for Sophie to adjust to my condominium overlooking the Park. After going and putting away my wallet and keys, I found her still standing in the living room, looking around. "This place is amazing."

"Thanks," I said honestly. "It took a lot of work and even more luck to get it. But I'm not thinking of stopping here."

"Oh?" Sophie said, breaking her temporary paralysis. "You plan on buying the penthouse or something?"

I laughed and went over to the glass door that led out to my balcony. Opening it, I let the night air in, enjoying the light chill. "Take a look," I said, waving Sophie over. "What do you see?"

"The Park, mostly," Sophie said, stepping outside and putting her hands on the railing. Her body was slightly bent over at the waist, giving me a wonderful view of her ass as she started swaying hypnotically back and forth, and I missed part of her next words. " . . . and, of course, the lights. Why do you ask?"

I pried my eyes away from the view of Sophie's posterior to lean on the railing next to her. I looked out at the city, and sighed. "I see a city that screams out, exploited by those who take advantage of it. I see pimps, hustlers, drug dealers and whores, all scrambling and fighting amongst each other while not realizing they are being held down by those with real power, the real crooks who pull the strings around here."

Sophie turned to look at me, her green eyes searching my face. "You have a pretty negative point of view."

"Sorry, don't mean to sound all down or anything," I said, "Especially after such a great date. But it's how I see this city. Anyway, my eventual goal is to go someplace where I'd not be afraid to raise a family."

"So you're thinking of having children?" Sophie asked, quirked her eyebrow. Those green eyes never left my face, and I stood up, returning her gaze.

"When the right woman agrees," I said, running my hand down her back. The feel of her back through the silky fabric of her dress was soft and amazing, and I leaned in closer. "But when she does, yes. I'd like to have children, at least two. A girl and a boy."

"Aren't you forgetting something?" Sophie asked, her smile disappearing. She rested, took her left hand off of the railing to cover mine. "You said the right woman. You have to find her first."

Instead of answering, I pulled her closer, whispering into her ear. "I think I already have," I said, hearing her breath catch. "That is, when she realizes that she's the right one."

"I see," Sophie replied. "Well, you might have to convince that woman that she should choose you. What more do you have to offer besides a very handsome face, an obviously large bank account, and a pretty good taste in music and movies?"

I laughed, and ran my hand down her back to rest on her hip. "I can also cook, and I promise that I'd never let her down."

"Really?" she said, turning totally to me and wrapping her arms around my waist. "That's quite a lot to live up to. You might be challenged to prove it every night. Your woman might have a very active libido, after all."

Picking her up in my arms, I turned and carried her inside, towards my bedroom. "I can't let her down," I said, burying my face into her neck and kissing the tender soft skin. "I guess I'll just have to show her what I'm made of."

I knew that satisfying her sexual needs would never be a problem. But the whole family thing was a fantasy for me. I wished it could someday be so, but in my line of work, I'm not sure if that day would ever come.

Chapter 11
Part 2 - Sophie

It was one of those dreams where you knew you were dreaming. I was swimming in the ocean at night, I think it was the Mediterranean, when suddenly my bikini was gone. I knew I was dreaming right then, because I never wear a bikini. The warm water flowed over my skin, caressing my body and giving me a languid, relaxed feeling. I turned over onto my back, letting my body float on the salty water. As I did, I could feel the small waves lapping against my legs, and my knees drifted apart on their own. The first wash of the warm sea water against my inner thighs sent warm waves of their own through my stomach, and my legs drifted farther apart.

I could feel something warm and wet trace the inside of my leg, sending little electric thrills to my stomach. In my dream I couldn't see anything, but the soft touches continued, and I could feel myself growing hotter and wetter with each thrilling stroke. I felt my dream start to break apart, and I felt a pang of regret at first, thinking I would be losing the erotic sensations. As the darkness of the starry night sky was replaced by the more common darkness of my closed eyelids, it took only a moment to realize that the warm, wet feeling between my legs wasn't going away.

My eyes fluttered open, and I could see that the soft light of the stars had been replaced by the mostly-full moon streaming in through the open window of Mark's bedroom. Before I could recognize anything else, the warm wonderful feeling came again, tracing so close to my labia that my eyes opened wide at the feeling. I could feel slightly shaggy hair against the inside of my legs, and I knew what was happening, even before I saw Mark kneeling on the bed, his tongue outlining my pussy. "What are you doing?" I asked, my words going from a sleepy whisper to a lusty moan as he licked around the soft edges of my lips. "mmmmm . . ."

"I woke up, it was a beautiful night, and you looked so sexy lying there in the moonlight, I couldn't resist," he said, his voice only slightly muffled by my thighs. "Should I stop?"

"No, please don't . . ." I answered, running my fingers through his hair. In the month we'd been going out, he'd let his hair grow a bit longer after I commented that I liked longer haired men. But he'd never gone down on me before, and while I didn't regret it, I had missed the feeling. I had almost resigned myself to being in one of those relationships where it just wasn't going to happen. I'm sure every woman's had one of those.

Now, though, I could feel Mark's tongue licking my wet folds lightly, just barely parting my outer lips to expose the reddish pink inner jewel hidden inside. He licked me from my clit all the way down to the entrance to my tunnel, gathering the nectar inside before repeating the motion. "MMmmmm, delicious," he muttered as his tongue stiffened and he began to literally tongue fuck me, reaching deep inside my body with each stabbing thrust. When I was almost delirious with pleasure, he stopped, sucking my lips and rolling them between his own, carefully keeping his teeth from my sensitive skin. "I should do this more often."

Pulling his lips back, I felt Mark's fingers pull my lips apart, teasing my clit from its hood. I trembled as the cool night air played with his breath on my fiery button, until I was ready to beg for him to end my anticipation. Before I could speak, though, the narrow tip of his tongue flicked over my clit, sending lightning coursing through my body. With every quick, feather light lick, the breath was driven out of me, until black dots swam in my vision. I pushed Mark's head back for just a moment to take a deep breath before pulling him back in, wrapping my legs around his head. "Don't stop, please."

Mark's licks took on a different quality, with long, broad sweeps, each sweep raising the temperature of my body while still allowing me to breathe. Within just a minute or two, I was on fire, and my juices flowed like water down my inner thighs. Mark pulled back, and smiled, his teeth white in the moonlight, his skin shining with my juices. "Beg for it."

Growling in frustration, I squirmed on the bed, trying not to be reduced to a begging, pleading, wanton slut for him again. It didn't matter though, and we both knew it. No matter how hard I tried to resist, the sparkle in his eyes and the feeling of his touch on my skin drove away all resistance from me, and I would do anything he asked. Coming straight from sleep and as aroused as I was, I didn't resist long. "Please Mark, please make me cum."

"Yes my little *hime*," he said, lowering his head again. He had started calling me his *hime* two weeks prior, and no matter how often I asked, he wouldn't tell me what it meant. I didn't have a chance to think about it more though as he resumed his flickering, light licks around my clit, circling and flicking until the tension built within me, like an over-tightened clock spring.

I was reduced to incoherent begging, my breath coming in deep gasps when Mark slid two fingers inside me, while at the same time just barely letting his teeth scape over my clit. The spring inside me broke, uncoiling a climax through my body that left my thighs shaking, and my feet drumming across the broad muscles of Mark's back. He took it all without a single complaint, lifting his head when my body had finally settled back. "That was wonderful, but I need more."

Barely giving me a chance to draw a breath, Mark took my right leg and turned me over, pulling my hips up into the air. Doggy style was his favorite position, and I felt my breath driven out of me again as his thick cock slid deep inside me. Despite the amount of lubrication my body had produced, I was still tight, his cock was so much thicker than his tongue or his two fingers, and I felt stretched almost to the point of pain as he pushed in without stopping until I could feel his hips settle against my ass. "You've got a great ass," Mark teased as he pulled back, leaving just the tip of his cock inside me. "I think next time I'm going to fuck it until we both come."

I had told him about my fantasy of anal, but my trepidation of having never experienced that. Mark had taken it all in stride, sometimes teasing me but never in ill will, instead using his almost uncanny sense of mental states to relax me to the idea. "Just go slow," I said, feeling a knot of fear unknot itself in my chest. I had never given him such explicit permission before. "And let me get some lube?"

"Another time then," Mark whispered, running his hands over my hips. He pushed in again as he did, and soon both of us were left breathless as he thrust in and out, his huge cock filling me over and over.

I hadn't expected him to last long. Most of my other lovers, after licking me to orgasm, always wanted to just get in and come as soon as they could. Mark instead kept his pace controlled, a tight reign on his pleasure as he let my body recover and build again. When I started pushing back into him, my forehead buried on the pillow and my breasts swaying with every thrust, he sped up. I could feel tears or sweat trickling down my cheeks as he drove us both higher and higher. My nipples were scraping over the light cotton of the bed sheet, adding to the pleasure I was feeling.

The sensation of him pounding me left me senseless, crying out into the pillow as I sped toward my second orgasm. Mark picked up his rhythm, his hips slapping against my wet skin until, with a harsh grunt, he drove his hips as hard as he could into me. His cock exploded inside me, and sent me crashing into another orgasm. I clamped down around his cock, not letting him go. I pulled hard on the bed sheets, and I could hear with what little was left of my mind the hard purring sound of them ripping, I was yanking so hard. With a final cry, I pitched forward, his cock pulling out of me, and I collapsed into the pillow.

Chapter 12
Mark

We didn't get up until ten o'clock the next morning. It was a Saturday, and Sophie didn't have a shift at the ER, which I was grateful for. With the unexpected luxury of the long morning, we both slept in, and I woke up with Sophie's leg draped over mine. It took me sixteen minutes to extract myself without waking her up, but the results were worth it, as I surprised her in bed with a quick brunch of scrambled eggs, some breakfast sausages, and some leftover potato hash I'd made for myself two nights before. "My my, wonderful midnight sex and then brunch in bed," she said, her smile angelic even after she pulled a spare t-shirt over her head. "Not too many women are as lucky as I am."

"No woman is as lucky as you are," I teased back. By this point in our relationship, we could tease each other easily without worry of the other getting offended, although Sophie did say she thought I was always quietly self-confident, which I liked. "So what would you like to do after your brunch? By the way, when do you go into the Shamrock tonight?"

"I start at six, so I'd like to leave around five, take my time getting there," Sophie replied. I watched, entranced as she daintily scooped a forkful of eggs and sausage into her mouth. It was just another of the things I found cute about her. I knew where she got it from, fighting her weight down during her undergraduate years. Taking small bites and chewing completely is an old trick in losing weight. "Also, I was wondering if you'd like to come by tonight."

"Really?" I said, surprised. "I thought you said I'd be too distracting coming around the Shamrock while you're working."

"Well, that's true," Sophie replied, blushing a bit while cutting through some sausage with her fork. "But Tabby has been insisting on meeting you, and I thought this would be a good chance for you two to meet. The Shamrock is a lively place, safe, and I can keep an eye on her. If I don't, she's more than likely going to hit on you."

"I thought you said she was your friend," I joked in return. "I mean, unless you're into that sort of thing. I'm not particularly. If I'm in a relationship, and at this point I think that's what we are, right?"

"Is that what this is? A real relationship?" Sophie asked quietly, setting her plate aside. It was one of her traits that still sometimes threw me off guard. I'd never had a girlfriend before who I couldn't keep totally enthralled with my body and my intellect. Sophie, on the hand, for all of her surface level shyness and uncertainty, had a deep reservoir of self-composure and strength that she could call upon. Maybe that was why, after a whole month, I was still seeing her. It was the longest relationship of my life so far. "Am I really important to you?"

I thought about how best to frame this answer. I could tell it was important, and I had to make sure I said things in exactly the right way. "Sophie, I've let you further into my life than I have any other woman," I began, sitting down on the bed next to her. "I think about you every day, and when you call me, it makes me smile, no matter what else is going on. My condo feels empty when you're not around, and I wake up every morning wanting to hear your soft breathing next to me. So yes, to me this is real. If it was just a fling or a booty call, I'd have ended it a long time ago. What about you?"

Before Sophie could answer, my front doorbell rang, startling me. My building had one of those systems where you had to buzz someone in, and any of the few neighbors who came around to my place would normally either call first or knock. Almost nobody used the doorbell. "Maybe a delivery?" I said, as the bell rang again. "Let me go check, hold that thought."

I made my way down the hallway, stopping only before I got to the door to pull on my leather jacket over my bare chest. On the inside of the sleeves I could feel the comforting weight of my two home defense knives tucked into the hidden sheaths sewn into the upper halves. I had tried on the inside of the arm, but the weight just didn't work. If I needed to have something on the inside of my arms, I preferred a strap on sheath.

I made a simple mistake at that point, opening the door without checking my peephole. I don't know why, that was very unlike me. Sophie had me off my game, perhaps I was distracted by the sound of her getting out of bed, and I knew she'd be pulling on some pajama bottoms. Instead, I opened the door. I was halfway to my left sleeve to pull my knife when the two men held up their hands, showing they were currently unarmed. "How are you doing, Snowman?"

Louis The Frog wasn't French, as best I could tell. And at five nine and barely breaking a hundred and fifty pounds, with dusky skin, brown hair and blue eyes, he didn't look like a frog either. Still, he was the top lieutenant to Salvatore Giordano, my main employer. With him was a man I didn't know, but I could be assured was reasonably well trained. "I was doing a lot better about thirty seconds ago, Louis.

How'd you find this address?"

"It's amazing what you can find on the Internet, Snowman. Like, how that stealth electric car of yours, while it's not registered to this address, well, it just happens to keep getting quick charges done at stations that have credit card receipts that do match this address. May we come in?"

I really couldn't say no. If I had, Louis would have accepted it with grace, but I know I would be getting a call from Sal Giordano himself later. "Okay, but keep it short, if you don't mind. I have company over."

"Ah, the beautiful Miss White. I must say, you have excellent taste in young women." Louis came in, ignoring the fact that my blood was running cold. They'd obviously been keeping tabs on me, I should've known. Still, I had a chance to detect the automatic slung underneath Louis' companion's coat. From the impression I could see, I was thinking a Colt 1911, most likely in .45 caliber. Definitely a lot of gun for a *friendly* visit. "Does she know what you do for a living?"

"He's a freelance troubleshooter," Sophie said, coming into the living room. She had pulled her hair back, and while she was still wearing the t-shirt she had pulled on in bed, she had also put on a loose pair of sweatpants that I had gotten for her when I noticed she found my air conditioning a bit cold for her liking. "Why?"

"Oh, nothing at all," Louis replied, giving her a predatory smile. Then again, every look that Louis had was predatory. I'm pretty sure he even gave his mother a predatory goodnight kiss when he was a child. "And you're right, Mr. Snow is a freelance troubleshooter for the group I work for. In fact, I was coming by to see if he was available for another job, but seeing as he has such lovely company, I think it'll keep until Monday. I'm sorry to have disturbed your Saturday morning Miss.....?"

"Sophie White," Sophie replied, and I inwardly winced. Louis hadn't said her first name before, I was hoping they didn't know. Either way, they did now, obviously. "Mister....?"

"Lefort. I should be going. Again, sorry to have disturbed your weekend. Mark, we'll be in touch when you have some free time, okay?"

Louis and his man left, closing the door behind them. It wasn't until I could latch and lock the door that I realized I had been holding my breath for almost a minute. Turning around, I saw Sophie standing behind the sofa, her arms crossed under her breasts. While normally a very attractive sight, the look on her face was dark and suspicious. "Who was that?"

"Like Louis said, just a business associate. Why?"

Sophie rolled her eyes and looked at me, and I could tell that she was getting angry. "You can stop lying to me now. I've never seen you upset or even rattled, until those two men showed up at your door. Now what the hell is going on?"

"Nothing," I said, trying to end the conversation. "I just was surprised, that's all. I'd been looking forward to an easy weekend."

Instead of replying, Sophie turned on her heel and stormed back to the bedroom. Before I could even get my jacket off, I heard her yanking open drawers, and the familiar sound of clothes being tossed into a bag. I rushed back to find Sophie jamming her t-shirts into a bag that she had used to bring some things over to my place. "What are you doing?"

She looked up at me, her eyes filled with fury. "What does it look like I'm doing? I'm packing my stuff. It's obvious you don't really see me as a real girlfriend. I should've never agreed to stay the weekend. I'm not going to stick around through one of these again."

I wanted to slam my hand against the door frame. I was frustrated with myself, frustrated at Sophie, but also angry as hell at Louis and Salvatore. Instead of letting my anger go physically, I clenched my fists as hard as I could behind my back. "Sophie, I do see you as a real girlfriend. Just because I haven't told you everything about my life doesn't mean I don't need you and want you."

"But you don't respect me," Sophie countered, zipping the bag closed angrily. "If you did, you wouldn't be lying to me right now. So let me ask again, who were those men?"

I was tempted to tell her about my work, but I knew if I answered her question, her life would be in danger, and it'd likely push her away even more. "Sophie, I can't.....there are things about my life that I just can't tell you. I'm not trying to lie, I just can't." I didn't know what else to say. I felt defeated, laid bare, and there was nothing I could do about it. My mouth opened and closed like a fish out of water for a few seconds, before I just sighed. "I'm sorry."

Sophie looked at me, her anger softening, but she still took her bag and slung the strap over her shoulder. "Me too. But until you can tell me more . . . I need to go."

Chapter 13
Sophie

By the time I got to the Shamrock that early evening for my shift, I was still in a downright shitty mood. The whole time going back to my apartment and then changing for work, my mind was whirling. Tabby had been disappointed that Mark wouldn't be at the pub, but told me she'd still come by around nine. In the meantime, I spent half my time calling myself a damn fool for walking out on Mark. He was more than a great lover. We enjoyed spending time together, whether we were hanging out and watching movies or having dinner he prepared for me, to just sitting around talking.

The other half of the time, I was telling myself I did the right thing. He kept secrets from me, that was obvious. I'd overlooked it for most of the month we'd been together since it was never in my face and as obvious as it was earlier. After all, every business has certain things they don't want other people to know. I'd dated a guy when I was an undergrad on and off for three months that worked at a Chinese restaurant. He told me that even though he'd worked there for five years, ever since high school, he'd never been allowed to learn what the chef used as his Mongolian barbecue sauce. Until Louis Lefort showed up at Mark's doorstep, I figured it was something as insignificant as that. But there was something about those two men, an almost palpable aura of danger and evil that made me feel uncomfortable the whole time they were inside. They looked like two men who really didn't care if I were alive or dead.

Also, what was up with Mark and that leather jacket? I'd never seen him wear it before, and the way he reached for the sleeves before stopping told me he had something in there, something he didn't want me or Lefort to see. It was just another thing that worried me, just like the worried expression that was on Mark's face the whole time they were there. I'd seen Mark confident, I'd seen him restful, I'd seen him thoughtful. But I'd never seen him worried or scared before.

All of these thoughts swirled through my mind as I entered the Shamrock and slung my backpack onto my coat hook in the back room. Taking a deep breath, I pulled my hair back into my work ponytail while knotting the Shamrock t-shirt near my left hip. It had taken me a while to catch on, but the tighter I made my shirt, the bigger the tips I got. I don't care what my feminist classmates might say; sex sells.

The bar was still pretty quiet when I clocked in, with a few folks enjoying early dinners. The Shamrock is a pub in the true Irish sense, so it had a chef in the back, a guy named Juan who turned out pretty good fish and chips, in my opinion. That an Irish pub had a Hispanic guy working the kitchen was just good irony. "How's the chips tonight, Juan?"

"*Hola* Sophie," he said. "You look down. You okay?"

"*No buena*," I said in reply. "But don't worry about it, I'll get through it all."

"Cool. Well, you know it's Saturday, so be on your toes."

"*Comprende*," I replied, going out behind the bar. The afternoon bartender, a nice older guy named Liam who was also the co-owner of the Shamrock along with his brother, gave me a smile and a nod before drawing a beer for a customer.

* * *

I was soon caught up in my work. After Liam got off, I was the main bartender, working with two others who shuttled beer and food out to the fifteen tables that dotted the area. About seven o'clock I was drawing a beer when I heard someone call out my name. "Hey, barkeeper?"

"Just a minute," I said, finishing off the pint of Guinness and drawing another of Kilkenny Red. I set the two pints on a tray and rang for Dave, the waiter working that table, for service. Wiping my hands on the towel I kept near my waist, I turned towards the voice. "What can I get you?"

The customer was one whose face I'd seen pretty often over the past three weeks. She was Asian, although I couldn't really tell you which origin. She'd been coming in almost every shift I was on, and I'd placed her as a new office worker in the area. She always wore a business suit, and she spoke with a bit of a British accent. I'd assumed she was a transfer from an overseas office, Royal Bank of Scotland had a regional office nearby. "I'll take a Porterhouse Oyster Stout, if you have them tonight," the woman asked, "I'm knackered."

"Good choice," I replied, grabbing a bottle from the cooler chest and popping the top. "Bottle or glass?"

"I'll take a glass if you don't mind," the woman replied. I poured carefully, making sure to get just the right amount of head, and set it along with the rest of the bottle in front of her. "Thanks. By the way, I'm Becky. Been seeing you around a lot lately."

"Sophie," I replied with a professional smile. "Well, my school work is wrapping up, and I haven't gotten any bites back on my resume yet. So, I asked and they let me pick up a few extra shifts."

"Well, it's good to have you around. The guy before you keeps giving me the horny eyeball, if you know what I mean. But you don't look yourself tonight. Everything okay?"

"Ah, not too bad. I had a bit of a falling out with a guy I've been seeing this morning."

Becky took a sip of her glass and sighed. "I know what you mean. What caused it? Caught him in bed with another woman? Text messages?"

I shook my head and chuckled. "Nothing so dramatic. Just.... he's got a secret side to him that he won't let me into."

"I understand. I've lost a few boyfriends to that myself. The last one turned out to not trust me when I told him that yes, I really was working late and no, I couldn't tell him. After all, if what I knew got out to the wrong people, the NASDAQ takes a hit and the SEC is knocking on my door."

"I know, I'd thought of that, but I met a few of his coworkers today. And let's just say they weren't very nice guys."

Our conversation continued on and off for the next hour, as I got called away to fill orders. Still, each time I ended up drifting back down the bar to where Becky was sitting, and we just kept talking. As we did, I just felt comfortable sharing with her everything I was worried about between Mark and I. His handsomeness, our economic differences, even our difference in education. Finally, Becky set down her glass after finishing off her second stout, and looked levelly at me. "You mind if I ask a blunt question?"

"Go ahead," I said, keeping my eyes on the bar. A guy down on the end gestured, and I got him a pint of Harp Lager before coming back. "Might want to hurry, though. The place is getting busy, and the band starts up in twenty minutes. Once they do, you won't be able to hear a damn thing most of the time."

"Sure. Listen, this man, is he a good man? Not the secrets, not the money, none of that other shite, but is he a good man?"

I didn't even need to think about my answer. "Yes. One of the best men I've ever known."

Becky smiled and drained her glass. "Then I think you know what you should do next. Listen, I gotta go, I love the beer here but I hate the band. I'll see you around." She handed me her glass and bottle, and by the time I got back she was gone, with a fifty dollar tip tucked under her coaster along with a note. "I kept you from enough customers, you deserve it. Call him. -B"

    I tucked the note into my pocket, stuck the fifty in the tip jar I shared with the other staff, and called out to the waiter on the floor. "Dave! Take the bar for five minutes, I need to step out."

Chapter 14
Mark

After Sophie walked out, I stared at my front door, for the first time since my mother died feeling mentally paralyzed. Hell, I'd celebrated when I left home when I graduated high school, my dad was too far into the bottle to give a damn anyway. There I was, standing half naked in my bedroom, and I couldn't figure out what to do. I'd already done my first paid job for some of my clients, running basic errands. I didn't graduate to my current line of work until a year later, and that was quite by accident. The sound of a helicopter flying over my building broke my fugue, and I shook my head. I couldn't just let Sophie walk out of my life, that was for sure. I grabbed the first thing in my dresser, a black t-shirt (not unexpected) and a pair of urban camo fatigue pants (a bit unexpected, I didn't wear those unless I was working in certain neighborhoods). I grabbed a pair of short boots, the type used by some of the SWAT teams in California and had the left one on when my cell phone rang. I snatched it up from my nightstand table, praying it was Sophie. I cursed silently when I saw who it was. "Hello, Sal."

"Marco, Marco . . . I just got a very disturbing report from Louis. The Frog says that the rumors of you having a romantic interest are true. You know we need to talk about this."

I pursed my lips, tempted to tell Salvatore Giardino to take a long leap from my balcony. First of all, I'm not Italian. Why the hell he kept turning my name into Marco was beyond me. However, I'm not the sort of person interested in making men like Sal angry, so I kept my reply polite. "I know you had some expectations for me, Sal. I'll be honest, though, I didn't think this was worth your attention."

"Now Marco, do you really think that I've gotten to the position I have without making sure nothing is beyond my attention? Since you've been such a valuable member of my team, I'm feeling generous. Where would you like to meet?"

Like it mattered. I knew Giordano would have men everywhere, regardless. I could have chosen the inside of a bank vault and it wouldn't have changed a thing. Still, I needed to at least make an effort to look like I was trying to cover my ass. "How about the Park? We can feed the ducks over by Hamilton Pond. Most of the old men who hang out there wouldn't care even if they could hear us."

Giordano laughed, an ugly sound that I detested. "All right. Thirty minutes by

Hamilton Pond. I'll even bring the breadcrumbs."

I hung up my phone and closed my eyes, letting my eyes close and forcing my breath to still. It's my greatest advantage, more than my physical strength, or my ability to set aside the better parts of me when I needed to and do the hard thing. Instead, I drew upon that inner pool of stillness I've had as long as I could remember. When I was a boy growing up in the country, I'd taken quite a few whitetail deer with that skill, more than hunters twice my age. My father, who usually ended our hunting trips drunk, kept swearing it was dumb luck. A seven-year-old boy does not take a ten point buck down with an old M-1 carbine at two hundred yards. You're not even supposed to shoot deer at that range with that size round, it's not powerful enough. But I knew, and the bullet took the buck just right, going between the thick ribs and piercing the heart. The buck dropped like a rock.

As I got older I explored meditation and various other ways to allow myself to quickly find that stillness. I learned how to be still while moving, and even in the midst of a whirlwind of activity my mind remained clear and perceptive. I yearned for this now, knowing I'd need it. It only took me a minute before I felt centered. I prepared for my meeting with Sal Giordano, and left for the Park. I knew it would be useless to sit down at a bench before Sal, he would be, as normal, extremely paranoid. Instead, I stood next to the railing overlooking the pond, keeping my eyes open. I didn't have to wait long.

Sal wasn't dressed like a man who owns four hotels in Atlantic City. Before you start thinking he was dressed like Tony Soprano or something, he wasn't dressed like your stereotypical Italian either. Instead, he was dressed kind of like you would expect your doctor to be on a Saturday afternoon, in a Ralph Lauren polo shirt, some Dockers khakis, and brown casual Skechers of all things. He approached me by himself, carrying a shopping bag, and I could immediately spot two of his men staying a respectful distance back. "Marco, it's good to see you."

"Thank you Sal. It's been a long time, hasn't it? You look like you're keeping yourself fit."

Sal patted his reasonably trim stomach for a fifty-year-old man and nodded. "New girlfriend, you know. To keep up with her, I've had to lay off the cannolis. Ah, but the benefits... those are worth a few cannolis. Sit down, let's talk."

Sal led me the short distance to an empty park bench before opening his bag. Inside there were three packs of Ritz crackers, still sealed in their foil tubes. "I couldn't find any bread that was dry enough on short notice," he explained, handing me one of the tubes. "But, my grandson says the birds like these just as much as bread, so I decided to give them a try."

"I hope the family is in good health," I said evenly, opening my pack after squeezing, crunching the crackers and making sure there wasn't something else inside. I took a few crumbs and tossed them onto the sidewalk in front of us, watching as pigeons waddled over and started to eat. These were city pigeons, they didn't feel the need to hurry for anything.

"They are, but let's get down to business," Sal said, his voice still friendly but his eyes going cold. "Marco, before I agreed to engage your services, I gave you some very specific rules. Do you remember what they were?"

"Of course, Sal."

"Really? Because one of the ones I remember being very explicit about was that if you were going to do contracts for me, you were not allowed to have any sort of romantic relationships. If you wanted to go out and fuck women, you could do that all you want. I don't expect a man to be a saint, even though I go to Mass every Sunday. But a girlfriend? No way Marco. No way."

As strict as it sounded, there was a sort of twisted logic to his rule. His brother, Vincenzo Giordano, had been ratted out by one of his men, after some of his competitors got a hold of the man's girlfriend. The man, who was a freelancer in the same job I did, rolled over as quick as he could to get his girlfriend freed. "I know Sal. But this girl, she's special. I know you hear it all the time, and I know you probably think I'm too young and stupid to really know what I'm saying, but she is special. I didn't exactly plan it, you know."

"I know, my boy. Which is why it was so surprising when Louis brought me the news that the best freelancer in this part of the country, a man I'd consider part of my own family if he wanted, was breaking one of my most important rules. And for who? Marco, your luck must be terrible when it comes to women, my boy."

"What do you mean, Sal? The girl has no family in the area, she comes from a working class background. What would be the problem?"

Sal looked at me with surprise in his features. "You really don't know, do you? Marco, she works at the Shamrock. Who owns the Shamrock?"

"Liam and Glenn Devitt. Two brothers, the place has been in the family for about fifty years. I checked."

Sal shook his head sadly. "No, son. The Devitt brothers may be the names on the business license and the IRS forms, but that pub is controlled by Owen Lynch."

Dammit. Owen Lynch was Sal Giordano's largest competitor, and also the man who had gotten Vinnie Giordano taken down. Also, Owen Lynch was the deputy mayor of the city, which tells you how corrupt the city was as well. "I'm sorry Sal, I didn't know. Honest to God."

"I know Marco, which is why you're meeting with me instead of with my men. But you know what has to be done, right? Marco, Owen knows about you and your girl. Just to let you know, he happens to be friends with a certain Doctor Green from the University Hospital Emergency Room, they were high school buddies. He cannot prove it, but suspects you in quite a few of the actions on my behalf over the past few years. Now, you are seeing a girl who works for him, even if it is only as a bartender."

I blinked, sideswiped by the fate of what had happened. "Sal, I'll stop seeing her I guess. Or I'll retire."

Sal shook his head. "Not good enough, Marco. First of all, she's still a liability. Second of all, you're one of the best assassins in the country, maybe even the world. You're more than that even. In the name of the Holy Mother, Marco, you're one of the best pure warriors I've ever known. You've taken out targets for me, both hard and soft, and for that you've been rewarded. You've worked for other men sure, but you've never crossed a client, never. Marco..... Sophie White has to die, one way or the other. Either Owen Lynch gets her and tortures her, trying to draw you out, or you take her out yourself. At least if you do it, it'll be quick and painless, I know that for sure."

I shook my head, perhaps the first time in all the years I'd worked for Sal that I'd ever rejected him so flat out. "No way, Sal. You talked about your rules, but you know I have rules too. I've killed a lot of men for you, and injured some more. But I've never, ever shed innocent blood. That isn't going to change. And Sophie is innocent."

Sal nodded slowly, almost sorrowfully. "Marco, I'm not asking you. I'm telling you. You know, I'm not the only man in the city you have worked for. All of us, well, we are in agreement. Owen Lynch cannot have an opportunity to exploit your weakness. This is an order from the Council, Marco. Sophie White must die."

"And if I don't?"

Sal looked at me as if my IQ had just dropped fifty points. "Then both of you will, by our own hands. Because of your loyalty, and because you've been such a good soldier for so long, I got the Council to agree. You have until midnight tonight.

If not, the Snowman goes into the broiler."

Without another word, Sal got up and left me on the park bench. I sat there for another thirty minutes, giving him and his men time to leave the Park. I checked my watch. Three in the afternoon. I had nine hours to make sure Sophie lived.

Chapter 15
Sophie

I was surprised when my phone buzzed just seconds after hitting the send button on my text message to Mark. "Hello?"

"Sophie, is everything all right?"

There was something strange about Mark's voice, it sounded strained and even a bit fearful. "Yes, everything is fine. Why?"

I could hear Mark let a long, shuddering breath go, and his voice sounded much closer to normal, although it was still not quite there. "I need to talk with you."

"Well, you can come by my place tomorrow if you want and we can....."

"Sophie, it can't wait until tomorrow. I need to talk with you as soon as possible. Please, is there any way you can get the rest of the night off? I promise, no deceptions, no hiding anything. But I need to talk to you immediately."

I knew I should have told him no, and that we'd get together the next day. But there was something in his voice that convinced me. "Okay. Where do you want to meet?"

"Your place, as soon as you can. I'll meet you in the parking lot, if that's okay."

"Yeah, sure," I replied, wishing I had given Mark a key. The idea of him hanging out in my parking lot made me feel like an idiot. "Say, a half hour or so?"

"Thirty minutes. I'll be there. Thank you, Sophie."

"It's all right. I'll see you then. Bye."

"I love you. Bye."

His last words stunned me, and I stared at my phone, which dumbly just said *Call Ended, 3:04*. I went to slip it in my pocket when it buzzed again, and I saw I had a text message. *Yes, I meant it. 30 mins. Mark.*

I don't really remember what excuse I gave to Juan and the two front house staff about needing to get out, but I knew I was probably going to get an ass chewing from Liam before my next shift. I really didn't care, though. The whole time, all I could think of were Mark's last words to me and then his text message. In my entire life, I'd never had a man say that he loved me before. I mean, sure my dad said it, and my grandfather, but you know what I mean. Driving back to my apartment, I'm glad I didn't run any red lights or hit anyone, I was so busy questioning myself about my feelings to really pay attention to how I was driving. After the secrets and the deception, did I trust Mark enough to give him my heart? While I'd never had a man say he loved me before, that didn't mean I hadn't fallen in love, myself. I thought I had, twice in fact, but both times I'd been hurt badly, and I didn't want to repeat the experience.

I was still undecided when I pulled into the parking lot of my apartment building, and I didn't see Mark's car. My heart dropped almost to my toes before I saw him climb out of a black Toyota pickup, wearing what looked to me like dark blue or black military clothes. My heart swelled in my chest, and I knew my decision. Shutting off my car, I jumped out and ran over to him, throwing my arms around his neck. "I love you too," I greeted him, pushing him back against his truck and mashing my lips against his before he could reply. "I love you, I love you, I love you."

Mark pushed me back slightly, his smile lighting a fire inside me. "Well, I guess that's the answer I was looking for," he said, smiling softly. Still, there was sadness in his face, and he looked down at my feet. "Listen, there's a lot we need to talk about, and not a lot of time to do it. Let's go inside, quickly."

Mark reached inside his truck and pulled out a small backpack that he slung over his shoulder while I locked up my car. Holding my hand, he led me up the stairs to my apartment, his eyes darting back and forth the whole time. "What's wrong?" I asked, perplexed. "It's just my apartment building. I mean, you were here just three days ago."

"Inside, I'll tell you everything," Mark replied, pausing at the top of the stairs to look back at me. "Sophie, I promise you, I'll tell you everything, the good and the bad."

Mark turned his back while I unlocked my door, putting his hand on my shoulder once the door was open to go in before me, his hand on his backpack. Once he turned the lights on, he let me in before closing and locking the door behind us. "You don't know how much I regret what happened this morning."

"Me too," I said, still confused as Mark set his backpack down on my coffee table, but staying standing behind it. "You said you'd tell me the whole truth. Mark, as much as I love you, I need the truth if there is to be a future between us."

Mark rubbed his hands through his hair and nodded. "You have no idea. Well, I guess I should start with the minor things. Like where my car is."

"Yeah, I was wondering about that. I've never seen that truck before."

Mark shrugged. "It's one of my backup vehicles. I don't keep it at my apartment, but in a storage unit over on the East side of town. You're probably now wondering why I have backup vehicles and why I'm talking about storage units and stuff like that. And I guess there's no way to tip toe around it. I've told you that I'm a freelance problem solver."

"Yeah.....?" I asked, confused. I mean, while I didn't know the details about his job, what could Mark have been, other than a freelancer? His work hours were weird, he worked seemingly out of his apartment, going to the clients, not to an office. What else could he be?

"Well, I'm a bit more than your normal freelancer. I'm kind of a...."

Before Mark could complete his sentence, the front door to my apartment crashed open, and two men came bursting through. Both of them were carrying guns, although I couldn't see what type other than that I'd seen them in action movies spitting out a lot of bullets really quickly. I thought I was going to die as the men started to raise their guns.

I barely saw Mark spring into action, and at the time I wasn't sure what happened, but over the next few days I had the chance to try and piece together what I saw. Mark first reached down and grabbed his backpack, swinging it in one smooth motion into the hands of the first gunman. Spinning with the force of his swing, Mark rotated towards the two men, his left arm cocked and catching the second gunman in the jaw with his elbow. The man sagged to his knees, stunned. Mark completed his turn, ending up behind the first man, whose gun hadn't even hit the ground yet. Mark grabbed the man's head and twisted, a sound like twigs snapping reaching my ears and the first gunman dropped, dead.

Turning his attention back to the still stunned second gunman, Mark's face grew hard as he stood above the man. Grabbing his hair, he cocked his right hand back in a strange sort of fist, where only the first set of knuckles on his fingers were bent before his hand flashed forward, the knuckles striking just below the gunman's chin, in the space right above his Adam's apple. A thick, gurgling sound came from the gunman and he dropped, his feet drumming weakly as his hands clawed at his throat. Mark studied him for a second before bringing his booted heel down on the side of the man's head, either knocking him out or killing him, I wasn't sure which.

"Holy shit," I whispered, the first words that came to my mind. It was over so fast I didn't even have time to scream, but just sat there in partial shock. "What the hell are you?"

Mark looked down at the two bodies, and I thought I heard him whisper to himself. "Seventy-five, seventy-six."

Chapter 16
Mark

Things moved fast once the two men the Confederation had sent were dead. I pulled both bodies inside, closing Sophie's door as best I could while she sat on the sofa, staring at me like I was something out of a video game or a horror movie. I turned my attention to the two men, and started searching the bodies while I talked. "After my father moved us up from South Carolina, I got in a lot of trouble," I said as I knelt. "Nothing too bad, a few fights, dealing with bullies in school. Things went bad though when my father got into debt with a group that is called the Confederation around here. They are one of two groups that control most of the crime in not just this city, but a lot of the East Coast. A night of drunken gambling in Atlantic City left him owing them about fifty thousand dollars. I was fifteen at the time."

"For the first few years, most of what I did was errand boy stuff, running packets from one side of town to another, and gathering intelligence. I've always been pretty good at blending into the background when I want to, and the Confederation saw to it that I learned from some of their best. Since I worked for all of the various members of the Confederation, I wasn't constrained by any cultural boundaries. I learned how to pick locks and avoid security sensors from a Japanese *ninjutsu* master, while at the same time did jumping exercises with a Chinese *kung-fu* teacher who was in debt to the local Triads. The Confederation used my skills against their enemies, and against each other. I did a lot of spy work to pay off my father's debt."

"To let me out of my debt, however, they upped the ante. My first hit was against one of the Confederation's own, a sick bastard named Clovis Methis, who was not only running a nightclub for the Confederation, but exploiting teenage girls. When he happened to get the daughter of a rather rich businessman drugged and more, the Confederation sent me to kill him. He was my first hit. For it, I got fifty thousand dollars. And the ability to work as a freelancer."

Sophie looked at the two men, then at me. "How many?"

"Seventy-six, seventy-four of which I was paid. In that time I've seen my fees raised to around a hundred thousand per hit. But, I've always had a rule that, until tonight, the Confederation respected. No innocent blood. Every death I've caused has been a piece of human scum that, if the police had caught him, would have earned him a life sentence at the very least, if not the death penalty."

"What do you mean, until tonight?"

I finished my sweep of the two bodies, taking the men's weapons, wallets, keys and other materials. While I'm sure the cops would investigate, it would at least throw them off the trail for a bit. I wasn't worried about my prints being on the bodies, I've never been fingerprinted in my life. "One of the Confederation members, in fact the most powerful member, is a man named Salvatore Giordano. He's what you might call the Godfather of this town. Sal had an extra rule, one that he had a reason for, but I broke. Sal's rule is that any hitman, even a freelancer like me, could not be in a relationship with anyone. My peers and I called it the two date rule. And until I met you, I had no problems following that rule. You changed that for me."

Sophie sat back, blinking. "I fell in love with a contract killer. Jesus."

"It gets worse," I said, hurriedly throwing the weapons into my backpack. "Sal found out about us. That man, Lefort, he's known as The Frog, and he's Giordano's top lieutenant. I didn't even know that they knew where I lived, that condo is owned under another name. Nothing I own is in my real name. Anyway, after you left, Giordano called me, set up a meeting. He said that I picked the worst woman in the world to have as a girlfriend. You know who Owen Lynch is?"

"Yes. He's the deputy mayor of the City. I've seen him at the Shamrock a few times, he's friends with the Devitts." Sophie looked like she didn't know if she was going to run, puke, or faint. I guessed it was better than screaming, so I just kept her talking, letting everything come out before she could stop me. "He's also the most corrupt criminal of them all. You ever watch that TV show, *Person of Interest*? You know, the one starring the guy who played Jesus in the movie?"

"Yeah, Tabby likes to watch. She thinks Jim Caviezel's cute."

"Well, the corrupt cops in the show, that group they called HR? Let's just say Owen Lynch and his group is about five times worse. There's a reason no cop has had charges brought on them for assault, attempted murder, or any form of homicide since Lynch has been in city government. And, he's the actual owner of the Shamrock. I don't know the two who hit us tonight, so I don't know if they are Confederation men who were sent by Sal because Sal knew I wouldn't do what he wanted, or if they're some of Lynch's boys who came to kidnap you to put pressure on me. But apparently everyone knows we're together, and neither side is happy about it."

Sophie's eyes narrowed as she looked at the two bodies still on her living room floor. "Just what did Giordano want you to do?"

I looked at the bodies, then looked at Sophie. "You weren't supposed to survive to see the sunrise. But I knew as soon as he ordered me, it was time for me to retire, and I knew I had to bring you with me."

Sophie wiped her hands over her pants and stood up. "And if I say no?"

"Then I'd at least ask you to come with me to a new city, somewhere you could set up a new life, a new identity, and then go away. If that didn't work, I was going to give you the backpack." I handed her my backpack and stepped back, keeping my eye on the door. Sophie opened it and gasped, before pulling out the first stack of wrapped twenty dollar bills. "There's exactly one million, two hundred and thirty thousand dollars in there. If you want to walk away, it's yours. It's the safe option. Once you drop out of sight, they'll lose interest in you pretty quickly. I'm the one with enough knowledge in my brain to take down criminal empires."

"Or?" Sophie asked, putting the money back and looking me in the eye. I sighed, and squatted down in front of her, wanting to reach out and take her hand but afraid to do so. I wasn't worthy of it, I never had been. But now she knew just what a disgusting creature I was.

"Or you come with me. Sophie, I'm not saying it's going to be paradise. We'd both be on the run for a long damn time, maybe for the rest of our lives. The men I worked for, they have connections all over the world. But as much as it is more dangerous for you, I can't imagine living my life without you. So yes, I'm greedy, I'm a taker, and I've caused enough death that I'm going to be answering to some immortal deity eventually, and I don't expect it to be a pleasant conversation. But I love you, and I want to at least see you to safety."

I watched Sophie ponder it for a minute, her eyes going from the bodies on the floor to me and back. I could almost see the thoughts running through her head, and the concerns she had. Going with me meant giving up any hope for a normal life, that was for sure. Finally, she turned and headed towards the bedroom of her apartment. "Where are you going?"

"To pack a couple of bags. I may be going on the run with you, but I'm going to at least take some of my clothes with me. Unless you happen to carry women's clothing with you in the back of that pickup you've got downstairs?"

"Okay, but I'd like to be out of here in five minutes. If those were Owen Lynch's men, his standard procedure is to send another team, usually corrupt cops, soon after. It covers their asses in more ways than one." I heard Sophie rustling around in her bedroom, hurriedly packing her bags, and I guessed more than a few times just jamming things in. Still, she came back out in less than four minutes, with a backpack and a large gym bag slung over her shoulders.

"If I forgot anything, I'm expecting you to pick up the tab," she said with a half grin. "So where are we going?"

Chapter 17
Sophie

We drove for four hours, until nearly midnight. We had taken the Interstate for most of the trip, stopping for gas once while Mark grabbed some snacks for us from the convenience store. While we munched on Fritos, he filled me in on his plan. "Ever since the first hit, I knew I didn't want to be stuck doing this my entire life. I met too many lifelong criminals in the years I worked for Sal and the Confederation, burned out by paranoia, and turning to drugs or other crutches to try and get through to the next day. So I started saving, and learning how to invest my money. I used a lot of shell corporations and dummy names, stuff I picked up from the same criminals I worked for. I took my laptop with me, it's in the back of the truck, although I plan on chucking it in a fire as soon as we can, just in case. I have a backup system anyway, one the Confederation can't track."

"Just how much money are we talking, anyway? I'm not trying to be a gold digger, but I am curious."

Mark thought for a second, then shrugged. "Well, there's a lot of things I'll have to give up in the city, stuff I bought under the alias I used for my condo. That kind of sucks, since that was a lot of my real estate investments. But my cash assets, my stocks, and my other investments I made under other names. I can't give you an exact amount, but I'd say if I liquidated everything that I could currently liquidate safely.... I'd have access to over a hundred and fifty million dollars."

I blinked, sure he had said something wrong. "A hundred and fifty million? That sounds like baseball player money."

Mark laughed and passed a minivan that was traveling fifty miles an hour on the highway. "Yeah, I guess so. Although most of it is locked up in investment vehicles that I specifically set up for long term usage, so the real value is higher. I mean, liquidating my gold assets and my mortgage securities would totally hose me on fees, and with the way the market is now I'd get soaked on my Asian investments too."

"Is that what you did with your spare time?" I asked, taking another few Fritos and chewing on them. The greasy corn flavor was a reminder of my childhood, as my grandfather loved the things, especially covered in chili con carne with cheese. "Become a business mogul?"

"I've tried to learn a lot of things," Mark replied without arrogance. "When you said that you thought I had an MBA, it really touched me. Most of the people I worked with, they wouldn't have noticed. They talk about my shooting skills, or my fighting skills, and lots of comments that I would never repeat to you that makes your average frat house sound like a highly cultured debate society. I hope I treat you better than how they treated the women in their lives."

I thought about it for a moment, then crunched on a few more Fritos. "You already are," I said, reaching over and squeezing his thigh. "Too many men would have continued to lie and try and bullshit me. You told me the truth. One question, though. If Lefort hadn't shown up at your door this morning, would you have told me eventually?"

"Eventually," he said, keeping his eyes on the road. "Actually, I don't know. I do know I was looking at getting out of the business anyway. I've made enough money, and I never did like it. It was just something I'm good at, I guess."

"Do you feel the need to kill?" I asked, looking over at him.

Mark smiled and shook his head. "No. While all of the men I've killed have been scum, I've lost sleep over them every time. I did it because I had to, at first to get out of the situation my father put us in, then later to get out of the situation I was in. You coming along was just the final little push I needed."

I wasn't sure if Mark was telling the total truth, and I looked in his direction. "Since we've met, tell me every job you've done over the past month."

Mark nodded and his face grew grim as his mind went back. "The night we met, I killed a Russian loan shark, Karl Vaslov. He went into business for himself, and the Confederation found out about it. He started trying to use his financial backing to expand into other fields, specifically the vice and drug trades. The next job I did for pay was an assault on a mixed martial arts fighter, spraining his left knee so that his opponent would have an advantage for their upcoming fight. I did two industrial espionage jobs, simple breaking and entering and getting files out of computers. The only unpaid criminal act I did was against Glen Green. I visited his house the night after we met. Other than a black eye, I didn't hurt him, but I did threaten him."

I nodded, not too surprised. "I'd wondered what happened to Green. He wouldn't tell anyone."

"Well, that's another way I got myself in trouble," Mark replied. "What I didn't know is that Glen Green was a frat brother with Owen Lynch. It was just one of the reasons that Owen wanted to use you to get to me."

Mark pulled off the Interstate, working his way along the minor roads. We drove for about another ten minutes before he pulled into a small motel, far away from the highway. "It's no luxury hotel, but it's safe, and they take cash," Mark explained as he shut off the engine. "It's one of four reservations I made this afternoon under false names from a burner phone. By the way, do you still have your cell phone?"

"Yeah," I said, pulling it out. "Do I need to get rid of it?"

"No, but shut it off and take out the battery for now," Mark explained. "Are there any very important numbers you have on there?"

"Just Tabby and a few other friends." A thought came to my mind, and I reached over to take his hand, which was still on the gear shift. "Mark, am I going to have to leave my entire life behind?"

Mark looked out the windshield, his face stony. "I don't know, Sophie. I hope not, but I honestly don't know. Let's go inside."

I grabbed our bags while Mark talked to the man at the front desk, coming back with a key. "Room seven," he said, "around back like I asked. It's not visible from the road at all."

The room was clean but obviously dated. The television looked like it was older than I was, and the wood paneling screamed nineteen seventies. Still, the bed was king sized and looked clean, the sheets were white and crisp. Mark brought in a gym bag with him, which he sat down on the small table next to the window. Pulling the single chair around, he sat down, his eyes looking out. "You need some sleep," he said quietly, keeping his vigil. "I'll make sure you're safe."

I watched him for a moment before going into the old fashioned bathroom, complete with a tiny shower that looked like it was maybe able to create a good steam if I wanted it, and a slightly warped mirror. I had packed my toothbrush, but forgot my toothpaste, so I just used water, scrubbing until my tongue squeaked over the enamel. Scrubbing my face with the cold water and provided washcloth, I then looked at myself in the mirror. A thousand questions whirled in my mind, the primary one being what my future with Mark entailed. Should I stay with him? Should I disappear? Should I just wait it out, then see if I could go back to my old life, secure that Owen Lynch or the Confederation wouldn't come after me?

On one hand, I was angry with Mark. His lies and deception had cost me, at least temporarily, everything. My friends, my job, my diploma, even my name I was sure. On the other hand, he had defended me without even blinking, taking out two armed men before they could even lay a scratch on me.

I came out of the bathroom after changing into one of Mark's undershirts, a habit I'd picked up over the past few weeks, and an old pair of light blue cotton shorts. As soon as I saw him sitting there, his eyes filled with pain but at the same time resolute. I could see, he did love me. And he'd never hit me, or hurt me, or mistreat me. Most of all though, I could see that if I asked him to, he'd die protecting me, and trying to keep me safe. It made my decision easy.

Coming over, I ran my hands over his shoulders, which tensed beneath the thick shirt he was wearing. I leaned down, letting my breasts rest on the back of his shoulders and neck, running my hands over his chest. "If you really want to make me feel safe," I whispered in his ear, while my hands worked on the buttons of his shirt, "you'll take me to bed and make love to me. Keep me next to you, safe through the night."

Mark took my hand and kissed the palm, before turning his head to look up at me. I was surprised and touched to see the glisten of tears in his eyes. "I'm sorry I've destroyed your life," he whispered. "I'll do what I can to rebuild it."

"Then make love to me," I repeated, coming around and pulling him to his feet. "We'll discuss the rest in the morning."

I pressed my body against his, letting my hands roam over his chest and around to pull Mark against me. Standing on my tiptoes I could just reach his chin with my lips, so I kissed him there, trailing kisses down the sides of his neck. He initially resisted me, still stiff and unsure, but when I pulled his shirt back and over his shoulders, he let me. He was wearing a black t-shirt underneath that curved and rippled over each muscle in his beautiful chest. Stepping back I growled lightly, running my hands over my breasts, making sure to rub my nipples which were already stiffening through the thin t-shirt. "Don't make me get on my knees and beg," I moaned, lightly pinching my right nipple. "Because if I do, I'm going to pull your cock out of your pants and suck you until you come in my mouth, and I don't want that tonight."

"What do you want?" Mark asked, his voice slightly husky. His eyes followed my hands as I ran them down my stomach and over my hips, slipping my right hand inside my shorts to lightly tease my pussy. I sighed and looked at him, my heart filled with desire and lust.

"I want you to fuck me until you fill me with your cream," I sighed, stepping backward until my knees bumped against the edge of the bed and I sat down. I spread my legs, feeling my juices already start to soak into the thick cotton. I pulled my hand out of my shorts and brought it under my nose, inhaling the spicy thickness. "Don't you want to taste?"

My last question broke Mark's reservations, and he walked over to the door of the room, double checking both locks before jamming the chair he'd been sitting in against the door. The window had security bars, which wouldn't stop a bullet but would stop an intruder at least momentarily, I guessed. Turning to me, he knelt down, quickly unlacing his boots before taking them off and placing them at the foot of the bed. He stood, unbuckling his belt and letting his cargo pants fall down his hips, his cock already straining against his underpants. I noticed he was wearing compression shorts. "Were you dressed for war or something?" I asked, propping myself up on my elbows. "You don't happen to have a knife or gun hidden anywhere on that body of yours, do you?"

"Just two," Mark teased, pulling his t-shirt off. I could see the first knife, a small little blade on a chain around his neck, and he knelt down to take off the other one, which had been strapped unseen near his right ankle. "There, now I'm unarmed."

"Except for that gun in your underpants," I teased, reaching out with my right foot. The Lycra of his shorts let my foot slide over his bulging cock like it was covered in oil. "Now tell me."

"Tell you?" Mark asked, a small smile on his face. He knew what I wanted. "I suppose you want me to tell you that you're the most beautiful woman in the world, and that every time I see your soft, beautiful skin it drives me wild?"

"Hmmmm, it's a start," I cooed, sliding my foot over his cock again. I hooked my big toe into the waistband and started to pull it down, which was more difficult than I had anticipated. After a few seconds, Mark helped, pushing the tight shorts down and off, his cock springing free. "But that, as sexy as it is, is not what I wanted to hear."

Mark smiled, pushing my legs to the side and crawling up on the bed next to me. "Maybe," he whispered as his hand came up to lift my t-shirt, cupping my left breast and driving the breath out of me when his thumb brushed my nipple, "what you want to hear is that if you give me the chance, I'm going to spoil you, and give you every little fantasy you've ever imagined, every little gift your heart desires."

"You know what my heart desires," I replied, pulling him in and kissing him.

Our tongues met, and we slowly kissed for what seemed like hours. Mark ran his hand down my body to slide my soaked cotton shorts off, leaving both of us in just our t-shirts. I wrapped my hand around the hard shaft of his cock, pumping him slowly while his fingers rubbed me. "But that's not what I want to hear."

Mark lifted my left leg up, sliding in between, forcing me to let him go. Taking his cock in his hand, he traced the thick head up and down my wet slit, teasing me with his eyes and with his cock. "I know what you want me to say. I want the same thing," he said honestly, his eyes deep with emotion. "I love you, Sophie White."

When he said my name, Mark pushed inside me, filling me with one stroke. Propping himself up on his knees, he lifted my hips up to him, then lifted me until I was sitting in his lap, my pussy stretched and filled by his wonderful cock. "I love you Sophie, and I always will."

The position we were in allowed me to control the pace of our lovemaking. Lifting myself up and down slowly, I luxuriated in the feeling of his cock slowly sliding in and out, each perfect inch different from the last it seemed, and each wonderful. Mark held me in his arms while I rode him, before I noticed a slight grimace on his face. "What is it?" I asked, pausing. "Am I hurting you?"

"No," Mark chuckled. "I did it to myself. My calves have gone to sleep kneeling like this."

We both ended up laughing, falling to the side so that I could keep Mark's cock inside me while still allowing him to stretch out his legs. Once on the mattress, I grinned and rolled him over onto his back, straddling his waist. "You didn't think I'd let go of such a wonderful position, did you?" I groaned, riding his cock. "It feels too good to let that happen."

Mark brought his hands up to cup my breasts, pinching and rolling the nipples between his fingers, and I threw my head back, crying out at the pleasure. My hips sped up, faster and faster until I was riding him as hard as I could. Leaning forward, I planted my hands on either side of his head while my breasts dangled in his face, letting my ass buck up and down, his cock filling me over and over. My clit rubbed against the hard muscles right above his cock, and I saw stars shoot across my vision.

Mark's lips never hesitated, sucking my nipple deep into his mouth and licking the sensitive tip with his tongue. I couldn't hold out much longer, so I poured my heart out as I rode him. "I love you, I love you," I said over and over as I plunged myself upon his cock.

Finally, I could take no more. Pushing back as hard as I could, I impaled myself on him, burying my face in his shoulder and screaming as a deep, hard orgasm gripped me. Mark held me tight, letting my body tense and quiver, until I started to relax. He suddenly held my hips tightly and bucked up, his legs propped up on the bed as he sought his own orgasm. In only four more strokes, he groaned and found his own release. I sagged against him, utterly spent.

* * *

I woke up in the middle of the night from a nightmare, in which the gunmen had shot first through the door, hitting Mark, before they came after me. I woke up with a short, startled scream before I felt Mark's presence behind me, holding me in his arms and soothing the fears away. "Shhh, you're safe," he whispered in my ear. Even in my half asleep state I could feel that he had changed back into his clothes, and was awake and aware. "Go back to sleep, I'll protect you all night. I love you."

Before I could protest, sleep hammered me back into the blackness, and I felt myself go. At least that time there weren't any more dreams.

* * *

Mark

The next morning, we had breakfast at a nearby Burger King, since I much prefer their breakfast burrito over anything on the McDonald's menu. As I munched, I lamented. "You know, it's been almost a decade since I left the South, but I miss Hardee's," I said as I squirted a bit of ketchup onto the eggs inside the tortilla. "They may say they merged with Carl's Jr, but it's not quite the same, I don't think."

"Never had either," Sophie replied, munching on her sausage biscuit. "In fact, this is the first fast food I've had in months."

"You've got a better diet than I do," I admitted, swallowing another bite. "They say you can't out train a bad diet, but I've been giving it my best shot for quite a while."

"I've noticed your training," Sophie said, half smiling. "Trust me, I enjoy it." We ate in comfortable silence for a bit before she swallowed the last of her breakfast and set her hands down on the table top, waiting for me. "So, what's next?"

"Well," I said, taking a sip of my orange juice, "it kind of depends on what you want to do. If you want to just disappear, I can arrange that. I have a few alternate IDs already, and know who I can talk to that can get one for you. Financially we are set, and I can get access to all of my accounts without them knowing what to look for. If you want to go back, things will be a bit more hands on, but we can start plans for that too."

"How will you get access? Can't they track you somehow?" Sophie asked, curious.

I grinned and reached into the thigh pocket on my pants. "Only if they know what to look for. I left my desktop at my apartment, to throw them off the trail. Even if they did trace my IP, they'd never see a single visit to any financial website where I have real money stashed, just a small account and some poker websites I throw some cash away on as a distraction. Instead, I did all my work on this." I pulled out what I called my smartbox, something Sophie had never seen before. "I know, it's not what you've seen, and there's been a reason for that. This little thing has in it a processor and about a two hundred gigabytes of memory, all able to be powered by a simple universal AC adapter. I can plug it into anything with an HDMI port, and connect through USB a keyboard and mouse. I'm running an encrypted Linux on it, and can jack into just about any WiFi I can find with its onboard cracking systems."

Sophie took the black plastic box from my hand, turning it over, looking at it. "It looks like a deck of cards. I mean, it's smaller than most tablets I've seen."

"More secure, too," I added. "The tradeoff is that I need to physically connect it to a keyboard and monitor."

"But can you get Netflix on it?" Sophie joked, smirking. "Seriously, though, that's pretty cool. What about physically, where are you wanting to go?"

"We can go just about anywhere," I replied, "although staying away from the big cities or places with a strong organization presence would be safer. While I've done most of my work in this half of the USA, I've pulled a few contracts overseas. The networks are more intertwined than you would imagine, and the farther I can get away from that the better."

"Hmmmm, well, I have always wanted to go to Fiji," Sophie said, before cocking her eyebrow. When I gave her no reaction one way or another, her face gaped in wonder. "You're serious, aren't you?"

"As long as I can get a satellite Internet connection I am," I said, tucking my smartbox back in my pocket. "And before you ask, yes I have a backup to the smartbox. Without one of those, however, nobody can get into my accounts. We're set for life if you want, Sophie."

Sophie thought it over for a bit, then looked at me. "Can I get in touch with my friends? I'm not saying permanently, but Tabby in particular has been my friend for years. I should at least tell her goodbye or something."

I thought about the safety risk. If the Confederation knew about Tabby, and if they had put a trace on her e-mail accounts, there was a chance that the mail could be traced back. This was especially true if Sophie's laptop had been hacked by Owen Lynch or the Confederation, and a tracer placed on it. Honestly, it was just one too many ifs to worry about. After all, they could already safely assume she was alive, and most likely with me, after the two men didn't report back successfully. I'd dumped their bodies in a river the night before, so they couldn't even be technically traced back to her place. "Not from just anywhere," I said, thinking quickly. "It'll need to be from a public place, few security cameras, public terminal, stuff like that. Is your e-mail accessible from a web browser?"

"Sure. Where then?"

About an hour later, we pulled up to a Best Buy, where Sophie gave me a suspicious look. "Keep your ball cap on, and we'll be fine," I said. "They sell prepaid phones here, I put it on my Mark Snow ID, and even if they trace it, they'll just know it was me. That's all."

We were in and out in a half-hour, and the clerk, a somewhat pimply faced high school kid, didn't even ask to see my ID. I filled out the form with total lies, and we walked out with a little web capable phone. As soon as we got to my truck, we plugged in the charger to my USB port I had replaced the cigarette lighter with, and turned it on. Two minutes later, Sophie was on the web, loading her mail. "The service here really sucks," she said as we drove down the road. "I mean, this thing is loading slowly."

"Well, what can you expect for a hundred dollars. The phone's probably cheap as hell too. Glad you're good with a stylus."

Sophie nodded, her head stilling as she loaded her message. "Mark, pull over."

"What is it?" I asked, pulling into a dry cleaners and putting the truck in park. "What's wrong?"

Sophie handed me her phone, which had an e-mail message up. "They took Tabby."

Miss White,

> *If you're reading this, then you've decided not to disappear as completely as I'm sure Mr. Snow advised you to. Our benefit, your mistake. We have Miss Williams with us, staying as a guest of our organization. She would like to have you come visit her. Even though we keep telling her that it can't rain all the time, she insists that you are the best person to help her. We tend to agree. Just remember Sophie, this is the really real world, there ain't no coming back. If you wish to visit, give Tabby's cell phone a call, she'll be happy to pick it up. We know you must feel like a little worm on a big fuckin' hook right now, but hey, are we having fun or what?*
>
> *Friends of Mark Snow*

"What's with all the cheesy lines?" I asked as I handed the phone back. "Nobody I worked with talked like that."

Sophie nodded and sighed. "A sign that they actually have or know Tabby. Back when we were in college Tabby went through a bit of a Goth-lite phase. She watched that old Brandon Lee movie *The Crow* at least twenty or thirty times on her computer, to the point that we could both quote lines to each other constantly. Last time I was over at her place, she still had a Brandon Lee poster and a copy of the DVD."

I didn't want to tell Sophie what I knew, which was that for any of the senders of the e-mail to get that information, they most likely tortured Tabby for it. I reached across the table and took her hand in mine. "What do you want to do?"

Sophie squeezed my hand and looked me in the eye. "Can you save Tabby?"

I thought it over, then nodded. "Maybe. I'd need some help and some luck, though."

"If you can't save her, what can you do?" she asked quietly, her eyes intense and her mouth tight. I squeezed her hand and looked her straight in the eye.

"If I answer, and you ask me to, you'll never be the same," I replied. "I'm not joking at all. I told you, I've got my own little corner of Hell on reservation. I'm willing to deal with that. Are you?"

Chapter 18
Sophie

I looked Mark in the eyes, and spoke from my heart. "You've done a lot of wrong things, Mark. They may not have been innocent, but you still helped men even more evil than the ones you handled to get stronger. You built up a huge debt, my love. And I will love you, no matter what. But in my opinion, you need to start paying off that debt. I don't know if you can ever fully repay it. We can start by saving Tabby, and making those bastards pay. If that damns me alongside you in the process, so be it."

We were on the road back within fifteen minutes, Mark letting me drive while he napped in the passenger seat. He hadn't slept at all the night before, even after the exhausting sex, staying awake to keep watch over me. I kept my eyes glued to the road, letting Phil Collins keep me company for the next three and a half hours back to the city. I pulled off across the river from the Tunnel, filling up on gas and waking Mark up. "Okay, we're close to the city now. Where do you want me to take us?"

"I'll drive," Mark said, yawning and stretching. He did a few jumping jacks, squats and other exercises while the gas filled up, and chugged a huge black iced coffee after we paid. "I'd go for a Monster or a Rockstar, but they tend to leave my hands jittery. That is not what I need right now," he explained as he grimaced and shotgunned the rest of the cup. He pulled into the driver's seat and started up the engine, pulling back into traffic. As he drove, he talked.

"I set up around the city five different bases of operation in addition to my condo. Three of them I used on a regular basis, the fourth I used rarely, and the fifth I set up, but never went to after initial setup. It was my emergency base, the one that I prepared for one reason only, and that was betrayal from inside the Confederation. We'll be going there, it's the safest place I know in the city."

"Where is it?" I asked, watching as the Tunnel gave way to Central Avenue. "And how do you know it is safe?"

"There's no place really safe," Mark replied, "But this place I only went to twice before. The building is totally owned by me, under one of my shell corporations. The building has motion detectors and alarms that never tripped. Also, this inside is very hard to access. Even if the Confederation knew about it, they'd probably not know what the hell it was for."

"So where is it?" I asked again, and Mark grinned and looked at me.

"You talked about redemption and paying my debts before, right? Well, I can't think of a better place to start than from Mount Zion."

"No way. Mount Zion?" Mount Zion was one of those sites that every city of sufficient age has. Built in the mid-1800's, it was originally a Methodist seminary before becoming an insane asylum (excuse me, hospital for the mentally disturbed) around World War I. After the war, the Methodist church wanted to unload the property, and it went into that limbo old properties tended to do. It was too old to get fixed up, but not quite old enough to become a historical monument. Besides, mental hospitals didn't exactly make good historical landmarks. There were dozens of stories about Mount Zion, your standard ghost story fare, but nobody really knew what was up with the property. "You're the owner of Mount Zion?"

"Well, the main church at least, with the minister's quarters upstairs," Mark replied. "The rest of the property I placed into a trust in order to take care of the taxes. The hospital is under an option to buy from three different developers who want to tear it down in order to put up things ranging from a strip mall to an apartment building. My shell corporation that controls the trust is playing them against each other, and the game could have gone on for a few more years."

We drove over to the Heights section of town, the rolling hills that the city had first been founded on, and Mark drove us to Mount Zion. As we approached I could see how perfect it was as a location. Relatively centrally located in the city, it was still isolated in the hills, with acres of unoccupied land around it. The driveway was nearly a half mile long, giving us plenty of isolation and warning if anyone wanted to drive up to the site. In addition, the ghost stories and other superstitions limited the number of teenage lovers or homeless who'd be willing to try and use the old buildings for unauthorized purposes. Mark pulled in, and shut off the engine.

"After I purchased the building, I used my corporation to hire a very discreet handyman, who came up here and did some renovations to the bell tower of the church. The old door was replaced with a steel core security door, and the stairs were reinforced along with the room at the top being cleaned and sparsely furnished. I apologize there is only a single thin mattress, but it was created as an emergency base, not a permanent residence."

"It'll be fine," I said, looking up at the old church. It still looked abandoned, but solid, in a Neo-Gothic style that intimidated. I thought about Tabby's fixation with *The Crow*, and thought it was an appropriate place to start from. "When we get

Tabby back, we should bring her here. She'd like this place."

We went inside with our bags, and I was surprised. While the main sanctuary was still an abandoned mess, the stairwell to the belfry was concealed well, looking like the door frame had been bricked over. Mark used a remote control that looked just like one for a car door to unlock the entrance. It even beeped like a car door system would. "Yeah, I copied it. A lot of supposedly high-tech gadgets are nothing more than applying old solutions in new ways."

The belfry itself was spartan, mostly scrubbed down hardwood that was stained almost black. "The handyman sent the lawyer for my shell corporation a few pics of what it was before, and I liked the old color, so I just had him seal all the wood after making sure none of it was rotted out. They built the platforms of cedar, actually, so it's still solid as a rock. I don't know if the color is a result of the original stain they used, age, bat guano, or a combination of all of them, but I liked it."

A little bit of natural light filtered in from the slat sides on the north side of the tower, which had years ago allowed the sound of the bells to come out. I could see the massive beams above us where they had once hung, but had been removed decades before. Along the other three walls the slats had been sealed up. There was a thin mattress on the floor along the west side of the floor, a small table, and a series of metal footlockers. "What's in these?" I asked, tapping them with my foot. "Your supplies?"

"And my tools," Mark replied, unlocking two of the lockers. The tops lifted open, revealing an arsenal. "We should contact the people who have Tabby, and learn more."

I took out my old cell phone, and looked at him. "Here?"

"No, we'll go back on the road," Mark said, taking out two pistols. "You ever fire a gun before?"

"Just on video games, and one time I did some paintball," I replied.

Mark nodded, put one of the pistols back, and pulled out another. He took a clip of ammunition from the trunk, slapped it in, and pulled back on the top, making a metallic, intimidating *snick*. He turned the gun around and held it out to me. "It's loaded, with one in the chamber. There's a safety on the left side, right now it's on. Push it in, and the red line disappears. See?"

I looked, and saw the button. I pushed it in, and heard a small click. I looked on the other side of the grip, and saw the button had popped out on the other side, this time with a red line visible. I pushed it, and the safety reengaged. "Okay, got it.

Now, how do I cock this thing?"

"You don't need to," Mark said. "Once the safety is off, just point and shoot. Listen, this thing is not very big, but it packs a punch. You more or less point and shoot, and can do it over and over again."

Mark took two more pistols from the footlocker, slid in clips, and tucked them under his shirt against his lower back. With his shirt hanging loosely over the top, I couldn't see anything. "Do you have a jacket or a sweatshirt?"

"I have a hoodie," I said, "but it's kind of tight. I couldn't wear that pistol in my jeans like you are."

"Then keep it in the pocket itself. If you stuff some other things in there, you should be fine. We're going to walk, so it should look like you have a cell phone or something like that in there. Don't pull it out unless you have to. You'll know when."

We left the belfry, and walked cross country until we were along a side street, near a preschool. "This was a lot easier when I started," Mark said as I pulled out my phone. "Back then, there were pay phones all over the place. Nowadays, neighborhoods like this don't have many at all. In some ways it makes it more flexible, since we can go anywhere. The bad part is you need to hang onto a phone. There's some VOIP and different masking programs out there, but in a lot of ways they are just as traceable as a normal cell phone. So, we do things like this, and travel. I'd prefer to get on a city bus or something and head downtown, but I don't want Tabby to be in any more danger."

I nodded and pulled out my phone, dialing Tabby's number. My hands shook as I waited for the call to be picked up. I didn't have to wait long. A rough-voiced man picked up the call after only three rings. "Miss White."

"Where is Tabby?" I asked immediately, before he could say anything else. "Is she safe?"

"She's fine," the man replied. "Although that may not last forever. Is the Snowman with you?"

"Yes," I said, looking up at Mark. "Why?"

"Put him on the phone," the voice commanded.

I handed the phone to Mark, who held the phone up to his ear. "I'm here...... okay...... okay..... not going to happen. Not there, I'm not a fool. That's fine. Just me and her. Fine. Three hours. Now put her on the line, let her verify her identity."

Mark handed the phone next to me, and nodded. "Tabby is supposed to be on the line."

"Tabby?" I asked, my throat tight and my eyes starting to water. "Are you all right?"

"Oh Sophie, I'm so scared!" It was definitely Tabby. Even with all the fear choking her voice, the accent, the intonation, everything was her. "They keep saying there's some guy they are interested in or something. What the hell is going on?"

Before I could answer, the phone was taken away. "You have your proof. Three hours."

The phone went dead in my ear, and I cursed, only muffling my voice enough to make sure the preschoolers in the area didn't hear me. I handed the phone back to Mark, who shut it off and took out the battery. "We meet in three hours, at the same nightclub where you and I met. Which at least confirms who took your friend. That club is owned by a Confederation member. Don't know how many in the Confederation are in on it, but it doesn't matter, I guess. Let's get back, I need to get us ready."

* * *

Mark

The club was dark, which I expected. I wished that I could have left Sophie behind, she wasn't prepared for this, but the men on the phone had been very clear, we had to come together. It made sense. They assumed that having Sophie nearby would reduce my combat efficiency, since I would spend energy and brain power trying to defend her at the expense of killing them. They were right. It came down to how much of a decrease in my abilities Sophie would cause, and if it would make them better than me. Honestly, it was an interesting conundrum, and one I would have enjoyed contemplating at any other time.

I didn't even try to hide what I was carrying, coming loaded full bore in a tactical vest, my Glocks in cross grab holsters against my ribs. I had my throwing knives in a thigh sheath on my right leg, and was as ready as I could get. Sophie, on the other hand, looked like she was wearing just a hooded sweatshirt, although it was different from the one she had worn earlier. She had borrowed one of mine, in order to fit the armored vest underneath. I just hoped she didn't have to use either of her two surprises she had under the shirt.

"Yo, I'm here," I called into the seemingly empty club. I knew all of the entrances and exits by heart, and immediately cut to my right, reaching for the Glock under my right arm, pulling it out and scanning. Sophie stayed right on my heels, exactly as I had asked her to do. She was quiet, her body semi-crouched as we made our way around the inside wall. Staying there had trade-offs. On one hand, I couldn't be crept up on from behind with my back to the wall. I could keep my eyes on the entire first floor of the club. However, I also couldn't see about two-thirds of the upper floor, especially directly above me. Thankfully, they couldn't see us either. "Come out, it's just the two of us, like you demanded."

There was motion near the VIP rooms, close to the hallway that led to the manager's office. Shaun, the manager, came out holding Tabby, along with two other men. He had his favorite pistol, a Colt 1911 in his hand by his side. "Snowman. I honestly didn't think you would do it. I mean, we all knew you'd stashed money away like my grandma used to. All those hits you made, and jobs you pulled, and you still didn't live anywhere near as good as you could have. I figured you for one, maybe two more years in the game. But I didn't think you'd go out like this. You were always too smart. I mean, it's not like you couldn't get yourself a dime bitch after you got out. Giordano wouldn't have had any problems with that, you know, after a year or two."

"So it was Sal who signed off on this?" I asked, trying to draw them out. Keeping them talking was vital to my plan. There was no way I could take them out without knowing exactly how many men Shaun had with him, or where they were located in the club. "He told me he gave me the rest of that night."

"Sal's a good judge of character, you know that. Didn't get to where he was without it. He saw in your eyes that you wouldn't take out your girl. Don't know why, either. I see better girls than her in here all the damn time."

"I'm not interested in girls, Shaun. I've always been interested in women."

Shaun laughed and stepped forward. "Come up here, man. Both of you. When you're at the bottom of the stairs, my boys will let the girl go."

"Fine. We'll come up the east side stairs. I see any of your boys anywhere near it, I start shooting. Let the girl go and she can come over to the east side as well. That cool?"

"Cool."

I nodded to Sophie, who followed me. I was proud of the fact that she hadn't said a word since we came in. There was no point in creeping up the stairs, they were open to the center of the club on all sides. Instead, Sophie and I took them at a quick but even pace, making sure my Glock in my left hand was visible, but not pointed in

Shaun's direction. I wanted him aware but distracted, not fearful.

When we reached the second floor, my eyes swept the walkway, spotting two other men. Shaun was smart, he knew me. In normal circumstances, five on one would be odds I would walk away from. "All right Shaun. Let her go."

Shaun laughed like I'd just told a funny joke. "Come on, Snowman, you think I'm stupid? I know how good you are. I let this bitch go, and before I can count to ten I'm a dead man. No way. Drop your guns, and then I let her go."

Now, I could have talked more. I could have dropped the guns. But one of the main personal rules of my training is that once you're in the zone, you just go. I felt that familiar, welcome coldness drop over my emotions, and I went with it. Squeezing the trigger on the Glock in my left hand, I put a round in the head of the man on Shaun's left before my right hand even cleared my other Glock from its holster. It is one of the secrets of my success, I'm not only almost totally ambidextrous with my hands, but with my eyes as well. I put a round in the thigh of the second bodyguard while my right hand snapped into place, firing as soon as I could. There was an instant when Shaun could have gotten the drop on me, while I was shooting his guards. If he had just raised his pistol in that split second, he could have gotten a shot off at me. Instead, he hesitated, torn between shooting me and trying to use Tabby as a human shield, and in that hesitation I had him dead to rights. The round took Shaun in between his eyes, the 9mm hollowpoint turning the back of his head into a giant bloody flower petal of bone, hair and skin. It took less than two seconds.

I whirled and dove while Sophie flattened herself on the floor. Rolling over a table in front of me I came up firing, catching one of the corner men before he could get a shot off at me. The second man was smarter, moving before trying to fire, and it took me an extra three seconds to find him and put a round into his shoulder. He spun, crashing over the railing to fall to the club floor below, head first. The dry twig sound of his neck snapping told me all I needed to know.

Suddenly there was a boom behind me, and I spun, both pistols ready, but it was already over. Sophie huddled on the floor, the pistol type shotgun I'd given her tight in her hands, smoke rising from the barrel. I'd never seen or even heard him, and he crashed to the floor, the deer slug obliterating most of the right side of his chest.

It was only then that sound came back into the world, and I realized the high pitch screaming in my ear wasn't my overtaxed nerves going nuts, but Tabby screaming hysterically. I swept the room with my eyes, then ran over and knelt next to Sophie. "You all right?"

She looked at me, her eyes calmer than I expected them to be. "Yeah. You?"

"Yeah. Get Tabby, I'll cover the room," I said, kneeling next to the man who had snuck up on me. I was curious, I hadn't had someone sneak up on me in years. Sophie started off, and I caught up, making sure the back of the club didn't have any more nasty surprises, then checked Shaun's body, taking his cell phone out of his right front pocket. Tabby was still in hysterics until Sophie pulled her into a hug, and between the two of us, we carried her out of the club. She passed out on the way to the truck, which I was grateful for. It made transporting her easier since she was already in a state of shock.

* * *

It was even more difficult two weeks later. "You're sure about this?"

It was the third time Sophie had asked Tabby since bringing her home. We were in her apartment, and while I was wearing jeans and a sweatshirt, I was still armed. There was no time I'd left the belfry in the last two weeks that I wasn't carrying something. We'd brought Tabby there, trusting her to keep the secret, to give her a chance to recover and adjust to the situation. I'd then spent the last week giving her a crash course on how to survive if organized crime was interested in you, and how to cover your tracks. Finally, I'd placed a few calls, and made a few inquiries to try and give her a bit of security in other ways too. Still, I agreed with Sophie. Tabby should have taken a vacation, preferably one of multiple months at least in a city far away. Europe would have been nice.

Tabby looked at Sophie in exasperation and smiled. "You know, just because I don't have Rambo for my boyfriend doesn't mean I can't take care of myself. Besides, you know what Mark told them."

It was true, I had used Shaun's cell phone to give Sal Giordano a call, warning him to stay away from Tabby, and that he'd made a big damn mistake doing what he did. I hoped that it would put a bit of caution into the Confederation, and have them spend more time trying to find me rather than going through Tabby. Still, I am only one man, and I couldn't protect her all the time. No matter how many times I tried to tell her though, she wouldn't listen. She was going to stay in the city.

"Tabby, I can't promise I can be here, but if you need me, you know the number to call." I'd bought half a dozen burner phones with some of the cash I had on hand, and had given her one with another of the numbers programmed in. I could ditch it whenever I wanted if I needed to. "Just remember, if you want to just talk, use your normal phone. Sophie's cell still works, it's been scrubbed."

Tabby nodded, only a bit exasperated with me. "I know, I know. Mark, you've been giving me lessons on how to survive for a week and a half now. I got it, really."

On the way back to the belfry, Sophie reached over and took my hand. "She'll be ok, you know. She may come off at a total ditz, but Tabby's got a decent brain inside that cute skull of hers. By the way, thank you for turning her down when she hit on you, even though she was just teasing me."

"She's not my type," I said. We reached the bell tower, and climbed the stairs. Once in the tiny room that had become our apartment, I pulled her into a deep kiss. "You are."

"For that I'm still confused, but very happy," she replied, her soft kiss matching the softness of her skin and body as she molded her body against me. "It has been a while, hasn't it?"

"Four days," I whispered into her ear. "Having a guest up here with us since the club kind of put a damper on doing what I wanted to do."

"Then let's not waste any time," Sophie replied, running her hands down my stomach and cupping my cock through my pants. Her gentle fingers massaged in a wave like fluttering, until I was aching and barely in control. Pushing her back to our mattress, we collapsed in a tangle of arms and legs, touching and stroking each other, Sophie ending up on top, straddling my hips. Sophie had lost a little bit of weight since we moved into the bell tower, but she was just as beautiful, with her long hair thick and silky in my fingers. Pulling her shirt off, I kissed the swells of her breasts, full and round against my face. Sophie was wearing a deep red satin bra that highlighted her skin perfectly. "You always have loved my boobs."

"They're works of natural art," I said, running my thumbs over her nipples. The dark pink skin crinkled and hardened, small little nubs that made my mouth water. Lifting her right breast to my lips, I kissed around her nipple, tickling her until she was moving from side to side, trying to bring it to my mouth and relieve her frustration. "You want more?"

"Dammit, you know what I need," Sophie growled, pushing me back onto the mattress. "And I know what you need." She slid down my legs, tugging at my belt and freeing my cock, which was already painfully hard, wrapping her breasts around my shaft. "Now, are you going to give me what I need, or am I going to have to tease you until your cock explodes and you pass out?"

"Okay, okay," I conceded, smiling and reaching down. "Bring something up here for me to give pleasure to."

I was happily surprised when Sophie almost spun around, swinging her pussy up and over my face. "Hmm, seems we've both found something the other does well," I joked before reaching out with my tongue, tracing the soft petals of her outer lips. Sophie didn't wax, but she kept herself well-trimmed, leaving just a small triangle of soft dark hair at the top. It left her lips smooth and satiny, beautiful to touch and kiss. Best of all was her flavor, spicy and tangy and exotic. Parting her lips with the tip of my tongue, I dipped at her nectar, relishing her sighs and soft cries as I licked up and down.

"Mark......" Sophie groaned, pumping my cock with her lightly clenched fist. I kept up my licks, delighting in both the sensual stroke of her hand and the beautiful flavor on my lips. I circled her clit and Sophie gasped, bending forward to swallow my cock, sucking hard. I barely held myself under control as Sophie licked and sucked, mirroring her actions to my own.

Our oral play became a game, a loving competition between the two of us. When I licked her clit, she would play her tongue around the head of my cock. When I kissed and licked deeper, Sophie sucked and tongued my shaft, both of us seeing how far we could bring the other.

Neither of us could take the game for too long. Sophie 'lost' only because of the fact she was on top, and could move easier than I could, pulling her hips off of me and sliding down my torso. Looking back over her shoulder as she positioned herself over my cock, her eyes were the sexiest look I'd ever seen in my life. If I live to be a thousand years old I'll still remember the half-open lips, shining in the afternoon light while her eyes shone with love and desire for me. Holding my cock in her hand, she sank down until the two perfect hemispheres of her ass touched my hips, and she settled down. "Hold on, cowboy," she grinned, flashing me a naughty smile. "This is going to be one hell of a ride."

Leaning forward and putting her hands on my thighs right above my knees, Sophie rose up, lifting and riding back and forth on my cock. It was sweet torture, pinned down under her as she pleasured herself. Her body gripped my shaft tightly, each nerve ending sending tingles through my body. "Faster," I said, just barely keeping from begging. I'd never given up so much control in bed to a woman before, but Sophie was like no other woman. "Fast and hard, babe."

Sophie's hips shook with each hard slap of her ass against my hips. We were both soon moaning and gasping, the rising orgasm expected to be loud and messy. Sweat stung my eyes as I bit my lip to keep from coming, the erotic sight of my cock disappearing into Sophie's body with every back and forth movement of her hips adding to the energy, until I lost all control. With a deep growl I grabbed Sophie's hips, planting my heels in the mattress and hammering her pussy, desperate for release. Our cries mixed, and when I heard Sophie's breath catch, I abandoned all restraint, racing towards my climax. "I'm going to come," I warned, my cock aching, so close I could feel it.

"Do it," Sophie screamed, her pussy clamping down on me. Her cry stretched out as her orgasm took over, her hair flying in a beautiful wave as she tossed her head back, her back arching. I pumped in one last time, letting my release rip through me. I could feel my balls actually cramp I was coming so hard, hissing the pain and pleasure together. It felt like it went on forever, until my hips relaxed, and we both sagged back onto the mattress. I was too weak to do anything but lay there while Sophie caught her breath, staying where she was until my softened cock slipped out of her, and she turned around to cuddle against me. "I love you," she whispered, kissing my jawline.

"I love you too," I said, wrapping my arm around her shoulders. We lay there in the dim afternoon light filtering through the slat sides of the tower for a few minutes before I spoke again. "What do you think about living here?"

"In the city?" Sophie asked. "It's a good city, but we're probably going to be in danger. Why do you ask?"

"I wasn't just thinking about the city," I said, gesturing around the room, "But here. The past few weeks, after we saved Tabby, I've been thinking. You're right, I have a lot of sins to atone for. What about using some of that blood money I've gathered over the years to try and clean up the city? I had five strike bases before, and my condo in the high rise. What if we do something the same, but use this place as our main base?"

Sophie thought about it for a while, running her hand over my chest. The effect was nice, and I could feel my body warming to the idea of another round of sex with the woman I love. "How do you plan on making sure we aren't tracked down? You start showing your face too much around here, and it's liable to get blown off."

I nodded and grinned. "You don't think I didn't plan on faking my own death? While it wouldn't be foolproof, you and I could take a vacation, say to South Korea.

They do plastic surgery there all the time, and we'd get a few changes made. Nothing too drastic, mostly I had planned a bit along my jawline and eyebrows, a bit of reshaping. Combine that with a change of hair color, and I'll be able to get by pretty well."

"A vacation to South Korea, huh?" Sophie replied, and I could hear her grin. "I could do that. But there's going to be a couple of rules in all of this."

"What's that?" I asked, rolling us both over so that I could lay on my side and look at her. It also pressed her breasts against me, and I had to fight not to be distracted.

"Rule number one," Sophie replied, running her hands over my lower back and stroking my backbone, a favorite site for her to explore as we spent time together, "is that I'm not going to be some passive little observer. I put a shotgun round into someone last time, and I'm still here. I didn't break down in hysterics. So if you want to turn into some cross between Batman and The Punisher, I'm not going to be your Alfred."

"Deal," I replied, kissing her forehead. "You're a lot cuter than any butler anyway. Although I'd love to see you in a French maid's outfit sometime."

"Maybe for Halloween," Sophie teased before growing serious again. "Rule two. You're going to train me. I damn near broke my wrists shooting that pistol in the club, and I'm not going into a situation so defenseless again. So you're going to train me how to shoot, and we'll work on how to fight."

"That's fine. I also was thinking you are going to want to continue your medical training as well. I'm good, but I'm not invincible. You're probably going to have to patch one or both of us up if you really want us to fight."

Sophie leaned up and kissed me, smiling. "Good. One final rule."

"What's that?" I asked, feeling my cock twitch and start to rise again.

Sophie opened her mouth to say something, then felt my cock poking against her thigh. She glanced down and smiled, wrapping her fingers around it and starting to pump. "I think you don't have to worry about rule three. You seem to be doing a very good job of that without any guidance from me."

Reaching up and cupping her breast, I smiled. "Well, I never went to college, but I do have a knack for learning."

Chapter 19
Part 3 - Sophie

The target was blurry in my sights, so I took a deep breath and readjusted. Pulling my head away, I realigned myself along the stock of the rifle, looking for that spot Mark had taught me was called the 'cheek weld.' It's supposed to be a perfect alignment, where your eye is just far enough from your scope that you can see perfectly, and your cheekbone rests lightly on the stock, reducing your need for muscular tension. Reminding myself of how it felt, I laid my cheek back along the cool hard line of the rifle, and sighted.

My target was almost totally stationary, tiny even in the magnification of my scope. Letting out half my breath, I slid my finger inside the trigger guard, resting the tip of my finger on the smooth curve inside. I stopped then, waiting for that magic moment when the heart would calm and everything would fall into place. At first it rarely, if ever, came but over the past month it had come much more often.

When everything clicked into place, I didn't even notice when my finger contracted the quarter inch needed. The rifle kicked in my hands, the scope going blurry as recoil jerked the rifle a bit. I quickly re-found my target, but a second shot was unneeded. The bottle dangled at the end of its string, swinging back and forth with red colored water shooting out of a hole in the middle, like it was pissing blood or something.

"Good hit!" I put my rifle on safe and set it on the bench in front of me, turning to smile as Mark nodded. "That's five for five today. Great work."

I gave him a quick hug, then we went down the short fifty meters to the target. Mark had hung a half liter bottle that used to contain Pepsi from a frame, letting the bottle swing back and forth in the breeze and with a bit of assistance from him. At the base of the frame were another four similar bottles, each with holes in them. While it wasn't exactly United States Marine Corps Scout Sniper level, for a girl who'd only fired her first real gun three months prior, I thought I was doing a pretty good job. "Still, it's only fifty meters, and I'm shooting bottles."

Mark considered the hole in my bottle and nodded. "Yeah, but the fact is that this bottle, when you consider the scale and the distance, won't be that much different. At three hundred meters, a six-foot man is the same as this bottle at fifty meters. Sure windage, elevation and things like that take a toll, but considering you're also shooting a tiny little .22 round right now, that'll be compensated too."

"And if I have to shoot longer than that?" I asked, untying the bottle and putting up a new one. We'd brought ten that day to use after I had fired another hundred rounds into stationary paper targets. My best so far in the exercise was five out of ten. I was hoping to get seven.

"Then we're in trouble," Mark replied with a grim smile. "Remember, we're going to be living in the city. If we have to start playing long range sniper with someone, either we're no longer in the city, or things have gone to hell. Either way, that's more of a time to run than a time to shoot."

"You forgot one other possibility," I said as we rigged the "wiggle string" that Mark used to make the bottle sway. He looked at me out of the corner of his eyes and squinted. I couldn't resist my smile any longer. "Zombie apocalypse. You can never forget the zombie apocalypse."

Mark rolled his eyes and turned, but I could hear the chuckle as I watched his back. Training with him had added a lot of depth to our relationship. Before, we were just like any other couple, friends and lovers. But by agreeing to train me in his skills in order to take on the crime that was crippling our city, we'd also become student and teacher. I had to say, Mark was an excellent instructor. He put up with my natural student irreverence very well, while at the same kept it focused and professional.

The education I went through was like nothing I'd ever done before. In addition to learning how to shoot, not just rifles but pistols, shotguns and even submachine guns, Mark had covered the basics of dirty fighting, knives, movement in and around an urban combat environment, surveillance, tracking, and a lot of others. We both knew that two months of training wasn't enough to even scratch the surface on some things, but I was making a lot of progress. The main things Mark focused on were firearms and movement. We'd spent hours running and moving through buildings, using the ideas of Parkour as a base movement. I was honestly in the best shape of my life and I felt incredible.

One of the things that had shocked me at first as Mark walked me through my lessons was the detailed knowledge he had of human anatomy. In some areas he even matched me after all the work I'd done to become a physician's assistant. Mark had explained it to me after I had asked one time. "We both studied, but two different sides of the same coin. You studied how to repair the body. I studied how to break it."

While we trained hard, it wasn't all we did. After the bandages came off of our plastic surgeries, Mark and I spent the rest of the month traveling around South Korea, enjoying the local food and seeing the sights. We even rented a car to go from Seoul to Busan and around the countryside in between. We left South Korea and went to the Balkans, where Mark conducted most of my firearms training. In addition to being able to speak passable Croat, he was fluent in German, and could communicate with almost all of the people we met. He chose the Balkans not because of the language, but because he knew we could cross from one country to another through poorly watched and barely defended national borders. This allowed us to fly into Athens on one set of passports and then use others later to establish histories to our false identities.

Mark Snow no longer existed, but instead, there was Marcus Smiley of Green Bay, Wisconsin. I was now Sophie Warbird, his girlfriend and a naturalized citizen originally from Canada. When I asked Mark about the similarity of our new names to our old identities, he nodded. "We've spent a very long time being called our old names. The fact is, while our family names could go away, we've spent too long being called 'Mark' and 'Sophie' to not slip up and ignore when someone says something to us, or to call each other those in public. The same with our signatures. The smaller the change, the easier it will be for us to adapt."

That day, I went one better than my goal of hitting seven of the ten swinging bottles. I actually hit eight, but Mark called it a non-fatal shot, as it just winged the bottle. "In a human, that would bleed like a stuck pig, but he wouldn't be out of action, and he'd recover," he explained. "A great day for you."

I smiled, a warm feeling in my chest at his compliment. It was something that I'd come to accept, the separation of Mark, my boyfriend and love of my life, and Mark the teacher and former contract killer. As a boyfriend, he was affectionate, warm, and kind. He would do all the little things that meant so much, and in terms of intimacy.... well, let's just say I'd lost weight due to more than just the Parkour running.

But Mark the teacher was different. It wasn't that he was cruel. It was just that he was all business. He didn't break me down, but he was a focused taskmaster. If I made a mistake, especially one that could have cost me my life, he made sure I knew in exact detail what I'd done wrong and how to do it right. We would then repeat it as many times as needed until I got the skill or the action down right.

For example, when he taught me how to shoot a pistol, he didn't start with a real pistol. Instead, we started with a BB gun, learning the different parts and how to aim and squeeze the trigger. From there we'd gone up to a .22 caliber round, his favorite training round because it was not only easy to get and cheap, but because it had a very small kick. Only after I could shoot the .22 properly did he move me up to a larger round. I particularly liked the 9mm, but we both knew that sometimes I wouldn't have a choice in what we might need to use.

He'd done the same for every weapon that I had learned how to use, going from small to larger. He'd even compensated for things like learning how to handle rifle kick by stifling any sort of recoil suppression device in the smaller rounds.

We shot in abandoned old buildings, and backwoods areas that nobody would come to bother us. Eastern Germany and Croatia were full of them, and we kept on the move often enough that no local police would get curious about us anyway. It was basic training, laying the foundations for a new life, and a vacation all rolled into one.

That night, we went back to the small inn where we were staying for a hearty dinner of what the locals called *zagrebački odrezak*, a veal steak that had ham and cheese stuffed inside before it was breaded and grilled. Absolutely delicious, and the glutton inside of me was well satiated. I looked at Mark, who was steadily working his way through his own, along with a bowl of the local polenta that the locals called *zganci*. "Is living this life going to mean I can eat like this every day and still lose weight?" I asked, patting my much firmer stomach. "This is amazing."

Mark chuckled and shook his head. "Sorry my love, but no. Eventually, your body will adapt, and we'll be back to eating normally. However, we should be back in the States by then, so I wouldn't worry about it for now."

It was the only undecided part of our plan. While Mark and I both wanted to launch our two person war on organized crime in our city, the fact of the matter was, I wasn't ready. I may have already killed a man, but that was more due to chance than anything else. The longer we could stay out of the city, and me training, the better off we'd be later on. It wasn't that we were lacking for funds, Mark had millions stashed in various accounts along with a core seed of money that he had invested in stocks, bonds, and various companies through aliases, shell corporations, and numbered accounts.

After dinner, we went back to our room. Croatian inns are not the same as American ones. Our bed was rustic, with a handmade comforter on top that most likely had been made by the owner's wife or mother. It had beautiful patterns interwoven into it, and smelled like it had been stored in a cedar chest when it wasn't being used. The bed itself was soft and thick, suspended on a real rope frame that actually worked better than any metal springs or frame I'd ever had.

Mark pulled out our tablet and turned on our little satellite uplink system. The speed wasn't exactly good enough to stream high definition video, but we didn't use it for such. Instead, we used it for keeping track of Mark's financial packages, read news, and keep in touch with certain people via e-mail. Tabby Williams, my best friend who we had saved from the Confederation, sometimes e-mailed us information about goings on in the city that you couldn't get from the local television stations. She'd become a good little intelligence officer. I hated involving her, but once Tabby sets her mind to something, you might as well agree or you're wasting your breath. The rest of the time we just swapped stories, although we were careful not to give away too many details.

"Anything new?" I asked as I quickly washed up and changed into light shorts and a tank top, not wanting to go to bed with the smell of gunpowder on my hands.

Mark sat silently for a minute, his brow furrowed. Finally, he turned to look at me, and nodded. "We need to go back. Take a look." He passed the tablet over, open to our secured e-mail. What I read shocked me. "See what I mean?"

Dear guys, the message began. Tabby was careful not to use names at all in the messages she sent us, and the address was nothing more than random numbers and letters. We had sent her the e-mail link through one of our burner phones, so there couldn't be any way to trace it back to us.

There's rumors that a certain party is about to bring in some interesting imports from out of town. Apparently, the current market share with his nearest competitor wasn't enough for him, and he wants to have the entire market to himself. The people I know don't have a lot of details, they just know it's going to be big, and it's coming into town soon. I'd say sweeps week is upon us!

That was another thing about Tabby, she always tried to write using circumspect language. Not that it helped, even a beginner could see what she was talking about. "So what do you think she means?"

Mark thought about it for a second while he turned the tablet off and shut down the satellite link. "Most likely Owen Lynch is making a play. The Confederation doesn't trust each other enough for them to allow a member to bring in an outside party into town, it would disrupt their own internal balance as much as the city-wide balance. And they have enough ears amongst their own that nobody could pull it off without the knowledge of the rest of the Confederation. But Owen

Lynch operates his group with him at the top. He doesn't need to answer to anyone. I'm not saying the Confederation couldn't be doing it, but more than likely it's Lynch."

I thought about it for a moment, then tilted my head. "So why not let him do it? He takes out the Confederation, we only have one enemy to worry about, right?"

Mark shook his head. "No, unfortunately it's not that easy. If Lynch can consolidate power, he'll be able to put himself in a position where our chances of taking him down dwindle to nothing. We're only two people, we can't stop everything at once. He'd have the manpower and the overall power to just flood the streets and take us out by sheer force of numbers. Secondly, if we take him out directly.... well, put it this way. Let's say a week after we get back, I find out he's going to be in public and I take him out. What do you think happens the very next day?"

I nodded, seeing where Mark was going. "All of his lieutenants and underlings go nuts trying to overtop each other, fighting for their scrap of his empire."

"Exactly. It would be a street war the likes our city hasn't seen since the Roaring Twenties. It'd make the Los Angeles Gang Wars of the eighties and nineties look like patty cake. There would be out-of-towners coming in, street gangs trying to move up the pecking order, and general chaos. There would be a lot of innocents caught right in the middle."

"So we go back."

Chapter 20
Mark

Stepping off the Lufthansa Airlines jetliner, it felt strange being back in the city. I knew that Sophie and I weren't being hunted by the authorities. After all, Mark Snow had never been fingerprinted in his life, and Sophie White had apparently accepted a job with a Christian missionary group providing health care in Southeast Asia, thanks to a little maneuvering. Besides that, the passports for Marcus Smiley and Sophie Warbird were totally legit, and totally clean. I'd paid good money for them, after all.

Still, we were back in enemy territory. Regardless of if the belfry tower was still secure or not, there wasn't any place in the city that we couldn't be found. Not between the Confederation and Owen Lynch. So, our plan hinged on something totally different, hiding in plain sight.

"Mr. Smiley! Mr. Smiley!" the newspaper reporter called over as soon as we left the baggage terminal. "Do you have any statement about your coming to town?"

"Of course," I said, grinning. "I'm glad to make this city my new home. With the opportunities that have been provided for me, I am certain I can provide plenty of opportunities for the people of this city as well."

To get this, you gotta understand my new identity. Marcus Smiley was an Internet millionaire. Starting with a small website, he built it to massive levels of traffic before cashing out, and reinvesting in various technology firms. Moving capital strategically around the globe, every company he touched seemed to turn to gold. Similarly, every company he pulled out of turned to dust almost as quickly. He'd been investigated by financial agencies all over the world, and with each of them he was as clean as freshly washed sheets.

The reality is, most of that money was pushed around within my own network of shell corporations. I'd always had Marcus Smiley in mind when I set up my retirement plan, along with a few other identities, and my accomplishments in his name were enough to set the media abuzz when the "reclusive business mogul" suddenly declared he was setting up his newest venture, along with a new home, within the city. He was even buying the old Mount Zion property from a local corporation and turning it into his personal home. The buzz within the technology sector, and the buzz within the society pages ensured our arrival would get local press.

The reporter looked next to me, where Sophie was smiling through a pair of sunglasses. "And who is this lovely woman next to you?" he asked, his eyes continually pulled to her hair. It was the most effective element of Sophie's disguise. As Sophie White, her most noticeable feature to most men were her large, perfect breasts. As Sophie Warbird, however, while still perfect, attention was diverted from her breasts to a shock of electric purple hair that ran all the way down to the middle of her back.

"This, my good man, is Sophie Warbird, my fiancee and vice president of Smiley Holdings. As you can tell, she's not only beautiful, but has the best sense of personal style on the entire East Coast." The purple was Sophie's choice, and I have to give her credit, I was inspired. We had both dyed our hair, but Sophie decided to go super extreme. Not exactly inconspicuous, but that was our plan, to stay in the open. In our bags, though, she also had a long black wig that she would use when she needed to not be recognized. That and a tight sports bra would hopefully combine to make her invisible at times. "We're both excited to be in town."

"Miss Warbird," the reporter said, swinging his little tape recorder away from me. "Anything you want to say to the people?"

Sophie smiled, and I could see the reporter's eyes glitter, enchanted. I could understand the sentiment. The three months we'd spent abroad had allowed her to blossom. She was pretty confident before, smart and lively, and sexy as hell, but now all of those qualities were dialed up to eleven. She had become the type of woman who walks into a room, and everyone stops to see what she's doing. What self-consciousness she did have before seemed to have disappeared. I had to intentionally become overly bombastic and attention grabbing just to get the first comments from people. "Well, like Marcus said, I'm glad to be here," Sophie said. "I'm a huge fan of football, and let's face it, no team has better fans than the Spartans."

The reporter smiled and nodded. He looked like he was getting ready to ask another question, but Sophie cut him off. "I'd love to talk more, but I'm very excited to see our new home. Maybe your office can contact us directly later?"

"Sure," the news guy said, mollified. He took out his business card and handed it to Sophie, who passed it along to me. "I know our style editor would love to talk with you about that hair."

Outside the airport, our rented BMW was waiting for us. It was one of the most frustrating parts about assuming the new identity of Marcus Smiley. As Mark Snow, I had various cars, properties, and other equipment ready for use. But, since the Confederation and probably Owen Lynch knew where most of it was, my tools were reduced to what I had in the Mount Zion belfry, and purchasing new equipment. A lot of it, like guns, was easily replaced, if a bit of a hassle. There was some of it though that was very difficult to replicate or replace.

"You know, I miss the Electric Dream Machine," Sophie said as we pulled away. I nodded. My all-electric Mercedes was one of the most noticeable trademarks of Mark Snow. It had gotten to the point that I didn't even need to do much more than drive it by the business or house of my target and they would fold. That is, if intimidation was my goal. Floating by silently, the blue GT-S got attention. Sadly, I'd never get to drive it again, it had been sold off through a third party, the funds donated to a charity to throw off any traces. I liked that car, too.

"Well, now that we're back in town, we'll see about getting something for each of us," I said. "After all, as the newest socialite millionaire, we're supposed to do at least a bit of conspicuous consumption."

Thankfully, there were no reporters waiting outside the Mount Zion property. I pulled in, shutting down the engine and looking over at her. "Well, we're home."

Sophie smiled, then looked down at her hands. They're beautiful, with graceful fingers and hidden strength. Even two months of hard training in Eastern Europe hadn't marred their beauty to me, although she had appreciated the manicure we'd gotten in London during our one-day stopover on the way home. She seemed to struggle with what she wanted to say, then looked over from the passenger seat at me. "Did you mean it?"

"Mean what?" I asked, taking the keys out and slipping them into the pocket of the Italian sport coat I was wearing. "That we're supposed to do some conspicuous consumption?"

"No, in the airport," she said, looking like the shy, somewhat insecure Sophie I'd met almost four months ago. "You told the reporter that I'm your fiancée."

The revelation hit me like a thunderbolt. In all the hurry and stress of training, and then getting back to the city to implement our rushed plan, I hadn't found the time to do what is most important. "Get out of the car."

Sophie looked at me like I was crazy, but I just smiled and got out, going around to her side. Opening her door, I held out my hand and helped her out before dropping to a knee. It was still a bit early, but I knew this woman was for me. I'd never met anyone like her, and when I know I want something, I'm not the type of man to waste time. "Sophie White…Warbird, will you marry me?"

Sophie blinked, and I could see the shine of tears in her eyes before she nodded. "Of course, you idiot," she said, pulling me to my feet and embracing me. Kisses rained down on my cheeks, and she jumped into my arms. "Now, take me into our new home and seal the deal."

"Mmmmm, yes ma'am," I teased, holding her easily as we headed towards the front door. "I just hope the renovations are complete."

Chapter 21
Sophie

Sadly, the renovations weren't complete, so Mark's initial idea of taking me into our new bedroom didn't work. Instead, he carried me up the steps to the bell tower, to the small strike base that we'd used to save Tabby from the Confederation. The entrance was still secret, as according to the plans we gave the contractor, the tower was sealed off. Never setting me down, Mark walked the distance from what had been the rectory to our hiding place. "Can you hit the switch, please?" he asked, pointing with his nose to the small, almost invisible button embedded into the wood beams of the tower. "My hands are wonderfully full."

You don't know how much of a turn on it is to be held in arms as strong as Mark's. I could barely feel a tremor of effort as he carried me up the thirty two stairs to the top of the tower. I could feel the bulge of his biceps against my back and under my legs, and the thick swell of his chest muscles against my side as he carried me, smiling at me the whole way. "Thank you," he said while he climbed. "You don't know how every day I'm grateful that you came into my life and saved me. You're making me into a better man, and for that I am eternally indebted."

"I love you," I replied, kissing him. He never lost a step, carrying me over to the thin mattress we had set up in one corner of the room at the top of the tower. He knelt and laid me down gently, kissing my lips before taking his arms out from underneath me. I giggled then sneezed, looking around. "We need to dust up here."

"It'll work for now," Mark replied, sitting down and taking off his sport coat. He was wearing a plain white button down shirt underneath, and simple charcoal gray slacks. Starting at the top, he took off his shirt, letting each inch exposed add to my growing excitement. "Well, aren't you going to join me?"

I looked down at my outfit, a light smock like blouse and designer jeans. Biting my lip, I ran my hands up and over my breasts, shaking my head. "I was thinking maybe I'd enjoy being stripped instead," I said. "Unless you don't want me naked."

"No, that wouldn't do," he replied, standing up. Finishing with his shirt, he pulled it off slowly, revealing his rippling torso. His new tattoos were dark against his skin, another part of his new identity as Marcus Smiley. With a Airborne Ranger tattoo on his left shoulder and a few other designs on his back, he looked different, but still the same love shone in his eyes. He gave me the same familiar smirk as his hands froze by the fastener of his pants, his eyebrow going up as he looked at me. "Should I take these off?"

"Please," I said, my breath thick in my chest. How is it that watching the sexiest man in the world makes it feel like you're breathing pleasant syrup?

"Since you said the magic word," Mark said, opening his pants and letting them fall to the floor. His cock was already semi-hard inside his boxer briefs, and he knelt down, crawling over to me.

Starting with my feet, he pulled my open-toed high heels off one by one, kissing and licking up my leg, starting at my feet. The feel of his tongue sliding up my leg sent heat straight through my body, and I groaned in anticipation. Kissing down the sole of my foot, he laid my feet together on the mattress so he could reach up and unsnap my jeans. My hips jerked in need as he pulled the form fitting denim down my legs, kissing my thighs as he went, skipping the ticklish area below my right kneecap and setting the jeans beside us on the floor. "You are more beautiful than ever," he whispered as he lifted my right foot up, kissing my calf muscle and working his way down to let his tongue lick behind my kneecap.

I don't know what the nerve connection is, but it felt like his tongue was just outside my pussy, and I could barely contain myself. "I need you."

"You have me," I replied, spreading my legs and letting the scent of my wetness flood the room. "Forever."

Mark answered by kneeling between my legs, kissing the soft skin above the waistband of my panties. Working his way up, he unbuttoned my top while his lips found all the little places that four months of lovemaking had allowed him to discover. He paused just below the cups of my bra, skipping my breasts to finish his unbuttoning and pulling my top off. Propped above me on his elbows, I could feel the warm thick bulge of his cock pushing against my panties, and I wrapped my legs around his waist. "So beautiful," he whispered before kissing me.

Our lips and tongues twisted and caressed each other, his hips working in small circles between my legs, rubbing and building electricity between us. Mark always favored compression style boxer briefs, the Lycra-like fabric sliding over my cotton bikini briefs and causing both of us to stop our kisses, small gasps filling the silence of the tower. Mark pulled back and knelt, letting his hands come to the front clasp of my bra. "May I?"

I was touched and moved by the sincere honesty in his voice. Here he was, the most powerful and sexual man I'd ever known, who literally could bring life or death with a single touch, and he was asking if he could take off my bra, even though we'd made love dozens of times before and he already knew the answer. "Yes," I said, placing my hands over his. "I'm yours."

I let go of Mark's hands and he undid the clasp tenderly, exposing my breasts to the warm air of the belfry. They felt full and heavy, and I could see my lover's eyes draw to them, even as his hands trailed down my body to take a hold of the waistband of my panties. He blinked and grinned, looking for all the world like a little boy who just found his favorite thing in the world before him.

Mark slid my panties off before pulling his own briefs down, his hard cock bouncing in the golden afternoon sunlight. My own lips spread in a smile, as I saw the thing I enjoyed most in the world before me. "Very nice, Mr. Smiley."

We both laughed, and Mark took his cock in his hand, stroking it slowly as he brought it closer and closer to my lips. It was so erotic to watch as he traced the blunt head up and down my lips, gathering my moisture on the pink tip of his cock. When he dragged it over my clit, a deep guttural rumble started in my chest and echoed through the room. He looked into my desperate eyes and nodded, lining himself up. "Hard or soft?"

"Hard," I barely whispered, "Give it to me rough" I added, after catching my breath.

Mark didn't disappoint, sliding himself in with one long, hard thrust that drove the breath from my lungs and sent sparks through my vision. Pausing just long enough for the flashes to dim, he pulled my legs up over his shoulders, pushing me deep into the mattress and pulling back before using his weight and the strength of his hips to pound into me, sheets of fiery lust coursing from my pussy to my head and back down. With my knees almost into my chest, I could only breathe in small, shallow sips of precious air, the lack of oxygen soon adding its own euphoric effect to the erotic buildup of energy.

I'm not into the whole erotic asphyxiation stuff, but if it was like this, then I guess I can understand the reason some people like it. There, pinned underneath Mark's muscular body, I could only submit to his power and his control. Pulling my arms up and over my head helped, giving me a bit more room, and I held my wrists there, crossed over my head. Mark's cock never stopped, the deep slaps of our hips creating a sharp cadence in counterpoint to my breathing and the rush of blood in my ears. His face was framed by what should have been the ridiculous sight of my feet and ankles next to his ears, but the look in his eyes bore deep into my heart and soul.

There is a reason that English has so many different words to describe the way that people can engage in sexual contact. I'm not talking just about words that describe the different actions or combinations. I mean the variations that carry with them the undertone of emotional content. Mark and I had done all of the consensual ones in the four months we'd been together. We'd fucked, we'd humped, we'd banged, we'd had sex, but this was my favorite. Despite the outer violence of our bodies slamming together, and the harsh sound of our breath as we both rushed towards our much needed climax, we were making love. The emotion in his eyes told me everything I ever needed to know about the man, and I could feel our souls come together and join, two becoming one.

My orgasm caught me by surprise, I was so lost in Mark's eyes and face. Suddenly my pussy tightened and then an explosion of pleasure ripped through me, my muscles clenching until it felt like a beautiful cramp flushed my entire body. I don't even know if I was making noise or not, my entire mind shut down temporarily from an overload of pleasure.

The next thing I could feel was Mark's body tightening and he let out a deep groan, his throat corded with effort as his own orgasm overtook him. I waited for Mark's breath to return before I gently pushed with my legs, the pleasure subsiding as my over-stretched muscles in my hips started calling for attention. "Oh, sorry," Mark said, climbing off of me and stretching out next to me on the narrow mattress. He gathered me in his arms and held me close, our scents mingling in the air. "I love you, my angel."

"I love you too," I whispered, letting my fingers play over his chest muscles. We lay like that for a few minutes before I worked up the nerve to voice my thoughts. "Mark?"

"Hmmm?" he asked, his chin in my hair. "Do you need to move?"

"No," I said, shifting to drape a thigh over his. "I wanted to ask you a question."

"Sure, go ahead."

"What would you think if I stopped taking my birth control?"

Chapter 22
Mark

Sophie's question rocked me even more than the orgasm I'd just had. Me? Possibly a father? I stuttered, rolling off the mattress. I went over to the refrigerator I had there, looking around inside for some of the bottled water that I had stashed. It was flat and stale, but it helped with my thirst as I thought.

I drained half the bottle before turning around, seeing Sophie sitting on the mattress with her knees pulled up to her chin, looking at me with her long purple hair hanging around her face like some sort of halo, her eyes filled with trepidation and fear. Even in my delay, I'd hurt her, but I didn't know what to say. I never thought a child would be possible for someone like me. I'd dreamed of it, and I'd even told Sophie that before, but I wasn't sure that day would ever come.

Finally, I drained the rest of my bottle and grabbed another to bring over to her. I knelt down and took her hands, clasping them in mine. "Sophie, it's not that I don't want to have a baby with you some day. I do. I most certainly do, and there's nobody in the world that I think would be a better mother than you. But.... right now I'm not sure I'm worthy of such a gift. I'm still an evil man, regardless of how redeeming your love is. I've still got a tab with the devil to account for. I have to make amends. The idea of having that debt passing onto a baby..... why would I ever be worthy of your love or your child?"

"So is that no?" she asked quietly, tears forming in her eyes. My heart broke, and I felt tears form in my own.

"Not a no, my love. Just.... we have to take care of some things before we can bring a child into our situation."

Sophie nodded, a single tear falling to trickle down one perfect cheek. While I knew she truly wanted to help rid the city of these criminals with me, I could also see she yearned for a normal life, something I'd taken from her when I fell for her. We sat there, side by side, and when she leaned into me, I held her and rocked her as the afternoon turned into an orange sunset.

* * *

Mark

"I've done some more investigating," Tabby said to us the next evening, as we met her for dinner at *Guliano*, one of the better Italian eateries in town that wasn't controlled by either the Confederation or Owen Lynch. Unfortunately, that meant it paid protection money to both organizations, and it showed in the decor. Guliano Dellacosta refused to let his food quality suffer, though, and I thought his lasagna was to die for. "Our deputy mayor is bringing in some out of town talent."

"Oh really?" I asked, keeping my voice low. Guliano had seated us in a booth, but since I was supposed to be famous, it wasn't a private corner one. Instead, everyone in the restaurant could see where I, Sophie and Tabby were sitting. Ostensibly, Tabby was there as our business consultant. She had her MBA now, and the firm she worked for did do real estate investing and venture capital marketing. She'd even brought along some information on real companies in the area, ones that she was reasonably sure were clean if I actually did want to invest.

I had to give the perky redhead credit, she was smarter than she let on a lot of the time. Sophie had told me her ditzy ginger act was just that, an act, but it was easy to forget even after having her live with us for a few weeks after her rescue. "Any idea who or what?"

Tabby nodded, and slid over a file folder. The outside read *Zen Nail Salon*, and I was going to remind Tabby to use real names and not sets from *Breaking Bad* when I opened it and found that there was, in fact, a nail salon named Zen just outside the city. Behind the business information, though, were two photographs that I slid out and looked over at Sophie. "They came in on an Aeroflot flight, but I don't know if that was because they are Russian or they just want to appear that way. I can't get into the Aeroflot data base, but a quick track of that flight number through their public information says the flight originated in Moscow before doing a stopover in Germany and then London before flying over here."

I nodded slowly and slid the photos back inside. "They're probably working for Lynch."

"Most likely. What are these guys if just two of them are supposed to unsettle the balance of power around here?"

I shook my head, and took another bite of my lasagna. "I'm not sure, but I have my suspicions."

Sophie, who had been quiet most of the day, took a sip of her red wine. I felt a twinge in my heart as I looked over at her. She was smiling and would talk when

Tabby asked her something, but ever since our discussion the day before about having a baby, she'd been withdrawn. She wasn't brooding, but sad, which hurt even more because I knew I was the cause of her sadness. If there was a way I could take away the pain while still being honest, I would have. But I knew if I said yes just to please her, I'd not only poison our relationship, but I'd be bringing a child into a dangerous situation.

This time though, she set her glass down, and I saw in her eyes the woman who'd become a reasonably proficient shooter and fighter in the few months of training she'd had. "Who could it be?"

"The men look like they could be Russian, but they could also be German," I said slowly, keeping my voice low. "If that's the case, then they most likely would be former Spetznatz. It's one of those open secrets in that part of Europe. The Russian government can't pay their commandos much, so a lot of them once they get their training and a tough reputation, they shop out their skills to those who can afford it. Most go to work for the Russian mob, although some go to the Germans, the Iranians, and the Chinese. About the only group they won't work directly for is ISIS or the various Muslim groups. They're fanatic Russian Orthodox Christians and hate Muslims."

Sophie blanched and looked at me. "Are they....?"

I nodded. "No restraints. They don't follow the rules everyone else plays by. It's how they're so effective. You know the rules I operated by? Well, they're nothing like that."

I didn't need to tell Sophie that in addition to their total lack of following the rules, they were truly some of the best-trained killers in the world. I'd had years of training under various teachers who, while strict, were at least willing to care about my wellbeing. These guys trained under a Darwinian system. Those who weren't strong enough to keep up were either dropped or got themselves killed. It encouraged a certain kind of crazy in those who survived, and a total disregard for human life, including their own.

Tabby gulped and took a drink of her ice water. "What are you going to do?"

I thought about it for a second, then took a drink of my own water. "I need to draw them out. The one advantage I have over them is that they don't know the city the way I do. They're probably studying it as fast as they can, but there's still things that I know that they don't. I need to draw them to a place where I control the terrain advantage. The question is how to do it."

Sophie and Tabby fell silent as the three of us thought. I finished my lasagna and waited for our waiter to bring dessert, a panna cotta with olive oil ice cream. Finally, Sophie looked up at me. "What about a baited trap?"

"What do you mean?" I asked, curious. Sophie's eyes had taken on the look not only of the woman I'd trained, but the natural hunter I'd sensed in her even before she knew who I was. There is a deep well of protective strength in Sophie, a heightened sense of the natural maternal protective instinct that, when she tuned into it, made her not just a capable protector, but a dangerous stalker and hunter. During some of the training exercises I'd had her do in Croatia, she'd done better than I had the first time I went through them, that's how natural she is.

"Well, we know who they work for. What if we give their boss a reason to come to us?"

I thought about it for a second. "You mean give him a reason to think we're not who we say we are."

"Exactly. Maybe the Snowman or Miss White need to come back for a single performance."

I thought about it for a second. It was risky, but it was bold. "But how? The surgeries were done for a reason."

Sophie chuckled and puffed out her cheeks and tightened her neck, pulling her shoulders up. It was startling in that it obliterated almost all of the change in her facial structure the surgeons had done. Instead of the slightly narrower jawline and long, swan like neck of Sophie Warbird, the more compact and in some ways cuter profile of Sophie White sat before me. The nose was still different, though. I blinked, and Sophie relaxed her features with a laugh. "I noticed it a few days after the bandages came off. I can't exactly hold it for a long time, but a still shot with a wig should handle things, don't you think?"

I nodded. "Tabby, you think you can find a t-shirt from the Shamrock?"

"I have one already," Tabby replied, "it's at my place. Sophie left it there one time after an early shift when I convinced her to come out partying with me."

"Then we can work a plan."

After the dinner was over, Sophie and I drove back to Mount Zion. Workers had been there most of the day, and the improvement was noticeable. At least our bedroom area was complete, as well as our kitchen. The bathrooms needed work still, so we couldn't take a shower until they were finished. Since we had both conspicuously joined a gym nearby, a total waste of money since Mount Zion's main sanctuary was being refitted for that exact purpose, we could at least use that, and the chemical toilet for another day or two.

"I'm going to get changed for bed," Sophie said quietly as we came in. She started towards the closet area, but I reached out to take her arm.

"Sophie, wait," I said, turning her around. She turned to look at me, and I took a deep breath as I considered what I was going to say. I just hoped that I wasn't making a mistake. I'd just have to try to wrap all this up as fast as possible, something easier said than done. Watching her over the past twenty-four hours had been the hardest thing I'd ever done in my life, and seeing the reanimation in her face as she applied her mind to the problems with the new players in town made up my mind. I was never going to let her feel that way again. "I've come to a decision."

"And?" she asked, her voice still not hopeful. When she saw me smile, her eyes lifted and the look of Sophie, my Sophie, came back into her face.

"Let's have a baby, but on two conditions," I said, pulling her in close and kissing her. "We wait until we've taken out these two men. You stay on your pills until then, and then we start trying. Second, if and when you get pregnant, all of this going after criminals stuff stops. You go straight to the day to day business of Smiley Consolidated. Okay?"

She nodded, and kissed me again. "I can do that. By the way, we have to actually make a Smiley Consolidated."

"Of course," I replied, our kiss growing deeper. "In fact, I was thinking we could do some consolidating right now."

Chapter 23
Sophie

Ironically, it was at the exact same nail salon that Tabby had showed us last night that we decided to do the first purchase for Smiley Consolidated. The owner, a pretty Southeast Asian lady named Ms. Wen, was ecstatic when we met. "Thank you so much, Mr. Smiley, Miss Warbird," she said in lightly accented English. "With your investment, I can make the expansion that we've needed for so long."

"We're glad to become your partners, Ms. Wen," I replied, offering my hand. We shook, and I leaned in, "Of course, the biggest mark in your favor is your reputation. I hear you do wonderful work with gel nails?"

"Best in the city," Ms. Wen said, taking a look at my hand. "Hmmm, maybe something to compliment that hair of yours? I must say, it's beautiful. So few Americans would have the courage to try something so out of the ordinary."

"Why thank you," I replied. "Let's talk about maybe next week. But I think if we do that now, my fiancée will be bored out of his mind."

Mark rolled his eyes melodramatically in good humor, as Tabby, who served as the facilitating agent, brought forth the paperwork. "It'll take about a week for this all to clear the county courthouse," she said as first Mark and then Ms. Wen signed. Tabby, who was required to get her notary public license by her new firm, stamped and signed in her spot as well. "But, once that is done, I'd say we can transfer the funds and get things rolling."

"That's perfect," Mark said, playing his role of business mogul to the limit. "Ms. Wen, if you could have the estimates and all the paperwork you have gathered for your expansion to my office soon, maybe you and I can sit down and figure out where best to start, and if there is a way to make our money go further. To be honest, I was surprised when Miss Tabby brought your company to my attention, you requested so little."

"We've been understaffed and working hard so long, we just need that little push. Once that is in, then the profits we can make can fuel the rest of the expansion by themselves."

Mark nodded, and smiled. "Well, we'll talk. In the mean time Ms. Wen,

Sophie and I have another business meeting. If you're going to come by my office, I need to have an office for you to come to."

We left Zen Nail Salon and climbed into our rental car. Tabby slid into the rear passenger seat, all smiles. "Well, that was easy. I like spending your money, Marcus."

"After we sign the lease on the office space, I want you to bring in more businesses like that one," Mark replied. "I'm going to put pressure on Owen Lynch and the Confederation by investing in businesses that they've been keeping down. Zen Nails, Guliano's, places like that. By the way, where are we leasing office space?"

Tabby and I both laughed. "You know love, for someone who's made a whole lotta money, you sure don't know a lot about how to do business," I said as we drove. "Not that I'm much better."

"Well, you know how I made a lot of my money. The rest I made using false identities and online companies. I never had to sign leases or paper agreements. Digital signatures and money transfers was all I needed. I made a million dollars sitting around in my underwear."

"With the way you're built, that could happen in about a dozen clubs around town," Tabby quipped, and I lost it, exploding in giggles as Mark tried his best to keep us on the road. "But seriously, face to face business isn't all that different, it just requires more paperwork. Didn't you tell me you had lawyers and stuff to handle this before?"

"None of them were local. They're in Bermuda I think. I need a local legal team, and you happen to represent what we need. That and I personally still want to keep tabs on you. I'd hire you directly, but that might create too much suspicion and keep you away from what you've done best, which is gather information for us. I never wanted you to do that, but it sure has helped. Anyway, I can keep you safe easier this way."

I could see Tabby blink back a few tears as Mark's words sunk in, and I turned to look out my passenger side window. "So, Tabby," I said after a few minutes. "Where exactly are you taking us for looking at office rentals?"

"In order to fit your profile, I had three options," Tabby said, and I could hear the relief as she could refocus on business instead of the danger she was most likely still in, even as diminished as it was.

"I wanted to run them by you. The first is downtown, in a high rise that also has three trading houses, a law firm, and some other similar things. Rent is reasonably high, visibility is good too. The second is in the North Valley, among the technology startups that are populating the area. You'll have less total visibility, but you'll be higher profile in the area, and your rent's going to be a lot less. The final one was the one that I had to do a double-take on when you asked me to look into it, but I found a commercial building close to the docks and the airport. It's been empty for the past three years, and while the neighborhood isn't exactly the DMZ, it's not great either. Three floors, but five stories tall, with the bottom two stories being a giant warehouse.

"Previously it was used by an assortment of shipping companies, the last one with ties to *La Cosa Nostra*. The owner got put in jail, and the property went into tax receivership six months ago. The advantage is you can buy it for a song. Outright you could have it tomorrow for just over two hundred thousand dollars. I've seen pictures of the inside, it's going to need more renovations than Mount Zion if you want to do the entire building."

"Let's check out the warehouse," Mark said. I glanced over, as all three of us were dressed for business, with Mark in a handmade suit we had picked up from a tailor in Hong Kong, while I was wearing a Donna Karan skirt and top. "I know, I know. But it fits better with my idea of how to stand out, and how to put our enemies off guard. Besides, that warehouse will give us the flexibility to use it as a potential base of operations. We can't do that in either of the other two locations, the neighbors will be too close and too nosy."

I couldn't deny his points, and sat back. "Babe, I don't want to sound too nosy, but just how much money are we going to use to set up this facade?"

Mark grinned and looked over at me. "Who says it's all a facade? If we do this right, we'll end up with more money than ever. But up front, I was thinking in the fifteen to twenty area."

"Fifteen to twenty thousand?" Tabby asked. "Your repairs to Mount Zion are going to be more than that."

I shook my head and turned around to look at her. "He means fifteen to twenty million."

I'd never seen Tabby's jaw drop the way it did when the numbers rolled over her, and she grasped just how much Mark was worth. Finally, she just shook her head and looked down at her tablet. "Go upstairs with him, I said. Go have some fun. Good luck, I hope he's a nice guy, I said. Sheesh, and I ended up being dry humped by a thirty-year-old loser with a mortgage," she muttered to herself, and I had to chuckle.

"You give good advice, Tabs."

"Yeah, yeah. Think someday I could get an advisor's fee out of it?"

"You keep bringing us targets like you have, and you're going to be a very well to do business advisor within four years," Mark replied. "What you decide to do with that money, well, that'll be the kicker, won't it?"

The warehouse was bigger than I'd expected, but wasn't the largest on the block. The bottom floor had just over five thousand square feet of empty space with thirty foot high ceilings. The second and third floors could be reached either by stairs or a freight elevator near the back of the huge space.

"We're going to have to take the stairs, the power's off right now," Tabby said, leading us over. We climbed up the steel grating steps, our footsteps echoing in the empty air. "I haven't been here yet personally, so I don't know what the space is like."

"So far so good though," Mark replied, looking around. When we reached the second floor, Tabby produced a key which she used to unlock the door. With the stairwell, the second floor was smaller, but still spacious, and had obviously been a shipping office as well as what looked like a break room and cafeteria for the workers at one point. There were even some tables still sitting around unused. "I like it. Third floor?"

The third floor was almost totally empty, with only a single folding chair off in one corner. We walked the entire floor, our feet crunching on the dust and dirt that covered the concrete floor, and I looked around. "Well, it could become an office if we wanted," I said. "A few coats of paint, one of those potted plants in the corner, and we'd be good to go."

"I agree," Mark said. "All right Tabby, get the documents drawn up. Once we have the building title, I want workers here within two weeks. Until then, we'll use Mount Zion as our office, and gather up some more businesses. In the mean time, it's time to draw out Owen Lynch's friends."

"And how are we going to do that?" I asked, happy that Mark was taking my idea of a baited trap to heart.

"Two things. First, I'm going to crash a party. Next, you're going to take a photo, and then, we're placing an Amazon order."

Chapter 24
Mark

The night was perfect as I walked up the flagstone walkway to the Mayor's official residence. It hadn't taken much to wrangle an invitation to the Fall Benefit for the city's youth. It was the Mayor's current pet project, and with Marcus Smiley already making headlines for the past two weeks, I could easily go. I only wished Sophie was with me, but according to our plan I needed to attend by myself. It would be vital for the timing of everything.

I checked my tuxedo, and chuckled to myself. Before meeting Sophie, I'd worn a tux less than ten times in my life. Sure I'd worn suits, some of the best money could buy, but a tuxedo sends a different message. When you wear a tux, you want to stand out, and as a hitman, that's not something you want to do.

Now though, as Marcus Smiley, I had to play a role on top of being my normal self. In some ways it was great. I could invest money cleanly, and make a difference in public. I felt like in that way I was helping to take down the criminal empire that had infested the city. Maybe I was buying some atonement for my sins, but then again, I've never been a churchgoing man.

"Marcus Smiley," I said to the assistant at the door, who was checking off names against a master list on the iPad she had in her hands. She looked like your standard intern, probably a college student who was majoring in political science and getting some kudos along with most likely a job recommendation when she graduated. She was cute in that innocent college co-ed kind of way.

"Marcus..... Smiley?" she asked, recognizing the name. She looked up at me, and I had to give credit to the newspaper reporter who Sophie was doing most of the dealing with. She had that star struck look in her eyes, I hoped from the good press and not from my looks. "Ah, yes, you're right here. Donation box is there on the right, and enjoy the party."

It was a masterful move on the Mayor's part, I thought. By making the pledge box sealed but transparent, there was technically no reason for someone to even donate. However, if they did, there was the tightrope that everyone walked. For a minute at least once your slip fluttered through the slot, it could land face up on the pile. If you donated freely and generously, it would be noticed and you'd get commendations socially. If you were a tight-ass, that'd get noted as well. It encouraged donations that would get the sort of quiet kudos that these sorts of events were famous for.

Striding up to the box, I took a quick glance at what was inside, and saw that most of the donations were in the five thousand dollar range. Not bad, considering the party was over two hundred people, with three corporations that were controlled by Owen Lynch already publicly stating they would absorb the cost of the event itself, but I wanted to really make a splash.

Taking the pledge slip from the pile, I smirked as I wrote my name in very bold, very dark letters across the top. In the donation slot I wrote smaller, but still clearly, twenty five thousand dollars. Owen Lynch might have been a criminal, but the mayor was actually trying to do something good. And the number was just high enough that it would get the attention I was looking for.

The party itself felt perhaps more dangerous than some of the hits I've done. Every face that greeted me, every person who shook my hand sized me up, every smile and every word uttered felt like there were multiple levels to the conversation. All in all, I enjoyed some of my meetings with criminals more than I did with the social elite of the city. At least with the criminals you knew they were trying to stab you in the back.

"Ah, Mr. Smiley!" I heard behind me. I turned, and saw the face of the man I had wanted to get the attention of all night, the man whose attention was worth twenty five thousand dollars to me.

"Deputy Mayor Lynch," I replied, offering my hand. I was nursing a single flute of champagne in the other, having drank about a third of it. I normally detest alcohol, but there was no way to get around it in this situation. I refuse to partake in a substance that dulls my senses. However, lots of repeated bringing the glass to my lips without actually taking a drink led people to believe I was drinking along with everyone else. "It's a pleasure to make your acquaintance."

"Why thank......" Lynch said, his voice faltering. He could see something in my face, which is exactly what I'd hoped for. The secret behind successful plastic surgery is not in dramatic reconstruction. People who go overboard end up with work that looks, well, plastic. The key is in subtle reshaping and changes. It was the type of work that Sophie and I had done. It was enough to fake most photo analysis done by computers, especially if the image used was of poor quality or taken from a distance.

Up close was different however. For example, think of a movie where one of the characters undergoes aging. I'm not talking a bad movie, I'm talking one of the real high quality ones that even may use a bit of CGI for the effects. You watch the movie long enough, and you can tell who the actor is under the makeup and effects. There's certain things that can't be changed without risking disability or death, such as the distance between your eyes, that just cannot be screwed with. It was why I made sure the few photographs that had been taken of Marcus Smiley had me wearing non-prescription glasses or other things that disguised the shape of my face more.

Owen Lynch was going through that now. For years, I'd been one of the best hitmen in the entire city, and aligned with the Confederation, although I'd also done work for him through third party contracts as well when they didn't conflict with the Confederation's own goals. I was dangerous, and one of those faces that he wanted to learn just to protect his own ass. It may have been four and a half months since Mark Snow had last been seen in town, but now here I was, standing less than two feet from him.

I smiled, putting just a bit of the predatory creature I am into it. "No, the honor is all mine Deputy Mayor. You look a little peaked, let's get you a drink," I said, grabbing a flute of champagne off the tray of one of the circulating waiters. Putting it in his hand, Lynch still looked perplexed. My plastic surgery was enough that he couldn't be sure, but there was still that little voice in his mind telling him he knew who I was. "Tell me, sir. I'm new to this fine town, and I must say it's more than lived up to its well earned reputation."

"Well, we work hard at it," Lynch, ever the politician, replied. We were surrounded by the social elite of the city, there was no way he'd risk a confrontation that would expose who he really was to the few who didn't already suspect.

"I'm sure. Although, after spending so much time overseas in warm climates recently, I'm not sure if I'm going to be ready for the upcoming winter," I segued, smiling tightly. "Although my fiancée Sophie is. She grew up in Canada, and really wants to teach me how to build a snowman. Do you know if many people have a snowman in the city?"

Lynch blanched at my words, stuttering for a moment before regaining his composure. "Well, I'm sure there are a few. Winter is not too bad here though. Have you ever been in a very cold winter, Mr. Smiley?"

I shook my head and smiled again. "Nope. I've been to Russia a few times, but only in the summer time."

Lynch nodded, and extended his hand. "Maybe someday you'll get the chance to visit it in winter. I have heard it is very harsh, and very cruel though. People who aren't prepared can be in very big trouble."

"I'm always prepared, Deputy Mayor. By the way, I was wondering, Smiley Consolidated is opening our new offices soon in the warehouse district. If it's at all possible with your busy schedule, I would love it if perhaps you could make an appearance for the grand opening? It would be a great motivator for my staff and such."

"I'd have to check my schedule. Perhaps your secretary could e-mail the information to my office?"

"I look forward to it. Well, I've taken enough of your time. Have a good evening, Deputy Mayor Lynch." I walked away, melting into the crowd before Lynch could have any hired muscle he had on hand converge on me. I had observed five different exits during my time at the party, along with at least a dozen security men, most of whom looked like off duty police. That didn't mean anything though, as Lynch owned the cops as well.

I made a beeline towards the east exit, which was the closest, but about three quarters of the way there turned and ducked around a table full of canapés and darted into the back garden, where a dance party was going on. While better than house music, the Mayor was pretty behind the times, and most of the music was from the eighties and nineties. I guess it made sense, considering his age, but I could have done without Madonna doing *Like a Prayer*. I don't even think the DJ had the original version, but some cover artist version.

I circulated through the group of about fifty or so in the dance area, which was actually a decently laid temporary floor. When *Like A Prayer* ended, I followed a small group of ladies towards the back door, until I could cut around the side of the house. I waited until I was in a very dark area before darting across the side lawn and leaping the wrought iron fence that surrounded the property. I had planned my escape earlier in that regard, and had parked my car not on the property, but in a Circle K parking lot a half mile away. I dropped into the seat and started the engine, glad it was my last night with the vehicle.

I checked my rearview mirror numerous times for signs of being tailed, but I seemed to be clear. Pulling a Bluetooth headset out of my inner jacket pocket, I slid it in my ear and tapped the power button, connecting it to the burner phone I had in on the dash. No use in getting pulled over for using a phone while driving if I didn't have to. "Dial memory 1," I said, pulling up the only programmed number in memory. The phone burred in my ear, and the call was picked up on the second ring. "Done. Now it's your turn."

Chapter 25
Mark

The next day, just as the clock in the University tower was chiming noon, I was able to meet with a man for the last part of my plan. It seemed strange to conduct a deal such as I was about to do in the middle of the day, but I'd learned that it was, in fact, the safest. During the day time, most of the police in the city were either rookies who didn't know what to look for, or cops who were tired of dealing with the corrupt bullshit that ran the force to do more than the bare minimum to get to retirement. Combine that with the deal going down in an upper-class neighborhood, and I think I could have bought a lot more than what I did.

"So what you've got here is your standard US Marine Corps M-14 rifle that fires a seven point six two millimeter round," the man I was making the deal with said. While the meeting was taking place in the open, I was still wearing a hooded sweatshirt and glasses, and driving one of my backup vehicles I had when I was Mark Snow. It was another calculated risk, but I didn't have the vehicles for Marcus Smiley yet, and I couldn't risk putting it in a rented vehicle, since it was connected to a credit card. "Depending on the round you fire, you can get a minute of angle accuracy out to about eight hundred meters or more."

"And the ammunition?" I asked, looking at the deep brown wooden stock. It was a beautiful weapon, and deadly in its intent. "I'm expecting armor."

"You have armor problems, I have armor solutions," he said, opening a small bag in the truck beside the rifle. "M61 Armor-Piercing Rounds. This will punch through up to a half inch of steel plating like it's nothing. It can defeat any ballistic vest material in use today. You wanna get more, you're going to have to upgrade to a fifty cal, or maybe a Winchester 300 Magnum."

I nodded and pulled out a thick envelope of cash, all twenties, and handed it over to the man. "You do good work."

"Pleasure doing business with you," the man replied. He took the bag of ammo and set it inside the case the rifle was in, which to the outside looked and was marked like one used for electric pianos. I pulled the case out and carried it over to my car and set it in the back seat. The dealer, an out-of-towner I'd only known through the Internet for a few months, got into his car and drove off. I waited two minutes before taking a circuitous route back to the warehouse. Once there, I dropped off the package before quickly driving my car to a paid parking lot on the other side of town, and hopped on a bus back to the warehouse area. It is one of the frustrating side effects of trying to be circumspect; you waste a lot of time.

Arriving at the warehouse, I took the elevator up to the third floor, where Sophie and Tabby were waiting. Sophie already had the rifle out, and had stripped it down to its parts. Considering I'd never covered the M-14 with her, I was impressed. "This is powerful enough?" she asked as she looked the receiver over with a careful eye. "I thought we were going for something higher caliber."

"It's more than powerful enough with the rounds he sold us," I said, indicating the black tipped armor piercing rounds. "It also has the advantage that I can put it on full auto if I need to. With two or more guys coming in, that could be useful."

"So what's the plan?" Tabby asked, carrying a briefcase with more business documents. It seemed out of place in the still barely cleaned room. We'd moved a table and some chairs from the second floor up to the third, and swept up, but the concrete was still raw, and the walls bare. "By the way, four more potential investments here."

"The plan is simple. They won't attack Mount Zion, the building is too identifiable, and they'll assume that if Marcus Smiley is Mark Snow, that I'd have already prepared. Also, it's in a rich area of town, which causes difficulties for Owen Lynch if there are suddenly a bunch of bodies found. So he'll want his men to hit us here. Besides, with Sophie's book delivery coming here, he won't want to pass up the opportunity to get two birds with one stone."

"I don't know, it sounds risky," Tabby said, flinching as Sophie slapped the bolt back into the upper receiver of the rifle with a loud metallic *schnick*.

"Tabby, both of you have had your homes invaded. I was lucky enough to be there for Sophie the last time. We basically have three choices. We can either let them come to our home, we can let them come to another place of our choosing, or we can take the fight to them and attack them where they live. There will come a time for us to attack. But this time, we'll let them come to us."

* * *

Sophie

After Tabby left, I turned to Mark, letting my inner nerves out. "The delivery is scheduled for tomorrow," I said, "you think he'll use that as the opening?"

"He'd be foolish not to," Mark replied. "Owen Lynch controls the shipping company that we're using for this delivery. You put it on Sophie White's credit card, and we scheduled it for a mid-afternoon delivery. It's in Sophie White's name. He'll bite if its only for curiosity sake."

We spent the rest of the afternoon setting up and checking out our sight lines and planning out angles of our ambush. With the sun going down, we locked up the warehouse and headed back to Mount Zion. "So after this," I said as I drove, Mark relaxing in the passenger seat, "I was thinking we need to go car shopping. This rental is nice, but I want something different."

"I agree. Besides, we need to set up our other facilities. That won't be done through Tabby by the way."

I pulled off the intercity parkway and started to break off towards Mount Zion, glad to see the gated driveway. Workers had been busy, and most of the work was now complete, so we could at least use our living areas. A lot of the other parts of the building were taking more time however, but it added to our security in a way. With workers going late, and lights on all over the property, there was less chance of things going down.

Still, we sealed the living quarters area with a steel core door that was about as strong as your average bank vault, turning the two thousand square foot living space into a giant panic room. While technically the windows could be penetrated, the construction of the Mount Zion building itself added to the safety factor. With the Neo-Gothic impressions, the old living quarters had only narrow, tall windows that let in light, but were barely a foot wide. Perhaps a six-year-old kid could get through, or a really narrow-headed contortionist, but that's about it.

We made dinner together, a simple mushroom risotto with grilled slices of duck breast and a kale salad. Among his other talents, Mark was a talented home cook, and even when we were overseas he would often spend some time learning bits and pieces of the local cuisine. Since coming home, he'd combined some of those spices into American favorites to let us both enjoy great home cooked meals. As we sat down, I grinned and took a drink of lemon water. "You know, it's going to be interesting."

"What's that?" Mark asked as he took a bit of the risotto. "Tomorrow?"

"No, I'm not worried about anything. Either we do it right or we don't. I was just thinking though that our married life is going to be very interesting." I tried some of the duck breast, which Mark had prepared using some Korean spices. It practically melted in my mouth, and I sighed happily. "I mean, not that it wasn't going to be anyway."

"I think that would be an understatement," Mark replied. "But what exactly do you mean?"

"Well, business owners by day, taking out the criminal underworld by night, and let's not forget getting married and maybe having a family somewhere in the mix. We're going to have a lot on our hands."

Mark thought about it, then smiled. He reached across the small table we were sitting at and took my hand. "There'd be nobody else in the world I would rather do it with," he said. "And as much as I'd enjoy making love to you for the rest of the night, we probably should get some sleep. Tomorrow's going to be very stressful."

Chapter 26
Sophie

We woke up before dawn the next day, after I had tossed and turned most of the night. Preparing for this ambush was different than when we'd rescued Tabby from the Confederation men at the club. Then, we'd been going off of three hours of preparation. Our entire plan was basically on the fly, and my role was to mostly try and keep myself from being blown away. Mark had been the one strapped up and responsible for dealing with the bad guys. Until I'd pulled the shotgun pistol and blasted the guy who was sneaking up on Mark from behind, I'd never expected to have to do anything.

This time was different. The two Russians we were expecting were seasoned pros. Mark was pretty sure he was better than either of them alone, but two working together would be dangerous. Therefore, he needed my help, and it was a great feeling. It was a different mental process, knowing that I was expected to try to kill someone.

Every time I closed my eyes, I could see in my mind the fight in the night club, and the feeling as I pulled the trigger on the shotgun pistol. The recoil hammered through my arms and sent my hands flying up and back, almost hitting me in the face as the unmuffled roar deafened me. My eyes would fly open, I'd be panting, and it would take me another ten minutes to try and close my eyes and get to sleep again.

Finally, around one in the morning, I dropped off into what could best be called a disturbed sleep. I won't even go into the dreams I had, full of death and violence and blood. I sat up with a scream barely contained behind my lips, and sweat dripping down my face. I glanced at the digital clock and saw that it was three fifty-eight in the morning. "Fuck," I muttered, running my hand down my face.

Mark, who I thought had been sleeping but had been lying quietly on his side of our bed, turned and looked at me with concern in his eyes. "If it's any consolation, I know how you feel."

I thought back to the first time he'd told me about what his job was, and how he'd killed seventy-six people so far. He had told me that for every single one of them, he had nightmares and regrets. It was one of the things that had helped me realize that despite the bloodiness of his profession, I felt that Mark was, in his heart, still a decent man; someone I could love. Now I was to join the brotherhood, it seemed. It was what I chose to do, but I had to admit I was scared that I was moving a little too fast, getting in over my head. "Does it get any easier?"

"For some of the men I used to call coworkers, yes," Mark said quietly, sitting up next to me. "They were the scary ones, and the ones that we knew once they reached a certain level, they couldn't be trusted any more. They were the ones who came to not only tolerate but even enjoy or need the violence and the blood. They were the ones we sometimes had to take out because they'd gone fully over the edge."

"Did you ever...?" I asked fearfully. Mark nodded his head.

"Number forty-seven. His name was Bob, probably not his real name, but he also worked for the Confederation. I had to hunt him down and put him out after he'd taken out not just his target, but the target's entire family just because he wanted to."

I shivered and leaned into Mark, who held me close. We lay back down on the bed, and for the first time all night I felt some comfort. Having his arms around me reassured me that I was still normal for feeling the way I did. "How many more will we need to kill?"

Mark shook his head. "Not as many as you fear, I think. The bigger weapon will be the use of information, spying, and media exposure. If we do those right, it'll be much cleaner. But yes, some will have to die."

I decided to change the subject, all the talk of killing started to bring me down a little. "How is it you get any rest beforehand? You don't sound exhausted or blurry in the least. I thought you were asleep."

"Meditation," Mark said, squeezing me in his arms and kissing my neck. "And one other thing, at least with this idea."

"What's that?"

Mark kissed the top of my head, and I could hear him inhale the scent of my hair deeply. "I think of you. The rest is easy."

* * *

Sophie

We got to the warehouse just after six in the morning. While I didn't think I'd be able to eat or drink anything, Mark insisted we have something on hand, so after leaving Mount Zion, we stopped at a convenience store to pick up some easy to digest groceries.

Mark didn't allow us to get anything with caffeine in it or anything overly greasy or dense. This, of course, eliminated about seventy percent of the store, and another fifteen percent was eliminated because it was cat food, motor oil, playing cards and the like. Still, we were able to find some juices, light fruits and packages of sliced chicken breasts that filled our needs. "I know you're cruising on nerves now," Mark said as we entered the warehouse, "but that's going to fade. You're going to start feeling hungry and thirsty eventually."

He was right, and by ten, I'd already drank one of the bottles of fruit juice. I kept glancing at the clock on the wall, while Mark made sure our video feed of the outside was clear. He'd installed obscure video cameras around the building to monitor everything. He'd even set up cameras on the inside of the building just in case the Russians tried something unexpected.

Around noon we were as set up as we could be. "The tough part is going to be if this delivery is legit," Mark said. "I wish I could just say *Hey, are you the two Russian hitmen* and shoot them, but we're going to need to be sure. It's one thing killing bad men, but it's something else entirely killing an innocent. I've went this long without doing that, and I'm not about to start now. Let's hope they are stupid and show guns outside."

We went down to the first floor, and I set up the M-14, which was my responsibility. Mark had originally thought to use the rifle himself, but he wanted me as far away as possible. By having me set up in a dim corner of the warehouse under some netting that from the outside looked like a pile of boxes, I could be safe. Or at least, as safe as I could be.

The beauty of the M-14 lies in its relative heaviness. The thick steel barrel and the wooden stock gave the rifle a lot of stability. Once I set the front part of the stock on the foam block I was using as a rest, it would fire straight and true. Since I only had to shoot less than a hundred feet, worrying about drop or anything like that was moot. Which was good, because while Mark had taught me about it, I was still a novice when it came to stuff like that.

I just had to aim at the belt line, hope that I could keep my nerve, and let the rifle take care of the rest. I took a quick view through the peep sight towards the cargo door, and nodded. If the delivery came when we asked, the interior of the warehouse would be in mostly darkness while the cargo door would be in relative shade. I wouldn't be blinded by glare.

"I'm ready," I said, coming out from behind the concealed position. "How're you looking?"

Mark's role was much simpler, but also much more dangerous. Answering the door, he carried with him a Desert Eagle pistol with Teflon coated armor piercing rounds. If he had to answer the door, he'd have the pistol with him next to his thigh underneath a long jacket. We were hoping, however, that we could use the intercom system attached to the door to bring them in without it.

"Good to go. When they trigger the intercom on the outside, I can buzz them in. If they're hostile, they'll use that as a chance to burst through the door. If they do, shoot as soon as you can. But stay in your position, the first guy through is probably going to be spraying the room and not really giving a fuck what's around. I'm going to be to the left the door, because it's the last place they see after initial entry. If your shot takes out the first guy, the second one will come through fast, and I'll take care of him. Just keep your fire contained and we'll be fine."

"Then why did you get something that shoots automatic?"

Mark took a deep breath and looked me in the eye. "In case I'm hit. You get those two and protect yourself. That's why you also have a backup weapon."

"Mark, you can't....."

He cut me off with a shake of his head. "Yes, I can. You know that. I'm good, but I'm not immortal."

I nodded, feeling tears come to my eyes unbidden. Before they could fall, he lifted my chin with his hand and gave me the same cocky grin he used whenever he was confident. "I'm not saying it's going to happen. In fact, I'm sure it won't today. But it could. If that happens, promise me you take them all out, and get your ass out of town."

"But what would I do then?"

Mark pointed upstairs. "You remember my smartbox? Login password is *sophie7891*, all in lower case. In the documents folder is a read me file, password locked, same password. Inside is instructions on how to access every dollar I have, along with account pass codes. The backup is at Mount Zion in the belfry. Take that and your passport and disappear. The smartbox has all sorts of information in the files that can help you."

"When did you put this all together?" I asked, my throat burning as I thought of even the possibility of living without Mark in my life.

"Over the past few nights. Wasn't all that hard, most of it was just collating the information already on there."

Before he could say anything else I wrapped my arms around him, and we held each other. It was strange, a moment of intimacy while we waited for what we expected to be a deadly fight. After a moment, we let go of each other, and looked around. The area was quiet, and the tension started to creep into the air. "Let's go upstairs and get the food and stuff," Mark said. "We can hang out next to your position and wait."

Chapter 27
Mark

The afternoon dragged on, something that Sophie wasn't accustomed to. I'd grown up in similar situations even before starting this line of work. It reminded me of times as a boy in South Carolina, sitting in a deer stand, waiting for the bucks to come through the woods. You had to remain quiet and ready, ready for the slightest movement. It could be minutes, it could be hours. So waiting for the delivery was actually easy for me, we didn't even have to be quiet.

The delivery was scheduled to happen between four and six in the afternoon, and we had Sophie's cell phone, along with the tablet, with us. We took turns watching the tablet, checking the security video feeds as the hours wore on. When we weren't watching the tablet, we studied the pictures of the two men that Tabby had provided for us. The image quality wasn't great, and I knew it would come down to waiting for them to pull their weapons. If we could shoot first in that situation, we'd win. If not, we could be in trouble.

I checked the clock, it was four fifty-seven when the delivery truck started down the street in front of our place. I sat up, jostling Sophie who I had let doze for a few minutes. The adrenalin had temporarily worn off, and her body was feeling the effects of the stress and lack of sleep the night before. "Delivery truck," I said, shaking her gently. "Get ready."

She blinked once before nodding, stretching her arms over her head and smacking her face. "I'm okay," she said, twisting and cracking her neck. "You okay?"

"Of course," I replied, picking up the shotgun pistol and holding it in my right hand. "Let's just see if this is who we're waiting for."

The van looked just like any of the other hundred delivery vans in the city, which I expected. Owen Lynch did own a legitimate delivery company, Capital City Deliveries, that was an affiliate of UPS. I had broken into the offices before on a few assignments, and had seen their files. With over a thousand employees in the region, the network was an efficient distributor of anything Owen Lynch wanted. Also, over ninety-five percent of the workers were innocent men and women whose only bad decision in life was to wear a hideous uniform to work every day.

The van stopped just past the normal entrance door, in front of the large rollup bay door that dominated the front of the building. It was a smart move, one I would have done. My suspicions were raised, although even a normal driver might do the same thing, considering the placement of the doors.

My mental alarms went off when two men got out of the truck. While Capital City Deliveries would often send two men on their trucks, that was for larger items. The order that Sophie had placed was for three books from Amazon, not something that would require two men. Both of them had packages under their arms, and that's when I knew for sure.

"You got that buzzer ready?" I asked, rechecking my pistol. My mind whirled, and suddenly a new plan dropped into place as the familiar emotional coldness I'd felt for every single kill shot I'd ever made fell over me. "When they buzz, trigger the intercom, say you're coming, and then three seconds later buzz them in."

I took off my jacket, leaving on the ballistic vest I was wearing underneath. Walking as quickly and quietly as I could, I made my way over to a pile of boxes and trash that the previous tenants had left behind. I'd discarded the idea of using them at first, the material was nothing more than cheap wood that is often used in wooden box pallets. But, I wanted a good sight line and concealment. The ability to stop bullets would have to take a back seat.

Sophie watched me move with eagle eyes, then settled behind her rifle. She rechecked her sight picture, and waited for the buzz. We didn't have to wait long. "Yes?" she said, triggering the intercom box.

"We have delivery, Sophie White?" the voice said in near perfect English, only slightly Russian-accented. I knew the Spetznatz were good, but I didn't think their English was that good. Maybe these two boys were more experienced within the States than I'd thought. "Amazon?"

"Oh, okay. I'll buzz you in, just a second."

Sophie settled herself against the rifle, and slid her right hand against the trigger. I took aim with my Desert Eagle, and nodded. Sophie reached over with her left hand and pressed the buzzer, which we could faintly hear.

I had to give it to the men, they were good. The door flew out and both men came diving through the door, their empty boxes disappearing to reveal bullpup-style carbines. Nasty little things that fired a Russian-made fifty caliber round, one that was designed for subsonic firing. If it hit a soft target, the damage was catastrophic, but Sophie was safe behind her thick wall of steel and cinder blocks. I, on the other hand, was not so fortunate.

Tracking the two Russians, I fired quickly, the small cannon in my hand booming in the confined space of the warehouse. The sound caught at least one of the men's attention, and he turned towards me in mid-air, squeezing his trigger as he dove and flattened out. I knew the impact of his chest on the concrete would hurt like hell, but it would give him an extra tenth of a second to try and get rounds off in my direction. I immediately flattened and dove myself, hoping that Sophie's shots would ring true.

With the booms of my Desert Eagle, and the muffled thuds from the Russian's weapons, the sharp crack of Sophie's M-14 stood out. Her shot was perfect, catching the second man, the one not yet firing at me, in his throat, and his lifeless body fell to the ground.

I felt a searing heat on the outside of my right thigh as I rolled over the concrete floor, and I knew I'd been hit. I just didn't know how bad. The pain washed through me but was clamped down as my mind refused to let it alter my perceptions of the world. I could still see the guy, who was now on his side, rolling and firing at the same time. Damn this guy was good.

I felt a sharp spray as another round ricocheted off the concrete near my head, and the sting as a fleck of the floor cut my face. I sighted and squeezed the trigger on my weapon, cursing as the Russian operative seemed to move with almost psychic abilities, pausing his roll just long enough that my round bounced off the pavement beside him instead of smashing through his head. He had also rolled out of Sophie's immediate ability to adjust, and I knew she would have to pick up the rifle to re-sight and fire.

I didn't have that much time, I could see in his eyes as he brought his rifle to bear. In that instant, I was faced with two choices. If I jerked my trigger, I'd die for certain unless I scared him. There was no way I could hit him, and his shot would probably take me in the belly. On the other hand, if I took the fraction of a second to steady my aim, I could take him out, but at the risk of not getting a shot off at all.

I thought of Sophie.

The rest was easy.

My bullet took him high in the forehead, painting a gigantic Rorsarch blot on the wall behind him in red and grayish tones. His rifle dropped to the concrete, going off, and I felt another sharp bite of pain as the round clipped off my right trapezius muscle before flattening against the far wall of the room. It was over.

The silence was immediate and immense. Sophie came around, her shotgun in her hands to run up to the automatic door, but it closed before she could get there.

The whole gunfight had taken less than the five seconds it normally took for the pneumatic hinge on the door to close.

"Sophie," I whispered, my Desert Eagle falling to the floor. I couldn't feel my right arm any longer, and I knew the hydrostatic shock of even the grazing hit on my right trapezius was disrupting the nerves to that arm. I only hoped that the feeling would return. Sometimes, in wounds like this, it didn't.

Sophie came over and looked at me, and at the blood already staining my pants and my shoulder. I could only watch in admiration as she quickly assessed my wounds and ran over to her position, where we'd stashed our medical kit. It was a full battle surgeon's kit, along with extra bandages and other things we thought we might need. Lying me on my back, she quickly pulled my armored vest off, and cut away my t-shirt to assess the damage, before repeating the process on my jeans. "Repeat after me," she said as she opened the kit. "Gunshot wound, right shoulder."

"G... gunshot wound, right shoulder." I knew what she was doing. By having me repeat, she could keep me conscious, and keep herself calm at the same time.

"Gunshot wound, graze, right outer thigh."

"Graze, right outer thigh."

"Stitches needed on shoulder, thigh can be bandaged."

"Stitches for shoulder, thigh can be bandaged."

Sophie nodded and pulled out the materials needed. "We don't have any anesthesia, so this is going to hurt," she said, taking out an ampoule of topical antiseptic. Cracking it open, she poured the whole thing on my thigh, sluicing the blood away and lighting up the entire area in fiery pain. I groaned from deep in my chest, which she ignored professionally while she applied a sterile gauze pad and taped it down. "Good, now for the fun part."

She repeated the process with my shoulder, then took out her suture kit. "You're lucky the wound isn't deeper into the muscle, I never learned how to do intramuscular sutures," she said in an almost conversational tone. I knew it was just detachment from the shock of what had just happened, and I let her continue. "You're going to have quite a nice little scar up there. It'll look like Dracula took a bite out of you."

I smiled, keeping the expression on my face even as I felt the needle slide into my flesh over and over. It took twenty stitches, forty punctures of my skin. I could feel each and every one, and it felt like forever before the last tug was done and Sophie snipped the thread. "Now lay back, I'll give you a shot of antibiotics," she said, filling a syringe and jabbing me in the uninjured shoulder.

"Thanks," I rasped, feeling the first tendrils of battle-shock drop over me. I groaned and lay back, letting Sophie elevate my left foot. "You need to get those bodies taken care of."

"After you're stabilized," she replied matter-of-factly. "You mentioned one time that Owen Lynch likes to send cop patrols as cleanup on hits. Think he'll do it this time?"

"No," I said, trying to focus. It was hard, like I was swimming in laughing gas or something. "These two were freelancers. He'd do that for his own boys, but not these two. Also, he probably suspected there'd be some sort of setup. If that was the case, he wouldn't want to send more men to their deaths. He's smart that way, knows when to cut his losses."

Sophie nodded and went over to her little hiding place, retrieving my jacket. She brought it over and covered my body. "Then rest for now. I'll clean up the mess after it gets dark. Now I'm glad we don't have too many neighbors."

"See, I told you." I grinned and laid my head back, letting my eyes close.

I heard Sophie get up, and go over to the bodies of the two men. She spoke so softly I could barely make out what she said. "Two."

"Seventy-seven," I whispered in reply, and let sleep overtake me. My last thought was just how high both counts would get before our war was over. Not a problem for me, but I just hoped that Sophie didn't let it overtake her.

Chapter 28
Mark

"Owen, this is the Snowman," I said over the burner phone Sophie had found in one of the Russians' pockets. "Your little delivery to Sophie White was not quite what I expected, but I must say it was quite a surprising welcome back to town gift. Unfortunately, your delivery men seem to have had problems, and found they needed to leave the country rather suddenly. Now, you don't have to worry about your Capital City Delivery truck, I've had that parked in the parking lot of the University Hospital. Maybe you can get Glen Green to check it out for you. It's been wiped down, by the way.

"Owen, by doing this, you did a very annoying thing. Now, my current business partners are not the type to engage in petty feuds, so they'll let this one slide. They knew you and I had history before they hired me. But Owen, I'm telling you now. Sophie White, Tabby Williams, and everyone and everything associated with Marcus Smiley are all, as of now, under my protection. Unless you want my employers to take a much more vested interest in this town, I suggest you keep that in mind. Take care Owen."

I hung up the phone, pulled the battery and crunched the phone under the heel of my left boot. My right leg still hurt too much two days later. I'd been asleep most of the time, waking up just enough to be amazed as Sophie had taken care of almost everything even without me instructing her, disposing of the bodies in the bay. The floors and walls of the building she'd first scrubbed down with bleach and water before digging out the slugs and patching them with cement. Once the workers came in next week and painted, you'd never be able to tell any patches had been applied at all.

"You think he'll buy it?" Sophie asked, beside me as I picked up the pieces of smashed cell phone and threw them into the bay. They disappeared under the water, and I turned to look at her. My right shoulder burned like hell, and I kept the hand tucked into the pocket of the hoodie I was wearing to try and support it somewhat.

"I'm pretty sure. Lynch and the Confederation were always worried about an outside party making a play in town. This city is too rich and too important for it to be just a two game town. The biggest worry they had was someone internal going into business with someone out of town like me. So Lynch is going to have to take time and try and verify if I really am as connected as that call makes it seem. He won't understand where I'm getting the money from, nor just how it all is working. He's a very cautious man, it's how he's gotten to where he is."

Sophie nodded. "What outside players would he be checking out?"

"The Korean gangs, the Triads, some of the operators in Italy. The Confederation has Sal Giordano from the Mafia, but his family isn't the only Mafia organization in the world. All of them have tried from time to time to make inroads here. We're going to have to watch for them too as we take Lynch and the Confederation down at the same time."

We turned and walked back to our vehicle, a lightly used Nissan Frontier that felt like an old friend. Not quite as good as my old pickup, but it still felt a lot better than a rental car. Sophie helped me into the passenger seat before going around to the driver's seat. "So where to now?"

I chuckled and looked over. "Now? Let's go home. I think Tabby can bring the paperwork to us at home for once."

* * *

Sophie

Mark's prediction was spot on. Lynch didn't move against us at all, although we both stayed hyper vigilant. It took a little over a week for Mark's wounds to heal, and he grimaced as I snipped the sutures and pulled them out in our bedroom. "Next time let's use dissolving sutures," he hissed in between snips. "Jesus, this hurts about as much as when you put them in."

I chuckled in reply. "Now, how's that feel?"

"Stiff," he replied, working his arm in tight circles. "I hope I don't need to exert the muscles for a while."

"Well, you'll be doing that this afternoon," I said as I put away the scissors and packed away my kit. "You need to start rehabilitating that shoulder."

Mark groaned and leaned back in the chair he was sitting in, sticking out his lip and pouting. I'm sure he knew how cute and adorable he was when he did that, but I wasn't going to let it deter me. "Now, let's get you into the shower to wash up and relax. We've got no business appointments today, just the workout and then some much needed private time together."

Mark smiled and went into our brand new bathroom. While Mount Zion originally didn't have very good water pipes, the workers we'd had on the property ever since we moved back had worked updating the utilities to modern standards. The scars across the turf around the building were still raw and fresh, but our new home was now fully equipped with all the amenities.

The bathroom was our biggest work, with an in ground deep tub that could go all the way to your neck without a problem. It was even environmentally friendly, using filtered and re-circulated water from the shower and the bath to do the laundry and toilets before finally doing some sort of whoopty-dos and irrigating the vegetable garden we'd had put in. It was another public relations coup for Marcus Smiley, and was getting us a write-up in the local paper the next week.

Right then though, Mark needed a shower, and I listened at the door as he got into the stall and the dual overhead sprays turned on. I gave him about two or three minutes to let himself get acclimated before slipping quietly into the bathroom and stripping, getting into the stall behind him while he shampooed his hair. "Mmmm, now that's something that will motivate any woman to work out," I said, running my hands over his chest. The muscles were slick with water and the runoff from his shampoo, and I relished the feeling of his skin under my fingertips. "Very sexy."

Mark sighed and leaned his head back, letting his arms rest on the granite tile of the stall. "You can do that all day."

I rubbed my breasts against his back, enjoying the feeling radiating out from my nipples. I continued my massage, tweaking his nipples and kissing the large muscles in between his shoulder blades. Keeping my right hand on his chest, I rubbed my left hand down to his waist, wrapping my fingers around his rapidly thickening cock. "Think I can do this part all day too?"

Mark's rumbling reply vibrated through his chest, and I slowly jacked his cock, until his head drooped and the breath tore through his body.

The feeling of having him in my control was exhilarating, and I paused as a kinky thought came to mind. "You know, in this position I'm the one in charge," I whispered into his ear. "You've taken me from behind so many times..... maybe I should return the favor?"

I heard Mark's breath catch, then he slid his feet apart, bracing them against the side of the stall. "I trust you," is all he said, his voice quiet and intense.

My heart swelled in my chest as I realized just how much Mark was giving me. He was the ultimate alpha male in my mind, strong, intelligent, decisive, powerful. Yet here he was, willing to let me have my way with him. The fact that he was so confident in himself and trusting of me made him even more masculine and alpha in my eyes. I slid beside him, and turned his chin until he could look at me. "I don't need to," I said, kissing him. "But maybe some other time."

We kissed, our lips meeting and the warm water running down our bodies. It was like kissing in a tropical rain shower, and before I knew it, Mark had wrapped his arms around me, holding me against him as our tongues and lips caressed one another and I could feel his cock press against my belly.

Mark pulled me in tighter. He lifted me up in his arms, his footing sure and stable even in the wet shower stall, pinning my body against the relatively cool tile of the shower wall. I wrapped my legs around him, both of us letting loose long groans as I sank down onto his wide, beautiful shaft. It didn't matter how often or how many times, having Mark's cock inside me was heaven on earth. "Did you stop the pills?"

I nodded, smiling. I'd thrown out the package the day after our fight with the two men, along with the M-14 rifle, all three being dumped into the ocean. "You said after the Russians were done."

Because of his wounds and the stress of everything, we hadn't made love since before the firefight, and we took our time. I was amazed at his strength, even after two weeks of relative inactivity. Mark held me effortlessly as he filled me over and over with small short strokes of his cock that had us both crying out softly. It was a perfect position for what we wanted. The thick spreading lit up the nerves in my pussy while my nipples dragged over his chest, sending fireworks through my body until I was almost begging for more. Mark was in the same situation, his cock squeezed and my fingernails dragging over his neck and back while we kissed.

At the same time though, because of our position, we couldn't go to that final level. Mark couldn't thrust deep enough without me sliding down the wall, and because of the difference in our heights, I couldn't put a foot down to help support myself. Instead we stayed in that prison of pleasure while he stabbed into me over and over with his cock, unable to stop but at the same time caught on an erotic plateau. I could hear myself groaning over and over, "Fuck me, fuck me, fuck me," in tune to his short viscous thrusts that pounded into me, wanting more than either of us could give.

My legs wrapped around his hips, pulling him in tighter, trying to use my own thighs to help lift and lower my body, but our skin was too wet and slick. I pushed with my arms, trying to add that, and it helped some. Our strokes became an inch longer, the extra distance exponentially increasing the sensations from the heated passion of our joining. My left breast lifted up high enough to catch on the hard line of Mark's collarbone, pinching for a moment before sliding down, a cry tearing from my lips as it shot pleasure down my body to the pit of my stomach and deep into my brain.

Finally, with an animal growl of frustration, Mark wrapped me up and took me to the floor of the shower, turning me over and setting me on my chest and knees. I could barely get my ass up as he lay on top of me, his cock impaling me over and over from behind. Both of us were almost drowning in the spray from overhead, but didn't care. My body was on fire with the pleasure tearing through me, and my mind flashed with colors with every slap of Mark's hips against mine.

I could feel my orgasm rushing up on me like a drag racer, and I clenched my fists, wanting to hold off for just a second or two longer. I couldn't stop it though, and it shattered through me, sharp shards of ecstasy that stabbed deep into my stomach and up my backbone before piercing my brain and leaving me senseless, red and white strobe lights behind my eyeballs that only grew brighter when I felt Mark's cock also explode.

We lay there under the spray for a long time, until the water heater finally gave up the ghost, and we shut it off. My body still felt boneless, my muscles weak as a kitten as Mark got out and found one of the large Egyptian cotton bath towels we bought, coming back in to wrap it around me and carry me into the bed room. He laid me on top of the comforter on the bed, and kissed my forehead. "Take a nap," he whispered. "We own the gym, remember? I think we can go in a bit later than we originally planned."

Chapter 29
Sophie

I checked my hair in the mirror, just now after almost a month and a half feeling comfortable and natural with the bright purple shade. It looked good, and the new manicure from Ms. Wen at her nail salon the day before made me feel pretty and feminine. It was a bit of a surprise, I thought. Six months prior, I'd felt overweight, lonely, and unloved. Since then I'd traveled the world, changed my identity, had some plastic surgery (none of it to my so-called problem areas), and had lost a grand total of five pounds. Yep, only five pounds. The difference was in how the rest of my body was laid out, and more importantly, in how my mind was laid out.

I didn't look in the mirror and see the soft bulge above my belt line, even though I still didn't have much in the way of abs. I didn't see the tired, desperate eyes of the girl who hustled between class, the emergency room, and slinging drinks at an Irish pub. Even though I was working longer hours than I ever did in school, I woke up every morning refreshed and eager to see what I could do that day. "Amazing what love and purpose can do for you," I said to the Sophie in the mirror, a women I couldn't quite believe was actually me. "You're looking pretty damn good, Sophie Warbird."

The door to the ladies room opened, and Tabby came in. "You get lost in here, or just going narcissistic on us?" she joked, coming over. "I mean, kickoff's in five minutes."

"Yeah, sorry, just gathering wool," I said, giving her shoulders a squeeze. "By the way, congratulations on the tickets. I'm glad your boss is rewarding you."

"Considering the amount of money you and Marcus have fed through my account sheets since you got back, I think using the company luxury box for the first game of the season is pretty small," Tabby said, "but thanks. Not that I did anything that spectacular."

"You kidding? You've brought us plenty of businesses that fit our needs. And of course, some of your other information you've gathered has proven more than helpful."

Tabby smiled, then shook her head. "You two have a lot more you're going to do. You know, I heard someone mention that Marcus should try running for Deputy Mayor next year, when the election is held. I had to laugh at that one."

"We've heard that one too. Yeah, that's poking the bear a bit too much right now." I heard a roar from outside the washroom, and I looked over at Tabby. "Think we should go. Can't wait to see if the Spartans can get a win against Central City."

We left the washroom, and found Marcus along with a dozen other various executives from Tabby's office along with their dates seated or enjoying the snacks and food from catering. I came up next to him and gave him a kiss. "Ready?"

"Oh yeah," Mark replied, smiling down at me. "You know, I think this is going to be a great season, and it's just kicking off."

Literally.

Chapter 30
Part 4 - Sophie

There are downsides to being the second most public face of a new and intentionally attention-grabbing company. While Marcus Smiley was the president and public head, in public I was his trusty assistant Sophie Warbird. With long, electric purple hair and a penchant for tight-waisted outfits that emphasized my cleavage and my hips, I showed up in the news almost as often as Marcus did. I had even been named one of the sexiest new trendsetters in the city in a recent Sunday supplement article. It was quite a change from being plain old Sophie White, medical student and part-time bartender. In fact, Mark and I had such a laugh over it we clipped it out of the paper and put it up on the refrigerator with magnets, like some school kids first A test or something.

But with all of the fun of becoming a sex symbol, there were things I didn't like. Besides the fact that I had to go to every public work appearance dressed like a walking anime fantasy, I had to sit through meetings. While *Marcus* and I kept things pretty loose due to the other activities in our life, we still had to go through the whole rigmarole every time we wanted to sink money into a new investment.

"So as you can see," the guy at the front of the room said as he turned his attention away from my breasts to the LCD display behind him, which dominated the west wall of the room. I'd have preferred a good projector myself, but the LCD was a product of one of our other investments, a tech company that was trying to make revolutionary ultra thin LCD's. I had to say the display was pretty good, to the point Marcus and I sometimes watched videos on it, and it could run off of a nine-volt battery if we wanted. I shook my head and tried to pay attention to the guy at the front of the room.

"We've increased sales by an average margin of twenty percent over the past five years," he said, pointing towards a bar chart on the screen. "But more importantly, we're poised for even more growth. The past two years I've intentionally held back on further growth options because I was worried about overreaching my company's ability to deliver quality service to our customers. This year though I'm at a plateau. If I don't get venture capital in order to expand into new facilities, I'm going to be stuck where I am."

"What's so wrong with that?" Marcus asked from his chair next to me. "You know that if I give you the money you're asking for, you're giving up at least twenty-five percent ownership in the company you founded. Isn't one hundred percent of a smaller pie better than seventy-five percent of a bigger pie?"

"Depends on the size of the bigger pie. I predict we can double in size. Mr. Smiley, I came to you because you've gained a reputation in the city of being able to help companies like mine when we cannot go through traditional channels. I've tried those ways, but each bank I've approached has turned me down. If you say no, I'm going to have to look outside the city for expansion capital."

"So you're this certain about your company?" I asked him. "Because while we provide money, the sweat equity and hard work comes from your end. Mr. Smiley makes his money by giving other people an opportunity, not handouts."

"Miss Warbird, I've already put everything into this company. My home is carrying two mortgages and I'm driving a fifteen-year-old Ford for a reason. I know that we can make ourselves into a great success. I'm just looking for that last little bit to prime the pump."

Marcus nodded. "Okay. Let me and my assistant look the figures and details over, and I'll give you an answer within twenty-four hours. Thank you for stopping by."

The man clicked the power button on the remote he was holding, and the LCD went blank. "No, thank you Mr. Smiley. I look forward to hearing from you."

After he left, *Marcus Smiley* was able to set his mask aside, and I was able to look at the face of the man I loved, Mark Snow. "So what do you think?"

I stood up and stretched, aware that my position was making my already enhanced bust line stick out even more. Since it was just Mark though, I didn't mind showing off a little bit. "I think he spent far too much time looking at my breasts for someone who was dedicated to growing his company."

Mark smiled and gestured with his hand. "Babe, with what you are wearing today, I had trouble not just jumping out of my chair and ending the meeting early myself. You look incredibly sexy today."

I could feel the blush creeping up my neck and waved off his compliment. "You tell me I look sexy, that's one thing," I said as I unbuttoned the form fitting suit jacket. "Hell, you tell me to dress like every guy's fantasy of an office vixen, and it turns me on, you know that. But when Mr. Potato Head is checking out my boobs too, no thanks. These belong to the Snowman only."

Mark got up out of his chair and pulled me to him, his strong hands holding my waist close to him. I could feel the lithe, powerful muscles under his navy blue Italian suit, and my heart sped up in my chest. "Mark....." I whispered, looking up into his eyes.

"Later, my love," he said, kissing my forehead regretfully. "If I do what I want, we're not going to have a chance to get the rest of the work day done."

Like I said, being Sophie Warbird was sometimes a drag.

Chapter 31
Sophie

Later that afternoon, after we had concluded the daily work, I got to do one of the more fun parts of being Sophie Warbird. I stretched my wrists, twirling the bamboo stick in my hand and looking over at Mark. My hair was pulled back, and I was wearing the lightly padded outfit that Mark still insisted that I wear. Mark's stick was also padded, giving me just enough protection to prevent bruises or injury while at the same time leaving enough feedback that I knew when I screwed up. Well that, and the fact that Mark was a great teacher and knew exactly how hard to take things to push me.

"Let's see how much you've learned," Mark said as he twirled his own stick.

Stick fighting isn't a big part of my training. With Mark and I taking on the organized crime elements of the city, firearms were much more important than anything else. However, Mark felt that understanding the basics of fear and how to react even when I was afraid was vital. I agreed, and besides, it was a lot of fun. Besides, it pushed us to another level of bonding.

Mark started slow, with simple single swings of the stick that I blocked and countered easily. He could dodge almost every blow that I returned, except for the minor ones that he wanted me to hit with. He didn't wear any protective clothing, depending on his skill and speed to keep himself safe. As our sparring continued, our speed and complexity increased more and more, until the two of us were swinging dual sticks at each other full speed. More than once I could hear the whoosh as Mark's stick whizzed by my ear, but instead of backing off, we pushed harder. The sparring ended when Mark's stick stopped a fraction of an inch from my neck, frozen in the middle of a swing that in real life would have most likely broken my neck, and definitely would have ruptured my carotid artery.

"Nice job," Mark replied, twirling his stick and stepping away. "You did a lot better."

"I've been working on it," I grinned. I rolled my left shoulder, which had taken a shot from him a few minutes prior. "So what percent were you going at today?"

"About eighty, a new high," Mark replied. "Seriously, I didn't think I'd ever be pushed to eighty percent by you."

"Because I'm a girl?" I asked with a smile. "Or because I'm your girlfriend?"

"Because you didn't start this until you were in your twenties," Mark replied. "It took me a long time to get the hang of this stuff, and I started a lot younger. The later you start this stuff, the longer it takes you to get the hang of it."

I smiled and dropped my stick. "Well, let's get the rest of our workout done, and then go home. I'm ready for an evening together. You owe me a bath and massage for that whack on my shoulder."

Mark grinned. "Sounds good."

* * *

Tabby

The day after Sophie and Mark's meeting with their most recent investment possibility, I was sitting in my office going over the financials on another one of the Smiley potentials when my office phone rang.

It was strange, the fact that I had my own office at Taylor & Hardwick's, one of the bigger financial firms in town, and I wasn't even twenty-five. I knew that it was all due to Sophie and Mark, but still I wanted to do my best to earn my spot. I had my MBA for a reason, after all. Still, the intern pool was filled with people who had degrees just as good as mine, and who worked just as hard as I did. I just happened to be lucky enough to have one of my best friends fall in love with a rich hitman who had a heart of gold, as well as a bank account that would make all of the senior partners in the firm green with envy.

As ridiculous as it sounds, it's totally true. Mark Snow was one of the best hitmen in the entire country, who knows, maybe one of the best in the world. I don't exactly keep track of these things. Tall, fit, and intelligent, he also had movie star looks to go along with it. Yeah, I was a little jealous when Sophie hooked up with him, but after knowing Mark the past few months, I couldn't be totally jealous any more.

There was only one area that I was still envious of Sophie, and that was *the look*. Any woman who has had a friend who gets a great lover knows *the look*. It's the look of a woman who just had every sexual desire satiated. For the average woman, you might see that once or twice in the course of a friendship. Hell, to be honest, you may never see it at all, even in our own mirrors. It's a look that says *The world's ending and the zombies are rampaging? Ah well, I'm cool with that.*

I've never had that feeling myself, although I've come damn close a few times. Despite my adventurous nature, I'm not an easy lay, so for me to be seeing it on Sophie's face on almost a daily basis was a little frustrating at first. Hell, Mark gets shot in the leg, she does emergency surgery on the man, and two weeks later she's back to looking like she's on permanent happy pills.

So I was sitting in my office going over the latest batch of potential investments for Mark and Sophie when my phone rang. I picked it up, tucking it between my shoulder and head. "Taylor & Hardwick's, Tabitha Williams."

"Tabby? Hi, it's Donna down in the intern pool. Got a minute?"

Donna was one of the girls who had started with me. Smarter than I was, she was a graduate of Penn State, and had been pegged as one of the fast risers in the intern pool almost as soon as we both started. Donna's main problem was the way that she presented herself. She lacked self-confidence, and it showed when she conducted business. It caused her to have a hard time getting traction in a business world where, quite frankly, appearance and personality got you clients in the beginning. Donna's advice was great, in fact she could outperform analysts with two and three times the years she had, but she was still slaving away in the intern pool until she got enough people who could get past her first impression and see the brain inside. I liked her, so I tried to help her when I could. "Yeah, what's up Donna?"

"I've got a company investment request that came across my desk, honestly it looks like one of those types of things that you tend to handle. Smallish company, local, looking for investment capital, and willing to give up a percentage of the business for it. I've done just the initial research, but I think it could be a Smiley investment. You mind if I come up and give you the info?"

"Heck no, I'd be all for it," I said. I knew that if Donna brought me the file, she and I would split the revenue for the investment. It could be enough that Donna could find herself the second member of our intern class to get their way into a real office, even if it was shared with another junior associate. "I'm in my office right now. You know where it is?"

"You kidding? Your office is like Valhalla for the interns right now. We all want to get in there."

I laughed. "Well, don't be too overwhelmed, it's not the greatest office in the building. I don't even have a window, and the air conditioner in here sucks."

"But you *do* have your own space. I'll be up in three minutes." The line went dead, and I waited for Donna to show up. She was true to her word, and knocked on my door, breathing just a bit heavily, three minutes later. She really needed to get more exercise, she spent too many hours working. "Hey Tabby, here you are."

I looked the file folder over. "Hmm, family owned HVAC installation and repair, looking at expanding their service from four trucks to seven, maybe open up a second location across the river to catch that traffic. How're the financials?"

"Solid. Good ROI, maybe twenty-five percent cash on cash yearly. They're only looking for twenty-five grand, I figure the Smileys can see that back within the first year even with the firm's percentage. Taxes might bite them in the ass a bit, but they're going to clear easy profit on it. I say let the accountants worry about the taxes, they're going to make money."

I nodded. "It's good. So why aren't you taking this to your current clients?"

Donna shook her head. "I don't have any angel investor clients. All I have currently is your standard stock market type crowd, mostly in mutual funds. Besides, my managerial portfolio is based around stocks and bonds. I'm currently fourth in the region in terms of highest performing fund managers, did you know that?"

"No, I didn't. Word of that gets out and you're going to be leapfrogging me on the firm's ladder very quickly," I said in true appreciation. Donna was that sort of woman, you couldn't get mad at her, she was just so sweet and kind. Also, she was just so unabashedly smart, you ended up feeling like a good high school player being jealous of Kobe Bryant or something, it just felt stupid. "So who are the top three?"

"Rob Viscount at East Street, Xavier Washington at Hammersmith, and an online guy, goes by the name of The Frost King. He's a freakin' legend amongst the market day traders, guy seriously has some sort of sixth sense when it comes to picking the right stocks to invest or short. He's down a bit from the past two years, and slipped to third, but he's still beating the market by twenty-five percent. God I'd love to meet him."

I smiled to myself and shrugged. "Who knows, maybe you'll get a chance some day. In any case, I'll take this to Marcus Smiley, and you get to keep your share of the credit for your portfolio. What is it now?"

"Thirty-three percent," Donna replied quickly before stopping and blushing. "Sorry, I took a moment to look it up before I called you."

"How about we make it fifty-fifty then?" I said. "You did most of the hard work on this I see, I don't want to take the credit from you."

I could see Donna considering. Was I being generous because I felt bad for her, or was I being truly rewarding because she was deserving of it? Finally, she smiled. "Okay, great. I'll get the papers drawn up. If you don't mind, can I get a chance to meet the Smileys some time? I've seen them on TV a few times, and they're just so cool."

"Sure. I'm sure Marcus and Sophie would love to meet you sometime. When I give them the brief on this I'll pass it along."

"Thanks."

* * *

Tabby

Pressman Contractors was a pretty standard looking industrial contractor's office, the building itself being cinderblock and concrete that could use a fresh coat of paint. Two trucks were parked outside, Ford F450's with the Pressman logo on the side and a back bed filled with tools and all the other things a repairman might need. I parked my little Prius in the spot marked for visitors and made my way inside. "Hello?"

"Just a moment!" a call came from the back. I heard a bit of frustrated grumbling and muffled curses, then the unmistakable sound of a wrench being dropped on a floor. "All right, there we go."

The guy who came out of the back was cute, plain and simple. He was about five ten, maybe a hundred and eighty or so, with brown hair and hazel eyes that went with a strong, square jawline. He was wearing a slightly tight polo shirt with the Pressman logo on it and some work pants, both of which he filled out nicely. He looked like the sort of guy that housewives called over to check out their units just to see him in tight jeans and a sweaty shirt as often as possible. "Hi, how can I help you?"

"Hi, I'm Tabitha Williams, from Taylor & Hardwick's, I'm a financial analyst. Is your boss around?" I asked, tossing my hair over my shoulder. My long auburn red hair is one of my favorite features, and I knew I was flirting. It's just in my nature, and besides, this guy was worth flirting with.

"Dad's out at a work-site right now," the young guy said, "but I'm sure I can help you. Are you here about the request for venture capital we submitted to you guys?"

I was impressed. This guy was smart, and yeah, he broke some of my preconceived notions of what an HVAC guy was supposed to sound like. "I am. I'm the account manager for Marcus Smiley's investments in the city, and I just wanted to see if I could look around some."

"Sure," the guy said, pulling a towel out of the back pocket of his jeans and wiping his hands. "I'm sorry for the greasy hands, but one of our guys just brought this unit in and I wanted to get it out of the shop quickly. We've got a lady over on the South Side without an air conditioner right now. By the way, I'm Scott. Scott Pressman."

"Nice to meet you. Sure you don't mind if I look around?" I asked, looking at the shop. "I don't want to get in your way."

"Not at all. If you want, you can even give me a hand if you want. I don't know why, but you look like the sort of girl who knows the difference between a socket wrench and a Phillips-head screwdriver."

Scott had me pegged. While since entering college I'd had the reputation and look of a sorority party girl, the fact was I'd grown up in a family that, while well to do, had gotten that way by owning three car dealerships down in Florida. I'd spent just as much time under the hood of a car as I had on the beaches, and could do an oil change by the time I was eight. "I think I can give you a hand if you want, just as long as I don't get dirty. I'm wearing a suit after all."

For the next hour and a half, I helped Scott break down and replace the parts that were going wrong on the AC unit. It was pretty similar to a car, really, and I could follow along as he walked me through the different systems and subsystems. It was a lot of fun, and as we worked, we got to know each other.

"So, how long have you been doing HVAC?" I asked.

"Officially only two years, but since Grandpa opened this place, I've been around it my whole life. After high school I went straight to my HVAC course, got my diploma, and came back to work the family business. Dad wants me to take night classes in business to get my associates, but I'm holding off for a year or two to get my feet underneath me again. What about you? You're not just a calculator type, I can tell that by the way you find the wrenches on sight without even needing to read the markings."

I felt a warmth in my cheeks from his compliment. "My family owns a couple of car dealerships in Florida. My father and brother run them now, and I kind of moved on. I enjoyed the family work, but I didn't want to spend the rest of my life working credit applications for new trucks or seeing if I can get someone into that convertible they insist they need. So I went to school, got my MBA, and started where I am now."

"I see. You enjoy it?" Scott asked as he attached a flywheel to the compressor. "I mean, I know it pays better than HVAC repair, but people don't work just for money."

"I know what you mean," I said, handing him a screwdriver. "And yes, I like my work. I'll admit I got lucky by being picked out by Marcus Smiley for his local investments, but that can make all the difference. We're spending his money not just for making profit, but to help real people make a real positive way in the world."

Scott set his wrench aside and looked at me. "And that's important to you. Making the world a better place."

I smiled and sat back on the small stool that we both had. "Yeah, I guess so."

"That's pretty cool. Uhm, I'm not sure if I'm supposed to do this or not, you being the financial analyst, but I was wondering if perhaps you and I could..." Scott said, looking even cuter as he nervously fidgeted.

I've always been kind of forward, and I answered him before he could even complete his question. "I'd love to. I'm into Italian food and I'm free this Thursday night."

"You ever been to Mar de Napoli?" Scott asked. "Real wood fired pizza oven, and the best *frutti di mare* you'll find in the city."

"You had me at wood fired pizza. Now, I really should do a walk around to do the work part of my job."

Scott smiled. "Of course. Dad should be back soon, and if you need anything I'll be happy to help you out."

Chapter 32
Mark

The night was cloudy and there was only a new moon in the sky, which is exactly what I was looking for. Pushing off from the observation deck of the Financial Tower, the tallest building in the city, I rode the updrafts from the sides of the surrounding buildings pretty well in my glider. Made of the lightest materials available, it was one of my newest purchases, and came in non-reflective black. While not totally invisible, I could be assured of a very quiet approach.

"So how's it going back there?" I whispered. The contact microphone taped to my throat worked perfectly, and I knew that Sophie could hear what I was saying. "I mean, instead of doing this, I'd much rather be having a relaxing bath with you."

"Hmm, well, you get out of there in one piece, and you can have more than a bath," Sophie purred back. "In fact, if it wasn't that you'd probably crash, I'd tell you right now what you could be having."

The sound quality on the radios was perfect, it sounded like I was sitting next to Sophie, who was back at our home in the bell tower where we had one of our headquarters for surreptitious activities. She wanted to come with me on this mission, but Sophie hadn't learned how to fly a hang glider yet, although it was something we were planning on doing soon.

I hung a right, catching the updraft coming off of the Huddleston Subway Terminal to get my final approach on my target. Landing was really the only tricky part of the entire flight. The top of the Hamilton Building wasn't at all like a lot of the other skyscrapers around town, with helipads and open gardens dotting their roofs. Nope, the Hamilton Building was covered in pipes, conduits, and a bunch of other crap that more or less make landing a very tricky proposition indeed. To do it the way I wanted, I actually needed to come in lower than the roof, then quickly pull up and bleed off speed to gain altitude, hopefully just clearing the lip of the building before settling down. I'd done a similar landing before on the top of our roof, which was much more comfortably laid out and was about ninety stories shorter.

Pulling back hard on my control bar, I cleared the lip, and found I was still too fast. I was going to keep gaining altitude, damn! Reaching out with my arms, I let go of the control and pulled in on the wing deployment, cutting the surface area in half within a blink of an eye. With so much less fabric to support my weight, I dropped somewhat under control, landing with a bit of a thump along the conduit lines that fed the building's backup generators. "I'm in."

"That's good. So I don't have to worry about the muttered *fuck* that I just heard then?" Sophie replied. That's the problem with throat mikes, if you want a truly hands-free experience, you have to transmit constantly.

"Nah, just came in a bit fast. But I'm down and safe. How about you?"

"Oh, nervous, sweating, and wearing nothing but those pajama pants that you like so much," Sophie teased. "Want me to tell you about it?"

Her next chuckle made me realize that I had probably groaned deep in my throat, and I tried to put my mind off of the image of my beautiful fiancée sitting in loose cotton pant and nothing else. Trust me, it was more difficult than I had hoped it would be.

"I swear," I finally told her once I had my glider stashed and my small satchel ready, "when I get home I'm going to make you pay for all this teasing."

"I look forward to it," Sophie replied. "But on to business, your target is five floors down. How're you planning on getting access?"

"Elevator shaft," I replied, pulling up a building schematic on the small tablet I had with me. I knew Sophie could see what I saw on her computer, which was hot-linked to my tablet. It allowed her to also send me data updates as well if she wanted to. "Just making my way down the stairs would be too big a chance of triggering some sort of alarm or getting caught by a patrol. And that whole rappel over the side and slide down a rope act may work in the movies, but I don't put a lot of faith in it myself. Nor do I plan on trying to cut holes in reinforced glass."

I went over to the elevator shaft, which hulked out of the top of the building. It's one of the classic challenges of an elevator system, namely, where do you put the motors and the cable? The easiest is to have them both stick out the top of your building in a miniature room. The bigger the building, and the bigger the elevator, the bigger a room you need. I found the elevator I wanted, which according to the schematics was marked as an executive elevator. I wanted that one because I didn't need anyone suddenly interrupting me while I was trying to work.

The cable descender I used is another one of the toys that I have come to enjoy about my new crusade against crime in the city. Made of a special type of braided nylon and Kevlar blend, it could support a full one thousand pounds while being flexible enough and small enough to wind onto a reel roughly the size of my hand. Really, more space was taken up by the ascender and descender mechanisms than by the filament itself. I used a carabiner to lock it onto the overhead beam of the shaft, then made my descent. It was easier than you'd think, I just had to hang and let my harness support me. Pretty soon I was five floors down, right where I wanted to be. Looking down the shaft, I double checked that I was still safe before jimmying the doors open.

It was strange, really. The place I was breaking into was one of the main computer centers for the Confederation, so security should have been tighter than Fort Knox. Instead, they went with hiding through deception, and made it no more noticeable than any other mainframe center in the city, just another one of thousands. If anything, I had expected that the elevator shaft doors themselves should have been rigged with an alarm. Instead, I was soon making my way down the corridor to the mainframe room, where I quickly picked the lock and went inside.

I had to expect that I'd tripped something by that point, so I didn't have a lot of time. Instead of trying to go databank by databank, I pulled out my little secret weapon; the cracker computer that I used for this sort of work. Not much bigger than an old Sony Walkman, it was packed with enough power and an adaptable AI that I could hack my way into almost any system within seconds. But I just needed data, so I slipped my cracker computer into the data port on the nearest mainframe and let it go to work.

The cracker program was able to get to the level of reading file folder names quickly, and then flash copied them to a custom made three terabyte USB flash stick. In less than a minute, it beeped, indicating that the job was done. I tapped in one more little program, uploading a file that buried itself quickly into a backup server. Easily traced, but that was what I wanted. I wanted the owners of the databases to know who had been there.

I made my way out to the elevator just as the radio in my ear buzzed again. "Hey, my systems are saying that you're going to get company," Sophie said. She had tied into the building's security system through their armed guard company, which was a private corporation with an office off-site, but not too great of a cyber security setup. "How far are you from extraction?"

"Twenty feet from the elevator, and then the roof," I replied. "You're going to drop off in the elevator shaft again. Too much metal and stuff in the way."

"All right. They're taking the freight elevator up, so you should have time. Maybe thirty seconds."

I hummed my understanding and got back to the elevator, where the doors had been left shimmed open. I clicked into my filament and carefully swung into the shaft. The scariest part was when I tapped the shim holding the shaft doors open with my foot, and the thin piece of wood went tumbling down the shaft. It was a long, long time before I heard it hit something below, hopefully shattering into a dozen pieces. Either way, I hadn't touched the wood with bare hands, only gloved.

Hitting the retract button on my belt, the powerful coiled springs whisked me up the shaft, stopping with my head six inches below the metal beam I had anchored to. I could hear the deafening roar of the freight elevator in the shaft next to me, and the rapidly approaching lights on top of the car. They had picked the right elevator, the rapid freight car would get them up faster than anything else. They just hadn't anticipated me.

I pulled myself back over and out onto the roof, finding my folded up miniature glider. I stepped off, letting my speed gather before pulling back and swooping off into the night, and I headed to my planned extraction point, a large self-storage company three miles away that happened to have five shipping container sized units rented out to me. "I'm away and safe," I told Sophie. "I'll be home before midnight."

"Good, I'll have our bath waiting for us," Sophie replied into my ear. "So did you get the little package in there?"

"Yeah, they're going to love that," I chuckled. The *package* was technically a virus, although all it did was change all of the system sounds of any Windows unit that downloaded it to *Do You Wanna Build A Snowman?* Sophie and I were having fun poking our targets.

Tonight's raid had been the data collection center for one of the biggest rackets run by the Confederation in the city. While insurance fraud had been one of their most profitable scams for years, recently the Confederation was getting pressure from Owen Lynch, who was using his political connections to revamp the state's insurance laws, limiting payouts. To counteract this, the Confederation was going back to an old stand-by, one that had been in use since the Roman Empire days, padding work claims and then short shifting the system. With hundreds of public works contracts, especially in the construction industry, they could easily say they sent eight people and only send seven. That doesn't sound like a lot, but when every crew was ten to twelve percent understaffed, it totaled millions of dollars a year.

I had downloaded all of their contracts, hoping to track down who was legit and who was a scam. And of course, left my little calling card. "Remind me again when I get back," I said as I approached the self-storage site, "I've got to do some musical research."

"Oh, what for?" Sophie asked. She could keep her headset in even as she moved around the house, and normally did whenever we were separated like this.

"I've got to find something more bad-ass than a song from a Disney movie as my calling card. Isn't there any heavy metal or something that uses the word snow?"

"I think the Red Hot Chili Peppers did something," Sophie said. "And of course, you could always use songs by the Canadian reggae guy, Snow."

"Ah hell no," I groaned. "I'd rather stick with Disney songs at that point."

"Well, get home quickly," Sophie said. "I've got the bath ready for you, with all your favorite oils and herbs on standby. And of course, two hands that are more than ready to give you a massage."

"I'll be there as soon as I can. I love you."

"I love you too."

Chapter 33
Tabby

I was kind of nervous as I waited outside my apartment for Scott to arrive. I was wearing one of my more polite first date outfits, a knee length decorated denim skirt and a white Bohemian-style top. It wasn't quite a poet blouse, but I couldn't call it a peasant blouse either. Either way, I liked it, and had worn it for years.

Scott was three minutes early by my watch, or as my Daddy used to say, right on time. He pulled up not in the pickup truck I'd expected, but a Buick Verano. I was surprised, I hadn't taken Scott for being a Buick type of guy.

"Hi," he said, getting out. At least he was wearing what I'd expected, black denim jeans and a khaki shirt with a green nylon flight jacket. He wasn't quite *GQ*, but he wasn't straight country either. Instead, he was somewhere in between, and he was handsome as hell doing it. "You look amazing."

"Thank you," I replied, giving him a little curtsey with my skirt. "And may I say, you look quite dashing as well. Is that jacket real?"

"If you mean is it really a military jacket, yes it is," Scott replied. "I had to laugh when I heard designers were coming out with six and seven hundred dollar imitation flight jackets when I was able to go down to an Army-Navy surplus store and get the real deal for under a hundred and fifty bucks. You like it?"

"It looks authentic on you," I replied honestly. "No froo-froo crap for you."

"Thanks," Scott replied. He led me around to the passenger side door of his Buick and held the door open for me like a real gentleman. "So what does it mean that I'm driving a Buick then?"

I waited for him to come around and sit down in the driver's seat. "It means you're looking for luxury, but are also smart enough to not over extend yourself by signing a lease for a BMW or Audi or some other sixty thousand dollar car," I replied. "I call that smart in my book."

Scott grinned at me, and turned over the engine. "Thanks. Now, how about some Italian?"

"Drive on, oh brave sir!" I said, both of us snickering at the jokes. It didn't take us long to drive to Mar De Napoli, and I had to admit, it was a cute little place. Near the Northside where the docks gave way to the beaches and the high-end houses of the Heights, it was built to look like a Mediterranean Villa, complete with white walls and blue accents. The smells coming from the pizza oven drifted deep into the parking lot, and I knew immediately what I wanted.

"Yeah, it's that good," Scott said, reading my expression. "Come on, we've got a table already reserved."

The atmosphere inside was quiet, mostly due to the design of the tables. The restaurant had done a masterful job of sound baffling, so that instead of echoing ceilings and sound drifting all over the restaurant, conversations were muted and you didn't feel like you were yelling over everyone else. The lights weren't exactly dim, but they weren't glaring either. Maybe the best you could describe it would be *cozy*. "So how'd you find this place?" I asked Scott after we had been seated.

"We do the HVAC for the restaurant," Scott said simply. "I wish that would score me some free food like we get from the chocolatiers near the Gaslight District, but I guess I'll just have to be content with the pizza instead. I'm just glad it wasn't the calzone."

"Oh, what's up with the calzone? Is it terrible?" I asked, curiously munching on a delicious oregano and parmesan breadstick.

Scott shook his head. "No, exactly the opposite. But, a pizza is big, it's open, it's supposed to be shared. A pizza is for a date. A calzone is closed up, it's by itself. It's the meal I order when I get stood up or I break up with someone. Trust me, I'm happy to be ordering a pizza tonight."

I was touched by his thinking, even if it was a bit weird. "As long as you don't like anchovies, I think I'm happy about it too."

"I promise, no anchovies. Hey, can I ask you a question?"

"Of course. Isn't that what dates are for, getting to know someone else," I said, taking a sip of my ice water. "And it's a lot more fun than just filling out a paper questionnaire."

"That is true," Scott told me, "then I know you'd turn me down due to my horrendous handwriting. I'm the sort of man that keyboards were invented for. But anyway, what led you to the financial services industry? You told me your family had car dealerships, and I understand not wanting to go into that if you don't want to, but why finances?"

"A couple of reasons," I said, my answer interrupted as the waitress brought our pizza. It was too hot to cut up yet, so we let it cool, the smell of the cheese and Italian sausage tantalizing us as I tried to finish my answer. "First, because I've always been good with numbers, but not so good I wanted to become an engineer or something like that. But second and more importantly, while I was in on the wrench side of things with my parents, I always loved the business side of it more. So when it came time for me to go to college, I knew I was going to go for business, and get at least my MBA. After that though, I just wanted to stand on my own two feet, and my current job allows me to do that."

"So how'd you get so lucky as to start working the Smiley contracts? I figured a high roller like him would be getting the VIP treatment from some higher ups or something," Scott said, dishing out the first slice of pizza onto a plate. He passed it over to me, then got a slice for himself, sprinkling extra Parmesan cheese and chili flakes over top. His taste in pizza was another thing to like about him, in my opinion.

"It was luck, actually," I said, falling into the story that Sophie, Mark and I had put together. "When I started with my current job, one of the things that every newbie is handed is a pile of dead weight files. These are ones that, if they pan out, gets you a nice bonus check, but nobody expects them to pan out. Estates that have been caught up in litigation for years, decades-long overseas claims, stuff like that. I happen to have been handed Mount Zion."

"Where the Smileys live," Scott said, doing the mental math. "So when they came to the firm, you met them."

"Something like that. Actually, Marcus' corporation bought the property before they ever arrived in town. However, our firm did have some property records that the Smileys wanted personally, so I was invited over and got to meet them at Mount Zion. Sophie Warbird and I are the same age, and as we started discussing things, Marcus asked me a few questions about business. I guess what I said impressed them, because the next week,I got a message from my bosses that I was to be the manager for the Smileys for all of their purchases in the city."

"So half luck, half your actual ability," Scott said, taking a bite of his pizza. "Don't sell yourself short."

The rest of the date went wonderfully, and I was more and more impressed by Scott's charm. I've never been snobby about who I date, I didn't care that he was an HVAC repairman, but I also want to have the complete package for someone I'm dating.

I want brains to go with looks if its going to be more than a one-night flirt session. Scott was checking all of the boxes. In addition to being cute, he was smart, in the sort of mix of street smarts and book smarts that told me he had taken what he'd learned in his HVAC license course, combined it with a high school education, and them swirled it all around with a few years of being out in the real world doing stuff. He had gaps in his knowledge, but admitted it, and not in that *yeah I'm ignorant and proud of it* way that a lot of insecure people get. He was just honest about it, while at the same time expressing a desire to learn more.

By the time the last slice of pizza was gone, I knew that I wanted to see Scott again. I hadn't had such a great date in at least a year, and I was enjoying every moment. "I suppose you have work tomorrow," Scott said as we left the restaurant. "I kind of wish you didn't."

"Oh, why's that?" I said as we walked through the parking lot. I entwined my arm with his, snuggling against him. "You think you'll get more than a shared pizza from me tonight?"

Scott actually blushed, and I could feel my heart and body react to the bashful look he gave me. "No, but a guy can wish," he said. "Actually, I just really enjoyed this, and don't want it to end."

"Neither do I," I said, "But yes, we both have work tomorrow. So, I had an idea that maybe could work for both of us."

"What's that?" Scott asked, giving me a small smile.

"Well, Friday and Saturdays are my social nights," I said. "I was thinking maybe you'd like to go out again tomorrow night? And if things go late tomorrow night, neither of us has our schedules too disturbed."

Scott's smile was electric and bright, and I could see the happiness in his eyes. "I think I'd like that. In the meantime, let me take you home like a gentleman, and we can discuss details on the way."

The drive home didn't take as long as finding Mar De Napoli, and by the time we'd gotten to my place we had barely set a time for when to pick me up the next night. I knew what I wanted though. After watching him work physically on the air conditioner, I'd seen his muscles at work, now I wanted to see him in a more sensual activity. "You're serious?" Scott said when I told him my plan. "A dance club?"

"Sure am. What, you don't want to see me in a short skirt?" I teased, crossing and uncrossing my legs for him.

Scott laughed and shook his head. "No, I just am a bit nervous of looking like a goofball trying to be coordinated on the floor. Promise to take it easy on me?"

"We'll see," I told him. We were soon at my apartment, and Scott stopped his car. "Thank you for a lovely dinner, Scott."

"Can I walk you to your door?" he asked. "I promise, just to the door."

"I'd like that," I said, and waited for him to come around and let me out. I could feel the pleasant tension as he led me to my door, something I hadn't felt in a long time from any date.

"I had a great time too," Scott said when we reached my door. "And I'm looking forward to tomorrow."

He leaned forward naturally, and our lips met. It was a good kiss, strong enough that I could appreciate his strength without being too forward. I let the kiss linger for a good amount of time before pulling back, smiling. "I'm looking forward to it too. Good night, Scott."

Chapter 34
Sophie

I was true to my word, waiting for Mark when he got back from his mission with my hair twisted into a thick cable braid and then laid over my left shoulder. Other than that, I wasn't wearing a thing when he came into the master bath suite of Mount Zion. Instead, I was sitting in the deep central tub, which was filled with milky colored water that covered me almost all the way to my chin. The tops of my breasts broke the surface of the water, but that was it. "My brave warrior returns."

Mark shrugged off his jacket and watched me as I slid through the water until I was on the other edge, facing him. I could feel my butt sticking out of the water, and knew I was enticing him. "I'm glad to see that you worried about my safety," he teased, pulling off his t-shirt. "What if I had gotten shot down or something?"

"Then I would have come to your rescue," I replied matter-of-factly. "Besides, I didn't start this bath until you were already down and in the car back here."

"I see. And you're not interested at all in what we learned from my little case of corporate espionage?" he asked, unbuckling his belt.

"Not as much as I am feeling you in this bath next to me. The data analysis can wait at least a few hours," I said. "That is, unless you happen to like analyzing data instead of spending time with me?"

Mark finished stripping off his clothes at what looked like warp speed, which was a shame. I enjoy watching him pull the fabric over his firm muscles, revealing himself to me. Even the scars on his body were sexy to me, and I shivered in anticipation as he stepped over the side of the tub and into the water, upon which I found the other drawback to the mineral salts I had used for the bath. While they provided a great scent and let me tease him by only giving Mark hints of my body underneath the water, now I couldn't see him the same way. I growled lightly in frustration and slid closer to him.

"I know that you're good, but that doesn't mean I don't worry," I said as our thighs brushed together. "All I can imagine is not being able to feel you again."

"You can feel me all you want," Mark whispered to me, pulling me onto his lap. Our kiss was hot and slippery, like the water we were in. I could feel our bodies pressed together, his skin electric over mine, and I could feel his cock already starting to swell in between us. I rubbed against his chest, letting my nipples rake over his skin, both of our hearts hammering in our chests.

"Tonight....." I said, breaking the kiss. I sat back in his lap, looking him deep into his eyes.

"I was safe," Mark whispered, stroking my back. "I promise."

I shook my head. "That wasn't what I was going to say."

Mark cocked an eyebrow at me, encouraging me to continue. "Tonight," I said, taking a deep breath, "I want you back there."

Mark's other eyebrow joined his cocked one in surprise. We'd discussed anal sex before, and in fact he'd used his fingers on me once or twice while he licked me, he'd never slid his cock back there before. In fact, nobody had.

But after the risks of our job, I needed this. It was one of the first dangerous missions he had undertaken since we'd been together without me, and it had scared me more than I was letting him know. "Are you ready?" Mark asked softly, kissing my neck. "Did you prepare?"

"A little," I said, "but not a lot."

"Then we'll take our time, and help you be ready," Mark replied, kissing down my neck to my collarbone. I groaned as his hands roamed up and down my back, stroking and massaging the muscles while his mouth feasted on my skin. His right hand disappeared under the water, cupping my butt cheek and massaging it.

"Yesss...." I sighed, lifting my breasts out of the water to his lips. Mark obliged me, kissing them quickly before raising his head up to kiss my lips again. While our tongues danced and twisted around each other, I felt his fingers slide into the cleft in between my cheeks, and I pushed back, opening myself for him. Mark's finger found my tight hole and rubbed slowly, in tight little circles.

"You told me you are virgin back there, yes?"

"I am."

Mark's solemn nod while he lowered his lips to my left breast again, reassured me while at the same time his lips and tongue sent tingles up and down my spine. I could feel the warm pleasure building in my chest, and barely noticed when he slipped his finger inside me. He pumped slowly, letting my body adjust to his graceful digit. On my end, it was absolute heaven. Mark's lips were sucking and pleasuring my breasts while his legs supported me, and at the same time let my pussy rub against the strong muscles of his thigh. Then, behind, I was wonderfully impaled, filled and taken by the man I loved.

I don't remember how long Mark kept up his digital stretching, but the next thing I was aware of was the tight coil of tension building in my stomach, one of the precursors of an orgasm that I knew meant I was going to lose it soon. Mark heard the change in my gasps and moans, and shifted his legs slightly, letting my clit rub directly against his thigh. I came quickly after that, moaning and calling his name softly while he supported me with his free hand.

When my climax had passed, he kissed my lips again. "Do you want me to stop?" he asked me, concern in his voice. "You don't have to do anything you don't want to."

"I know that," I told him, stroking his face and looking him in the eye. "It's why I know you're the only person I trust with this."

I reached down under the water and wrapped my hand around his cock, which was still rock hard and thick. There was no way I was ready at that point. "What do we need to do?"

"Bend over the edge of the tub," Mark said, slipping out of the water and going to the medicine cabinet. Inside we had a few of the various toys we'd collected, but he came back with a large tube of lubricant. "This might feel cold after the bath water, I'm sorry about that."

"Well then," I teased, wiggling my bent over backside at him. "I guess you'll need to warm it up then."

Mark coated two of his fingers in the shiny, clear gel before capping it and setting the tube in the overflow area of the tub. It made sense, it was almost as warm as the bath water. "Okay, now look at the wall, and push back, see yourself opening up," he said.

I did as he asked, in my mind's eye imagining my ass opening up to allow him in. There was a moment of tightness, but suddenly both of his fingers were inside me, massaging my inner walls and filling me with delicious fullness. At the same time, his other hand continued to rub and massage my back, relaxing me and letting me feel calm and at peace.

Just when I thought I could actually feel my body start to rise again towards another climax, Mark pulled his fingers out. Getting out of the bath, he lay down on the thick faux fur rug that we use for catching drops and smeared another glistening dollop of lubricant on his cock, until it was shiny and ready. "You control your depth," he said simply.

I nodded and got out, making sure my feet were dry before squatting over top of him. I could feel my ass still wet and ready for him, and I took him in my hand, looking into his eyes. "I love you, Mark."

"I love you too, Sophie," he said, and I lowered myself down. It's one of the benefits of having a super-fit hitman as your fiancee, you get lots of exercise. My legs, which couldn't have supported the squatting position for very long before, gave me plenty of control as I felt the blunt spongy head of his cock push against my ass. It was bigger than his fingers, but it wasn't too much for me, and except for a momentary twinge of pain, I guided myself down onto his cock in a smooth, amazingly sexy descent.

"Oh fuck," I groaned as my hips settled against Mark. I'd read about anal sex before. Hell, it's not exactly a subject that you go into blind nowadays. I'd read both the good and the bad, and all I can say is, the good paled in comparison to how I actually felt. It wasn't just the fact that I had Mark inside me in a way no man had ever been before. It was the look in his eyes, and the calm assurance in his face as he held my hips in his hands. There were no words to describe it.

"I'll go slow," Mark promised me as he lifted my hips up slightly before holding me there. He began to thrust, slowly at first, letting me feel the taboo pleasure make its way through my body as our eyes stayed gazing into each other. I swore I could see into Mark's soul, which was just as beautiful as it was tortured. Still, his love burned bright for me, and as his hips increased in pace, I could feel that burning start up again deep in my belly.

I pushed back, stroking my ass up and down Mark's cock as my own desires took over. As I did, I marveled at how perfect our position was. My breasts dragged against the strong muscles of his chest, while at the bottom of each filling thrust my clit ground against the flat muscle below his belly button. I was filled, I was taken, and I was safe all at the same time.

The only thing that our position wouldn't let us do was last. It just felt too damn good. My hips sped up, to be met by Mark's thrusts, and soon both of us were trembling on the edge of another orgasm. I looked up into Mark's eyes and nodded, pushing myself back and squeezing down. I saw his eyes roll up in his head and I knew he was ready. My clit ground as I rode his orgasm, until my own followed behind, reducing me to a trembling, teary mass on the rug. Mark's arms held me tight through my convulsions, his body never pushing me away or pulling me too tightly against him. Finally, my convulsions passed, and we lay against each other until I started to shiver. "What's wrong?" Mark asked.

"I'm cold," I told him. "Let's get back in the bath."

* * *

Sophie

The next day, we started to pour over the data that Mark had stolen. "I think we've got a lot here," Mark said as he skimmed the file headers. "I recognize a lot of these businesses, they're ones that the Confederation used to launder their money."

"That's a lot of businesses," I said as we looked at the long list of file folders. Even on the huge thirty inch monitor we were plugged into, the list of names filled the screen. "How are we going to get through them all?"

"We probably won't need to," Mark said. "If we take down random ones, it'll put pressure on the others. Since I know quite a few of them myself, I was actually thinking of saving some of those for last. Let Sal Giordano and the rest of the Confederation keep guessing. Also, we don't have to take down these companies. We can just monitor them, get the dirt on them, and then turn them over to the Feds. Even if the FBI is pretty incompetent, they have their uses."

"You don't like the FBI, I take it."

Mark chuckled. "Considering the rings I ran around them for years? Nah. But I give the FBI credit on one thing. Once they know where to apply pressure, they are like millstones, they grind very very fine. We just have to make sure that we're not in their path when they let loose their juggernaut."

"Can you do it?" I asked. Mark grinned and nodded.

"Of course. With this amount of data, it's not a matter of if the FBI will get involved, but when."

Our conversation was interrupted as Tabby Williams buzzed for entrance. We were on the fourth floor of the Smiley Headquarters, far enough away from the noise and music of the gym on the first floor that we could work uninterrupted. After buzzing her in, Mark shut down the files we were looking at and went back to his normal desktop. Tabby may have known our real identities, but there was no reason to put her at risk by letting her in on more secrets than she already knew. "Hey you guys."

I could tell as soon as she came in the door that something was different with her. Tabby was always bubbly, but this was almost perky. "Hey Tabby. What's up?"

"Oh, just wanted to drop off some more files for your perusal," Tabby said, practically skipping across the floor. "How's life in Mount Zion?"

"Good," Mark replied, turning towards her. "You seem rather chipper this morning. Get some extra caffeine in your latte or something?"

"I just had a really good night last night, that's all," Tabby said, starting to blush. I looked at Mark, who nodded.

"What was his name?" Mark asked with a smile. "And just how good a night was it?"

"Marcus Smiley!" Tabby said in mock outrage. I was glad that Tabby knew Mark more under his assumed alias than as Mark Snow, because you could tell she was being flippant and not really thinking. "I will let you know, Sir, that despite all appearances, I am a very hard to please woman. In fact, I'm just the sort to take home to your mother for Sunday dinner."

"Uh-huh. So is he or she cute?"

Tabby rolled her eyes and nodded. "Yes, HE is very cute. But more than that, he was a total gentleman the whole time. In fact, we only kissed once, when he walked me to the door of my apartment."

I was surprised. Tabby was no slut, but she rarely played hard to get like this. "Really? And you're seeing him again?"

Tabby smiled and started giggling. "Tonight, in fact."

I was flabbergasted. "Whoa, two dates in two nights with the same guy? He must be a good one."

"He is. Listen, I'd love to tell the two of you all about it, but I just barely had time to drop these files off before getting to the office. I have a meeting in thirty minutes that I can't be late for."

"Okay. Well, give me a call tomorrow or something, we can talk all about it," I said, picking up the inch thick pile of file folders. "And when do you need these back?"

"I don't," she replied, heading for the elevator. "Those are your copies now. See you!"

As quickly as she arrived, Tabby was gone, the elevator taking her down stairs. I turned to Mark, who had a careful look on his face. "What is it?"

"Have you ever known anyone interested in Tabby who was willing to settle for just a kiss at her front door at the end of a good date?"

"No, but that doesn't mean it can't happen," I said. "Maybe Tabby has finally run into a guy who will treat her with respect and admiration. Trust me, when that happens, it feels great for a woman."

I saw Mark blush, and he turned back to his computer without a reply. "Okay, well, could you start taking a look at the businesses while I work my way through the files from last night?"

"Okay," I said, starting with the top folder on the pile. The first sort was easy, really. While we had given Tabby very specific ideas on companies that we wanted to look at in terms of income, potential for growth and other hard data, there were factors that we hadn't told her.

For example, one of our rules was that we didn't invest over a hundred thousand dollars unless the company was either offering very close to a majority stake, or that the company was already so wealthy that the stake offered was under ten percent. The first group of companies were true angel investments, meant to provide people with the ability to achieve their dream. They were relatively high risk, but still we did it to help people. The other group were companies that we were assured to get our money back, and we used them for growth of our total portfolio. Companies who were in neither group were eliminated because they either didn't need us, or were high enough risk that it wasn't a good investment for the amount of potential return.

That rule alone eliminated roughly a third of the pile. The second pass was more careful, as I geographically mapped each of the potential investments. Mark wanted Smiley companies all over the city, but especially in the areas that were being taken advantage of by either the Confederation or Owen Lynch's organization. The reason was simple, to give the neighborhoods that were being exploited by these groups something to rally around. After the second pass, which took close to two hours, I was left with four potential businesses. I set them aside for a final pass through with Mark after he was done and stretched. "How're you looking over there?"

"There's hundreds of companies here. I'm going to need to set up a database program to help us classify them and sort them according to a bunch of different factors. Just getting them all plotted on a map is going to take a long damn time," Mark said, rubbing his tired eyes. "Tell me you at least have something positive over there."

"Four potentials," I said, "but nothing that can't wait until after lunch. Besides, you still have your other investments to look after and everything. You can't be Marcus Smiley all the time, my love."

Mark hummed his assent and stretched, his back popping in three places. He walked away from his desk, a slight limp in his leg from where he had been shot. I knew he had to be tired, he only showed that limp when he was exhausted. "Come on," I said, making a decision, "let's get some lunch, come back, get our workouts in, and then go home. You're too blitzed to get anything else done."

"Okay," Mark said, sighing. "You're right, this was a lot easier when all I had to do was stay fit, cruise the markets, and do my other work. Not that I want to go back to that, no matter what."

Chapter 35
Mark

After a relaxing lunch at a Chinese restaurant that we were funding in the middle of the Triad-controlled part of Chinatown, Sophie and I drove back to the warehouse that was our headquarters as well as the first floor being another one of our investments, one of the most advanced fitness facilities in the entire state. The owner, a former NCAA strength coach who got frustrated with the limitations of college politics, was a nice guy in his thirties who knew a lot about fitness. Between his knowledge, Sophie's training as a physician's assistant, and my own prior knowledge of the body's systems from my training, I doubt there was any place in the country that could give me a better place to do what I needed to do.

"Good afternoon Marcus!" the staff member on duty said as Sophie and I came through the door. I was on strict terms with the owner that I was not to be called *sir* or *Mr. Smiley* by anyone in the gym. I may have been thirty-five percent owner, but I was still just there to do a workout just like everyone else. "What's on the agenda for today?"

"Legs," Sophie answered for me. I inwardly winced, as I knew that Sophie's idea of a good leg workout usually left me feeling like my muscles were made of burning kerosene and my heart pounding somewhere between my throat and my eyeballs.

"Did I do something to upset you?" I asked as we headed towards the one nod I had to being the owner, an executive locker room that Sophie and I could use together. "I thought you felt good after last night."

"Oh, I did," Sophie replied with a twinkle in her eye. "In fact, the better you do during your workout today, the sooner you get to do that again."

During the course of my free-wheeling, scattergun approach to higher education after leaving high school, I took a course on basic human psychology online from Stanford. In it, we covered quite a few lessons talking about motivation, and I still remember from the videos that the professor was talking about the difference between internal and external motivation.

Internal motivation, as you can guess, comes from inside, the professor had said, *while external motivation is imposed on us from an outside source. Both of these can be either positive or negative methods of motivation, but what psychologists have found is that for most people, in most circumstances, internal motivation is greater than external motivation. Basically, the fire that burns inside of us will often far outstrip anything that is imposed on us from outside.*

Of course, I thought as I cinched my back support belt tight for my last set of squats, when internal and external motivational factors worked together, the results were damn near nuclear. That was what that day felt like. Sure, I knew Sophie's promise for more sex was just a silly tease, but it worked, even though I knew exactly what she was doing. She was pushing me to get my leg back in tip-top shape after I'd been shot. I was almost there, but not quite.

I nodded and positioned myself under the bar. The deep criss-cross pattern of knurling cut into the bar bit into the skin in between my shoulder blades even with the t-shirt I was wearing, a welcome pain. I knew the bar wouldn't slip and screw me up. Taking a final deep breath, I squared my feet and stood, clearing the bar from the hooks. I had worked this pattern over and over, three steps back, the first for distance, then adjusting my feet to exactly where I needed them to be. My back and shoulder muscles trembled with tension of supporting the bar. Sophie watched me with a careful eye. She would call me on my downs and ups. "Down!"

The pressure in my head increased with every inch that I descended. I knew my face was almost bright pink, and would only get worse as the set wore on. I focused on pushing my hips back, keeping the bar moving straight up and down, with as little forward and back motion as possible. Just as I felt like I was about to be crushed, I heard Sophie call. "Up!"

I pushed hard, about halfway between my heels and the balls of my feet, driving my head up as I accelerated. A deep grunt came through my clenched teeth as I pushed, and I knew why some very heavy squatters would wear mouthpieces to prevent dental damage. With a slight rattle, I reached the top of my squat, and I grinned as I took a deep breath. "Down!"

Sophie was relentless, giving me enough of a break in between heavy pushes to get another deep breath before commanding me down again. My leg where I'd been shot screamed in fire, and I knew Sophie would have to help me out of the car when we got home to Mount Zion. "Up!"

I pushed, my deep bellow of effort becoming an epic roar as I put everything into getting that bar two more inches up, and then the next two, and then the next. It felt like the squat took days, and dark spots danced before my eyes when I finally got up and could breathe again. Sophie leaned next to me, speaking quietly. "You can do one more. Don't think about the pain, or the weight, or anything else. Listen to my voice, and think about the fact that I love you."

She stepped back and resumed her studying stance. "Down!"

For me, the entire world became the narrow focus of my eyes in the mirror in front of me, and Sophie's voice in my ear. She kept up her command, repeating down in a calm, quiet voice that cooled the fire in my spine and legs. Even the pressure of the bar seemed to disappear as Sophie's voice switched from "Down," to "UP! PUSH!"

The fire in her command gave me the energy, that's all there was to it. My mind went blank as I pushed, and the next thing I knew, I was standing up, my entire body trembling. Sophie was there along with two other gym members, who helped me take the bar into the hooks. As soon as the bar rattled into the hooks, I pitched forward, stopped only by Sophie's arms around my chest. She guided me down onto my hands and knees, rubbing my back the whole time.

"Beautiful, baby," she whispered into my ear as sound started coming back into the world. "Sorry, I know you're good, but I need that leg back one-hundred percent, I worry enough as it is."

Sophie reached around and pulled the lever release on my back support belt, letting my stomach expand and my body to flood with precious oxygen. I stayed there for a good minute, until the black roses stopped blooming in my vision.

"Ready for a massage and about two straight hours of nothing but Netflix and popcorn?" Sophie asked.

"That's exactly what I need."

* * *

That night, after a relaxing evening and some gentle lovemaking, Sophie and I lay in bed, too tired or perhaps too satiated to want to get up, but too awake to fall asleep.

"Sorry about today, I just want one less thing to worry about when you go on some of these crazy missions," Sophie said, her head laid in the crook of my shoulder. I swear, I could die a happy man as long as that woman is snuggled against me, her warm body pressed against my side. Hell, maybe if I'm lucky, in sixty or seventy years that might happen. "You know that, right?"

"I know," I said, pulling her close and kissing her purple hair. Once you got used to it, it was really damn sexy. I had to give her credit for the idea, choosing electric purple. "After seeing what I could do today, I think I'm almost there."

Sophie sighed, rubbing my chest. "I just...there's a part of me that hopes someday this little dual life war we're fighting ends."

"I know, my love. Me too. After all, raising a family in the middle of a war is not in my plans."

Sophie tensed for a second and moved her head to look at me. Her beautiful eyes bore into mine, heavy with meaning. "You really want to have children?"

"Someday," I said, kissing her forehead. "Sophie, there's a very boring, very normal streak running underneath the business peacock and trained killer sides of my personality. So yeah, I want to have you with me, in some quiet house somewhere peaceful and boring, with two or three kids running around the house, maybe a dog or two."

"And of course the obstacle course with salmon ladder in the back yard," Sophie teased me, reaching up and tweaking my nose. "Mark Snow, I know you too well after the amount of time we've been together. Boring and you do not go together. Now, I can be on board with the kids, and the house, and the dog, but let's be honest, our lives are never going to be so boring that you're going to be normal."

"Good point," I said, sliding down and kissing her lips. "But then again, you seem to like me just the way I am."

"Not quite," she said, stroking my arm muscles

"How so?" I said, kissing her lips again and running my hands down to cup her backside. Sophie moaned and kissed me back, and I knew exactly what changes she wanted me to make.

I was more than happy to make them.

Chapter 36
Tabby

I looked myself up and down in the mirror, wondering for the third time if I was dressing too slutty for my date. I was wearing one of my favorite clubbing dresses, a tight red piece that was just a shade brighter than my hair. It actually covered a lot of skin, there was nothing that was see through, but the sexiness was from just how tight everything was. There was just enough thickness in the cloth over my breasts and my hips that I could wear my thinnest pair of thong panties, but that was it. I could see the dip of my belly button in the outfit, and even the flex of my leg muscles as I turned. It was the sexiest thing I had, but was it too much?

"Scott sees you in this and he's going to have just one thought on his mind," I said to my reflection, pondering. "Then again, that's been about the only thing on your mind since last night too."

It was true. I'd stayed up until almost one in the morning after my date, tossing and turning as I struggled with my inner desires. Part of it is just flat-out physical. I've always had a very high, very voracious sex drive. It started when I was a teenager, and I'll admit that it took me a few years to learn how to keep it under control. There were, of course, benefits. I've been able to do things that most people only read about, but I'm not stupid, I'd always been safe.

At the same time, though, there were drawbacks. First of all, when you have a sexual appetite that never seems satisfied, a lot of partners saw you as just being a casual thing. While I had no problem with having a friend with benefits, everyone wants to have a real relationship. It was perhaps the main thing that I was jealous about with Sophie and Mark.

I looked myself up and down in the mirror once again, and decided to take a risk. Reaching for the zipper, I unzipped and pulled the dress down, exposing my body. True to my Irish blood, I'm about as white as you can get without being a vampire, but with my red hair, it works. Also, thankfully, my skin tone has been described as "pale creamy" and not "ghostly pale." And I don't have any freckles, so I avoided the 'ginger' tag as well. Going into my closet, I pulled my tissue paper thin panties off and chose a more reasonable blue satin number along with it's matching pushup bra. Next was a black skirt and electric blue sleeveless blouse that was almost the same color as my lingerie. It was a few steps too sexy for office wear, but still had that naughty executive vibe that I sometimes liked to play.

I was just finishing the last button on my blouse when my doorbell rang, which I guess is a good thing. I would have fussed with the button until Scott came otherwise, and I had just enough time to grab my "club purse" which held one of my ID's, a pair of tightly folded twenty dollar bills, a disposable cell phone that I could use if I needed a taxi, and nothing else. I didn't even carry an apartment key after having one of these purses stolen in a club, which is why I used an old student ID for the clubs now. No need to risk my driver's license or something.

I opened the door to my apartment and felt my entire body skip a beat. Scott wasn't dressed in the most fashionable of clothes, a simple pair of black slacks and shirt that looked like he was trying to be something between Johnny Cash and Neo. Sure, it was off, but it worked for him. "Good evening."

Scott gaped for just a moment, and I felt better about picking the outfit I had. He probably would have had a coronary if I'd worn the red dress. "Good evening. Wow, you look amazing. Seriously, like, movie star amazing."

I smiled, and looked around. "So are you ready to go?"

Scott started and shook his head, smiling sheepishly. "Yeah, I guess I am. Sorry. By the way, you didn't say where we were going."

"Hold on," I said, turning and locking my front door from the inside. The manager and I were on good terms, and kept a copy of my key underneath the second flower pot next to his door, which I used whenever I went out clubbing. It was a nice safety feature, that was for sure. "Okay, ready. As for where we're going, there's a nice club over on Southeast and Monroe that I think we can have some fun at."

Scott nodded. "Okay, although the way you say that, it makes me think you know more clubs than I have ever heard of."

I smiled, not letting Scott know just how right his statement was. I knew a lot about the clubs in town, even Sophie didn't know just how deep down the rabbit hole I'd gone there. "Well, maybe. But tonight I just wanted to have a nice date with a nice guy, if you can believe that. So shall we?"

"We shall, beautiful lady," Scott said, offering me his arm. I could quickly become charmed by his almost old fashioned gentlemanly manners, and the walk to his car was pleasant. He let me mess with his in-dash navigation system for a moment before figuring out how to input the address, and we were off.

"Sorry, I'm just too easily distracted by stuff outside to be a good navigator," I told him as he drove. "Much better for you to just follow R2-D2 on your dash."

Scott chuckled. "I wouldn't have taken you for a Star Wars fan."

I laughed. "Oh, that I totally am. I've even forced myself to like Jar-Jar Binks, or at least tolerate him enough to watch the prequels without going into a homicidal rage. Besides, let's face it, Natalie Portman was hot in a lot of those outfits."

Scott gave me a double take, then turned his attention back to the road.

I knew maybe I'd said a little too much. It was a habit of mine sometimes, I talked just to talk, and sometimes I said a little too much. "Don't worry, it was a phase I went through. And my constant talking like this is what earned me my nickname in college."

"Oh, what was that?" Scott asked, taking it in stride.

"One of the other girls in my dorm called me Deadpool."

"Ah, the Merc with the Mouth," Scott said gleefully. "Red outfit, hits or tries to hit on just about every other character, and a total wiseass. Just tell me you're not deadly with pistols?"

I laughed, shaking my head. "Negative. Never fired a gun in my life before. So you're into comics too?"

"It helps on slow days around the shop," Scott said. "Normally into DC, but since they re-launched The New 52, I've been dabbling around. Not a problem I take it?"

"I just told you I thought Natalie Portman was hot in Star Wars, and you're worried that I think you liking comic books is weird? Scott, just where do they make you, because you are too good to be true."

"You'd be surprised."

We got to the club, and Scott found a parking spot underneath one of the lights in the parking lot. It was one of the safer clubs in town, but still, young people, alcohol, and semi-sexual activity didn't lead to always peaceful behavior. The line was pretty short for a Friday night, which I had anticipated. There was a big act in town at one of the other local clubs, and I was sure it was going to be packed. That meant that this club was going to be a little more laid back, which is what I thought Scott would be ready for.

The doorman and I were on a nodding acquaintance, and let Scott and me in through the velvet rope without even waiting in line. "Nice to see you, Tabs."

"Thanks, Tank. Enjoy tonight."

Inside, Scott gave me a look after we'd checked my purse and his light jacket with his wallet and stuff in. "You know the doorman?"

"Just a bit. He broke up a fight once between two guys who thought I was a piece of meat to snarl over."

"Really? What did he do?"

"Threw one into the side of a car, and kicked the other in the balls," I said with a grin. "Tank doesn't fight fair. Enough of that, though, let's dance!"

The music was pretty typical club fare, but I wasn't interested in whether the songs were hot or not. Instead, my eyes were caught up with Scott, who moved better than I had feared as the beat moved into his body. He relaxed pretty well, and while he wasn't going to win Dancing with the Stars anytime soon, he knew what to do as our bodies came closer and closer together. The first brush of my hip against his sent a jolt through both of our bodies, and as the music stopped, both of us were breathing a bit faster.

"This is more fun than I thought it would be," Scott said in the slightly less deafening sound of the club as we made our way off the floor. "Thanks!"

We got drinks, nothing alcoholic for me. Sophie has seen me act tipsy with men in clubs all the time, but the reality is unless I was with female platonic friends, I never drink alcohol in nightclubs. First of all, it's too damn easy to get your drink spiked nowadays. Like I said, I'm a little wild and free, but I'm smart. Secondly though for me, it actually takes that delicious sexual edge off of the dance floor, and who wants to mess with that? Scott just had a beer, which totally fit his personality, straightforward with no bull crap. Just as he finished, he set his cup (sadly, the club didn't allow bottles after a fight a few years before) and smiled at me. "You wanna dance again?"

For the next few hours, Scott and I engaged in an erotic, sensual foreplay on the dance floor that left my heart thumping and my body buzzing. He seemed to know exactly where and when to move closer, and his touches, while never naughty, were always in such a way that it lit the nerves of my skin on fire. When the last set came on and the bass picked up while the beat slowed down, we were nearly grinding on each other, and all I could do was stop myself from ripping his shirt off and having sex with him right there on the dance floor.

His hand slid around to my lower back, his eyes locked with mine as we came closer, my legs parting on their own, yearning for him to be between them. Scott obliged with one well-muscled leg, pushing closer to me to the point I could feel the sweat dampened fabric touch against my soaked panties. I gasped, throwing my arms around his neck and wantonly dry humping his leg, rubbing my aching pussy against the fabric, hungry for release. "Oh God," I moaned, leaning into him.

"Whenever you need to, you can," he said into my ear before pulling back and looking me in the eye. The music picked up pace, the bass thumping harder and harder, and my hips increased their rubbing back and forth. I was aware on the edges of my consciousness that some of the other couples were looking at us, but I really didn't give a damn, this was something I needed. I needed this man, and I needed to come so badly I could taste it.

With a sick drop in beat that ended in a vibrating bass pulse, my orgasm clamped down on me. I leaned my head back and moaned, unheard above the music, and not caring if anyone heard me or not. Scott held me carefully, letting my body ride out the wonderful wave until it released, and he pulled me in close for a final kiss as the song wrapped up. "That was the most beautiful thing I've ever seen," he said in the momentary silence. "Let's get out of here."

"Anywhere," I replied breathlessly, following him on shaking legs to the coat check area and then back out to his car. We were mostly silent on the road, and I was surprised when he pulled into my apartment.

"What are we doing here?" I asked, confused. "I thought when you wanted to get out of there..."

"I do," Scott said, an intense look in his eyes. "But Tabby, when we do what I want to do so badly, I don't want it to be because some music, a little bit of drink, and an awesome dance scrambles our brain circuits. I want it to be because we both want it, clear-headed, and that it is all we can think about."

"What do you mean? It's all I've been thinking about since last night!" I practically wailed. "For fuck's sake Scott, I'm telling you I want you to take me to bed and fuck me senseless, do you need a more open invitation than that?"

Scott cut off my complaints with a finger on my chin, and a soft kiss on my lips. "Yes," he said once our lips parted and I could listen again. "I don't want to just fuck you, Tabby. I'm sure that will be great, and there may be a time for it. But I want to make love before we just fuck."

The look in his eyes struck me dumb, and I nodded in understanding. Could Scott be the one, the one to accept who I am? "Scott, that's hard for me. I'm a pretty sexual person."

"I know," he said, smiling. "I saw that from the first moment I saw you in the shop, and in everything you've done since then from sipping a soda to dancing with me. And you can do whatever you need to relieve those desires. But I want our first time to be special. Can you make me a promise?"

"I can try," I said, in a small voice that was totally unlike me.

"Just give me one day," Scott said. "If you wake up in the morning and can think of nothing but me, not sexually but just as me, like I've been thinking of you, then call me at lunch. I'll come over at dinner time, and we'll see what happens then."

"Okay," I said in a shaky voice. "Well, I have to go rescue my door key from my apartment manager. You mind walking with me to the gate at least?"

"I'd like that," Scott said with a smile. He came around and opened my door, helping me out of the car. We held hands like a couple of teenage sweethearts until the gate, where I stepped into the manager's alcove and retrieved my key. "You should find a different plant next time. You never know, I could be some creepy stalker dude."

"I doubt that," I said as we stood there, holding hands. I hadn't felt this way about a guy since my teen years, honestly. "Are you sure I can't convince you to come upstairs with me?"

"My body wants it so bad right now my balls are kicking themselves," Scott said softly, "and the rest of my body is joining in. But my brain and my heart want more, Tabby. Call me greedy, but I want more than some nights of what I anticipate would be some incredible, memorable, mind altering passion. I want the whole package. And the only way I can get that is to wait, at least until tomorrow."

I nodded, and pulled him in for another kiss. Our lips and tongues twisted slowly around each other, and I was moaning in frustration when we finally broke apart. "I swear to all that it supernatural that tomorrow night, I will extract a measure of revenge on you for this," I groaned, already feeling my nipples hardening again inside my bra. "You are never going to be the same, boy."

"You know what I need, Tabby," he said, and I could see the painful grimace on his face when he adjusted his feet, and the hard bulge in his pants. It looked so delicious I wanted to go to my knees and suck it right there. "If you can give that to me, then call me at lunch tomorrow. Good night."

Scott turned and, while not exactly gracefully, at least walked back to his car. I watched him go, and turned, a tear trickling down my face. There were two reasons for the tear. Part of it was frustration, I was so aroused I thought I could wear out a fresh set of batteries on my favorite vibrator at that point and still not be satisfied. But the other part of the tear was the happy side, the side that thought that perhaps, in accepting the frustration, I was seeing the chance to have more than just sexual satisfaction, something I'd dreamed of for a long time.

Chapter 37
Sophie

"You really want to work on Saturday?" I asked, as Mark and I walked up the stairs to the bell tower at Mount Zion. "Are you planning another operation or something?"

"No, it's just something that I saw when I glanced at your final pile yesterday before we went to lunch that has been on my mind all day since I woke up, and I wanted to do some cross checking," he said. He sealed the steel core door that was at the bottom of the staircase, and we went up to the top, which had thankfully been refitted somewhat since he had first brought me there. The thin foam mattress was gone, replaced by a full workstation along with locked steel cabinets for the small arsenal we kept at Mount Zion. While the bell tower was not our main strike base, the fact was, we could easily outfit ourselves to take on just about anything short of an armored assault with what we kept there. "I just didn't think I could get it out of my mind until I had done this one thing."

"Okay, but why the tower? You could have used your pocket computer with any of the in-house monitors, you know that."

"Just a gut feeling," Mark said, sitting down and turning on the small cubical computer he used for secure purposes. Barely bigger than a deck of cards, it was the twin of the one we had at our main offices, and backed up with it nightly.

I'd come to trust Mark's gut, because usually what Mark called a gut feeling was more due to the constant awareness of everything that went on around him. One time, when we were on our trip through Eastern Europe to facilitate my training, he allowed me to test his awareness. I went into a hotel room, and put the items exactly the way I wanted. He hadn't ever been in the room before. When I was ready, I took photographs and stored them on a camera. Mark then walked through the room and spent thirty seconds walking around, looking at things. We then went into an adjoining room and described the room.

His recollection bordered on freaky. He started with interesting but not outlandish things, such as that the television was a Samsung, and that the clock radio's display was green. It then went on to borderline amazing, as he noted that the toothpaste tube visible in the bathroom had a pink label, and that the gel inside was dark red. By the end though, it was almost totally insane, as he recalled things like a stray hair I had laid on the pillowcase, and how it was on the opposite side of a crease that I had caused by running my hand across the upper corner of the pillow. He even saw things that I had missed, like the light tea stain on the carpet next to the window, so faint that I had to go back into the room and look more closely, as it hadn't shown up on the digital photos I took.

Mark's ability to gather information was just as sharp when it came to business and facts. He'd read the newspaper, and make connections between stories that sounded almost paranoid, but they would either turn out to have connections later, and would affect the investments he moved around in response to his connections. Sometimes these connections were so subtle even he couldn't put a name to them, and they were gut feelings. So when Mark told me he had a gut feeling, I didn't discount it in the least.

Mark pulled up the spreadsheet of the hacked companies he'd stolen from the Confederation servers a few nights before, and then next to it my final list of candidate companies for our next round of investments. He blinked a few times, then tapped a few controls. It took the computer less than a second for words on both windows to flash bright blue. "I thought so," Mark said as he tapped the screen.

"Pressman Contractors," I said, reading the screen over his shoulder. "HVAC company. I remember the portfolio, actually. Good ROI, small, ticked all the right boxes."

"Except for one," Mark said, sighing. "They're a front for the Confederation. It's not unexpected, I didn't know every company that fronted the Confederation and there was bound to be some that matched everything else we're looking for. It's the biggest problem with the Confederation."

"They're a Hydra, with more heads than we know about," I said. "What about Owen Lynch?"

"Lynch's power is more concentrated, and more narrowly focused. Taking him down is different in that he isn't worried about money or traditional things like that. He just wants control and power. Which kind of makes sense. I mean, seriously, after the first couple of million, what is more money to a man like him? If you can buy three Ferraris, who cares about being able to buy a Bentley as well? He uses his money like we are, using it to finance power. The Confederation though, with so many players, has to care about money more, and has more little things like this."

"So what are we going to do?" I asked. Mark clicked on the file on Pressman Contractors, reading what he had gathered. "What is Pressman?"

"On one hand, they're a pretty typical money laundering front, using construction contracts to filter Confederation money in and out of circulation. They've got the receipts here to back that up, the bank transfers and other stuff. This is full of second level connections that I'm going to need weeks to fully analyze, with all these companies. But there are a few other things here that concern me."

"How so?" I asked, looking over his shoulder still at the spreadsheet on the screen. It looked a lot like a normal accounting spreadsheet to me.

"This accounting code," Mark said, tapping one of the cells, "is the same one that Sal Giordano used with me when he hired me out for contracts. I don't think that Pressman has another hitman working for it, I knew that group very well. It pays to know the men who might be putting a bullet in your back. But that doesn't mean that there isn't some other sort of Confederation operative working for Pressman."

"Like what?" I asked, finally taking a seat and looking at the screen, my imagination whirling.

"Oh, there are all sorts of different operatives. A place like this would be a good place to stash an arsonist, a bomber, drug maker, burglar, spy, quite a few different jobs. They'd have access to buildings, deeper than a lot of others go, and they don't look out of place carrying tools and weird bundles of stuff."

I shook my head in amazement. "And you knew the Confederation had these sorts of men."

"And more, my love. Why else am I taking so many precautions with our own actions?" Mark replied. "Well, we know what we have to do now."

"What's that?" I asked, as Mark shut down the computer and unplugged it from its monitor and keyboard.

"We have to go down there, see if we can get eyes on someone, maybe figure out what is going on. You think Sophie Warbird and Marcus Smiley might be up for a weekend visit to our most recent potential investment?"

"Why not wait until Monday?" I asked as he sat back. We faced each other, and I could tell that Mark was nervous. "Come on, talk to me."

"I'm concerned that the Confederation may be making the same connections that I'm sure Owen Lynch is doing," Mark replied after a moment. "They know that coming after Marcus Smiley directly creates too much danger to their operations, but by putting out these sorts of poisoned pills, these land mines if you can think of it that way, they can derail us without risk of exposing themselves. I want to go down there today for two reasons.

"First, they won't know we're coming, so they can't be prepared. If we call Tabby and go down there Monday, they'll know it and be prepared, giving us a whole dog and pony show that will surely be ninety-nine percent bullshit. We go down there today, and we might learn something."

"What's your other reasons?" I asked. "You said first as if you had others."

Mark nodded. "Yes. Tabby. You saw the way she acted the other day, I'm sure."

"Of course. We even joked about it."

"I remember. Sophie, what concerns me is if there is a connection between this guy that Tabby met, and Pressman Contractors. If there is, and they know who you and I are, then Tabby may have gotten herself into trouble again."

"Oh God," I moaned, standing up. "We should call her."

Mark stood up and took my hands. "No, there's no reason to panic," he said, giving me a reassuring look. "First of all, we don't know for sure. Also, even in Confederation companies, a lot of the workers are just ordinary people who are making a living. Only a small percentage are the real criminals. Finally, if they are trying to use Tabby to get to me, they're playing a long ball game. They know it didn't work before when they rushed it. Their most likely plan is to try and use her as a blind mole, someone who funnels them information on our operations without ever knowing they are doing what they're doing. She's not in immediate physical danger."

I felt Mark pull me into an embrace, and I relaxed, letting my tension flow into him. "Okay," I said after I was calm. Actually, I was a bit more than calm, but that's normal every time Mark hugs me. "So we go down there, and what do we do?"

"We be flamboyant," Mark said with a grin. "Rattle their cages, see what falls out. Is your Sexy Executive Suit still clean and ready?"

I grinned. "I have three of those, you know I have one ready. Which do you want, black or white?"

Mark thought for a second, then smiled. "White. It contrasts your hair more, and if you just happen to get a grease stain on it that pulls attention to your breasts, well, shucks, guess it can't be avoided."

* * *

Pressman Contractors looked like any of a half dozen other industrial companies Mark and I had visited for potential investment during our work. The front windows showed a somewhat cluttered but semi-organized mess of machine parts that I couldn't even begin to identify. The shop was somewhat dark, with a bored looking guy manning the counter. We drove up in our customized Bentley and got out, Marcus in his skinny-panted suit with counter stitching and pocket watch, me looking like an anime wet dream. Thankfully the suit was mostly Lycra, I doubt it would have been able to move otherwise.

As expected, the counterman first caught sight of the car, then of me. Marcus' plan to be a "business peacock" depended on me pulling as much attention from his face as possible, especially when he went into areas that the Confederation or Owen Lynch could have men who knew his old face. That and it helped distract from the spring-loaded knife blade he kept attached to his left wrist. A twist of his clenched left hand, and the top of his forearm would grow a ten-inch razor sharp spike faster than you could blink.

"Good afternoon," Marcus said as he came in. "This is Pressman's, right?"

The counter clerk, a reasonably handsome kid who stood about five-ten, nodded. "Yes, how can I help you guys?"

It was my cue to take over. "I'm Sophie Warbird, and this is Marcus Smiley," I said, offering my hand in such a way as to make my already noticeable cleavage roughly the size of the Grand Canyon. "Our investment firm brought over a file on this company, and while we understand it is a bit strange to be visiting on a Saturday, do you think it would be okay if we looked around, get a feel for things?"

"Ah, sure," the kid said. He looked like he was about seventeen, maybe eighteen, and I was sure that with the show I was giving him, I'd filed a long-term spot in his spank bank. "I'm Mike Pressman, my dad owns the place."

"Really?" Marcus said, reaching over and shaking the kid's hand. "Well, you're just the sort of person I wanted to meet. So what are you doing here on a Saturday afternoon when I guess most guys your age are out with a pretty girl?"

"Covering for my brother Scott, mostly," Mike said. "He was supposed to work the afternoon Saturday shift, but he begged me to cover for him. He's got a new girlfriend, and he wanted time with her enough to not only give me his pay, but an extra hundred bucks."

"Sounds like a good deal for you," Marcus said with a disarming smile. "I do hope the young lady is worth it for your brother. Tell me, is your father around?"

"No, but I can give him a call if you want," Mike replied. "As for my brother, he told me she was gorgeous. Redhead, which my brother is weak for."

"Sure, if your dad could come down for a few minutes I'd appreciate it. In the meantime, you think you could show me around the shop?"

"Sure," Mike replied. "Let me give him a call. Uh, there's some chemicals and stuff around the shop, so it's best if you guys stay inside and don't touch much until I get back, but you can look around if you want. Three minutes or so."

Mike disappeared into the back, and Mark looked at me, for the moment his Marcus persona dropped. "Keep your eyes open," he mouthed to me while he stepped around the shop, his eyes taking in everything.

I kept most of my attention on the back, where I could hear Mike talking excitedly to someone on the phone, while Mark walked around the shop. He looked closely at a few of the items before circling the shop some more, semi-casually strutting while Mike finished up his phone call. As he came back into the room, Marcus was back, looking around at the disassembled window air conditioner unit on one of the benches. "It's been a long time since I've seen one of these monsters," he said to Mike, who came over after giving me a once-over with his eyes. "Are these still popular?"

"That's actually not an air conditioner, but I can see why you'd think it," Mike said. "That's actually part of an industrial freezer. Works the same way as an air conditioner, but it obviously blows a lot colder. This one is just in for a bi-annual checkup and recharge of the coolant, I think."

"So are you trained in the HVAC business?" Marcus asked, letting his natural charisma pull Mike in. It was safe, the kid was so young that there was no way he knew the full extent of his family's business. "No offense Mike, but you look like you're a junior in high school."

"Sophomore, actually," Mike bashfully said. "I know it's against state law for me to be here by myself, but Scott really likes this girl, and all I do is answer the phones."

"Don't worry, it won't affect my investment decision," Marcus replied. He and Mike small talked until a large Pressman truck pulled up in front, and a beefy upper middle aged man got out. His polo shirt was stretched across a stomach that looked like it had seen more than its fair share of good steaks in its time. Marcus looked at the man, then over at me, flicking his head. I read his signal, he wanted me to be in full distraction mode.

"Hello, you must be Mr. Pressman. I'm Sophie Warbird, Mr. Smiley's personal assistant."

Papa Pressman was just like his son, and could barely keep his eyes off of my cleavage and at least somewhat politely on my face. "Nice to meet you Miss Warbird.

I have to say, this is highly irregular."

"We understand Mr. Pressman, and we apologize for that. It was just that Mr. Smiley was so intrigued by your petition for an investor that he wanted to move quickly. As you know, we just moved into the Mount Zion property."

"Yes, I've heard about that," Pressman said. "I have a friend who was contacted about some of the electrical work, but had to pass on the job."

"I'm sorry to hear that. While we have good heating and air now, the process taught us a lot about the importance of a good contractor. So we've been looking for a place to invest in."

"And of course maybe having someone on call who can come fix that place," Pressman said with a knowing grin. "Let's face it, places like that need repair all the time."

"They do," I conceded. "If you don't mind Mr. Pressman, let's you and I talk while Marcus gets a knowledge lesson from your son. I do most of the investment decisions for Mr. Smiley."

"Of course, but I'll be honest I'm not exactly ready to talk numbers," Pressman said.

I waved it off with a small laugh. "That's okay, neither am I. I have all the numbers I need back at the office, in fact probably too many. I just agree with my fiancée in that the numbers don't tell us everything. The people are just as important."

"Well, the people I can talk about all day." Pressman grinned and looked over at his son. "He's the reason I asked for investment. Him and my son Scott. A single shop with four trucks is enough for me. I raised a family and I set up a good retirement for myself in about a decade. But it's not enough for two sons. So I want to spend this next decade expanding, setting everything up so that Scott and Mike can be set up in a better place than I am."

I nodded, drawing out the conversation. Pressman continued to blather on, and I could see that while part of him was trying to tell the truth, he was far too well off to be worried. I didn't know any other air conditioning repair shop owners who wore thousand dollar dive watches while at the same time trying to put himself off as only upper middle class. Eventually, I saw Marcus pat Mike on the shoulder and come over. "Sorry about that Mr. Pressman. You have a remarkable son."

"Thank you, Mr. Smiley," Pressman said. He tilted his head for a moment before shaking it. "Sorry, you just reminded me of someone for a moment."

"I get that a lot," Marcus replied. "I just seem to have one of those familiar faces to some people, I guess."

Chapter 38
Tabby

I could barely contain my trembling fingers as I reached for my cell phone. It was exactly twelve-fifteen, and I'd already been up since five in the morning, after a night of tossing and turning.

Scott had never left my thoughts the entire night. I'd even gotten up at about two to take an Ambien, which I hadn't done since my college days to try and reset my body clock after a weekend long party. It took a bit of the edge off, but I didn't get more than two hours of sleep all night.

I knew what Scott was asking for. And I knew what I wanted. That was all there was to it. I needed him, and I needed him like I needed air or water.

Growling in frustration, I cleared my phone's dial for the third time. My fingers were trembling so much that I was double typing numbers all the time. Finally, I took a deep breath, and tried for the fourth time. The call went through, and I prayed to whatever deities listened to women like me that I had the right number. "Hello?"

Relief and desire washed over me in alternating waves as I heard Scott's voice in my ear. "Scott, hi. This is Tabby."

I could hear a bit of a chuckle in his voice. "You waited all the way until twelve fifteen. I was beginning to think that I had guessed wrong."

"No, you guessed right," I said, feeling my heart swell and tears come to my eyes. "You don't know just how right."

"I can bet," he said, his words like honeyed potion in my ear. "And because I only got about four hours of sleep myself."

"Twice what I got," I replied. "Scott, I need you. I want you. Please, come over."

The delay while Scott formulated his answer was almost torturous. "Okay. I'm at work right now, I'll need to call my little brother to cover the rest of my shift. Can you give me an hour?"

"It'll feel like a hundred years," I said honestly, aware I sounded like a melodramatic teenager. "Can you do it any faster?"

"I'll try, but I had another idea," he said, his voice soft in my ear. "You must be exhausted. Use the hour I'm not there to lay down on your couch and take a nap.

I promise, when I get there I'll wake you gently, and we'll see what happens from there, okay?"

His suggestion hit me like a ton of bricks, and my body cried out in exhaustion as well. "I think that could work," I said, stifling a sudden yawn. "One thing though, promise me."

"What's that?"

"Bring a Rockstar with you when you come. An hour nap is going to need a jolt to get me awake, and I want to be very, very awake when you get here."

"Deal. One Rockstar, as fast as I can get there. And Tabby?"

"Yes, Scott?"

"Thank you." The phone went dead in my ear, and I collapsed back on my sofa. I was asleep before my head hit the cushion I think.

The next thing I knew, I felt a gentle shaking of my shoulder. I opened my eyes to see Scott kneeling next to me, a smile on his face. "Don't freak out, I just remembered where you left your key last night," he whispered, brushing a lock of hair out of my eyes. I looked at the sunlight on the wall behind him, and was surprised at how orange it looked. "I let you sleep some more."

"How long?" I asked, sitting up. I should have been weirded out, I mean, the guy just more or less broke into my house and sat there watching me sleep for what had to be an hour or more, based off of the sunlight. Then again, it wasn't the strangest thing to happen in my love life.

"It's three thirty," Scott replied, standing up and heading into my kitchen. He came back a second later with a familiar looking black can. "Here. They didn't have any Rockstars, but I was able to grab you a Monster Zero. Hope that works?"

"Yeah, I can do that," I said, popping the tab and chugging half the can in one long draw. I finished with a burp that would have impressed Homer Simpson, before covering my mouth and blushing. "Sorry, I guess that wasn't the sexiest thing I've done."

Scott shook his head and smiled, taking another can out from behind his back. "Tell you what, let's share in the disgusting bodily functions," he said, popping his own tab before chugging the entire can in a performance that would have left any frat boy I dated in college envious, and then letting loose a burp that sounded like a cross between Chewbacca and a fog horn. "There, we're even."

The disgustingly humorous romantic gesture touched me, and we both ended up laughing as I took careful sips of the rest of my can, not wanting to choke or have energy drink shoot out my nose. I've had that happen, and it burns *bad*, even worse than alcohol because of the carbonation. "So how long were you sitting there, anyway?"

"Oh, I got here at one thirty, like I said," Scott replied. "But the look on your face was so precious I couldn't bear to shake you awake, and then when I did try, you were so out that you didn't even respond at first. So I just sat back and watched, thinking about you and what we're about to do."

"So you still want to, even after watching me belch like some biker mama?" I said, smiling. "Good, because it's all I could think of too."

Scott stood up and held out his hand, helping me to my feet before pulling me in close and kissing me. The slightly tangy taste of the energy drink was on our lips, and I thought it was appropriate, since Scott was that sort of interesting tangy sort of person. He could have had me twice, and yet here we were, and it felt more momentous than ever. Maybe he was right, and holding back made it better.

We stood there in my living room, kissing gently, and I felt happier than I'd ever been in my life. Scott held me in his arms, and I felt both powerful and protected, his lips dancing over my neck and behind my ear. Tingles ran up and down my spine as he bit my earlobe softly before tracing it with the tip of his tongue, and I could feel fresh heat radiate down to between my legs. "Oh damn, that is amazing."

"Let's head back to the bedroom," Scott said, taking my hand. "Lead the way? I only found your kitchen."

I smiled and led him back, where I had only a momentary flash of embarrassment at my unmade sheets. Sophie can tell you, I never make my bed, usually just yanking my blanket around me from wherever it happened to have ended up when I got up in the morning. My sheets were clean at least though.

Standing next to the bed, our kisses took on a feather light, tender quality as our hands took over, pulling at each other's clothes. I was wearing just a t-shirt and some jeans, not even worrying about a bra before falling asleep. I was sure Scott could see my nipples standing out against the thin cotton of my shirt, but I wanted him to look, and see how much he aroused me. "You can touch me if you want."

"First let's get this off," he said, lifting at the hem of his work shirt. The polo was the same one I'd seen him in the first time I saw him, creating kind of a time warp effect that made the previous days seem like nothing more than a surreal dream. I pulled the shirt up, and was more than happy with what I saw.

Dancing the night before I'd felt plenty of lean muscle and strength, but with his shirt off it was even more evident, the only flaw in his body being a pair of long scars that stretched from his left collarbone almost all the way to his belt. They looked like a matching set, and were a few years old at least. "What happened there?"

"Another time," he said, silencing my questions with another kiss. His lips trailed hot electricity down my neck as he sat down on my bed. I followed him, not letting his lips leave me as I pushed him back onto the sheets, both of us scooting until he was laying fully on the mattress. Straddling his waist, we kissed, while Scott ran his hands under my shirt and stroked the skin of my back, sending ripples of pleasure through my spine.

I giggled when he touched one of my ticklish points, sitting up. "You can take my clothes off too, you know," I said, reaching down and pulling my shirt up. Freed from my shirt, I dangled my breasts in front of Scott's lips, sure he would know what I wanted. He didn't need much more encouragement, kissing my pale pink nipples, and sucking my left one into his mouth. I sighed contentedly, letting him suckle and please my skin, collapsing to the side as my happiness became too much. I could feel tears in the corners of my eyes as Scott rolled with me, pinning me to the bed even as he continued to suck, tenderly biting my nipple and causing me to cry out.

"Did I hurt you?" he asked, looking up at me with concern. I shook my head, stroking my fingers through his hair.

"No, it feels wonderful," I replied. "But you can help me by helping me out of my jeans and panties."

Scott grinned at my suggestion, and nodded. "Well, if I do that, I think it's only fair if I get to take mine off as well."

I nodded hungrily, excited to see what I wanted. Scott smirked at my enthusiasm and scooted back, knee walking backward until he was on the edge of the bed, rolling to his feet in a smooth athletic motion. Unbuttoning his cargo pants, he slid them down his hips, and I was again happily pleased. His cock was nice sized, and very veiny, almost rigid and bumpy. I could already imagine what those ridges and veins would feel like rubbing against my nerves inside my body, and I felt a fresh wave of juices flood my pussy. "You're a very sexy man."

Scott smiled and got back on the bed, his cock bobbing as he crawled towards my legs, reaching up to unbutton my jeans and slowly, almost tantalizingly, pull my zipper down. I was happy I hadn't worn my tight jeans that day, I didn't want the process to take any longer, and as soon as the jeans were loose enough, I lifted my hips, pushing them down along with Scott's assistance.

Scott came up to kiss me again, his fingers continuing to stroke and tease my hair. The gentle touch set me afire even more, and I pulled him close to me, sweat starting to come out on my forehead. "You're burning me up inside," I said in between kisses. "Why are you burning me up?"

"Because I'm on fire too," Scott replied as he continued to stroke. "You've lit my heart on fire."

His words touched me, and I looked him in the eyes. "I know what you mean," I said, stroking his face. "I feel the same way."

Scott's smile told me everything I needed to know, and I opened my legs more for him. "Make love to me, Scott."

He slid over my outstretched left leg and positioned himself in between, my anticipation growing with every beat of my heart.

He positioned himself at my entrance and pushed forward. The head of his cock slipped easily inside me, and then the most amazing sensations started. Scott's cock was even harder and more ridged than it had looked, and with every millimeter of penetration, the nerve endings inside my pussy were lit off in ways I'd never experienced before. Almost immediately, my hands were clawing at his shoulders, and I was caught up in a wave of sensation that drove all conscious thought from my mind. It was better than any toy or experiment I'd ever had before, and I couldn't believe that this was from a real, breathing man. He was just too perfect, yet there he was, sliding in and out of my body, shockwaves of pleasure coming from every motion of his cock slipping in and out of my body.

I let it go, and trusted in my body's wants and needs. Instead of words, I let my lips and my hands convey my desire on Scott's skin, while his tongue traced erotic runes on my neck. Our bodies moved in a liquid, primal harmony, and I could feel my soul shatter to be reformed in his hands by every unbelievable thrust inside of me.

He knew, without me saying a word, exactly how to please me. When he thrust long and slow, it built a bubble of passion inside me, which slowly expanded and grew bigger, until the size of it was almost a bit scary. Before I could say anything though, his movements changed, into quick little fun motions that brought a smile to both of our faces even as it shaped the orgasm that was inside me, forming it into something that I knew I'd never felt before. When it was ready, like an artist, Scott looked me in the eye and started thrusting hard and fast, his balls slapping against me as he drove himself as deep as he could with each and every movement.

It was the last bit, when he went to long, fast, deep pounding strokes that I felt my body begin to shiver, starting in my toes. I'd heard about orgasms like this before, but I'd never felt one, and I prepared myself as best I could. The trembles continued, starting in my fingers and then working up my legs and down my arms until I could feel the muscles in my chest and stomach quivering, waiting for that last touch I needed to push myself over the edge.

Scott could see the condition I was in, and smiled. He pulled back, until just the head of his cock was inside me, and paused. Looking me in the eye, his lips whispered something I couldn't hear before he drove forward one last time. The white hot sensation exploded out from there, and my entire body sang with pleasure. A high pitched, almost angelic sound came to my ears, and it took me a moment to realize that it was me, and the sound was my cries of release as my orgasm shook me from head to toe.

I hung on, knowing that Scott was there above me, an angel to take care of me, to be there for me. I'd found the man I'd been searching for my entire life, and there was no way I'd ever let him go.

Chapter 39
Mark

"His name, at least among the Confederation, is the Knave of Hearts," I told Sophie as we drove away. "I wasn't sure when I saw the brother, but when I saw the materials they have around the shop, I knew for sure."

"What do you mean?" Sophie asked me as she made the turn and we headed back towards downtown. "Did everyone in the Confederation have jolly pirate nicknames or something?"

"There you go with your *Crow* references again," I said with a chuckle. Sophie stuck her tongue out at me and made another turn. "But actually, you'd be surprised. A lot of us had nicknames, used either because we had secret identities that we didn't want the rest of the Confederation to know, or because we needed a way to talk business or discuss people without outsiders knowing who we were talking about. Not that it always worked, of course. Some names became more famous than our real identities."

"So tell me about the Knave of Hearts," Sophie said, making another turn. She was following our standard procedure, which was to never drive directly back from a business meeting, just in case we were being tailed. "Who is he?"

"The family has been a minor set of players in the Confederation for a very long time," I said, going deep into my memory. "You met his father, the so-called King of Hearts. His mother is the Queen, and while I doubt Mike Pressman is fully involved in the family business, I'd suspect he'd be called the Jack. But the Knave is the one who's currently really dangerous. The King and Queen, they became famous in the Confederation for being breaking and entering thieves, although the Queen was quite a beauty in her day. It's what earned her nickname, and her husband became the King after they got married. They both more or less retired before I came on the scene, but I see how they did it now. In their shop they had, in addition to the normal tools you'd expect an HVAC repair facility to have, a lot of carefully disguised other goodies. The one I noticed first was a canister that had no chance to contain coolant, it was totally shaped wrong. Instead, it was a disguised pressure container for a plasma cutting torch. I saw the rest of the setup broken down on the bench, but it was all there. The Pressman's used their company as a front, doing pretty standard burglaries and thefts until the Knave got involved."

"What did he do differently?"

"He's not into straight burglaries," I told her. "In fact, the Knave steals in a whole different way. He's a bit of a confidence man, a bit of a Lothario, and one hundred percent thief. He gets his way in by seduction normally, and from his reputation, he's very, very good. From what I know, and I only know him by reputation, he works his way into the woman's heart, and turns her into whatever he wants her to be."

"Damn," Sophie seethed, echoing my own personal feelings. I had always detested the methods employed by the Knave, even during my own days of being a bit of a womanizer. I never used emotions to try and get to my targets, and I never, ever twisted a woman the way the Knave did.

"That's not the worst," I said, as Sophie finally made the last of our misdirection turns and started back towards Mount Zion. "The worst part is, he's married. His reputation is that he looks young, maybe just twenty-three or four, but he's actually pushing thirty or so. It's part of his game, he comes off as this barely out of high school guy, but he's actually got a wife at home."

"How can his wife be cool with that?" Sophie asked, disgusted.

I shook my head. "I don't know. From what the rumors have told me, she's the same as him, a Mata Hari type who left the business when she couldn't pass as a teenager anymore, and wasn't quite old enough for the MILF act yet. But if this guy is the one who I think has been seeing Tabby, your friend is being played."

"So what do we do?"

I clenched my fists, the knuckles cracking as I thought of all I'd like to do to the man. However, he did have a wife, and I don't like killing people with families, if it can be avoided. I know how hypocritical that sounds, and I know I've killed men with wives and even children, but they were jobs I never enjoyed doing. "Let's go to the bell tower," I said, thinking. "I have an idea."

"You going to fill me in on the idea?" Sophie asked as she made the turn towards Mount Zion. "Please tell me it's painful and slow-acting."

"Slow-acting it isn't, but painful? You can say that for sure," I said, thinking of some of the alternative lessons I had gotten from some of my instructors over the years.

There's an old song from the Wu-Tang Clan member Redman that includes the line *six million ways to die*. The line is actually older than that, but he's probably the most famous user of the line. In any case, the truth is there are less than that, but the number is still pretty high. While I doubt there is anyone in the world who knows all of the different ways that the human body can be killed, the really creative methods are actually quite useful. Any idiot can pull a trigger, just look at the gun violence statistics. The same is almost true for bladed weapons as well. Even the most pacifistic person can be pushed to the point they'll bury a knife in someone's guts, especially if you don't give them a chance to think about it first.

But the creative methods are a sort of deadly art, or a deadly science, depending on your point of view. The martial arts are filled with methods of shattering bone, cutting off blood flow to the brain, and potentially stopping the heart with just your bare hands. When you add in hand held weapons, the possibilities increase. When you then add in the use of chemicals, electricity, and other means, well, you understand. You can go slow, you can go quick. You can be painless or mind-breakingly painful. You can affect any of a dozen systems in the body, if you want. Someone could study to a Ph.D. level and still not fully know every way to kill someone. In fact, I studied under a teacher who was called Doctor Death, and he willingly admitted he didn't know everything.

But there was another level underneath just death that was just as large, and sometimes even more useful, that was manipulation of the body. Truth serums, minor poisons, crippling agents, all of them were just the beginning. I had a better idea in mind.

"I learned a few combinations, some things that I keep in the bell tower," I said, running through the list of stuff in one of my cabinets. "He'll be alive, but he's going to be out of the seduction business for the rest of his life. His wife might not like how he ends up either, but at least he'll be alive."

"I can deal with that."

* * *

Mark

The night was colder than it had been in a long time, fall was coming on again. It wasn't cold enough to snow, we wouldn't get that until mid-winter, but it still was cool enough that I wore my lightweight tactical jacket. I had gone to one of our alternative bases, where I had a nondescript car. While I had been mixing up my little surprise for the Knave, Sophie had tried calling Tabby, using both our normal phones and her old personal phone, which we had reserved only for emergencies.

Tabby hadn't picked up either, which told me she was probably either distracted or asleep. Either way, her apartment was the best place to start looking.

I had been waiting about twenty minutes outside Tabby's place when the door opened, and she came out with a man, five foot ten, who was wearing the same sort of polo shirt that Pressman had been wearing earlier that day. He looked a lot like Mike Pressman, but slightly bigger, more filled out. He was definitely Scott Pressman. The Knave of Hearts.

My emotions lurched as I saw the look on Tabby's face when she walked with him towards his Buick, which was pretty nice looking. The kiss she gave him when he went to get in his car told me everything I needed to know. She was so head over heels enamored with him that I wondered how the hell the paint on his car didn't blister from the heat.

He fired up his engine and drove off after the kiss, and I followed him, keeping a decent distance between us. I wanted to get him alone, and try to find a way to implement my plan.

Thankfully, he made a move that I hadn't expected. Instead of going home, he turned towards the industrial district and the Pressman Contractors office. I wondered what he was up to, but decided not to look a gift horse in the mouth. Instead, I drove past, pulling around a building down the block and shutting off my engine. Getting out, the dome light gave away nothing, I'd turned it off long ago. From the back seat I took out my equipment and checked my load. I was ready.

I approached the Pressman building silently, doing my best to avoid any cameras or other surveillance equipment. I was wearing a skull cap and camouflage face paint, so I doubted I could be identified by image, but still I wanted to take as few chances as possible.

I didn't wear a full ski mask. I've done it before, and it does have its uses. If you are in an ambush, or in a long range sniping situation, they can be great for retaining body heat. However, there is one flaw in even the highest tech ski mask, and that is that it changes the way you hear, and the way you breathe. I didn't want either problem during a fluid, sensory driven stalk.

As I came around the side of the Pressman building, I heard the key rattle in the front door, and Scott Pressman came out. I flattened myself against one of the company trucks, close enough that I could hear him and even see when he moved. What he said was helpful.

"Yeah, it's me baby," he said, obviously talking into a cell phone. "Who, the redhead? Yeah, she's going to be ripe for the picking soon. I've got her so hopped up on my act that she'll give us anything we want. Info on Smiley, his bank account numbers, anything we want. Sure, it wasn't as good as taking out that girl with him, Warbird, but still, getting his main financial advisor is a good in."

He paused, listening to whatever the person on the other side said. "No, you'd of had fun with her too if you'd tried. She seems to have had a thing for women, she'd have been putty in your hands. Ha, maybe sometime later, if we could figure out the angle to play it. No, she was pretty good, a lot better than a lot of the marks I hit. No baby, she was nowhere near as good as you of course. Hey, I'll be home soon, I'm going to check in with a buddy on some computer cracking gear, I hear that Smiley's a real bear when it comes to cyber security. The redhead might get us in the door, but I doubt she's got Smiley's passwords. I love you too, baby. Bye."

He hung up the phone, and rattled the keys in the lock again. I heard a deadbolt shoot, and I made my move. Easing around the side of the truck, I saw Scott Pressman pull out a keyring from the door and turn to his right, pocketing the keys. He never saw me approaching from the left, and my tranquilizer dart caught him right where I wanted, close to the carotid artery. He barely had time to swat at his neck before his legs went to jelly, and he collapsed on the ground.

Scott woke up ten minutes later, the sedative was fast acting but also short term. I didn't take him far, in fact we were inside the Pressman building. He struggled a bit against his bonds, but couldn't break the plastic zip-strips I had tied his arms and legs to the office chair with, they were rated to four hundred pounds of pressure each, and I'd used two on each limb, as well as a conveniently left lying piece of rope to tie his waist to the seat as well. He wasn't going anywhere. "What the.....?"

"How's it going, Knave?" I asked. This was the difficult part of my act, and the only part I had to somewhat play by ear. I tapped a small button on my belt, and the digital video recorder I had in my back pocket turned on. The lens and microphone was attached to my shirt, so as long as I kept Scott in my sight, I was good. The lights were dim though, so the image wasn't great. It helped protect me. "Thought you and I should become better acquainted."

"Who are you?" he asked, trying to see in the murky darkness. I was sure he could see my outline against the slightly lighter darkness outside, but that was about it. Meanwhile, the very dim light allowed me to see him in pastel blues, grays and blacks, like some sort of *anime noir*. "Who is this Knave?"

"Oh, don't be shy, you're damn near a legend," I said, teasing him. "I mean, I was pretty well known, but you'd expect that. My job depended on fear and intimidation, people needed to know at least my nickname if nothing else. But you, oh you are the opposite, the fewer people know who the Knave of Hearts is, the better, especially those with wives or daughters who might be your targets. But you're so damn good that even a simple leg breaker like me knew who you were, dude. The Knave of Hearts, best damn dick in the city. The Lothario of Larceny, the Corrupting Cock of Cons, Don Juan de Thievio!"

Pressman dropped the act, and sat up straighter in the chair. "Okay, okay. Fuck man, did you make that last one up yourself?"

"Kinda did. Watched *Rocky IV* before coming over, and loved how Apollo Creed got himself a ton of nicknames. But that's not the point. I've been a big admirer of your work, man."

Pressman laughed. "Which is why I'm zip-tied to an office chair. Nice choice, by the way, choosing the wheeled one that I can't tip over because the base is too wide. And you attached my feet in such a way pushing off the floor is impossible too. You've had training. So can I ask your name, or are you going to just be my secret admirer?"

"Oh, how remiss of me!" I said with a big, fake Southern accent. Actually, all I did was take my native South Carolina accent and turn it up to eleven. "Of course you may know who I am. I mean, after all, when we're done, I'm just going to have to let you go, let you go, can't hold you back any more....."

The hokey singing got the point across, and Pressman grimaced slightly in the dim light. "Fuck, Snowman, I thought you were a hitman, not a torturer. You could just introduce yourself instead of the goddamn Disney tunes. By the way, you know Sal is looking for you."

"I'm sure. It's one of the reasons I'm back in town, actually. Sal and I have unfinished business. He took away the only damn thing I've loved in my life, you know." It was a play, but I hoped it worked. I wanted the Confederation wondering if I was Marcus Smiley, and the more deception I could give them, the better. "Yeah, Sal and I have a date in the future for sure."

"So what's that got to do with me?" Pressman said, frustrated. I could see him testing his bonds, but there was no way he was getting out. I couldn't have pulled those bonds free, and I was stronger and better trained in escapes than he was. "I'm just an operative. I had nothing to do with you or that hospital girl you were caught with."

"No, but you did stumble by bad luck into my business. You see, I happen to work with your latest seduction, Tabitha Williams. We all have to have day jobs, you know. Very few of us can get by just working our night shift work. By the way, nice gig with the HVAC. You and your folks must get plenty of loot that way. You bringing your little brother into the business as well? Your wife too, that's a full house of hearts, quite a strong hand."

My implied threat was clear, and I knew that when Tabby heard this point she'd feel like she'd been stabbed in the heart herself. "Leave my kid brother and wife out of this, Snowman. I'm asking you. He's innocent for the most part, he just thinks I'm in an open relationship sort of thing, and my wife.... man, my wife's retired. She's six months pregnant for Christ's sake."

"Really? I got a different impression listening to you on the phone earlier. Should I go to your home at...... 3457 Hampstead Lane and check it out myself? Or maybe go visit your little brother at your parents' house?" I'd pulled his wallet while he was out, and had read his driver's license. It was standard procedure in things like this.

"FUCK! No, man, shit! I'm not lying to you, okay? Yes my wife is pregnant, and she's out of the game. Hell, I was going to get out too once I was done with this redhead, just use the money I could get from Marcus Smiley to set up my dad's business. Drain Smiley dry, and have a good retirement nest egg for my folks. Have a nice one for me too, really. Mike would be set up to take the whole HVAC thing if he wanted, above board. This place actually does clear a good profit you know."

"After you get rid of the plasma torches and safe cracking devices, of course," I said dryly. "Okay, let's just say I believe you. Still, I work with Miss Williams. In fact, she introduced me to the girl that Sal had killed, did you know that? She's the only thing I have left of the girl I loved. No, you probably didn't know any of that, that sort of thing doesn't get out too often. But Tabitha, she's off limits. I thought I had made that clear to the Confederation when I took out that night club. But it seems like Sal needs another lesson in that regard."

"Whoa, whoa, whoa!" Pressman said, desperation in his voice. "Listen, Sal didn't know who I was going after! He just knew I asked permission to try and get to Marcus Smiley. Hell, he probably thought I was going to try for Smiley's purple haired hottie, Warbird. It was my original plan, but when Tabby came by, I just went with my gut. I figured I could get her to get me in some other way, and who knew, maybe I could drain a few other clients as well. She is a financial advisor, after all. I swear to God man, I didn't know she was on any sort of protected list, I didn't know who she was. She was just another short term pump and dump, that's all."

"I see," I said, tapping the button to my recorder again, stopping the recording. I had what I needed. "Still Knave, you seriously fucked up. Now, I'm not the sort to be overly vindictive, despite my reputation. So I'm not going to kill you."

I could hear the relief in Pressman's voice as he exhaled, followed by a quizzical tilt of his head. "If you're not going to kill me, then what?"

"Well, you've got a job I want you to do," I said. "You're going to go to Sal, and tell him everything we talked about tonight. Tell him that Tabby Williams is protected, plain and simple. Next time she gets messed with, I kill five Confederation soldiers for every scratch on her body. If any of Owen Lynch's men mess with her, I kill five Confederation men and five of Lynch's men, so make sure the message is passed along."

"Okay, okay, I can do that," Pressman said, nodding like an eager puppy. He was just glad he was going to survive the night. I could understand the sentiment. He had a few things going for him. First off, my reputation was never one of being a guaranteed killer, I had let victims go before. But I was known as an enforcer, a person who applied force, not just a killer.

"I'm not finished," I said, pulling out my dart gun from my coat again. "Next thing is, you are going to retire. In fact, I'm retiring you tonight. Hold still, this might sting a bit otherwise."

I shot Pressman in the chest with the dart before he could ask what I meant. The dart was much larger in dose than the first one, a special concoction that was based a bit on LSD, a bit on the drugs used in chemical castration, and a few other darker items that I wasn't sure were in the list of drugs any pharmacist or doctor in the city knew about. I saw Pressman's head roll back and forth as the hallucinogenics started to take effect, and I pulled the last item from my jacket, a carefully prepared and designed mp3 player with headphones that I taped in. I then injected another syringe of the mix into his right thigh, just to make sure there was enough to do what I wanted. I hit the play button on the player, and walked out, locking the door and closing the security gate behind me.

Chapter 40
Tabby

When Scott didn't call me Sunday morning like he said he was going to, I wasn't worried at first. After all, we'd basically spent the past three days together, and I was still physically exhausted from our passionate lovemaking the day before. I was so exhausted, in fact, that I rolled over and stretched my arms over my head for the first time at nearly eleven in the morning. The sun was shining, and I swore I could hear songbirds twittering outside my window. *All you need is some violin music and you sound like a fairytale princess*, I said to myself. *God it's good to be in love.*

The words stunned me. In love? Already? I mean, I know the last few days were amazing, but love? Was I really in love with him after just three days? I lay back and closed my eyes and knew the answer. If I wasn't in love, I was already ninety-nine percent of the way there, that was for sure. I'd never felt that way about anyone, man or woman, before.

The thought made me smile, and I lay there on my sofa for a good ten minutes, a silly little half smile on my face. I was tempted to just lay there, sure that my prince would come and find his willing lady lying ready for him on the couch, but after about twenty minutes, my grumbling insides forced me up and to the kitchen. A girl has to eat, after all.

I finished slicing up the apple I had found when I saw that both of my cell phones were flashing. I'd missed at least one call, and most likely from Sophie, since she was the only one who had that number. I opened my regular phone, and saw that not only had she tried with her Sophie Warbird phone, but also with her old Sophie White phone. Concerned, I immediately picked up the secure phone that Marcus had given me and called her back.

"Sophie, it's Tabby. What's wrong?"

Sophie's voice sounded both tired and concerned. "Tabby, we need to talk. Can I come over to your apartment?"

"Sure," I said, looking around. "I can have this place kinda ready for company by the time you get here. Anything in particular we need to talk about?"

"That would be better discussed in person," Sophie said. "So please, just you and me, okay? I'm coming over alone."

"All right, see you when you get here," I said, hanging up the phone. While her tone of voice somewhat concerned me, I was still so over the moon about Scott that I barely heard her tone of voice. Instead, I flitted around my apartment for the next twenty minutes or so, making sure my stuff was kind of picked up, and eating my apple as I did. I had just tossed my crumpled up jeans into the hamper when Sophie knocked on my door.

"Hey babe, what's up?" I said, giving her a friendly hug. She was dressed down that day, just some track pants and an old sweatshirt that she'd picked up in Europe along with a backpack. She looked more like the college student I'd roomed with for four years than the sexy executive ass kicker I knew she was now. I felt some nostalgia, and was glad to see that girl back. "You want some coffee? I'm sorry I missed your call last night, I was kind of distracted."

"I know," Sophie said. She came in, and instead of sitting down, pulled out a palm-sized device. Turning it on, she walked through my apartment, talking the whole time. "I just had some business stuff I wanted to talk about, sorry if I worried you."

I followed her, confused, as she completed the swift walk around of my apartment, staring at the little thing in her hand. When she reached my bedroom, she barely gave my stripped mattress a glance as she finished what I could only describe as a sweep, then stopped and nodded. "Okay, we're clear."

"Clear of what?" I asked, curious.

"Bugs. Mark and I were worried he may have planted a bug in your place while you were distracted or something." She took the device and put it into her backpack, and looked at me with a weight in her eyes I hadn't seen in a very long time.

I shook my head, confused. "Sophie, what the hell is going on. You're acting totally weird."

Sophie sighed, and led me back into the living room. "Tabby, we need to talk about Scott Pressman. And if you don't mind, I think I'll have that coffee, if you can ice it for me."

After I got Sophie her iced coffee, she handed me a tablet. "There's no other way to put this, so I might as well be direct. Scott Pressman is a member of the Confederation, Tabby," she said with a sigh. "He's a seduction specialist, in fact."

I couldn't believe it. I shook my head, over and over, refusing to listen to anything Sophie was saying. "No. No no nononononononononononono!"

I had to give it to Sophie, she stayed calm through my rant and sipped at her coffee, waiting me out. Finally, she took the tablet from my hands and tapped the screen a few times. I heard Scott's voice, cutting through my denial like a knife, and stopped cold. I watched the ten-minute video twice, before setting the tablet aside with trembling hands. "What an idiot I've been."

"No you haven't," Sophie said, sipping her coffee. "You were played, yes, but from what Mark tells me, Scott Pressman is one of the best in the world at what he did."

I felt the first red flushes of anger creep into my mind as I kept thinking about everything that Scott had said about me. "Tell me one thing."

"Sure."

"Tell me he paid for it, that the video cut off because Mark didn't want to show blood on screen."

Sophie shook her head. "He's still alive, but he's not going to bother you again. Mark made sure of that."

"What do you mean?"

Sophie shook her head again. "He didn't tell me everything. I just know he put together a couple of mixes of chemicals, and when he came home this morning he told me that Scott Pressman was not going to be a problem ever again. He did tell me he was alive, but that was it."

I nodded my head, then looked at her. "I want to talk to Mark about this. No offense, but you don't have the answers I want right now."

"No offense taken. He wanted you and I to talk first, he thought you'd take the news easier from me than from him. But if you want, he can meet you. You want him to come here?"

"No, not here. In fact, I think I'm going to start shopping for a new apartment. But, I do know a place that we can meet."

* * *

Tabby

Mar de Napoli didn't look all that different from when I'd been there with Scott just a few days before. Still, it wasn't the same restaurant. The atmosphere seemed contrived, the rustic Italian cheer forced. I knew what was different, and it wasn't the music. It was not having Scott.

After Sophie left the apartment, I spent the next two hours alternating between fits of rage and fits of self-recrimination. How could I have been so damn stupid? Finally, I put it temporarily aside by contacting a few real estate agents, and setting up apartment viewings for the following day. My agreement was month to month, so I wasn't going to be out too much. Besides, maybe a slightly better apartment was needed, I could afford to not live in the same place I had crashed when I was an undergrad after all.

I had been sitting, nursing an ice water for about ten minutes when Mark showed up, looking nothing at all like Marcus Smiley. It was really the first time since he had rescued me from the club that I saw the guy that Sophie fell in love with, the real guy inside there. He was wearing a navy blue t-shirt and jeans, and looked like just a really handsome regular guy in his mid-twenties. "Hey, have you been waiting long?"

"Not too long," I said, gesturing. "Have a seat."

"Thanks," Mark said. "I'm sorry about what happened, Tabby."

"Can I ask you why you acted so fast, instead of talking with me about it first?" I said, pausing to allow him to order from the waiter who came by. It was still pretty early, just past five thirty, so the dinner crowd wasn't in yet. Other than a few golden agers in the corner, the restaurant was ours.

"Threat level and opportunity," Mark replied. "I drove by your place last night because I wanted to get eyes on him. Yes I was prepared to act, but I had anticipated having to tail and prepare the takedown. Sophie would have talked to you either way, but when he went back to his office instead of home, I moved. There wasn't going to be another easy chance like that for a while."

I nodded in understanding. When I was working the stock market, sometimes you had to make snap decisions like that as well. "So tell me the details that I didn't see on the video."

"What do you want to know?" Mark asked, thanking the waiter when he brought him his Coke. Mark took a sip, then set it down. "I'll tell you whatever I can."

"Tabby said you retired him. How?"

"Mix of drug therapy and psychological conditioning. The second dart I shot him with had a powerful mix of hallucinogenics and some other things that make the mind very plastic. It can't change his memories, not with the time I had, but it can change a few other things."

"Like what?"

"Like the fact he's now permanently impotent," Mark said. I felt a little side of me, the part interested in revenge, growl in triumph at what he said. Another side of me, the side that remembered the feeling of him inside me and the earth shaking orgasm he'd given me, recoiled in agony. "But even after that, he's not going to be able to go back to what he did."

"Why?" I asked, intrigued. I couldn't help it, the angry side of me was stronger than the rest of me right then.

"Any time he gets sexually excited by anyone other than his wife from now on, he's going to have some pretty severe physiological reactions, including a blinding headache, stomach cramps, and loss of bladder control. Basically, if he sees a woman who he wants to make a pass at, he'll piss himself and go blind for fifteen minutes."

"Damn," I said, impressed. "You could do all that with just an injection?"

"That and about eight hours of psychological conditioning using auditory inputs," he replied. "The player was specially made to play the track once, then melt and destroy itself, so they didn't even have a chance to recover what the exact commands were. All anyone would know is the effects."

"So it's permanent?"

Mark shrugged. "If not permanent, at least long lasting enough that he's not going to be able to do the same scam. I'm sure some really good psychiatrist could fix it in time, but he's going to have gray hair, jowls like his father and some other not so handsome traits by the time it all gets reversed. Oh, and I added a few other things to keep you safe from him as well. If he thinks getting aroused will be painful, you don't want to know what getting within eyesight of you will do to him."

I sighed. The waiter came, and we ordered a basket of cheesy garlic sticks, just a small appetizer, I wasn't ready to seriously eat yet. After we were alone again, I asked the next question on my mind. "Can I ask why you didn't do more?"

"You mean why I didn't kill him?" Mark said quietly. "He has family, and a child on the way. Perhaps it would be better for the child to not have a father like him, but I thought with a mother like that already, there was a small chance that it would actually be helpful. I hope that maybe Pressman turns to the right path, although I don't know. Also, I thought the message I could send by him staying in the condition he's in would be a better warning to those who might target the two of us later on."

I nodded, then asked the questions that had been running through my head since I saw the video Sophie had shown me. "What did I do wrong, Mark? Why do I feel this way? What the hell am I supposed to do now?"

The waiter brought our cheese sticks, and Mark offered me one with some marinara sauce on it. The cheesy tomato flavor awoke the growling little demon in my stomach, and before I knew it I had wolfed it down. Wordlessly, he offered me another before taking one for himself.

"That's a lot of questions, Tabby, so give me a chance to try and answer them all. As for what you did wrong, you did nothing wrong. You followed your heart, and unfortunately you were taken in by someone who knew exactly how to manipulate you. Don't be ashamed, even though I know you feel that way right now. He could have done it to almost any woman, especially a single one like yourself. As for your second question, can I ask you bluntly, how do you feel?"

I huffed and wolfed down another bread stick, considering my answer. "Is it wrong that part of me feels like I love him?"

Mark shook his head, his gentle smile sending a hammer blow to the dam of emotions that I'd stored inside me for most of the day. I held on however, and listened to what Mark had to say. "Should I feel pride in my skills? I do, even as dark and as evil as they are. We cannot help who we love, Tabby. My father was a gambling, addicted wretch, whose mistakes got me into this life before he died. I still love him. So no, it's not wrong to feel that way right now. Just like it's not wrong to feel anger, hurt, rage, and a bunch of others. I wouldn't be surprised if you feel a bit of hatred towards me right this second."

"You see pretty deep," I replied. "Does that psychological insight help in your work as well?"

"A bit," Mark replied, "But I've carried it into other areas as well. You've got a deep streak of it too, you are like most people though in that it's most difficult to turn that lens on ourselves."

"So what now? Am I supposed to spend the rest of my life double guessing every man who approaches me, or living without love? No offense Mark, but considering what you and Sophie have, that's pretty damn harsh to ask."

Mark shook his head. He started to reach for my hand, and stopped, pulling back. "You're never without love, Tabby. Sophie loves you, and I love you too. Maybe not in the way that people may think, but you're vital to our lives. Sophie said you are thinking of moving, right?"

"Yeah, I just don't feel safe in there right now. I think a change of apartments might be in order, if only so I can sleep soundly at night."

Mark nodded. "You know if you want, if it helps you feel safe, you can live for as long as you like at Mount Zion. We didn't do that before because we felt you wanted your independence, and it would protect our identities better. But your safety is more important than that. Hell, I'd sleep outside your bedroom door guarding you if it helped you feel better. And I know there is a real man out there for you. They'll be kind, they'll be grumpy at times, they'll be imperfect to everyone else, but they'll be perfect for you. And when that happens, Sophie and I will be the first people to congratulate you and make sure you have the wedding of your dreams."

I looked at this kind, gentle man in front of me, and realized again how lucky Sophie was to have him in her life. I could see that he was speaking the truth, and that he would protect me and Sophie with his very life if need be. If there was a purer expression of love than that, I didn't know what it was. "Thank you," I said. "And in fact, I'll probably take you up on it while I'm apartment hunting. I'll make sure to vet any potential places through you too."

Mark nodded. "That's fine. We're here for you if you want, Tabby."

I nodded. "Thanks. Listen, I know this sounds bad, but if you don't mind, I'd like to have some private time to think about all this. You mind if I come by the house later, maybe just me and Sophie and our old boyfriends Ben and Jerry?"

"Sure. I'll be in another part of the house, you two have any room you want all to yourselves. What's your favorite, I'll make sure to pick you guys up some on the way home."

"I think tonight's a Chubby Hubby night, actually. I don't know what Sophie's current is, I guess I should keep track of that sort of thing more often." I felt a tinge of sadness that I'd lost track so much of my best friend, especially after everything she was doing to make my life better, and after all we'd been through.

"Nah, you remember the important things instead," Mark said. "So, a pint of Chubby Hubby, and a pint of Peanut Butter World, and a pint of Cherry Garcia. I love Peanut Butter World."

He got up and patted me on the shoulder, then walked off. I saw him talk quietly to the waiter, and there was a passing of a small wad of cash, so I figured he paid for the meal as well. The waiter tucked the cash into his apron, and came over after Mark had walked off. "Are you ready to order, miss?" he said, a professional smile on his face.

"Yeah," I said, trusting my gut. "One calzone."

"Great choice. Sausage or pepperoni or veggie?"

I chuckled darkly. I was already blowing my diet, why not? "Sausage please. And can I get a second Coke to go with the calzone?"

"Of course. Anything else?"

"No, I think that's enough."

I polished off the rest of the bread sticks while waiting, keeping myself somewhat under control. When the calzone was brought to the table though, I could barely thank the waiter before the tears started to trickle down my cheeks, and the world blurred.

Chapter 41
Part 5 - Sophie

I enjoy a good bath. In fact, I think it's one of the greatest luxuries in the entire world. My favorite bath of all time was one Mark and I took when I was in training in Eastern Europe. I know it's a bit confusing considering I spent time in South Korea where, like the Japanese, hot baths are a way of life, but it was the setting of this particular bath that left such an impression on me. It was a totally natural spring, isolated in the woods on the border area between Greece and Macedonia. While the region itself is not exactly the safest place in the world to do things, this natural bath was idyllic. The water was crystal clear, and so pure you could drink it safely with no problems. However, it was warmed from deep in the Earth, so the water was warm. Mark and I had spent four hours hiking to the bath from the nearest place we could park our car, and had bathed, soaked, and made love for hours in the private little grove.

While our bath at home was not as good, it was still wonderful. In addition to specialized water heaters that could filter and recirculate the bath water to take it from a refreshing cool to an almost painful hot, the black marble interior was perfect for a long soak after a day at work or training with Mark, and the decoration, instead of being ostentatious, was actually subdued. I felt relaxed rather than pampered, and grounded rather than elevated and luxurious.

It was needed. There were times, living as Sophie Warbird, where it was very easy to slip into the fantasy of being the executive assistant and fiancee to one of the richest investors in the city. Just in the last week I had signed documents shifting over half a million dollars around, and had also signed off on financial reports from my friend Tabby that had more zeros than I thought I would ever see in my life on a bank account.

The craziest part of it all was that Mark and I hadn't even touched either our core savings or Mark's own stock market investments that he managed himself through a couple of shell companies and online aliases. While it wasn't mine technically, just over a year prior I had been nothing more than a college student who slung beers at night to make ends meet, still Mark and I were as close as we'd ever been.

I lay there in the warm water, letting my muscles relax, when I heard the door to the bath area open and I opened my eyes to see Mark standing there.

"Hey beautiful," he said, his eyes taking in my body through the clear waters.

Considering he was wearing just a pair of athletic shorts that he had worn for our workout that day, I had quite a view too. Steely muscles swept like liquid from every one of Mark's joints, sweeping and curving in all the ways that spoke of the graceful power contained within his body. I loved his legs, especially the scar where he'd been shot by a Russian commando. The scar was thicker than what could have been, forming a slight hook on the outside of his quadriceps because it had only been a flesh wound. But that, in addition to the thin scar where I had stitched up his right shoulder muscle, in some small way seemed to mark him as mine. Especially the shoulder scar where my own handiwork contributed to the final look of his skin. Thankfully, I hadn't needed to do any more stitching since then.

"Hey babe," I replied, scooting over. "The water's nice if you want to join me. After that gym session, I think you might need it as much as I do."

Mark smiled and shrugged. "Trust me, just looking at you stretched out like that washes away any soreness and gives me enough strength to take on a hundred men barehanded."

I cupped a bit of the water in my hands and let it run down over my chest, intentionally dribbling it between my breasts. "Is that so? Well, maybe I could use you in the bath with me then."

"I could never refuse a request from you, my love," Mark said, hooking his thumbs into the waistband of his shorts and pushing them down. Did I say earlier I liked Mark's legs? Yeah, they looked even better with nothing on, especially that *third leg* that he could use to give me so much pleasure. "My eyes are up here, you know."

I laughed at the corny comeback and scooted over in the water. Mark slipped in, stretching out next to me. When we installed the bath, we made sure that the one side was sloped so that two people could recline easily next to each other. Stretching his long legs out, Mark lay back next to me, looking up at the ceiling before closing his eyes. "It was a good day today," he said, a gentle smile on his face. "I was happy."

"Considering you handstand walked across the entire floor, you should be," I replied, turning to study his face. While Mark's body was more than impressive, what always intrigues me about him is the way his face can change. When he was in public as Marcus Smiley, he wore this sort of mask, a cocky, somewhat affable look. It wasn't exactly unintelligent, but slightly open, a look that often put some of our investment targets off guard, miscalculating what they wanted to tell us. That, and the fact that I also wore tight suits with lots of cleavage to throw them off even more.

When he was in action as what I could best call the Snowman, Mark's face was set, cold and distant. It took me a while to recognize that it wasn't that Mark didn't feel anything during those times, but instead he was compartmentalizing himself, setting aside the immediate visceral emotional reactions for later. He was focused, and yes, a little bit scary.

But these were the times that I enjoyed most, looking at Mark as Mark, the man I loved. With me, and with a very select few other people he had let into his life, they got to see him as he really was.

It was the little things, like the fact that despite being a very high level athlete and financial genius, he still enjoyed eating Reese's Peanut Butter Puff cereal for breakfast or snacks, or that he had the world's cheesiest air guitar routine while jamming along to old Queen tracks. Those were the things that really were endearing about him, and what let me know just how amazing he was and how comfortable he felt around me.

"What are you looking at?" Mark said without opening his eyes. His ability to sense those things was another of his unique gifts.

"I was just thinking," I said, turning on my side and brushing a bit of hair off his forehead.

"About what?"

"How much I love you," I said, causing him to smile, "and something else."

"Hmmm? What's that?"

I took a deep breath, and said what was in my heart. "I want to have a baby with you."

Mark opened his eyes and looked over at me. "Seriously?"

"Seriously," I said. "I know we've talked about it before, and I know that our lives are full of danger, but I don't see that ending for a while. In the meantime, I can't think of a better man to be with, nor someone who would make a better father than you. I know we got rid of my birth control a while back, but I was thinking maybe we could really try, you know, timing things and trying to get it right with my cycle."

Mark blinked, and peered into my soul with his piercing eyes. "Are you sure about this?" he asked, his voice soft and contemplative. "After all the terrible things I've done?"

"You're the only one I could think of doing this with, I know that for sure," I said, turning over to kiss him. In between the soft, warm kisses I continued. "You protect me, you have a good heart, and you're everything a woman could ever want."

Mark smiled at me. "You've made me into a better man, Sophie. But when?"

"You are a good man. And you're all mine," I said, claiming his mouth again in a kiss. "As for when, well, according to the websites, the next four days would be best."

Running my hands over his body, I couldn't suppress the small giggle as the tip of Mark's cock rose to break the surface of the water. "Seems someone else wants a kiss too? He's certainly not shy tonight."

"Maybe," Mark replied, stroking his hands through my purple hair. "But I don't think the bath is the right place for it to happen, you know?"

"Why?" I said, reaching down and taking him in my hand. "We've never done it in here before."

Mark was distracted as I stroked his cock slowly, a playful smile on my face. Finally, he took a deep breath and replied. "For all the erotic look," he said in between small groans, "the hot water would leave us drained. I don't need either of us passing out from heat exhaustion during sex."

I couldn't refute his argument, I already had a fine sheen of sweat on my body from the soaking. Still, part of me regretted getting out of the tub, and watching the water glisten as it ran over Mark's body. Waiting just until he was out of the bath, I pulled him down with my left hand for another kiss while my right hand grasped his cock lightly again, pumping it slowly while we kissed. The feel of his rock hard shaft in my hand and pressing against my lower belly filled me with a thick liquid heat, like melted caramel.

Leading him playfully by his cock, I retreated down the hallway, all the way to our bedroom. The large bed was exactly what I wanted, turning and pushing Mark onto the crisp cotton sheets. "I'm still dripping wet," Mark laughed when he hit.

"So am I," I said, the double meaning clear in my voice. "We can change the sheets later, or go sleep on the sofa. Right now I want to make love with you."

I fell on top of Mark, letting gravity dangle my breasts in front of his face. Despite his strong, tender lovemaking skills that doesn't ignore a single erogenous zone on my body, Mark definitely loves my breasts. I have to say I love teasing him by just brushing them in front of his lips, pulling them back if he reaches up for them. Normally, I could keep the game up for a very long time, but Mark and I were both too eager that night, and he pulled me down, his hands playing a symphony of sensation on my back while his lips feasted, going back and forth from one side to the other, sucking and nipping at my pale skin. When his tongue traced circles around my right nipple, I saw stars shoot across my vision.

Pulling back, I slid down until I could feel Mark's cock pressing against the wet juncture between my thighs. Looking him in the eyes, I kissed him again, resisting the urge to lift my hips up so I could impale myself on him. Instead we rubbed slowly, grinding against each other, my juices coating his hard shaft while my clit ground into the firm muscles of his lower stomach.

"I love you so much," I groaned as my hips circled, while his hands massaged my hips.

"I'll be with you forever," Mark said. He lowered his lips to the curve of my neck, sucking and licking the secret spot that only he knew about. "I swear."

"I swear," I echoed, lifting my hips up until I could feel his cock pressing against my entrance. Lowering myself slowly, not because I needed to but because I wanted to prolong the wonderful sensation of being filled by the greatest man in the world, my body trembled in lustful want as I felt his cock slowly, inch by beautiful inch, spread me open and fill me up. Finally, I pushed back off of Mark's chest to let that last inch push deep into me, my body's nerves singing heavenly choruses as it did.

"I never get tired of this," I sighed as my hips started to move back and forth. I put my hands on Mark's chest, teasing his own nipples with my thumbs while I slowly rode him.

"Me either," Mark said, running his hands over my arms. "And I've thought about it."

"What?" I said, my hips slipping back and forth in their own subconscious harmonious wave. Mark's own hips started to rise up and down as well, meeting my hips in soft little explosions.

"What you asked for in the bath. I agree," he said, his eyes full of intense emotion. "I want to have a baby with you too."

His words added fuel to my fire, and I moved my hips faster, my clit dragging deliciously against him with every thrust of our hips. I could feel the rising bubble of passion within me, and I let myself enjoy it, going faster and faster. Mark let go of my arms to cup my breasts, teasing my nipples with his fingers while I rode him, throwing back my head and groaning thickly. I was close, so close, and I knew what I needed.

"Fuck me, Mark. Please fuck me," I groaned into the air. I needed him, and sobbed for a moment as Mark lifted me off of him. "What?"

Mark kissed my lips quickly as he guided me onto my knees, and he slid behind me. "One shot knockout for both of us, baby."

I grinned and nodded at Mark's term, one we had picked up from some strange combination of our mutual martial arts training and something I had read for fun soon afterwards. Bending over, I let my breasts press into the the damp sheets and held on. I closed my eyes, letting my skin tell me everything I needed to know.

Mark's hands stroked my ass and back for a moment, and I knew what he was doing, looking at me bent over open and ready for him. The first stroke of Mark's cock up and down my labia sent electric shivers up my spine, and I could feel the muscles on the inside of my thighs jump in anticipation. "Ready?"

"Oh yeah," I barely breathed, "I'm so ready."

Mark took my waist in his hands, sliding inside me with one beautiful, breath driving thrust of his hips. He didn't hold back, his cock driving in and out of me quickly, barely giving me the chance to breathe before another soul-searing cascade of pleasure tore through my body. I buried my face in the sheets and screamed my joy as I clenched and pushed back into him. For all of the bitching I sometimes do about working out with Mark, being in good shape has a wonderful effect on sex. Being able to keep going, even as the breath burned in my lungs from the gasps and the sweat dripped off of me added to the pleasure.

Still, even with all of that, neither of us could hold back much longer. Mark's thrusts came faster and deeper, my ass warming as our hips slapped together harder and harder. My ears could hear the dual gasps and grunts coming from his and my lips as we sought our climax, and I squeezed as tight as I could with my inner muscles.

The feeling of Mark's cock swelling inside me is perhaps the greatest joy I have in making love with him outside of an actual orgasm. It's the sensation that not only takes my already full pussy and stretches it that much more, but it also tells me that he only has a few seconds, ten or fifteen at most, before he comes. It's so wonderful because it's so fleeting, and when I felt it then, I was overjoyed. I was holding back my own orgasm by only sheer force of will, and feeling him swell shattered even the illusion of control I had. My world paused, teetering on the razor's edge of insanity for a mere heartbeat before my orgasm exploded, and my wails of passion became a single long, undulating scream of joy and pleasure. I could feel

Mark's hands clamp almost painfully on my waist as he also came, and we both froze, his arms tight on me.

In my mind I could see the swell of his biceps as he pulled, and the clear definition of his stomach muscles as his cock pumped and filled me up. The moment passed, and both of us collapsed to the side, Mark keeping himself buried inside me while we spooned, and we let the warm afterglow wash over us.

"God you're amazing," I breathed as I felt him wrap me in his arms and kiss the back of my neck.

Chapter 42
Mark

Sophie found me the next morning typing away at my computer. She came padding in from the living room with her beautiful purple hair tousled and stringy. With one of my large white t-shirts being stretched out quite seductively by her breasts, I doubt there was a more beautiful sight a man could see in the morning.

"Wow, if you wanted to tempt me, I could think of worse looks," I said, standing up and pulling her into a good morning kiss.

"You're sweet, and I have horrible morning breath," Sophie said after we stepped apart. It was true, she did have morning breath, but still, kissing her was nice. "So what are you looking at?"

"The end game," I said, showing her the monitor I was plugged into. "It's a plan I've been working on for quite a while now. The final piece of the puzzle was using the information we stole from the Confederation computers."

Sophie nodded, studying the plan I had mapped out. I was worried she would object to the amount of bloodshed that could be required, and I prepared myself for the flood of concerns about the danger and violence. As Sophie's studying grew longer, punctuated with a few hums and other small sounds, I grew more and more nervous. Finally, she turned away from the plan and looked me in the eyes. "It's okay, but you left a lot of stuff out."

That was not the answer I'd been expecting, to say the least. It took me a moment not to just smile defensively, and clear my mind to hear what she had to say. "What did I leave out?" I asked, when I could let my curiosity be stronger than my ego or surprise.

"The biggest thing you left out is me," she replied, tapping the screen. "You're planning on taking out four of the Confederation heads and you have yourself taking the shot each and every time."

"Yeah, I didn't want to place you in danger, and I figured that it would be best if I did...." I said, before Sophie cut me off.

"When I agreed to come back to the city, I told you I wanted to be fully involved, not sit and watch while you do everything," she said, shaking her head. "I've worn the stupid suits, I've dealt with the danger, I shot a Spetznatz commando, all because I'm not your sidekick. I'm your partner, remember? Now, if I'm reading this plan right, you think that by taking out these four Confederation family heads, you can trigger a self consuming battle between the various Confederation members and Owen Lynch. But, you want to try and take each of these people out on separate days."

"Of course. Prepping a hit on people as protected as these people are takes either planning and patience, an overwhelming attack force, a shitload of luck, or a bit of all three. We don't have an overwhelming attack force."

Sophie chuckled. "You working by yourself isn't overwhelming at all. But the two of us working together, we can double our forces, and at the same time I was looking here at the first two hits."

"What about them?" I said, grudgingly admitting that Sophie had a point. Still, I wanted to start this damn war to clean up the city to protect her, not to put her into firefights with criminals.

"If you and I strike the first two targets on your list at the same time, we can increase the panic within the Confederation. Also, they'll start to doubt that it was Owen Lynch, because we can hit them where Lynch won't or can't. This first target, Han Faoxin, is the head of the local Chinese, right?"

"Yeah."

"But you note here that Owen Lynch doesn't know who he is. Of all the hits, his is actually the hardest because very few people know who he is. So if we take him and the second target, Illyusas Petrokias out at the same time, it turns the Confederation immediately against each other, and makes them unwilling to trust each other. Then their deaths can't be seen as either accidents or random chance."

I started laughing, causing Sophie to frown. "What? Did I say something wrong?"

"No, your logic is totally sound," I said after calming down. "It's just that you made the same mistake that a lot of people do with Han Faoxin."

"What?" Sophie said, getting a little peeved. I leaned down and kissed her on the cheek, and grabbed a chair. Sophie was right, I needed to bring her into the plan, and to let her know everything I knew.

"Han Faoxin is a woman," I said. I grabbed the wireless trackball for the computer and went into the file explorer. I quickly navigated to the profiles I had compiled over the years for the various criminals I had worked with, targeted, or were somehow related to either the Confederation or Owen Lynch. Pulling up Han Faoxin's file folder, I opened her personal profile.

"Han Faoxin, daughter of Han Gaotan, is the third generation of her family to control the Asian crime syndicate in the city. One of the things that made her control so different from her father's is that she's been able to cross the cultural lines that divided the various Asian groups. While the Yakuza aren't happy about it, being mostly locked out, she created an amalgamation of Chinese, Korean, Vietnamese, Thai, and independent Japanese criminal groups that gave her total control over anything coming into the city from eastern Asia. She doesn't have control of the Middle Eastern groups, but has a good working relationship with them. Considering how relatively young she is, she's been considered next in line when Sal Giodano retires for taking control of the entire Confederation."

Sophie looked closely at the picture I had of her, the only picture I knew in existence of Faoxin that tied her to criminal activity. "Is that.... is that you next to her?"

Blushing, I nodded. "Yes. Just before she took over from her father, Faoxin and I were.... well, it was complicated."

"How so?"

"This isn't the conversation I thought I'd be having with my fiancée," I said sheepishly. "I guess you could say that while Faoxin and I weren't exactly dating, I was more than a hook-up to her as well. Perhaps you could say I was one of her steady boys for about a year. She had a penchant for younger men."

"Really?" Sophie said with a smirk. "So she was the one who taught you all those ancient Asian bedroom techniques you use on me. I'm not sure if we should kill her, or send her a thank you card."

I groaned and shook my head. "Note to self, hold off on discussing prior partners until after breakfast."

Sophie leaned over and kissed my cheek. "Don't worry, I'm not jealous," she said. "I can see from the picture that this was years ago, you could pass as a high schooler almost. And since you and I came together, you've been nothing but a loyal, wonderful boyfriend and lover. It's not like I expected that either of us came into this as pristine virgins. Although I do have to say one thing."

"What's that?"

"Faoxin, she's quite beautiful. It's kind of good for my ego to know that I can tempt you away from such a beautiful and powerful woman. How old is she anyway?"

I laughed and stood up, pulling Sophie to her feet. "First of all, you are far more beautiful than Faoxin," I said, kissing her nose. "Not just on the outside, but far more on the inside. That woman is as evil as she is beautiful, trust me on that. Now, before we discuss anything else, we're getting some breakfast, and then we have to put in our daily appearance as Marcus Smiley and Sophie Warbird."

"So how old is she?"

* * *

That night, up on the third floor of what had come to be known as the Smiley Building, if such a grand name could be given to a four story converted warehouse in the industrial district near the docks, I started the more difficult part, which was prepping my hit. The key to my plan was using a mix of styles. If each of the four hits were done in my preferred manner, a long range sniper shot using a heavy caliber rifle, I'd leave too consistent a trail, one that could be assigned to an individual. That individual was most likely me, since both Lynch and the Confederation knew I was active in town again. That was the last thing I wanted. I wanted the Confederation looking at each other and Owen Lynch first.

Sophie and I had agreed on one thing, and that was I needed to do the hit on Faoxin. There were a lot of reasons for this. First of all, while I had a picture of Faoxin, it was older, and I had enough memories of her that I could pick her out easily. Secondly, with Sophie taking at least one of the four hits, I wanted her to use her best skill, which was the long range rifle shot. While she wasn't as good as me, with the setup we had agreed on for the hit on Illyusas Petrokias, she didn't need to be, taking only a three hundred meter shot. That left me to focus on Faoxin.

A long range shot wouldn't work for a hit on Faoxin anyway. The key to her effectiveness was that, like me and Sophie, she lived a double life. Most of her communication with her soldiers was through scrambled voice calls. While she spent lots of time around her territory, she didn't advertise who she was. In fact, I knew of at least three times she had gone into various clubs or massage parlors she controlled as nothing more than either a customer or even an employee.

During the day however, Han Faoxin lived under her Americanized name, Anita Han. She was a high school teacher, who for ten years had taught advanced placement history at William Henry Harrison High School. Trust me, if she had been my history teacher, I probably would have paid attention a lot more in class. I don't know if I would have scored any better on my tests, but I would have certainly paid attention in class. I'm sure her students, at least the male ones, were the same way.

I didn't like my plan, but it was the easiest way for me to get to her. During the night, Han Faoxin was either protected or within structures that were controlled by the various Asian crime groups. There was little chance I could get in and out safely. But at Harrison High, I only had to worry about the security systems in place of a rather prestigious private high school and whatever weapon, if any, she had on her.

Not that Faoxin was a pushover. Trained from birth, she could more than handle herself, and I could be assured that she was carrying some form of weapon on her. Still, it was my best shot, and I couldn't think of a better chance.

Chapter 43
Sophie

While Mark was preparing himself for Han Faoxin, I was across town, taking a moment to see an old friend. Since being played and having her heart broken by Scott Pressman, the Knave of Hearts, I'd been worried about her. Tabby Williams was my best friend for a very long time, going on nine years. I'd never seen her as messed up as she was when Mark and I revealed who Scott Pressman was, and in the weeks since, something just hadn't been right with her.

Knocking lightly on the frame of her office door, Tabby looked up from her desk, long after most of the other financial analysts in her firm had left. "You know, I think it'll wait until tomorrow," I said with a smile, before doing a double take.

For as long as I'd known her, Tabby had long, lustrous auburn hair. It was the perfect color of red, dark enough so that she couldn't really call herself a "ginger" except as a joke, but bright enough that she was striking. Combined with her natural beauty, and Tabby had been a head turner as long as I'd known her.

One of her old flames, one who had come over to the dorm room Tabby and I shared and ended up spilling his guts, told me that Tabby had the kind of hair that wound through your fantasies, spread out over a pillow or draped over your vision. "The sun filtered through her hair would look blood red, like a ruby trapped in a web," he said while sipping at the beer I had offered him. "The thing is, that ruby could easily be your heart, and you knew it, but didn't care. When she was on top of me like that, none of it mattered."

Yeah, that was Tabby. Now, instead of the vivacious redhead, a raven haired woman with slightly drawn cheekbones looked up at me. Her normally creamy pale skin was bordering on sickly white, and she looked cadaverous. I realized I had gotten so busy over the past two weeks that even when she stopped by the office, I'd not looked at her as closely as I should have, and was put off by her bluff and bluster. The hair was new though, I was sure of that.

"Hey Sophie," Tabby said, trying to give me a smile. It didn't work, and looked more like a grimace of pain than a genuine smile. "What's up?"

"It doesn't matter," I said, coming over and closing her laptop. "You're coming with me, now."

"But I have a ton of work....." Tabby said before I cut her off. I seemed to be doing that a lot recently.

"Nothing that won't keep for a day, since I control eighty percent of your workload anyway," I said, taking her by the hand. "You're sitting here looking more like the Bride of Dracula than the woman who means most to my life, so we're getting out of here. If you insist, I'll bring your laptop with me, but you're not opening it until tomorrow morning, and then only at my house. You can send your bosses a note saying that Marcus and I got you up at six in the morning for a business meeting or some other sort of lie. I'll back you up on it."

Tabby looked like she was about to protest again, when I played my best weapon. Taking her other hand, I looked her in the eyes and smiled. "Come on, it'll be fun. Just the two of us."

It was obvious that she needed me. For all of Tabby's playful flirting, and underneath that sex kitten exterior that she likes to put on, she has a deep romantic streak. She wanted more than anything to find someone that she could give her heart to, to share her soul with. And yes, someone who could keep up in bed with her. You think someone who studied for her freshman psychology final by listening to Bryan Adams ballads doesn't have a romantic streak?

"I guess I have been a bit too focused on work," she said, resting her head on my shoulder. She felt feather light, and I wondered if the ten pounds of weight loss was more. "I just haven't been able to sleep well."

"Even in your new place?" I asked. After Scott Pressman had broken her heart, she hadn't felt safe in her old apartment, so Mark and I had helped her move into a better place, one with security and no criminal control. Mark had also surreptitiously placed extra security measures that only the three of us knew about and made her apartment just about one of the most secure places in the entire city.

"Yes," Tabby said, lifting her head. "I just... I can't fall asleep without thinking he's going to be there. I know Mark took care of him, but still, it's hard."

"Then tonight you come home with me," I said. "We're watching *The Crow*, and if you haven't gotten sleepy after that, I'm soaking you in my bathtub until you feel like nothing but silly putty. Oh, that and we're both stuffing our faces and having a girl's night. If Mark comes home in the middle of it, well, he can be our man servant and paint our toenails or something."

For the first time, I saw Tabby smile, even if faintly. "You boss him around like that, huh?"

I smirked and rolled my eyes. "Not quite, but I can get away with it sometimes. When it's important. He's a pretty good sport like that."

"Deal," Tabby said, letting go of me to pack her bag. "So what's got you two out so late anyway?"

"Big plans," I said. "I'll tell you about them at home."

I led Tabby down to the parking lot where she saw as I put my hand inside my purse as I walked. It was one of the little tricks Mark had taught me. "What's in there, anyway?" Tabby asked after she had gotten into the passenger seat of my Jaguar. "Don't tell me you're carrying."

I sat down in the driver's seat and started the engine, which growled with muted power. "Not unless I plan on using it," I said, "but it sometimes pays to look like I am, even if I'm not. Here, take a look."

I handed over my bag and backed out while Tabby rooted through my little purse, which contained nothing more than my Sophie Warbird driver's license, a box of Tic-Tacs, my phone, and seventy three dollars in bills. "No credit card even?" Tabby asked.

"The phone's got a chip built into it, I can use it as a credit card or even access a Paypal account if I want to," I said. "But as you can clearly see, no 007 Walter PPK or even a knife in there."

Tabby relaxed and chuckled, closing my purse and setting it on the floor between her legs. "You know, I should get you to give me a ride in this thing more often. You know I took the light rail to work today?"

"No, but I'm not surprised," I said. "Your place is less than two blocks from a station, and there's a station a block from here. It's gotta be cheaper than a car."

"It is, but that doesn't mean I can't enjoy the luxury of Italian leather seats," Tabby replied, leaning back and closing her eyes.

She was silent for the rest of the drive, so much so that I thought she had fallen asleep by the time I pulled in. When I shut down the engine, I saw that Tabby was looking at me with a look I had seen before in her eyes. "Why do you keep doing this, Sophie?"

"What's that, Tabs?" I said, hitting the button for the automatic garage door. I waited for the door to close and the extra locks to engage. Yes, the door was solid, and was technically rated against an F-5 tornado, although our city hadn't had a tornado recorded in the past century. Just another Marcus Smiley quirk that conveniently doubled as a good security feature.

"Why do you keep looking out for me? You win the lottery of all lotteries in life, finding a wonderful guy who loves you for who you are, is totally loaded in addition to being a hottie and good in bed, and you could have run away with him anywhere on the planet. But you came back, have saved me twice now, and have set me up for career success. Why?"

"Because I love you," I said simply. "What other reason do I need?"

I got out of the car and waited for Tabby to get out. I could see the questions in her eyes, and I took her hand. "Tabs, you're a wonderful woman, I've said that so often I feel like it's running on repeat in my head sometimes. I pray every day that there is someone out there for you like Mark is for me. I'm sure there is, I have no doubt. Until you find him, I'm here for you."

Tabby swallowed and nodded, smiling at me with a bittersweetness that broke my heart. "I know. Trust me, I know. Thank you."

I decided to deflect the situation with some levity. I could tell that she needed to relax and have some fun. "Good. Then let's get some sweats on, get a bit of cheesecake, and Brandon Lee on the big screen. Did you know Mark outfitted one of the rooms in here with super sized two person bean bag chairs, a HD projector and surround sound?"

"Oooooh. You know just how to speak my language," Tabby said, her smile more relaxed and natural.

"Excellent. One more thing," I said as we went inside the main portion of Mount Zion. "We're giving you back your natural red, or at least something approximating it."

"Why? If you get to go purple, why can't I go black?"

"Because our friendship demands at least one redhead, and if I do it, it's going to be fire engine red."

"Good point."

* * *

Around midnight, the closing credits of the movie were rolling. Tabby was asleep next to me, her left leg thrown over my thigh and her head pillowed on my breast when Mark came in. "Shhh," I said quietly after he had done his double take and realized who it was. The movie was a big hint, I think. "We have a visitor."

"I see," he whispered, carefully taking the quarter of a cheesecake from me and taking a bite. "Thanks for leaving me some dessert."

"She needed it," I said, stroking her hair. "She was pretty messed up, but she'll get better."

"Okay," Mark replied, not needing any other commentary. He trusted me, which is spoke deeply to me. "Should I just bring you two a blanket?"

"That'd be nice," I said, smiling. "Thanks. How was your work?"

"I'm prepped as much as I can," he said. "Need a few little tools, but we can discuss that in the morning. I'll help you with yours tomorrow."

"Okay. I love you," I whispered. Mark smiled, blew me a kiss and stood up, taking the rest of the cheesecake with him. I turned and pulled Tabby a little bit tighter, wrapping both arms around her before dropping off to sleep myself, barely feeling it when Mark draped the blanket over us.

Chapter 44
Mark

Both Sophie and Tabby were pleasantly surprised when I brought them breakfast the next morning, about the only breakfast I knew how to make well, Southern style biscuits and sausage gravy. I found them spooned together on the large bean bag, both of them looking tiny in the middle of the immense sack, which I had ordered to be more than large enough for me and Sophie. Setting the two plates on the low coffee table in front of them, I went and got my own plate and set it down before waking them up. "Good morning ladies," I said, sitting cross legged on the far side of the table.

Tabby groaned, while Sophie rolled and stretched before blinking and looking at me. Tabby sat up, giving Sophie a chance to finish rolling and start rubbing circulation back into her left arm. I could understand, she and I had fallen asleep on the bean bag before, and it was tricky. The surface was shifting and soft enough that you could stay that way all night, but you still woke up with a pretty wicked case of pins and needles in your forearm. "Wow, breakfast in bed," Tabby said sleepily. "He is perfect."

"Not quite, but I'll keep him," Sophie said, running her fingers through her hair. "Hold that thought though, I need to use the potty."

Tabby apparently had to as well, as both girls disappeared for a few minutes, coming back looking like they'd both washed their faces and maybe swirled some mouthwash before coming back. In any case, both girls looked much more refreshed, Tabby pulling her hair back into a quick ponytail.

"Wow, country boys can survive," she said after taking a bite of her biscuits and gravy. "Now, if you tell me you made these biscuits from scratch, I'm going to have to kidnap you and keep you for my own. Or just invite myself to live here permanently."

"Actually, I wanted to talk to the two of you about that," I said, setting my spoon aside. While you can eat biscuits and gravy with a fork, spoons work much better for scooping the gravy up into your mouth. "How would you like to live here?"

"What do you mean?" Tabby said, grinning foolishly. "Mark, just because I slept together with Sophie doesn't mean I need to move in with you guys."

"You wouldn't be," I said, causing both women to look at me like I was crazy. I looked from Sophie to Tabby. "You didn't fill her in on our plan?"

Sophie shook her head. "I was going to leave that decision to you."

"What plan?" Tabby asked.

"We're going to go into our end game," I said, leaving out a lot of details. Sophie could understand that people had to die, I wasn't sure if Tabby could. "If our plan goes well, then both sides of this criminal chokehold on the city will get broken."

Tabby took another bite of her breakfast, chewing while she digested the information I'd just given her. "Okay, so what part of that means I live here and you don't?"

I shrugged. "If things go well, Marcus Smiley and Sophie Warbird will have to disappear. But that puts us in a bit of a pickle. You see, one of the things we've used in our long term game plan is the financial investments that you set up for us. We're tied in with how many companies now in the city?"

"You're approaching forty," Tabby said after a moment. "I was just working on your quarterly report last night when Sophie rescued me from the office."

I nodded. "That sounds about right, and there's a lot of money that is in our investment fund that we haven't even touched yet. Tabby, I can't just disappear without those companies going through hell, especially if it comes to light that the money is tainted. So I need another way out."

"What's that?" Sophie asked, curious. I hadn't filled her in on this, but I figured we had time to discuss it later.

"Another layer to our corporation," I said simply. "Before the final steps of our plan, Marcus Smiley and Sophie Warbird make a very public departure from the city, supposedly to look at more investments overseas. We come back into the city discreetly, and take down Lynch and the Confederation. In the meantime, our local investments are put into a corporate trust, with the manager and president of Smiley Investments here in town being Tabitha Williams."

Tabby thought about it for a moment, eating the rest of her breakfast. "If you two do that, are you going to disappear again afterwards? Permanently?"

I shook my head. "Marcus Smiley and Sophie Warbird might, but there's a set of backup identities I prepared for us. It might be a bit quieter, less purple hair and flamboyant fashions, but we wouldn't disappear forever."

"More plastic surgery?" Sophie asked.

I shook my head. "No, I don't think it'll be needed. But even if we are recognized, we can still go back to the Smiley and Warbird identities. It'll just be a more low-key version." I turned my attention to Tabby. "So what do you think?"

"Hmmm," she said, pretending to consider the option even though I could read the truth in her eyes. "Good salary package?"

"I was thinking a percentage of all profits, and a low end guaranteed package," I said, "I'll trust you to draw up the contracts and stuff like that. But you'll also get a nice benefits package as well. I was thinking housing, a car, and of course other things if you can think of them."

"Can I play with your guys' guns too?" Tabby asked, grinning. "I know you have an arsenal or two around this city."

"We have four," I replied, "and no. You'll know where they are, but you don't want the heat that some of that stuff would bring down on you if the ATF ever really searched them."

"What sort of heat?" Tabby asked, smirking. The smile faded as she saw the look on my face. "No, seriously, what kind of heat?"

"Minimum of fifteen years, Federal prison," I replied. "Maximum, if they ever tie in some of those weapons to the stuff they've been used for? Life."

Tabby gulped and nodded. "Well, I've already been involved in one shootout with you guys, I guess I might as well accept it. So by keeping me out, they can see I never used them, and I'd just be able to play dumb."

"Pretty much. So, what do you think?"

Tabby looked at Sophie, then over at me. "When you're ready, I'm ready. Just give me a few weeks warning to put in my resignation at the office."

I nodded, and finished off breakfast. "Deal. Draw up the paperwork, this plan of ours isn't going to take long."

After breakfast, Tabby took a shower while Sophie and I washed up. "Sorry I didn't tell you about my plan for Tabby," I said as I used a soapy sponge on the frying pan I'd used for making my gravy. "I was going to talk to you about it today, but after finding you two last night, I didn't want to wait."

Sophie, who was drying off the plates, shook her head and kissed me on the cheek. "No, I totally understand. The only thing I would have done differently is give Tabby the option to come with us, but if you want to come back, well, that's okay too."

"She means a lot to you, doesn't she?" I said, finishing the pan and setting it to dry on the hook on the rack.

"She's like a sister to me," Sophie said softly, in a tone that told me she cared for Tabby deeply, although it wasn't something I didn't already know. She's the second most important person in my life."

"Then she's the second most important person in mine too," I said simply. "If you want, we can talk to her about all three of us leaving, but if she can get by for three or four months without us again, we'll be back. Besides, if things go right, there's another reason I'll want to be back in town by then."

"Oh, what's that?" Sophie asked, putting her towel away.

I put my hand on her belly, smiling. "If things go right, Tabby can become an aunt."

* * *

William Henry Harrison High School was one of the oldest, most prestigious private high schools our entire part of the country. Graduates routinely were admitted into Ivy League universities, and sported a performing arts program that was so strong it routinely was compared to New York's LaGuardia High School. In fact, the school counted five Grammy winners among its alumni.

Getting on the grounds wasn't too hard, actually. The school used janitors that were outside contractors, one that despite claims to the contrary, used a lot of day laborers. It was pretty easy to use a bit of special effects makeup to add a scar to my cheek, some temporary hair color to turn my hair a two tone brown and blonde, and fake a contract with the day labor company that dispatched the janitors.

That morning, I used my freshly minted ID badge to scan my way through security just like the other three guys on the cleaning team. It was getting late, just after five thirty in the evening, but I knew that Han Faoxin would still be at work. Despite her second life as one of the biggest crime lords (or Lady) of the city, she was a pretty good teacher, and that day she had debate team that lasted until six o'clock. Afterwards she would probably stick around another hour before any of her night time work began.

My plan was simple, to take her out in her room when she wasn't prepared. Unfortunately, the school's scanners were much more advanced than a simple metal detector, so I couldn't even bring a ceramic knife onto the grounds. Instead, I had to made do with what I could get within the school.

I was pushing a mop bucket slowly down the hallway when "Anita Han" came around the corner, chatting with one of her students.

"So next week I want you to focus on tightening up your rebuttals. You have the facts down, and your rhetoric is good, but you tend to ramble a bit too much in between points. Remember, debate isn't quite the same as public speaking where you can keep the audience in the palm of your hand for twenty minutes. In debate, you're being held to a very strict timeline, and the moderator will cut you off if you go over that time."

"Okay Ms. Han," the student, a pretty little girl who was probably a junior or senior, replied. She looked like the sort of girl who was probably involved in student government, and in a more innocent time would have been dating the quarterback of the football team. She had that sort of innocent sweetness to her. "Is there anything else?"

"Not at all Stacey," Faoxin replied. "Just remember that next practice you're doing the moderator's role, so I want you listening and giving good feedback to your teammates. They kind of let you down today, so that's why I asked you to stay late. See you tomorrow."

Stacey disappeared around the corner, and I waited another minute before making my move. Pushing my mop past the now open door to Faoxin's room, I saw her sitting at her desk, checking a pile of papers that looked like they might have been a set of tests or something similar. In any case, her head was down, which is what I wanted. Pushing my mop and bucket inside, I went inside the room.

"One of you guys already got the garbage," Faoxin said, not raising her head. I was glad, since it meant there was a greater chance of her not being totally focused on who I was.

"Mopping," I said, intentionally pitching my voice soft and slightly lispy. I didn't want her knowing who I was just yet. "Sorry."

Faoxin kept her head down, and I took the opportunity to pull the door closed behind me. I didn't know if the other door to the room was locked or not, but it at least cut off the room visually. Faoxin looked up when she heard the door close, her eyes wary. She looked at me for the first time, her eyes widening as she realized who I was. "Snowman."

"Fao," I replied, using the shortened name we had used years before when I had been her bed partner. "Long time no see."

Faoxin set her papers aside, keeping her hands where I could see them. That didn't mean I didn't think she wasn't hitting some sort of panic button with her foot, and we had less than five minutes to finish this. "I didn't think I'd see you so soon," she said, smiling. "I was kind of hoping that our history would have given me a bit more time to enjoy my life, or maybe you'd let me walk away without having to be killed."

"After what you've done since your father died, did you really think that was an option, Fao?" I asked, setting my foot against the shaft of my mop. I stepped hard and twisted, snapping the wood a bit shorter than I would have liked, but still giving me a stick that was just over two and a half feet long. "Han Faoxin, you have failed this city."

Faoxin rolled her eyes and got to her feet, picking the pen up off her desk. She reached down and pulled a long metal ruler from under her desk blotter, and even from across the room I could see the glitter of the sharpened edge. I suspected that while perhaps not as sturdy as a real sword, the wrapped end and relatively hefty weight would give her more than enough cutting ability to inflict major damage if she had the chance.

"You know, that was one of the reasons I stopped seeing you," she said as I closed the distance between us. She swung her blade, and I pulled back, just out of range before trying to dart in with my own thrust with the partially sharp point of the break. "You were never short for cheesy one liners."

"You always said it was cute when we were out together," I retorted, whipping my thrust to the side and smacking into the hand that held the pen. I knew that once the distance was closed between us, she would use it like a shank, stabbing me with it.

I had to circle around her desk, or in some way get it from between us. Stepping to my right, I saw Faoxin retreat to her own, starting to circle. I kept it up until we switched places when I went for it, using what I'd been hiding in my left hand. It had hurt, but it was effective, a handful of thumbtacks. It caused Faoxin to at least try to ward off the projectiles for a moment, allowing me to dive over the desk and tackle her to the ground. The impact drove the wind out of her, although she retained enough sense of mind to lift her legs and push me over, flipping me. I rolled through, shoving a desk out of the way as I went.

Finding my feet, I spun, pouncing back on Faoxin just as she was getting to her knees, her face red and gasping from the pain of the tackle. Taking her back, I wrapped my arm around her throat, not for a choke but rather to bring her chin and around to the locked position. From there I could twist and easily break her neck. Faoxin clawed at my arm, but the janitor's coveralls I was wearing prevented her from doing much, especially with my weight bearing down on her back.

"Goodbye, Han Faoxin," I said sadly, twisting. It had to be done, but it didn't mean I had to enjoy it. A sharp brittle crack reached my ears, and she collapsed, face first onto the floor. I looked in her eyes, and could see that there was still a glimmer of consciousness in her eyes. I could see her still trying to form words, even as her lungs failed to breathe, and her heart stopped getting the signals it had gotten for over thirty years. She mouthed something, I wasn't sure what, and then the light faded as her brain slowly died.

"Eighty one."

Chapter 45
Sophie

When Mark left that day for the hit on Han Faoxin, I was in one of our strike bases near the red light district of the city. It was a crummy tenement actually, one that Mark had owned since before he had met me, and the strike base was actually the basement, which was only reached from an outside steel door that for most people was rusted shut. Inside the basement, I found what Mark had told me was there, an AR-15 configured in a heavier caliber than the normal M-16. We were using it because Mark had trained me so much in Europe on the AR-15 and it's main rival, the AK-47. With the ability to attach a scope the same way each and every time, all I had to do was bring the scope that I had already adjusted for my own uses. It wasn't going to put a bullet through a playing card at half a mile, but it would do its job.

Checking the cabinet, I pulled out the heavy caliber AR and attached the scope. Bringing it up to my cheek, I sighted down the dimly lit basement, impressed. The scope wasn't super powerful, only magnifying things by a factor of seven, but it was enough. I could easily see the writing on the paper down at the end of the basement which was taped to the wall.

"Remember, find the cold place," I repeated to myself before smirking and pulling the rifle away. It was one of the lessons Mark had taught me, and perhaps the hardest for me to internalize. Watching Mark, even when we were sparring in martial arts or working out, it was easy to see when he went to his cold place. There was something in his eyes, something in the way he held his jaw that told me the warm-hearted man that I knew had dropped away, and I was looking at another side of Mark, the survivalist side that would have no problems slaying a thousand men if it meant they were in his way. I once told him that if there ever was a zombie apocalypse, that was the side of him that would make sure the two of us survived.

For me though, finding the cold place when it came to violence was more difficult. Sure, I could do it, I had done it when the Russians had attacked us, but it was much easier when I was saving lives rather than taking them. The most recent time I could think of was when I had stitched up Mark after the Russians had shot him, and I had to not only stabilize him but dispose of the bodies and evidence. Once I'd treated Mark, staying in my cold place was easy. Getting there however was difficult.

Still, I thought I could do what needed to be done. In a lot of ways, Mark had given me the easier of the two hits. Illyusas Petrokias was the biggest controller of the sex trade in the city. Whether it was men, women, old, young, or even more "exotic" if you wanted it, chances were you'd find it under Petrokias' control. He was of course also heavily involved in the sex slave trade, trafficking girls and young boys both in and out of the city. When the newspapers came out with a story of a young undocumented immigrant found dead, if they carried it at all, nine out of ten times they were a worker for Petrokias who had outlived their usefulness.

So it was very, very easy to want to put a bullet in the man's head. I say head because I doubted he had an actual heart with the disgusting things I read he was involved in. There was still a challenge however in setting aside my disgust to complete the shot.

I triple checked the rifle, then checked that the sound baffles were still good in the basement. While I was sure the scope was good, my training taught me to always confirm the zero on any attachment to a rifle, especially if I was taking a shot over two hundred meters. Since our plan called for me to make a shot that was close to three hundred, I retreated to the far end of the basement, where a small pile of sandbags waited. Setting the rifle down, I then went to the other end of the building. The building was only a little over forty meters long, and the padding and absorbing material at the far end meant I could only make a thirty meter shot, but that was enough. Taking out a small paper target, I pinned it to the foam, which could absorb anything short of a fifty caliber shot or an elephant gun. I went back to the rifle, and put in a twenty round magazine. I wouldn't need all twenty rounds, I was hoping to need no more than two, but still, better to be prepared than to be sorry.

Getting down on the floor, I got into the prone position, the most stable position I could get. I looked through my scope, centering on the small X in the middle of the target. I chambered a round, took the rifle off of safe, and reacquired my target. The trigger was touchy, barely taking more than a caress of my finger to fire the rifle. The target blurred in my vision as the recoil shifted the rifle, but I quickly found the spot again, with a neat little hole just a shade over the X. Considering I was firing a hot round that was going to fly high at only twenty five meters, I knew I was ready. Even if I aimed at the head, I'd only miss low, dropping one right into Petrokias' torso.

Who knew? If I aimed for his chest, I might just blow off his balls.

The thought, while a little sick, comforted me as I removed the magazine and cleared the rifle, making sure I was ready to go. Concealing the rifle and my backup weapon, a Glock 19 pistol, in a electric keyboard case, I shouldered the heavy bag along with a small bag of other supplies and checked the way I looked in the mirror. My purple hair was concealed under a black wig and baseball cap, while my pants and outfit made me look like any of the other thousand struggling musicians in the city. As opposed to Mark, I couldn't use any sort of makeup, I was going to be sweating too much, but my skin tone was nondescript anyway.

Leaving the strike base, I hiked the near mile over to my shooting position, a cheap hotel that was often used by Petrokias' lower priced whores who would bring their johns over for the cheap hourly rates. I rented a room for five hours, laying down an additional fifty bucks to ensure the clerk at the desk wouldn't bother me.

"What's in the case?" the clerk asked as I scribbled an illegible muck of a name in the register.

"Piano and a CD player," I said, tugging at the thin leather gloves I had been wearing since unlocking the strike base. It was another one of Mark's rules, and one I had learned to work with. "I have an audition next week. Need to practice."

"Here?" the clerk asked. "Why in the hell would you want to practice at this dump?"

I shrugged. "It's better and quieter than where I live," I said. "Music is okay, right?"

The clerk shrugged. "As long as you don't mind a thumping headboard back beat, I don't care," he said, handing me the key. "Here you are, room five fifteen, just like you asked. Has a western view so you can get your sunset and everything. Hope you're inspired."

"Thanks," I said, picking up my case. I trudged up the five flights of stairs, glad that working out with Mark got me in such great physical condition. The girl who'd met Mark Snow over a year ago wouldn't have made it, not with the thirty pounds of stuff on my back. As it was, my legs were still a bit pumped up when I got to the fifth floor, which was the top floor. Mark had chosen it for two reasons. First, the top floor had the least amount of visibility to surrounding buildings. Secondly, I could escape both up and down. The cheap hotel was so close to its neighbors that I could leap from rooftop to rooftop for close to two blocks to make my escape. It was my preferred method of egress, actually. Going back down five flights of stairs and out the front or the most likely malfunctioning fire door would be too dangerous in terms of being spotted, especially since I planned on carrying the Glock with me.

Setting my case down, I went out of the room and over to the stairs to the roof, quickly checking the access. The door was locked, but I was able to pick it quickly, leaving me with a clear path. I went back to my room and locked the door, taking out the CD player. The main purpose of the player wasn't to give me background music to play piano to, but rather was an hour long mix of synthesizer heavy music from the eighties, which was enjoying a resurgence in certain hipster circles in the city recently. Anyone who listened would think I was playing along with the tracks. It would also hopefully, if someone was a total idiot, mask the rifle shot as well, since a lot of the tracks also had a lot of snare drum in them as well. I wouldn't notice, since I would be wearing heavy hearing protection for the shot itself.

That ready, I set up my sniper shot. Petrokias was one of the more predictable members of the Confederation, having dinner and drinks at the same one of his so called "gentlemen's clubs" every night starting at seven. He had created "Pollux and Castor" to cater to his more wealthy clientèle, along with some of the best Cretian cuisine in the state. A very deep fondness for the Greek dish *moussaka* had him eating at Pollux and Castor five or six nights a week. He always took the balcony table, where he could look over his ill begotten empire and enjoy the finest Greek wines.

Looking out the window, I could see the building. Taking out my rifle, I looked through the scope, and even through the late afternoon glare, I could see the small white "reserved" tag on the table. I looked around the room for something to use for a rifle rest since I didn't want to stick the muzzle out the window. Finally, I decided to use the two chairs that were in the room. The taller one, a mostly straight backed wooden affair that looked like it came out of someone's old dining room set, had little knobs on each side of the back that created a rest I could wedge the barrel against. With the heavy weight of the piano itself sitting on the seat, it was a very stable rest. The other chair was a shade too tall for me to sit straight in, but by reversing it and leaning into it, my upper body was also supported for the shot. I was ready, I just had to wait for Petrokias to arrive for dinner.

Setting up my CD player, I started the music, listening along as Dire Straits filled the minutes, along with Kenny Rogers, a bit of Van Halen, Bonnie Tyler, and a-ha!. As bad as it was, at least it wasn't nineties boy bands. I might have had to shoot myself if I had to listen to that too much. As the CD repeated, I turned it up a few notches, hoping the johns with their girls didn't mind listening to *Total Eclipse of the Heart*. Just as the CD was starting for the third time, I saw movement at the club, and

I looked through my scope.

What I saw nearly floored me. In addition to Petrokias, who was clearly identifiable by his haircut, a silvery fox look that looked a lot like he should have been a televangelist, I saw Sal Giordano. I'd studied his picture for hours on end after he'd ordered my death, and there had been shot after shot that I'd imagined returning the favor.

My fingers itched as the two Confederation bosses sat down, Petrokias pouring what looked like a deep red wine for both of them. I wanted to take down Giordano, but I couldn't. Mark had been very specific on that fact, if either of us had a chance to take down Sal Giodano, we had to pass. "If Sal goes down, the entire Confederation will blame Owen Lynch, and they'll go to war with him, united," Mark had said as we had gone over the plan again. "If we do that, this city will run with blood, and neither of us could do a damn thing to stop it. We want the Confederation distrustful and broken up, so that when they do go to war with each other, they'll be able to be taken down by Federal and state law enforcement."

Still, I wished I could take the shot. Instead, I focused, searching for the cold place that Mark had trained me for. Taking deep, calming breaths, I blanked out everything but my target, and then even lost that. Instead of seeing Petrokias the criminal, I saw just a target, like any of a thousand other practice targets I'd shot at. It took me a long time, a lot longer than Mark would, but by the time I opened my eyes and looked down the scope, I was ready.

My timing couldn't have been any more perfect. Petrokias and Giordano were deep into what looked like massive plates of either *moussaka* or lasagna, perhaps each man enjoying their particular culture's specialty. I turned up the CD to maximum volume and put in my ear plugs, muffling the noise. Sitting back down, I needed only a moment to find my target, sight for his head, and stroke my trigger.

As soon as I took the shot, I knew I had hit. Everything was exactly like Mark had taught me it would feel. There was no betraying quiver of muscle, or tightly held bit of breath. The rifle shot had actually surprised me, and in the moment I took to reacquire my target, I saw that I'd struck him in the throat. Sal Giordano was already down, crawling for safety and people were yelling. I pulled back and tossed the rifle on the bed, grabbing my Glock and headed for the door.

"Three," I whispered into the cacophony of the CD player music, opening the door and slipping into the hallway. The hallway was clear, I had been lucky so far. Either nobody had seen the shot, or they weren't sure where it had come from yet.

Still, I didn't expect my luck to hold out forever, so I jogged down the hallway to the stairs to the roof, making my way up and out. The late twilight gave little illumination to the rooftop, but it was helped by the diffused city lights around. Moving quickly but not rushing, I made my way to the end of the roof, looking across at the next roof. It wasn't too far, just over seven feet, so I backed up a little bit and took a light running jump, landing with a little thrill on the other side.

"Didn't suck," I said to myself, enjoying the adrenalin rush. I heard yelling from below and behind me, someone had found my room. Picking up the pace, I started running, not even pausing as I jumped the next two roofs, before facing the big choice. If I was confident, I could take this building's fire escape down to the street level and disappear onto the light rail system. If not, I could turn right and flee another three blocks before taking another fire escape, but my escape route would then be going through the city storm drains for over a mile before emerging and then catching a city bus.

Looking behind me, I couldn't see anyone. While my lead may only have been a few minutes, it was enough. Chucking my Glock to the side, not wanting to get caught with one by a local cop, I took the fire escape, controlling my slide down the ladder using my hands. It's harder than it looks, especially when the ladder is old and a bit rusty. The hardest part actually was the end, when I was faced with a twelve foot drop. They make those fire escapes hard to climb up for a reason, after all. Still, even dangling, I was a good six feet above the ground, and the drop onto the trash littered street below didn't look all that inviting. Saying a quick prayer that there were no rusty nails or drug needles below me, I let go.

Thankfully, the worst that I landed on was an old flyer for the weekly discounts at the local department store. Brushing off my hands, I pulled the gloves off and tucked them in my pocket to be washed and disposed of later. Walking calmly to the train stop, I only had to wait three minutes before the next train. Stepping on, I held my cool until the doors closed, and I found a seat. Only then did I start to let the tremors begin in my hands.

Chapter 46
Mark

The news of Illuysas Petrokias' death barely made page four of the local papers. He was a low life who got shot in a club that was known more for the size of the waitresses' breasts than those of the chicken dishes. His death was only notable because of the fact that he had been sniped from a long distance, although the police would only say they were following leads. Considering that the police worked for Owen Lynch, I doubted they would get too far, although I pitied the poor detective who had been assigned the case. I was sure they would get stonewalled at every turn.

Han Faoxin, or more accurately Anita Han, on the other hand, was front page news. A celebrated, popular, and quite beautiful teacher at one of the best high schools in the state being killed in her own classroom was the stuff of television reports and lots of press coverage. For the next three days, there were daily reports and updates from obviously flummoxed reporters who kept trying to put a new spin on what obviously was no new information.

I had to admit, it was quite dramatic. The grainy images of me, clad in my loose fitting coveralls and my false ID soon flooded the local newscasts, highlighted by the fact that after the kill, I had apparently just walked off casually, like I didn't have a single care in the world. One local newscaster had even put forth the theory that I was some sort of new serial killer, even though there was no other crime like it in recent memory. I didn't like that I had to do it in the school, but any other way would have been very dangerous.

On a quieter level, I could see the effect the two deaths had caused. The signs were subtle, but in my next few night patrols, I saw there was less cooperation among the street level thugs used by the various Confederation members. Members working for one member who were in the territory of another were treated with more suspicion, and each person's territory was patrolled a bit more vigilantly than before.

Sal Giordano being at Petrokias' shooting actually was a lucky break in our favor. I could understand why. After all, why was the smaller Confederation member hit while the big boss man himself not even shot at? The fact that Sophie had used a specially configured AR-15, a weapon that I was known to favor, raised even more questions. Was the hit done by me? But if so, how, when the room was rented to a woman, and the clerk swore that nobody else went in the room? If it was me, why didn't I take a shot at Sal, or was I working for him again? Was this just a way for Sal to unleash an unknown factor into the carefully balanced Confederation system?

Of course there were questions pointed at Owen Lynch as well. However, the death of Han Faoxin sowed even more confusion in that area. The Confederation wasn't sure what to think once the word got out who had actually been killed. The suspicion on Sal Giordano increased even further, as he was one of the few Confederation members who knew who she was, and routinely claimed to meet her in person.

"All in all, a good start," I told Sophie a week after the hits, as we were reviewing the paperwork to put Tabby in charge of our investments in the city. The biggest headache was setting up another shell corporation, which we named MJT Holdings. Thankfully, while a basic pain in the ass, I'd done shell corporations plenty of times before, and had a connection with a lawyer's office in Connecticut that could get us the paperwork quickly.

"So what's next?" Sophie asked, rubbing at her stomach.

I noticed she was looking a bit pale, and was concerned. "Are you okay?"

She nodded, her eyes tightening a little bit. "Yeah, just feeling a bit weird. I hope it's what we're wanting, and not that my smoothie I had for a mid-morning snack was bad."

My pulse quickened at the idea, and a silly little smile crept up my face. "You think it could be?"

"That my smoothie was off? It's a distinct possibility," Sophie joked, before giving me a kiss on the cheek. "Relax, my love. Let's just wait until I miss a period, then get a home test. It's only been a few weeks, you can't tell this fast, not that I know of anyway. We've got other things to think about anyway."

"Yeah, like how we're going to entertain our houseguest," I said, thinking of Tabby. Since finding her in such a depressed state, Sophie had insisted, although I couldn't argue, and besides, it was nice having another person around such a large home. While Sophie and I did have a cleaning service come by twice a week, it was a large house, and I honestly felt like we were rattling around in it half the time. "By the way, I like the new red. A bit more flamboyant than before, isn't it?"

"It was, but we both agreed that a bit of overcompensation would help her mood. You know, kind of the whole fake it until you make it sort of thing," she replied, flipping a page on the document she was reading. I had to give Sophie credit, perhaps it was because of all the years of reading complicated medical stuff, but she had picked up reading business contracts with an eerie speed. There were a few times at first that I'd had to explain a few of the legal terms to her, but after that she was off and running on her own. "Caught something."

"What?" I asked, looking over from my computer where I was focusing on the next steps of our end game plan.

"Just a number error. On page four it says that Tabby will be compensated with fifteen percent of net profit, while on page six it says that she would be compensated with twenty five percent. Which do you want?"

"Twenty five," I said automatically. "What did we decide was the low ball of her pay?"

"Two hundred thousand a year, plus the house, cars, and other stuff. Not that she'd even be close to it with the twenty five percent. She'll be rubbing elbows with the one percenters very quickly with this."

I nodded. "Good. I was thinking, when we come back into town, we're going to need new identities."

"Yeah, you mentioned that before. I know you have the documents ready, but what did you have in mind?"

"I was thinking," I said, typing a few words on my keyboard to adjust something in our plan, "that Tabby could use a butler and maid."

Sophie looked over at me, making sure I was serious before grinning. "I think she just might. After all, this property is large enough for a servant's quarters. It would most likely be a very luxurious servant's quarters as well."

"Damn right," I said. "Maybe we can tell her about it this evening. By the way, how was her return to work today?"

"Seamless," Sophie said. "Our cover story of having her do out of office business trips went over perfectly with her bosses, especially when I came in there and stuck my boobs in their faces along with a pile of contracts for three more businesses."

I laughed and looked over, admitting to myself that Sophie looked especially beautiful that day. "Okay then. And she knows to use the excuse of a business dinner to get out of there by six tonight, right?"

"Either that or you show up as the business peacock and start making a scene," Sophie answered.

"There are downsides to every plan."

* * *

That evening, Tabby was shocked into silence as we showed her the contract for her new position. She read it over twice, her jaw dropping in more than one place as details jumped out at her. "You're serious with this?"

"Dead serious," I replied, muting the television. "Tabby, it's not just a cushy little job, you realize. While there is a basement level compensation there, your job won't be about just the money."

"What will it be?" Tabby asked. "The details are pretty generic honestly."

Sophie took over for me, which I was glad for. "Once our plan goes down, the city is going to have some very gigantic power vacuums. The political one should be filled relatively quickly, there are too many politicians who are more than willing to step up into Owen Lynch's shoes. By using some financial pressure, we can guide them quietly. But the bigger and more dangerous area is going to be in those very businesses that Mark and I have invested in. Tell me, what do they all have in common?"

"Just like you told me to look for, all of them are physically located in areas that are normally considered gang areas, but are clean themselves. Most of them are also in fields of business that have had a high level of corruption from the Confederation."

"Exactly. What do you think is going to happen in those neighborhoods when the Confederation goes down, and Owen Lynch's corruption is rooted out?" Sophie sat forward, resting her elbows on her knees while I listened the intensity creep into her voice. It was a part of Sophie that had never changed from her days working in the hospital. She was a person who wanted a better world than the one we were living in.

"In the long term, I hope that things are better for everyone," Tabby said, "But the short term is going to be turbulent."

"Turbulent is a mild word," I interjected. "The fact is Tabby, things are going to be seriously fucked up. Once the state and Feds come through, a lot of high up cops are going to be arrested, and the department is going to not have the support of the community. Meanwhile, the Confederation imploding doesn't mean that all of them are going to be arrested. Most of them won't, in fact. A lot of the higher ups are going to be dead, but the low level guys, the street soldiers, they're still going to be out there. Your job is to guide the businesses, keep them clean, and prevent them from being taken advantage of by the leftover criminals. Those neighborhoods and industries are going to need bedrocks to lean on, and the MJT Holdings are going to be those bedrocks."

Tabby sat back and considered the ramifications of what we were asking her to do. "The rebuilding is going to be harder than taking these guys down."

"It always is," I said. "So are you up for it?"

Tabby thought for only a second. "It says in here that I get a maid and butler. What's up with that?"

"You're going to need your own street soldiers," I said. "And with me out playing Dark Knight, I'm going to need a good place for my wife and child to grow up, somewhere safe where they have family with them all the time."

Tabby took the news in, then without another word got up from the couch and walked to the kitchen. I heard her rummaging around in a drawer for a moment before it slammed, then a moment later she came back in, handing me the document. "Deal. I'll notify the firm tomorrow that I'm resigning."

After Tabby had gone off to the bath, Sophie came over and sat in my lap. "Thank you," she said, kissing me on the lips. "Although it still worries me that you still think you have to be a street level operative."

"I do," I said quietly, kissing her back. "The nice part is though that I shouldn't have to be in direct violence as often. Patrols, the proper use of fear, and dropping information to the suddenly more honest police force will be far more effective than what we have to do now."

"Do you really think I'm going to let you go out there by yourself all the time?" Sophie asked, kissing me again. "Maybe I like the vigilante life too."

"I'm not surprised, but you have a more important job," I said, pulling her close. Our kisses grew softer, and I moaned when Sophie climbed into my lap. "You're going to be raising the next generation, remember?"

"You too," Sophie replied, stroking my face and kissing me. Her tongue traced along my lower lip, and I could feel the slowly growing pressure of my cock hardening inside my loose house pants. Pressing her body against mine, we kissed slowly and sensuously. I stroked my hands up and down the soft skin of her back, relishing the amazing blend of soft curves and firm muscle I found underneath. She was quite the femme fatale compared to the medical student I'd fallen in love with while discussing Hans Zimmer music. Still, she was just as wonderful, and I was more in love with Sophie than ever.

Sophie wiggled her hips in my lap, grinding against my erection, both of us moaning at the feelings. I tugged at the edge of her shirt, trying to slide my hand underneath to cup her breast when we were interrupted by a polite cough from the doorway.

"Sorry guys, I just wanted to know where you kept the bath oils," Tabby said, wrapped up in a terrycloth robe. "I didn't mean to interrupt."

"Ah, not at all," Sophie said, tugging her shirt down and climbing off my lap. "I'll show you where they are. Mark and I just need to remember that we have someone else here right now."

I stayed where I was, knowing that if I stood up my already painful erection would become even more visible than it probably already was. Sophie leaned down and gave me a peck on the lips, then whispered in my ear. "Later tonight, my love. I promise you that."

I nodded and watched as the two beautiful women turned to leave the living room. "For what it was worth, it was a hell of a show," Tabby said to Sophie as they walked away. "I hope I only paused the action, and didn't cancel it."

"Tabs, it would take wild horses, an ice storm, and probably the sun exploding to totally cancel it," Sophie replied. "Trust me on that."

"You still haven't given me all the details," I heard Tabby joke. I couldn't hear Sophie's reply, but Tabby's reply of "whooo-oooo-oooo" certainly did wonders for my self esteem.

Chapter 47
Sophie

The next day, Tabby and I went shopping. Unfortunately, it wasn't quite the sort of shopping trip that she and I had indulged in when we were students.

"I can't even pronounce some of this stuff," Tabby said as she looked at the list Mark had given us. "Is this in Latin?"

"Not quite," I replied with a laugh. "It's just chemistry with a good smattering of brand names thrown in. Remember, you majored in business, I majored in medicine. I got exposed to a lot of this stuff during my undergrad and medical classes."

"So what is all this stuff supposed to make, anyway?" she asked, as she ran her finger underneath the third ingredient on the list. "And what is di-methyl-po..... I dunno?"

"Well, depends on what you want to use it for," I replied. "From what Mark told me, he's going to use it to make a bomb."

"A buh...?" Tabby said.

"Not a buh, a bomb," I said, unable to resist indulging in the classic corny joke line. Tabby also had a chuckle before I continued. "It's part of Mark's plan. To really keep the Confederation confused, each of the four eliminations we're making are going to be done in different ways. Han Faoxin was hand to hand. Illuysas Petrokias by long range shot. The next two are going to be done by bomb, and by poison."

"Which is what we're shopping for," Tabby said. "I don't think they have this sort of stuff over at Wal-Mart."

"You'd be surprised," I said in reply. "Actually, other than one or two things that Mark wants me to get at a medical supply place, we can get most of it at Home Depot."

"Really? I would have thought that it would be harder to get the stuff for a bomb or a poison."

"It is, normally. But so much of the regular world runs on chemicals nowadays, its impossible to control fully. Did you know that the difference between aspirin and LSD is really only a few molecules?" We pulled into the parking lot of the Home Depot, and got out. "And that you can, with a few interesting additions you can get from here, you can convert one into the other?"

Tabby shook her head, and looked at me, impressed. "I guess you learn something new every day. It's going to be fun working with you guys. You ever whip something up just for fun?"

I shook my head. After one time being slipped some Ecstasy at a dance party that had left me with a splitting headache and not much else, I didn't mess with mind altering chemicals. "Nope. You?"

Tabby grinned at me as I shut off the engine. "Hell no, it's too much fun being me most of the time. But I gotta keep my eye on my staff, you know. After all, I already found you trying to have sex in my entertainment room."

"Were you not entertained?" I replied, causing her to laugh and blush at the same time. Since staying with us every day other than work, Tabby had returned to her former self, although there was still an undercurrent of seriousness that hadn't been there before. In some ways it was refreshing, but still I missed the irreverent girl she'd always been.

The inside of the home shopping center was cavernous, and I tried to think back to the last time I had been inside such a place. Finally it came to me, it had been when I had needed to get some plaster patch for Tabby and my dorm room after she and a nighttime visitor had gotten a little too enthusiastic, and had put two divots in the wall above her headboard. I'd also bought a pair of foam pads that had been taped to the headboard to prevent further incidents, which Tabby had gleefully left there for the rest of our time living together.

Our first stop was in the car supplies, where we picked up road flares, some power steering fluid, a jug of antifreeze and a canister of refrigerant for air conditioning. After that we went over to plumbing where I got a jug of industrial strength drain cleaner, before swinging through the kitchen section for a hand mixer, and then finally picking up a five pound can of honey roasted peanuts next to the checkout. "What are the peanuts for?"

"I'm hungry, and they are awesome in homemade peanut butter," I replied. "So I decided on the really big can. Besides, looks a little better this way, doesn't it?"

Tabby thought for a moment before grabbing two root beers from the cooler next to the register. "No, now it looks better. Root beer goes great with peanut butter."

The rest of our shopping went equally smooth, with at each of our stops Tabby or I added a few other items to make it look like we weren't just shopping for chemicals. Still, it took half a dozen stops to complete our errands, and it was already early afternoon by the time we got back to Mount Zion. "You have a lab here?"

"We have a former mental hospital, remember?" I said, indicating the larger building. "It's not as clean as a chemistry lab, but we don't need it to be. Mark assures me that just a regular room will be just fine."

"Then why use the old outbuilding?" I asked as I pulled the SUV we were driving that day in front of it. "Why not just the house?"

"Mark said that making this stuff smells like crap," I replied. "Maybe not cooking meth bad, but still not exactly an odor you want lingering around the kitchen. This outbuilding will work just fine, as long as we're careful."

Taking our bags inside, I saw that Mark already set up his materials. "Okay guys, thanks, but I'm going to need to make this stuff myself," Mark said. He was dressed in a set of coveralls and had a rebreather around his neck, and all I could think of was Walter White crossed with a fitness model. "Some of these steps are a bit nasty, and I don't want you guys to risk getting injured."

"Are you sure?" I asked nervously. "We can't help at all?"

Mark shook his head and smiled. "Not this time, babe. Maybe I'll teach you how at some point, but I'll take care of this."

I nodded, worried. "Be careful, okay?"

"I will. This one's actually easy. Plastique is pretty easy, and the poison's not that hard to control. But still, you two get inside, and I'll be in for dinner."

Tabby and I left, leaving Mark alone. "So what should we do?" Tabby asked as we walked across the overgrown grass that separated the outbuilding from our house. "I don't suppose you're in the mood for another cheesy movie."

"No, but I could use something to distract myself," I said, thinking. "I know. Mark and I have some workout equipment here, how about joining me in working up a sweat? I remember you used to drag me to the university fitness center all the time."

Tabby grinned and nodded. "Okay. But I suspect that it'll be me dragging ass trying to keep up with you this time. I've heard the stories from your place downtown, you're turning heads for more than just your hair and boobs."

"They like my ass too?" I teased, cocking a hip. I was a little surprised when Tabby reached back and slapped my butt, rather hard too. "Ouch!"

"Sorry, couldn't resist," Tabby said while grinning wolfishly. "Now I just have to figure out what to wear. I didn't exactly pack a full wardrobe for my stay here."

"You're still a size four, right?" I asked, knowing already that she was.

"Yep, why, you going to loan me your stuff?" she said with a cocked eyebrow.

"You might have to cinch the waistband some, but I think I got your hookup," I replied. "I'm a size six now, so we're pretty close."

As it was, one of my tighter pairs of shorts fit her just fine, and we had a fun workout that left both of us sweaty, Tabby more than me. When we finally finished, I lay back on the hardwood floor of our little home gym and smiled. "Thanks. You really helped me push."

Tabby grinned from her position leaning against the wall, shaking her head. "You were the one pushing me. I think you were sandbagging to make me not feel bad."

I shrugged. "A little. I still got good work in though."

"That's good to know. So when you come back, think I can start joining you and Mark for your workouts? I may not turn into a sexy ninja girl like you, but I certainly could use the push and the company."

"I'd love that," I said. "I was thinking, since Mark and I can't go back to the other gym where we are now once we come back, either setting up a room here with more stuff, or maybe you can invest in another place closer to here while we're gone. What do you think?"

"Sounds good. Let's go get washed up though, unless you want Mark to walk in on two sweaty hot women lying around waiting for him."

I laughed. "We do that, and he'll faint from lack of blood to the brain as it all goes somewhere else."

Tabby grinned. "Don't tempt me. I may be getting my emotional needs met having you two around taking care of me, but there are some itches that aren't being scratched, if you know what I mean."

I grew more serious and looked over at Tabby. "Are you okay with that for now?"

Tabby's face grew contemplative, and she thought for a moment before nodding. "Actually, I am. I've been a flirt for so long, maybe a bit of forced celibacy other than what I can do for myself is helpful. It's maybe time that I start really looking for Mister Right rather than just Right Now."

"Sounds good," I said, coming over and helping her to her feet.

"It's going to be a bit difficult," Tabby said as she climbed up. She looked me in the eyes, her gaze filled with meaning. "Whoever it is, they're going to have to be willing to share my heart, you know."

I nodded and patted her on the shoulder. Acknowledging the depth of her feelings for me was a great thing. "I know. And Mark knows he's sharing my heart too. He's cool with it."

"He's a great man like that. Think there's another man like him around?"

I shrugged. "I don't know. But I'm sure there's someone out there for you. Now, let's go get washed up."

After my shower, I waited in the kitchen for either Tabby or Mark to come in. Mark was first, his coverall unzipped to his waist and carrying two bags. "Done," he said, his hair damp and sweaty. "You look refreshed."

"Tabby and I grabbed a quick bit of exercise and a shower. She's still using the hot water, not surprising me in the least."

Mark smiled and gave me a kiss on the cheek. "Are the gas bills going to go up with her living here?"

"Most likely, but since we recycle most of our water, that won't be affected too much. She told me something really awesome after the workout, too." I opened the fridge and took out some salmon, which I thought would make a good dinner for all of us. "She's thinking it's time for her to find her one."

"One what?" Mark asked, setting his bags on the floor near the back door. "By the way, don't use those. It's plastique and poison."

"I won't. And as for her one, she's looking for her version of you. She knows that's going to be pretty hard to find. Perfection is pretty hard to repeat."

"Keep talking like that, and I'm going to have a problem fitting in the door," Mark said as he headed for the back to change clothes. "My head's going to be too big."

I messed around in the kitchen while Mark and Tabby got ready, marinating the fish and prepping some couscous and some grilled asparagus. The fish was ready to go into the broiler when Tabby came out, wearing some casual clothes that we preferred for around the house. They weren't quite pajamas, but I wouldn't go grocery shopping in them. Still, Tabby made them look like a million bucks, and it was good to see her so relaxed and happy. "Hey, Mark's getting changed, and dinner will be ready in ten."

"Great. So is that what I think it is by the door?" she asked, pointing to Mark's bag. "The party favors?"

"You could say that. If you want, Mark can tell you what it's for when he gets out here." I took down some plates from the cupboard, along with silverware. Without a word, Tabby set the table while I started the fish. Our timing was perfect, and Mark came out just as I was setting the fish on the table.

"That looks amazing. And I'm not talking about the fish," he said, giving Tabby's shoulders a squeeze before coming over to kiss me on the cheek.

"Thanks," Tabby said, sitting down. "Now Mark, after we get this dished out, I want to hear everything you have planned for what's in that bag."

Chapter 48
Mark

The pre-dawn hours are one of the few times when the city's pulse was at its slowest. The city never really slept, but the time between four and five thirty in the morning or so was as close as it got. Most of the nightlife was done, and except for some newspaper deliverymen and bakers, the morning hadn't started yet. It was the best chance I had to do what I needed to do.

Of all the spots that were slow around the city, the airport was one of the deadest at four in the morning. Other than a few cargo flights and air mail, there were few flights going in and out. Security was lax, especially where I was going.

Taylor Broadwell was perhaps the richest member of the Confederation. If it wasn't that he didn't enjoy bloodshed, and that he was a first generation gangster, he probably could have run the whole damn thing. As it was however, he was fourth in power to Sal Giordano. Taylor's money came from the simple fact that he controlled trafficking in the city. Whether it was drugs, guns, or anything else; if it came by plane, by train, in a semi truck or buried in the trunk of a 1979 Oldsmobile, Taylor Broadwell was the man who controlled over ninety percent of it.

The only weakness that Broadwell had, besides his hesitancy to get his hands personally dirty, was that his operation was just a bit too loud. As such, even though he was a major player in the Confederation, he was paying just as much money to Owen Lynch for his police and other people to look the other way. As such, it hurt his standing, as some of the other Confederation members didn't trust him as much as they could have.

The plan was simple. Broadwell had a very unique schedule among the criminal element, in that he actually worked banker's hours. I got access to the airport by going through the marshes, which bordered the airport on its southern edge. The entire airport had been reclaimed marsh from the World War II era, and had in fact once been a B-17 crew training site. Afterwards, a lot of the old Quonset huts had been converted into the first generation of warehouses and privately owned buildings as runways were expanded and regular air traffic started up in the nineteen fifties.

Taylor Broadwell had bought them, giving him a secure cargo area. The southern edge of the airport however had been mostly ignored, being deemed too wet and too difficult to finish reclaiming. It was along that edge that most of

Broadwell's warehouses were, along with the one he used as his office.

The biggest danger of penetrating the airport perimeter from the south was the snakes. Ten workers had died in the nineteen thirties in the initial construction of the airfield from copperhead bites, a subspecies that had adapted to the marshy land and stagnant water. They were smaller than your average copperhead, but because of the fact that the marshes contained a lot of other large predators, they were especially venomous. I don't mean yellow bellied sea snake venomous, but not something you wanted to mess with. I wore high hip waders and thick clothing making my way through the marshes, along with night vision goggles that helped.

I started my trek through the swamps at midnight, going slow. Broadwell knew that the southern edge of his warehouses were undefended, so in addition to normal airport security, he had his own security patrols that went around all of his warehouses. Still, I had good training, and slipped out of the water at just after three in the morning. The narrow blacktop road was quiet, and I ditched the heavy waders and outer heavy waterproof jacket for what I carried in my backpack, a pair of wrestling shoes that gave me both grip and flexibility.

I got into Broadwell's office through a window in the back of the building, picking the lock. Slipping inside just fifteen seconds before a searchlight from a security patrol bathed the back of the building, I took a moment to calm my nerves and slow my breathing. While I doubted that he had any men inside the building, I couldn't be sure.

Broadwell's office was cluttered, the man hated using computers. He had an overwhelming paranoia of storing anything on computers, even those that weren't networked, convinced that someone could hack into them at any time. I may have played a part in that, actually, considering some of the things I'd told him during the times I had done contracts for him. It was ironic, then, that I was going to use a network connection in order to kill the man.

Looking over his desk, it took me a few minutes to find Broadwell's day planner. I looked up that day's schedule, and saw that he had a lunch appointment at one in the afternoon. The morning however was clear, and I knew he would be in his office, overseeing his men loading and unloading his illicit packages. I had noticed the crates already in the warehouse, and wondered how many contained cocaine, heroin, or meth, and how many contained other materials. Thankfully he didn't have any human cargo in at the time. With Petrokias' death, those shipments were at least temporarily suspended.

I got down on my knees and slipped my package underneath his antique desk, which filled half the damn office it was so large. I had once joked to Broadwell that he could keep a midget under his desk and not find him for a week, to which he had replied to me, "Snowman, I've found that after a hard day at work, nothing beats getting a blowjob while I fill out my paperwork. With this desk, I can do both very easily."

Like I said, my former associates were not good people. In any case, I put the shaped charges in the lower corners of the desk, angled in such a manner that when they went off, they would scatter a rain of shrapnel into Broadwell's legs and lower torso, kind of like a miniature Claymore mine.

The final touch was the trigger. In my old life, it would have been far too easy to just put in a simple timer, one that would go off at about ten thirty. But I wanted to make sure, and I also wanted to make sure that Broadwell was the person taken out. My message wouldn't be anywhere near as effective if my bomb killed a secretary who just happened to be using the boss's desk to answer the phone when it went off. So, I connected the trigger to a WiFi capable video camera. Piggybacking off the signal that the airport used, I could monitor it from anywhere I wanted, and with just a click of a mouse, trigger the bomb to go off.

I checked the connection on a prepaid smartphone and made my way out. The exit was more difficult than getting in, because I couldn't go through the marshes again. With daylight coming in soon I instead made my way building to building, over two miles to a FedEx processing center. At seven, the shifts changed, and I walked out the front gate towards the employee parking lot, flashing a fake ID badge to the security guard as I went.

Two rows from the back of the lot, Tabby was waiting for me behind the wheel of a used Ford that was another one of my small fleet. She was wearing a baggy sweatshirt and track pants, and looked like a normal working class girl. "Wow, you've got camouflage skills," I said, plopping down into the passenger seat. "No offense, but you look like a regular girl."

Tabby laughed and rubbed her head. "None taken, it was what I was going for. Besides, if you're saying that, you also mean you think I look pretty when I'm doing my normal thing. So everything is set?"

"Yeah, we're good. We need to check the feed in about three hours. According to his schedule he'll be there by himself."

Tabby made a right turn and headed away from the airport. "And if someone else is there?"

"It shouldn't affect anyone on the other side of the desk, but we can take our time," I said. "We just trigger it when he's in there by himself for the added margin of safety. I'll tell you a rule that one of my teachers had told me. Indiscriminate killing only works to paralyze your enemy in the short term. Targeted eliminations though, they create long term effects."

Tabby thought about it, and nodded in understanding. "I learned something similar in business. If you just throw more money across the whole company that you need to turn around, all you end up doing is strengthening the things you want to get rid of along with the things you want to keep. So you end up with just a more expensive crippled company. But if you can target your changes, you can create a long term effect that reforms the company."

"I knew I hired the right person to run MJT," I said, leaning back and rubbing my eyes. "Now if you don't mind, I need to grab some sleep. Wake me up when we get back to the base?"

Tabby nodded. "You got it. Sophie told me to tell you she's going to take care of some stuff as Sophie Warbird today, to keep the public image up and everything. She's actually scheduled to meet with the mayor this afternoon."

"I remember," I mumbled, letting my eyes close. "If I have time, I'll crash the meeting. Marcus Smiley hasn't grabbed too many headlines in the past week or so."

I think Tabby said something in reply, but I was already mostly asleep, and didn't answer. The next thing I was aware of, Tabby was shaking my shoulder. I came awake instantly, a side effect of my training. I can turn it on and turn it off pretty much at the drop of a hat. "Hey, we're back. This is the place you wanted, right?"

I sat up and looked around, recognizing the small mobile home that I had about thirty minutes outside the city in the middle of some pretty crappy scrub land that developers hadn't touched yet. It was listed as a hunting cabin, and I usually stayed there about one week a year just to keep up appearances. Tabby had already parked the car under the tree around back, and I could see my SUV parked nearby. "Yeah, you found it again. Not bad, considering we came out here at midnight."

"I thought for sure you'd have woken up when I hit that pothole about a mile back, but you just slept like a baby. I didn't think a hitman would sleep so deeply."

I smirked and got out of the car. "You'd be surprised. But there was a simple reason I didn't wake up. I knew you were in control, and I trust you. Now, let's get back to Mount Zion and get ready for the day. You've got to go in and start handover of your accounts that aren't related to MJT, and I've got a meeting with the mayor to be late for."

"Good deal. You want to drive or sleep?"

"What time is it?"

"Seven thirty. I got caught in some roadwork coming out of the city. Morning rush hour is starting, so it's going to be an hour at least before we get back to Zion."

I yawned and ran my hand through my hair, and reached into my pocket to toss her the keys. "You drive. I can use another hour of sleep."

* * *

"Mr. Smiley, the Mayor is in a meeting right now," the flummoxed secretary said to me as I came in wearing what was perhaps the most obnoxious looking suit ever. A black suit jacket with red contrast stitching paired with a silk wine colored cravat and white shirt was bad enough, but the custom tailored red and black plaid suit pants put it over the top. I'd copied it from an Australian food critic and television personality, although I think I looked a lot better in it than he did.

"But of course, lovely girl!" I said in my boisterous and overly loud *Marcus Smiley voice*. "But what you forget is that the person the mayor is meeting with is my lovely fiancee and assistant."

"Well, her and and five other business leaders," the secretary countered, her eyes pointedly flickering towards the clock on the wall which declared I was thirty minutes late for the meeting. "His Honor...."

"Wouldn't dare think of having an assembly of local financial movers and shakers without the largest private investor over the past twelve months in the city, would he?" I replied, giving the secretary a disarming grin that I love to call my *Han Solo* and a bit of a basketball double fake to get around her.

Before she could say anything else I threw open the double doors to the conference room, causing two of the security guards near the podium to reach for their guns before they realized who I was.

"My friends, so sorry for the tardiness," I said, while the secretary fluttered behind me ineffectually. The Mayor, I had to give him credit, played it pretty cool, waving the guards and his secretary off. Sophie, who I had texted ten minutes before and was aware of my arrival, hid a small smile behind a polite hand while I made my way around the large round table and sat down. "My my, what a table. I think I'll sit here between Queen Guinevere and Sir Galahad, if you all don't mind."

"Thank you for joining us, Mr. Smiley," the Mayor replied. "And I have to love the subtlety of your suit for today. Are you going to a bagpipe concert after this?"

"You know how it is, Mr. Mayor. Being understated is my strong suit," I said, breaking the tension and letting things continue. "But please, continue. What did I miss?"

"The Mayor was discussing the recent news reports about increased tension on the streets and how it might affect community relations," Bill Franklin, the president of the largest bank in the city said. He was part of the old guard, and while I knew he personally was clean, I also knew that his bank served as one of the various filtering mediums for both the Confederation and Owen Lynch. Hell, I even had an account there under one of my alternate identities. "He's also concerned about recent economic shifts that might affect employment in the city. With an election coming up soon, he'd rather not have a poor economy being a distraction from the important social issues he wants to focus on."

"I see," I said, looking around at the other people seated at the table. They represented the apathetic monied interests that frustrated me, but couldn't fight against yet. I needed leverage, and my war with the Confederation and Owen Lynch was the tool I needed. "Well, please go on."

The Mayor continued, and I listened with half an ear as he droned on, while I scribbled a note on the legal pad that Sophie had out. *Anything of importance?*

Not really. BTW, how was your nap?

Useful. Will tell you about it later.

OK.

I listened as the rest of the meeting went on, the other so-called financial and business leaders blathering on, using big words to basically say they didn't want to do anything other than cover their own asses. Finally, when I couldn't stand it any longer, I spoke up. "Mr. Mayor, no offense, but this meeting seems like a giant waste of time."

"I beg your pardon, Mr. Smiley?" Francine Berkowitz, who represented one of the city's unions sputtered. I had cut her off in the middle of a long winded speech where basically she was saying the unions were going to play ball with the status quo, which I knew meant with either Owen Lynch or the Confederation, depending on which union she was talking about. "How dare you..."

"No Ms. Berkowitz, how dare you," I interjected, cutting her off for a second time. "Let's speak honestly for a moment. This city is on a razor's edge because the criminal elements that have controlled the streets for so long are at each other's throats. Just before coming here, I saw on the local news that a bomb just went off at an airport warehouse, killing one man at his desk. Instead of terrorism, the first idea out of the news reporter's mouth is that it was another strike on whoever is trying to control crime in this city, I didn't have a chance to listen to the theory before coming over here. The fact is that crime controls this town, and all of you have either ignored it, condoned it, or are actively working with it. As a result, while you may have lined your own pockets, the life blood of this city has been slowly choked off for far too long."

I turned to the Mayor, looking him in the eye. "Nobody here has the, excuse the term, the stones to do a damn thing about it. So here's what's going to happen. Me and Sophie here, we're leaving. But before we leave, we're making sure that in the next election, this city gets a Mayor that will actually stand up and try to make things better. I don't give a damn about the party, or what their stance is on Common Core education standards, or whether they like their pizza crust thick or thin. What I care about is if they are willing to do what is needed to break the stranglehold that the criminals in this city have on it."

"That's a lofty goal for someone who's going to cut and run," Berkowitz retorted. "And just how are you planning on accomplishing this goal?"

"The same way that I went from being a nobody in this city to being able to arrive a half hour late for a meeting and get more done in fifteen minutes than you have in years," I said simply, standing up. "By the way, Ms. Berkowitz, how is it that a simple community organizer and union member can afford a custom tailored suits with handmade Italian leather high heels for a business meeting? Mr. Mayor, we can talk later. Have a good day."

The room rumbled while Sophie and I left, and I heard comments behind us. As Sophie and I were making our way through the marble halls of the foyer, I heard someone calling my name behind us. "Marcus! Marcus Smiley!"

I turned and saw the Mayor walking with a purpose towards me, trying not to look like he was rushing after me, but not doing too good of a job. "Mr. Mayor. When I said we could talk later, I didn't think you would want to five minutes later."

"You pissed off a lot of very powerful people in there, Marcus," the Mayor replied, as we turned and kept walking. Coming out into the sunlight of the mid afternoon, we walked across Civic Plaza, stopping by a hot dog cart to grab some food.

"Four big dogs," I told the cart vendor, while Sophie pulled some cash out of her purse. Nodding to her, I turned my attention back to the Mayor. "I know I pissed them off, Mr. Mayor. But those people need to get pissed off. They've been sitting in ivory towers for far too long, meanwhile the very foundation of their towers are sinking in a flood of sewage and shit."

"You have quite a way with words, Marcus," the Mayor replied. "By the way, outside just call me Joe. That Mayor stuff can be saved for the press and official duties. I hope one of those dogs is for me."

"Of course, although don't think I'm trying to influence you with it," I said with a smirk. I handed one to Sophie and one to the Mayor, and all of us put our toppings on. The Mayor was a chili and ketchup man, not too bad in my opinion. You can tell a lot about someone by their taste in hotdog toppings. "So what did you want to talk about?"

"Walk with me," the Mayor said, indicating towards the rest of the plaza. I nodded, and the three of us walked and ate at the same time, a rather impressive feat for Sophie who was wearing one of her sexy suits and carrying a purse and briefcase along with eating a hot dog. "You pissed off some people, but I agree with you overall."

"Then why did you have the meeting with them?" I asked, not mentioning the fact that his very own deputy mayor was one of the biggest criminals in the city. The time wasn't right yet. "You look like a hypocrite doing so."

"Most politicians have to be," the Mayor replied. "But I'd like it to be different."

"I'm sure, but I'm afraid it might be too late for you," I said, looking around. I could see that while a few people were looking at us, there was nobody who might be eavesdropping. "You know that the biggest criminal in the city works for you. Or do you work for him?"

The Mayor looked at me with a moment of panic on his face, and almost choked on the last bite of his hotdog. I, on the other hand, finished off my first dog and started on my second. "So you know too."

"For quite a while," I said, stopping and casually tucking another bit of hotdog into my mouth. I don't know what the City Hall hot dog vendors used for their product, but it was the best damn dog in the city. "And I know something else, too."

"What?" the Mayor said shakily, still recovering from the news that I knew.

"Owen Lynch is going to be caught up in all this, very soon now. If you want any chance of surviving this politically, you need to distance yourself from him immediately. Tell me, who is honest and has the balls to take him down in the state level?"

"At the state level? Nobody. Owen's got connections up there too, he's tied in with all the movers and shakers all the way to the governor's office. But if you're looking for a cop or prosecutor who's willing to take him down, Bennie Fernandez at the DOJ is your man. He's as clean as a whistle, and Owen hates his guts. If it wasn't that Bennie is kept busy chasing the small fish, Owen would have had him taken out long ago."

"I know who Fernandez is," I said. "And you're sure that he can take Lynch down?"

"If there's any evidence. But Owen didn't get to where he is without being slippery. Guy makes Teflon look like super glue."

"I know. Okay, Joe. Thanks for the information. Trust what I said though, you need to dump Lynch now. As for me and Sophie, we're leaving town tonight. We won't be back."

The Mayor nodded, and held out his hand. We shook, and the Mayor turned to leave. About halfway there, he turned back, a questioning look in his eyes. "Who are you, Marcus Smiley? Really?"

I shrugged and gave him a grin. "It's not who I am underneath that counts, but what I do that is important."

The Mayor looked at me quizzically for a moment before turning and going back towards City Hall. Sophie, who had watched the entire exchange silently, watched him go. "You think you can trust him?"

"Yeah. He knows he's in league with dirt, but he's tried his best to be as clean as a politician can be in this city. Besides, he was legit on Bennie Fernandez. Sal Giordano hates that guy too. I'm only worried about one thing."

Sophie watched the Mayor start up the steps to City Hall. "What's that?"

"How anyone can consider themselves worthy of leading a city and not get such an obvious Batman reference. Come on, let's go home."

Chapter 49
Sophie

The news reports were buzzing when Mark and I came home that evening. The bomb at the airport had gotten the attention of Homeland Security and the FBI since it happened on an airfield, and rumors were already swirling that there were things found in the warehouse that were connected to Owen Lynch. I sipped at my tea and looked at Mark. "Had you planned on that?"

"No, but I'm not surprised. Actually it's a bit of a setback," I said. "While it hurts Lynch, the problem is it takes heat out of the Confederation. We're going to have to really make sure the next one goes smooth."

Tabby came in, dressed to kill in a business suit that looked more appropriate on Sophie Warbird than Tabby Williams. Still, she filled it well. "Hey you two, you need to make your departure."

"You're right," Mark said, sighing and finishing off his own tea. He was dressed in cargo pants and a sweatshirt, and I had a moment of deja vu as I thought of the night that Mark and I had first fled the city, the clothes were so similar. "You ready?"

I nodded my head and got up. "I'm going to miss the purple hair," I said, running my fingers through it. As part of our plan to disappear, I was going to go back to my regular shade of brown while also getting a short haircut. "I kinda felt like a superhero with it."

"You did give off the Psylocke vibe," Tabby said. "By the way, you like the suit?"

"You can raid that part of my closet all you want," I said in way of reply. She did look good, and the red was perhaps even more striking than the purple I'd been rocking. "Just remember that you're not officially President of MJT until two weeks from now, so until then, just be normal Tabby."

"I know, but I figured I'd send you two off with a good feeling that things are in good hands," she said, spinning on a heel. "I know you'll be gone only a few days, but still."

Mark came over and wrapped his arms around her, hugging her tightly. "We'll miss you too. Watch the fort, and you'll have us back before you know it. Just lay low, okay?"

"I will. I'm planning on my last trip to the old office tomorrow, to do final handover of my accounts to Donna. She's a good girl, and this bumps her out of the intern pool. She's going to be one to keep your eye on, she's smart as all hell." Tabby released Mark's hug and came over to me, wrapping me up as well.

I could feel her holding tight, and I clung back. "It's just a few days, sweetie. Then you get to boss me and Mark around, at least in public," I whispered in her ear, patting her back. "You're strong, and if things get scary, you know how to reach us. Just chill for three or four days, we'll be back."

Tabby nodded, then kissed me on the cheek. "Do me a favor while you're gone," she said when Mark left to go out to the garage.

"What?"

Tabby looked over her shoulder towards the door to the garage, then turned back to me with that familiar Tabby grin. "Take at least one night and rock that man's world. You both deserve it."

I couldn't help it, I laughed. Nodding, I kissed Tabby on the cheek and stepped back. "Damn right. What do you think we're going to do besides rest up during the next few days?"

"And your tummy?" Tabby asked, looking down. "Everything okay down there?"

"We'll check while we're gone. I'll tell you when we get back."

I heard the SUV that we were using start up, and I patted Tabby on the shoulder again. "Okay. See you when we get back. We'll text you when we get there."

Tabby followed me out to the garage, where Mark was already sitting behind the driver's seat. "See you in a few days," Mark said, hitting the garage door opener. "Don't eat all the ice cream."

"I won't," Tabby said with a laugh. The door rattled up, and we pulled out. Down at the street level, we could see a few paparazzi, exactly as we'd planned. Marcus Smiley's leaving town wasn't going to be front page news, but it did establish that we were leaving.

"Mr. Smiley!" one of the reporters, from the local ABC affiliate yelled.

Mark pulled through the gate and let it close behind us, then opened his window. "Yes, but only a minute. We do have to hit the road."

"Rumors are swirling that you're leaving the city permanently. Is there any truth to that?"

"Well, financially I'm always going to be here," Mark replied, pitching his voice in the Marcus Smiley persona. "You guys will get some more information on that soon. As for where Miss Warbird and I will live, well, we're exploring our options. We were thinking maybe Hawaii, maybe the West Coast, maybe overseas. But yes, we've both decided as great as this city is, it's not the place for us to get married and raise a family."

"Does that mean you two are going to tie the knot soon?" another reporter hollered. "What about kids?"

"No comment," Mark said, smirking. "But maybe you all can get some honeymoon photos. Thanks guys, you've been pretty wonderful and respectful. Take care."

Rolling up the window, we crept along until the last cameraman was clear before driving down the street and towards the highway. As Mark drove, he had a strange little smile on his face. "What?" I asked, unable to resist smiling myself. "Why are you smiling?"

"Just thinking about what that reporter asked as we were leaving," Mark said, turning and getting on the Interstate. "What about it?"

"What about what?" I said. I knew the plan at this point, we were going to head north and cross the Canadian border, then sell the car before crossing back over under our new identities. It'd be a supposed disappearing celebrity mystery, made even more weird as we had booked flights to five different international locations along with a yacht. The tickets would be used, but not by us. It was an elaborate scheme, but we hoped it would let Marcus Smiley disappear.

"Getting married. When we cross back over, we can stop off in Las Vegas, get married if you want. It'd be pushing the schedule, but I think it could work."

I grinned and nodded. "Why the hell not? Think you can charter us a plane to get us to Vegas in time?"

"Of course I can," Mark replied, giving me another smile. "But first we're going to need to get some haircuts and stuff."

"No, first we need to get to Canada."

* * *

The famous Las Vegas strip was amazing, even more than all the times I'd seen it on TV. Flying in on a Lear jet, I felt giddy as I looked over at Mark. Excuse me, at Mathew Mark Bylur, originally of Phoenix, Arizona. I had laughed when he had told me what his name meant.

"Bylur is an Icelandic word, it means severe snowstorm," he told me as he handed me my new American passport. It had been brought over the border three days prior by an associate of Mark's, who then snuck back over the border after dropping it off in a train station coin locker in Toronto. "You think it works?"

"I think I'll come to adore it," I said. "I think Joanna Bylur has a certain charm to it."

After living my entire life as Sophie, first Sophie White then Sophie Warbird, I was now Joanna Smith, at least for the next two days. I'd stopped asking Mark how he was able to get such good fake identification papers, but I knew it involved hacking a lot of government databases. I'd done a search using the plane's WiFi while we flew, and I had a complete credit history, records from the University of Washington saying I graduated with a degree in sociology, as well as a Tinder account. I didn't even want to know how much it had cost.

"In any case, we'll be landing soon," Mark said, patting my knee. "Then we have to check in at the chapel, they'll have us sign the basic paperwork, and the ceremony is tomorrow."

"Did you book the one with the Elvis impersonators?" I said with a laugh.

"No, another one that actually looks a little bit classy," he said. "It's still on the strip though, and we'll be within walking distance of our hotel."

"But we're still getting married in shorts and tank tops, right?" I asked. It was my only insistence about the whole deal. I'd dreamed as a little girl about my perfect wedding and my traditional wedding dress, but now all I wanted was Mark. None of the other stuff mattered, and I wanted this to be fun.

"Of course. I told the chapel in an e-mail, and they replied that they would be fine with it. Even offered to have the preacher and organ player in Hawaiian shirts if we wanted."

"What did you say?"

The plane banked, and we started our final descent into the Las Vegas airport. "I told them we'd tell them when we get there today," Mark replied. "I'd leave it up to you."

After landing and getting our bags, we took a taxi to our hotel. Mark had been able to book us a room at the Bellagio, and I was absolutely blown away as we made our way through the luxurious lobby, past the casino and to the reception desk. I almost forgot to respond when the clerk called my name, and had to have Mark jostle my arm. "Sorry," I said apologetically as I handed over my driver's license. "First time in Vegas."

"No problem, Miss Smith," the clerk replied. "It happens all the time. Okay, well, here are your room keys, and we've included complimentary tickets to the buffet as well. There's a map inside your guest packet if you need help finding it. Enjoy your stay."

Up in the hotel room, I stared, transfixed at the sights outside our room. "It's amazing," I said as I watched the lights and the cars far below. "I can see why people become enchanted with this place."

"It is," Mark replied, coming up behind me and giving me a hug. "But I see something even more enchanting."

I smiled, resting my head against the glass while Mark held me from behind, his hand rubbing my belly. "Mark?"

"Yes babe?"

"I know it'll be tough, but tonight, can we not have sex?" I asked him, entwining my fingers with his. "I just.... I dunno, I want to save it for tomorrow after the ceremony."

Mark kissed the back of my neck, and let go. "Of course. Just don't mind me if I have to take a very cold shower tonight. Say, are you ready to go to the chapel?"

"Yeah, let's go."

The pre-wedding part was easy, and the chapel staff was actually pretty nice. Walking back to the hotel, I stopped when I saw a pharmacy. "Hold on," I said, pulling him inside. Once there, I went over to the pregnancy test aisles, picking one up. "A wedding gift for both of us."

"You want to open it tonight or tomorrow?" Mark asked as I paid for the test and put it in the backpack I was using as a purse. It felt strange and comfortable, not using something from Gucci or Dolce Gabbana for a purse again. I was going to enjoy being Joanna Bylur.

"Tomorrow, after the ceremony. Come on, let's get back. I've never played poker before for real money, and wanted to try. Don't worry, I'm going to keep to a very strict budget. I walk away if we win more than two thousand, or lose more than two hundred."

"That won't take long either way," Mark said as we walked. "The Bellagio tables are some of the biggest in the world. Have you ever played before?"

"Just online against computers," I said. "But hey, I'm on my honeymoon. Why not live a little?"

Chapter 50
Mark

As it turned out, Sophie was a better poker player than I'd expected, or perhaps just a luckier one. Using the Texas Hold 'Em tables, she walked away with four thousand dollars in her pocket and another comped meal from the pit boss after just an hour of play. The last hand, she'd gone all in with two other players when she had just over thirteen hundred dollars. The final two cards had given her a full house, beating both other players and pushing her over her limit. I was more impressed however as Sophie calmly cashed out and walked away after the hand, despite being on a hot streak, and we went to dinner at Le Cirque.

The next morning neither of us could eat much, nerves prompting both of us to skip the buffet. Instead, we made our way down to the chapel early, arriving a good forty five minutes earlier than we had to for our ceremony check in. The staff who greeted us laughed and showed us to the garden. "We get this every day," she told us as she left. "I'd much rather have that than the ones who get sudden jitters and don't show up until five minutes late or something. Those are a pain. I'll bring you two some iced tea. Enjoy."

As it was, we ended up doing more than enjoying, as the couple before us, two kids from California who were most definitely eloping, didn't have witnesses. While Nevada law said that the staff could witness, the kids didn't have the extra money for the staff, so Sophie and I agreed to stand in for free. It was sweet to watch, and helped us calm down.

Our ceremony, I can barely remember, which tells you just how dumbstruck I was by the whole thing. I remember that the organ player had a kind of jazzy sound to his playing, and that the minister was balding, and slightly overweight. Things didn't really start to speed up again until we got into the limo, and I was sitting there with the wedding certificate in my hand. "Mathew Marcus Bylur and Joanna Bylur. I still can't believe it."

"Well, believe it," Sophie said. "Tabby is going to be so flipped out when we show her the pictures."

"There were pictures?"

Sophie looked over at me and laughed. "Yes there were, Mr. I Notice Almost Everything Around Me. You have been looking a little dopey, you sure your mind is right?"

I blinked and nodded. "Yeah, it's just that I still feel blown away by all this. So what's next?"

Sophie slid across the seat and into my lap, giving me a very nice view of her breasts underneath her tank top. "Next, my sexy husband, I'm taking you back to our hotel room and doing what Tabby told me I needed to do. She told me that at least once I needed to rock your world, and I think this is the perfect occasion to do so."

For the rest of the short ride back to the hotel, Sophie and I kissed and made out in the back of the limo, an experience I hadn't done in a very long time, although this time it was much more meaningful than the last. Getting out, we rushed through the lobby to our room. Shutting the door and locking it, Sophie took two steps and launched herself into a full on flying leap, crashing into the bed with an explosion of giggles. Her short, now nearly black hair was the only thing that stopped it from being perfect, as I kind of wished I could have seen her do the same thing with her old purple locks. Ah well, it was still funny, sexy, and just everything that made Sophie perfect to me.

"You going to join me or just stare?" she asked as she posed with her legs in the air, arms open for me.

"If I jump on the bed like that, I'll break the damn thing," I said, pulling my tank top up and over my head. "But I am more than happy to join you."

Coming over to the bed, I took Sophie's feet in my hands. I pretended to consider which foot to work over first before setting her right leg aside and untying her left shoe, pulling it off along with her sock. I was pleasantly surprised as I saw her toenails were painted a dark, lustrous purple. "I knew you were missing the color."

Rubbing my thumbs up and down the sole of her foot, I brought her foot up to my lips and kissed each one, smiling in between. "I have, but the color isn't as important as the rest of you," I said, kneading her foot until Sophie was groaning in appreciation. "I think I might make foot massages a staple of our marriage."

"I can get used to that," Sophie replied, her words slurring slightly as I worked up her calf muscle. There were quite a few knots in the shapely muscle, and I wondered just how hard she'd been pushing her workouts. "Oh God that feels good. I thought I was supposed to be rocking your world."

"You do with every touch, every kiss, and every time you say you love me," I replied, setting her left leg down on the mattress. I picked up her right foot and took off her shoe and sock, before playfully teasing a puff ball of fuzz out from between two of her toes and blowing them off.

Laying her leg to the side, I backed up, then lowered my face to Sophie's thighs, kissing each of them chastely before kissing higher and more intimately. Finding the waistband of her shorts, I pulled, and was surprised by what I found. Sophie, who had always just neatly trimmed our entire relationship, had shaved herself totally bare. The skin was so smooth and fresh she must have done it just the night before, or maybe that morning before our ceremony. "Wha...?"

"You don't mind?"

"Not at all," I said, kissing the soft skin on the inside of her thigh. Sophie trembled, and I could see her breath catch in anticipation of what I was going to do. "May I?"

"Yes, of course..... my husband," she said, the words causing both of us to shiver in happiness. Her hand came down to stroke through my hair, and I kissed her thighs again, pushing them apart just a bit to keep her tender skin from the slight roughness of my cheeks. Reaching out with my tongue, I traced the silky soft skin of her outer lips, reveling in the taste.

Licking up and down her outer lips, I slowly darted my tongue inside, listening as Sophie's breathy moans guided me in my caresses. Her sticky juices coated my tongue, a flavor that I will never get enough of regardless of whether I live to a thousand years old. Reaching deeper, I found the entrance to her pussy and licked as deeply as I could, feasting on her nectar until it ran down my lips. Sophie groaned deeply, her hands pulling me into her before tensing and pulling me higher, toward what I knew she wanted.

I withdrew my tongue with only a momentary flicker of regret, longing for more of her perfect essence before licking higher, searching for the tender button of her clit. It lay there at the top of her labia like a perfect round little pink ruby, shyly poking out from between the coral pink petals of her labia, wanting my attention. I kissed it first, my lips causing Sophie to cry out with a gasp. I traced around the nub with the tip of my tongue before flicking my tongue over it, her gasp becoming a sharp cry of pleasure. Her fingers tightening almost painfully in my hair, and she bucked into my tongue, nearly losing control. I repeated the flicks, my tongue barely brushing over the tip of her clit over and over, before I started circling again, this time my tongue dragging against her clit with every circle.

I felt Sophie's fists tighten again, and her pull went all the way to totally painful as her hips lifted off the bed, and her cries reached a fever pitch. Her thighs clamped around my head as her orgasm washed over her, and I rode out the pain, even as the blood thundered in my ears and I could feel my hair being literally torn out of my scalp. Finally, Sophie's hands relaxed, and her legs fell to the side, her body sated momentarily. "Holy shit."

"I aim to please," I said, kissing her belly button before slowly moving next to her on the bed. Sophie is very sensitive after an orgasm, to the point that anything more than holding her hand can be painful to her, and it takes her a few moments to recover. I lay there, holding her hand as she clasped it in between her breasts, taking deep breaths and staring at the ceiling.

Finally, she turned her head to look me in the eyes, a single tear falling from her right eye to trickle down her cheek. "You're amazing."

"I just love you," I said. "That's all."

Sophie snorted and looked at the ceiling. "That's all."

We lay there for another few moments before she turned on her side and kissed me. "And I love you with all my heart. And with all my body, too."

Sophie's eyes glimmered with a kittenish sparkle that I knew so well, and was so happy to see. Reaching down, the nimble fingers of her right hand quickly unsnapped the button on my shorts and reached inside, finding my semi-hard cock. "What, you lost interest?" she teased, stroking me with her hand. "I've heard that happens in marriage."

"No way, ever," I semi-replied. I know I wasn't that coherent, but I had the most beautiful woman I'd ever known smiling at me with a seductive look that was hot enough to melt titanium and stroking my cock right after I'd given her a pretty good climax. The only reason I was only half hard was because I had been so into using my tongue that my attention had wandered from my cock to my wife. As it was, I was raging hard again before I could answer, and I was pushing painfully against the constriction of my shorts. Worst of all, I had chosen shorts with a button fly, which meant that it took Sophie an extra ten seconds to get my shorts off, since she used just her right hand while her lips made little kisses on my jaw and neck that felt like they barely touched my skin, but each one of them left a trail of fire behind it.

Kissing her way down my chest, Sophie let her movement drag her t-shirt up, although I must admit I helped by pulling on it from the back. When it was all the way under her armpits she sat up to quickly pull it over her head, giving me an amazing look of her body. Grinning, she shook her head, letting her breasts sway from side to side in front of me. "You're never going to get tired of these, are you?"

"Never," I said, pulling her back down into a kiss. Rolling to the side, I cupped her left breast as we kissed, my thumb running over her nipple while our tongues darted and swept around each other, kissing. I found one of the nice advantages of Sophie having short hair, as stroking and caressing her face was easier by far.

Suddenly, I felt something that caused me to break our kiss, surprised. Using her thighs, Sophie had trapped me between her legs, wrapping my cock in a warm, smooth, strong vise that felt nearly as good as being inside her. Sophie grinned and leaned forward, biting my lower lip gently while she squeezed her thighs around my cock, growling sexily.

Our lovemaking took on a feral quality, and Sophie dragged her fingernails down my back, both of us gasping in the mix of pain and pleasure. We wrestled around on the bed, both of us highly trained in martial arts, both of us in top shape. Still, we were making love, not fighting, and I had a nearly seventy pound weight advantage. Also, Sophie couldn't use her legs, keeping her thighs clamped around my cock with delicious results. I was hard and oozing precum, creating enough lubrication that I was actually thrusting in between her legs as we moved. Stopping, I used my strength to pin Sophie to the bed, her wrists held in my left hand above the bed. Sophie struggled for a moment, then relaxed, surrendering to me. Her thighs unclenched, and her knees splayed open, letting me in between. "You are mine," I growled, kissing her fiercely. "Forever."

"Forever," she said, pulling her legs up. I could feel the hot, wet entrance to her pussy, as she angled her hips to give herself fully to me.

I let go of her hands to pull her on top of me, reversing our positions.

Turning around, she pushed my legs together, my cock pointing straight up. Facing away from me, Sophie put her hands on my knees and slid back, my cock pushing inside her with both of us groaning with the wonderful sensation. Riding me in this cowgirl position, Sophie slid back and forth, her inner muscles squeezing me even more wonderfully than her thighs had.

One of the many reasons that Sophie was perfect for me was the way I was able to fit inside her. One of the first times we made love, she had remarked at how large I was as she had wrapped her breasts around my cock and gave me a boob job. She didn't know, but she was closer to the truth than she had ever known. Most women were timid of my size, or were drunken size queens who just wanted me to pound them mercilessly.

Sophie was neither. Her beautiful body accepted me as it was, and wrapped itself lovingly around me, regardless of what we did. And yes, we had done almost everything. This time, she rode me slowly, letting her body build up slowly from the orgasm she had been through already.

For long, wonderful minutes, I felt the slow penetration and withdrawal of Sophie's pussy around my cock. I watched, fascinated as her hips flexed and pushed. It gave me a mental cue to the wonderful waves of pleasure that would wash through me, and building my anticipation. Sophie's hips moved faster, her own body's urges taking over.

"Mark...." she sighed, starting to lift her hips as well as ride back and forth. My cock slid in and out in longer, mind numbing strokes, both of us giving ourselves to the feeling. Sophie took her hands off my knees and sat up, using her thighs to push herself up and down, taking me inside her in longer movements than ever.

I put my hands on her hips, helping Sophie as she pulled her knees underneath her as she leaned back, letting me thrust with my hips as well. Holding her up with my arms, we rode each other, my thrusts meeting her knees. Sweat beaded my forehead and I couldn't hold out much longer, but I didn't need to. I felt the flutters of Sophie's pussy around me, and I knew she was oh so close to another orgasm.

"Forever," I said again into her ear, the emotional stimulation combining with the physical feelings tearing through our bodies. With a final thrust I felt Sophie start to come, and I gave in, giving one more thrust of my own before my own climax tore through me, and I gave myself to my wife, my soul mate.

Chapter 51
Sophie

A hundred years ago, the city's central train terminal had been a marvel of early twentieth century architecture. With high vaulted ceilings, sweeping arches, lots and lots of marble, and a style that seemed to be a blend of Neo-Gothic and Art Deco, for a long time it had been almost as much a tourist attraction as it had been travel hub. Millions of people every day swarmed the platforms, and quite a few classic movies had been filmed in the main hall.

After World War II however, with the rise of air travel and the increased use of cars, the now thirty year old station lost some of its luster. It wasn't noticeable at first, and in fact for nearly twenty years afterward the station serviced more passengers than ever, mainly due to the ever increasing population of the city. But more and more people were using cars or planes to get to the city.

By the seventies, the decline was obvious, and an overly stressed city budget just didn't want to invest the amount of money necessary on upkeep of the now 'classic' building. Murals on the walls weren't cleaned with the same care, and the marble stairs started to gather a certain hollowed out look from the millions of feet that tread upon them every day.

Around the turn of the century, there was an attempt at renovating the station, so some of the biggest eyesores were fixed, but some of the magic had been lost, forever. It was this station that Mark and I stepped into, our bags slung over our shoulders and my still unfamiliar feeling wedding band pressing into my left ring finger from where he and I were holding hands. "You know, that's the first time I've ever ridden the train cross-country," I said as we walked through the main hall. "It was a lot of fun."

Mark grinned. "Considering that we used the *ka-tan-ka-tun* of the wheels to such good effect, I agree."

I blushed lightly and slapped his chest, earning a wistful look from a housewife who could obviously see how much we were in love. Mark was right, however. We had used the rhythm of the wheels and the bed in the sleeper car to very good effect.

"Actually, I was thinking of your little karaoke session in the dining car last night."

It was Mark's turn to blush. The night before, after dinner had been cleared away, an informal karaoke session had broken out on the train. I could understand. For a lot of the passengers, it was still early in the evening, and Amtrak doesn't put televisions or Internet on those sleeper cars. For the passengers who hadn't paid for a sleeper car, it was even worse, as they could only look forward to an evening in a seat not much more comfortable than the type you get on an airliner. The dining car, at least, offered some space to try and stretch your arms and legs, and talk to other people.

I don't know who had started the session, but it built up quite a little crowd, maybe about a dozen or more. The dining car actually did have a sound system with instrumental music, so the bartender helped out by letting us select tracks from the three CDs.

The highlight for me, however, was when during a lull, Mark got up from our little chairs and sat down on the bar stool. The group quieted down, curious as Mark waved the bartender off.

"It's been a while since I did a lot of singing, but I'll try my best," he said, before clearing his throat. With his new identity, he was letting more of his soft natural Southern into his speech patterns again, and smiled. "*A long, long time ago, I can still remember, how that music used to make me smile....*"

I don't really know if Mark made any mistakes in the lyrics of the old Don McLean song, but I do know that his resonant voice filled the car with music, as another patron, a older black man who looked like he had grown up in the Motown do-wop era, backed him up with a pretty good imitation of the music using just his voice and tapping his table. By the final round of the chorus, most of us were singing along, and the whole group applauded at the end.

"I just felt like singing," Mark deflected, his blush deepening as I grinned at him. Mark was very, very cute when he was embarrassed. "Come on, we need to catch a bus."

To give at least a veneer of appearance to our re-entering the city, Mark and I were officially staying at one of the buildings that Mark owned in the city. The small efficiency apartment was smaller than even the one I'd had when I was a medical student, but it worked for the few days we needed. "So do you think Tabby will be surprised with our present?"

"Of course. I'm still giddy about it myself. By the way, once we get this all settled, we're finding you a doctor for your first check-up. You may be trained, and I know you're healthy, but I'm not taking any chances."

Smiling, I came over to the bed where Mark was sitting and took his face in my hands, kissing him on the nose, then on the lips, then on the nose again. "You, my dear husband, are going to be the best father in the whole damn world."

We held each other for a few minutes, just enjoying the closeness, not needing anything else. Finally, I let go. "Come on, let's call Tabby, and set up our job interview."

The next day, both of us felt weird dressed in off the rack "business clothes" that we had just bought that morning, walking up towards Mount Zion from the closest bus stop. We were glad to see that the press media were no longer camped out front. While my appearance was different enough that most people wouldn't mistake me for Sophie Warbird, Mark's build and face couldn't be disguised, even with two days' growth of stubble on it. We'd considered some more drastic options for changing his appearance, but first we had some things to do.

Knocking on the front door, I could see in Mark's eyes the trepidation, which helped me. Regardless of whether it was a real job interview or not, there was something about the whole thing that felt real. Maybe you never get past that feeling, I don't know for sure.

When Tabby opened the door, it was hard for the three of us to carry on with the charade just in case someone was watching. "Please, come in," she said, holding the door open for us as we walked in. As soon as the door was closed however, all pretenses were dropped and she grabbed both of us in a hug. "God I missed you both! How was your trip?"

I showed Tabby my wedding band, upon which she grabbed both my hands and started hopping up and down like an overly excited preschooler. "Oh, I'm so happy!" she almost yelled, pulling me in for another hug. "I only wish I could have been there. I mean, I assumed when you said the two of you were going to be stopping by Las Vegas before coming back, but still, this is awesome. Really awesome."

"I know, but we have pictures and video of the whole thing if you want to watch," I said, prying her arms from around my neck. "I promise. Also, we brought you a gift."

"Ooooh. You didn't happen to bring me some decks of cards from the Mirage or something, did you?"

"No, but we thought you might like this," Mark said, handing over the small gift box.

"What is it? A pen?" Tabby asked, taking the case. I could understand her confusion, the case had originally belonged to a Mont Blanc pen set in fact, and we had those pens set aside as well if she wanted them.

"Open it and find out," I said, trying hard to not grin like a fool. Tabby opened the the small case, her eyes puzzled for a second before she realized what the little device inside said. "Oh my God. Really?"

"Read the note underneath," I said, letting the smile come out. "It's for you."

Tabby took the test, which had a big pink plus sign on the side of it, out and looked at the folded note underneath. *Hi Tabby! I'm looking forward to meeting you! Will you be my Auntie?*

"Oh hell yeah," Tabby said, before closing the case. Tear glittered in her eyes. "Okay, well, I guess I can hire the two of you then. Come on, we have some video magic to do and you've got some other things I know you need to do."

The video magic was actually pretty simple. Mark, using a quick temporary color dye to shift his hair back to what Marcus Smiley had, along with a shower and shave, filmed a quick ten minute video in front of a green screen in which he announced the forming of MJT Consolidated Holdings which would be a subsidiary of the overall Smiley operations. Since Marcus wouldn't be able to oversee the day to day operations, he was vesting full corporate powers with Tabitha Williams, naming her as President and CEO of MJT, while he and Sophie Warbird would have advisory roles with the company.

A bit of video magic later, and it looked like Marcus was making the speech from inside a tropical hotel room. That, combined with the paperwork we had already filed, would totally pave the way for Tabby to take over.

"Now just a few more things to do," Mark said, taking off his Marcus Smiley suit coat. It, along with most of his Marcus Smiley clothes, were going to be donated through MJT to a shelter for disadvantaged people who needed a hand in outfitting themselves for job interviews. Tabby herself would be making the delivery that day, and the press conference announcing her hiring would be the next day. If things went according to plan, Marcus Smiley and MJT would be very small news.

Chapter 52
Mark

While I'd done it before, breaking into a Federal building always made my palms sweat. In addition to the fact that most of them operated twenty four hours a day, the pure fact was that the FBI, the NSA, and quite a few other members of the alphabet soup that is Federal law enforcement had their fingers in the pie. With none of them really trusting the others, everyone in the Federal building had sphincters that were water tight, which meant that there was always the chance that some security measure I hadn't expected could trip me up.

Oh, and let's not add the fact that quite a few people in there carried guns and weren't afraid to use them. So as I worked my way down the air conditioning vent, I kept my eyes open. Thankfully, the Federal Prosecutor's office wasn't quite as locked up as, say, the ATF offices on the fourth floor.

Creeping along, I used the small smartphone strapped to my forearm both as a flashlight and a guide. Bennie Fernandez didn't have his own office, but instead shared one with two other Federal prosecutors. Looking through the grate, I saw that nobody was there, which I had hoped for. It was midnight, after all, and none of them were on any high powered cases at the moment. If Bennie was half as smart as I thought, that would change.

I eased the vent cover out, dropping to the ground softly. I'd taken no chances, if there were any video surveillance, they wouldn't see me. I'd gone the whole face mask route. Taking the envelope with a letter and dual flash cards out of my vest pocket, I taped it to the monitor of his computer, his name written on it in block letters in black magic marker. My delivery complete, I made my way out the same way I came in, emerging on the roof just as my phone buzzed, telling me it was one in the morning. Time to make a phone call.

Sure, it isn't exactly polite to call someone's house at one in the morning, especially someone like Bennie Fernandez with a wife and young baby at home. But this time I think it was worth it.

"Hello?" a sleepy man's voice said once the call was picked up. "You know what time it is?"

"I've been told you're an honest prosecutor," I said. I was using a scrambler to disguise my voice, although I was still pitching it in such a way that it would be different from my normal voice. Okay, so a computer could match certain things, but you'd be surprised how many people are fooled when you just try to talk like James Earl Jones as Darth Vader. "Is that true?"

"Who is this?" Fernandez replied, his voice sharpening immediately.

"Relax, Mr. Fernandez, I'm a friend," I replied. "I ask because I just left a little present for you taped to the monitor of your computer in your office. Nice desk, by the way, but I'd get rid of the Patriots coffee cup. At least in this town." I added the little tidbit to convince him I'd been there. The cup wasn't actually on his desk, but on a small bookshelf next to his desk, right next to a copy of the Abridged Federal Rules of Evidence. "There's two data cards and a note. Go ahead and have them verified if you want, but keep one for yourself."

"Why?"

Instead of answering, I asked another question. "I asked you earlier if you were honest. I have another one. Do you have any guts, Mr. Fernandez. Any *cojones*?"

Bennie Fernandez may have been a well educated Federal prosecutor, but he was still Latin at heart, and calling a Latin man's balls into question is going to get a reaction, regardless of who it is. "Give me a chance, and you'll find out."

"Good. Because if you do have guts, then you're going to make a career. I'm going to give you a name. Owen Lynch. Have a good evening, Mr. Fernandez."

I hung up, then put the phone on the roof before bringing my boot heel down on the phone, shattering it before I pulled the battery. I'd throw the whole thing into the ocean later, but I had another delivery to make before the night was up.

* * *

Louis the Frog, despite being the second most powerful man in Sal Giodano's crime syndicate, lived like a poor man. I had never understood why, although I could understand why he lived alone. He was the closest thing I'd seen outside of fiction to a true sociopath. It wasn't that he didn't have a code that he lived by, just that his rules were almost the antithesis of what every other person lived by.

He was loyal to only one man, Sal himself. Other than that, dealing with Louis was kind of like fucking around with a jar of nitroglycerin or maybe nerve gas. One wrong move, and you just might end up dead. He'd killed plenty of people, far more than I had, and had no rules at all as to who he killed. Man, woman, child, innocent or guilty, he didn't give a damn.

The scariest part about Louis though was that he was smart, smarter than a lot of people gave him credit for. They were so intimidated by his propensity for violence that they overlooked just how smart he was. While Sophie often called me a genius for what I'd been able to pick up through just the Internet and my own thinking in terms of business, I think Louis may have been even smarter than me. He just wasn't interested in legitimate business, but instead in making Sal Giordano the most powerful man in the city. Why, I never did figure out.

Louis and I had, for the most part, a respectful relationship prior to the time he'd visited my old Mark Snow apartment. Part of it was that I gave Louis the right amount of respect, which mainly meant I never lowered my guard around him. For his part, Louis recognized that I knew he was dangerous, and I was a touch faster and perhaps more skilled than he was.

So I guess that Louis living in a cheap hotel room made perfect sense, in his own way. The hotel, one of those down on your luck places that catered to illegal aliens that would cram a family of eight into a two person room, desperate to make a new future for themselves in a new country. I had to respect them, considering the guts it took. Or just down on your luck losers who usually checked out via gunshot or hanging rather than by credit card,. The hotel took payment in cash only, paid a week in advance.

Louis had what I guess you could call the penthouse, if a flop house like that could have anything that could be considered a penthouse. The top floor, due to the manager's apartment being next door, had fewer rooms which were just a little bit larger than the normal spots. Still, the bed was sagging, and the walls rattled with the scratching and clawing of rodents as I stepped through the window. I was quite sure that below me, in the rooms below, there were more than a few mothers who were engaged in their nightly battles with the rats and the cockroaches to keep them from feasting on their babies.

To be honest, I was tempted to burn the whole damn place down after pulling the fire alarm. The only thing stopping me was I knew that for many of the other residents of the hotel, the only other option was living on the streets, or in the netherworld of the homeless that congregated in the storm drains and sewers. I'd been down there on missions for Sal, and I never wanted to go there again. It was the sort of place you carried a gun for protection from the wildlife, or at the minimum a machete.

If Louis the Frog had one indulgence, it was scotch whiskey. He was practically a connoisseur, and had in fact gathered bottles from every medal winning producer, from Scotland to North America to the more recent Japanese winners. Still, he had a favorite, forty year old Glenfarclas Scotch at over four hundred dollars a bottle. A single malt, he had once told me in an unexpected moment of introspection that he never went to bed without having a glass.

I found his bottle, which was only had a few shots left in it. Perfect, I didn't want somebody killing themselves by accident after Louis.

Taking the vial from my small pack, I emptied the contents into the scotch. I had crafted it from some of the nastier little tricks that I had been taught during my so-called education as a hitman, and knew that the flavor of the Glenfarclas would cover the chemicals I had used. The poison itself was totally colorless and odorless. I had, in fact, learned the basic recipe from a Japanese teacher of mine, whose family had developed it for mixing into Japanese *shochu* rice wine during the feudal period. With a few tweaks, I'd made it more powerful, and knew that as soon as Louis took even a small drink, he'd be counting the minutes to his death. There was no cure.

Still, I wanted to make sure, so I took up a position on the roof across the street. Using a periscope, I was able to see Louis' room while still staying behind the low brick wall that ringed the roof. I stayed there for hours, making sure to move around enough to keep myself from getting stiff, as the night wore on. Louis was a night owl for sure, and it was nearly three before he came home.

He was dressed in his trademark coat and fedora, which kind of made him look something like a comic book character or something. He just needed to wear crimson lensed glasses and be bald to really cross the line from frightening to nightmare inducing, in my opinion.

Taking off his coat, he hung it up on the hook behind his door along with his hat, rolling his shoulders. Without taking off his jacket, he immediately went to his scotch, pouring himself half a tumbler, no ice. I watched, a grim smile on my face as he tossed it back in two swallows, sealing his fate. Finding his bottle empty, he went to his cabinet and pulled another out. He cracked the seal and was pouring himself another tumbler before the first tremors hit his hand, and the rim of the bottle chattered against the glass.

Louis set the bottle down and looked at his hand, before looking down at his feet, which I was sure were also tingling and losing sensation. Staggering back, Louis tried to go to the door of his place, but his legs lost all feeling before he could reach the knob, and he collapsed on the floor. I turned away, not needing to see anything else. Reaching into my pocket, I pulled out my old cell phone, the one that Mark Snow had used, and dialed a number I hadn't used in a very, very long time.

As I expected, it kicked immediately to voicemail. "Sal, it's the Snowman. I think you and I should talk. How about the Park near the duck pond like last time? This time though Sal, you come alone. I see anyone with you, or even suspect it, and you'll be sitting on that park bench when the cops come to arrest you. You do, and we'll have a chat, and then go our separate ways. You have my word. I'll see you for lunch at noon."

Hanging up, I checked my periscope one last time. Louis lie on the floor, not moving. I knew from descriptions that the poison was supposed to be relatively painless, and that after losing control of his limbs Louis would have felt a creeping numbness spread throughout his body. While he would have been awake the whole time, in my opinion it was a gift for a man as evil as him to die the way he did. He'd done far worse to others.

Chapter 53
Mark

The duck pond was as quiet as it had been the day that Sal had told me I had to kill Sophie. I'd observed the bench for thirty minutes, since before Sal had arrived. He had followed my instructions, arriving alone with no bodyguards.

It was amazing how much a year could change a man. When I'd last laid eyes on Sal, he had been healthy looking, even if he had been older. His clothes had fit him well, although the stomach of his shirts swelled out a bit much for a man of his age.

A little over a year later, his pants hung baggy on his hips, and his shoulders were stooped and broken. His weight loss had been rapid too, from the jowly, hangdog way it looked on him. If I had to guess, most of it had come in the past six weeks or so. He looked like a sick man.

Making my way across the short distance between us, I kept my jacket collar turned up and my baseball cap on. I wasn't wearing sunglasses, but it didn't matter. In my left hand I carried a bag from Burger King, and my right was tucked in my pocket. For all the world I looked like a man just going to have some lunch by the duck pond.

"Hello, Sal."

Sal almost jumped out of his skin, and I knew in an instant his empire was crushed. The early daytime news had been filled with movements on all sorts of fronts. Bennie Fernandez was even more ambitious than I'd thought. Not only had the FBI already arrested Owen Lynch, as well as brought in over two dozen members of the city's police department for questioning, but members of the ATF, the FBI, and the state police had swept through much of the Confederation as well. Hell, even the IRS was getting a piece of the action, and once those buzzards were in on you, it was just a matter of time. I'd planned on them, at least, and was as secure as I could be.

"Hello, Marco. Well, as you can see, I'm here."

I sat down next to Sal and looked out on the pond. "You know why I did all this, don't you Sal?"

Sal nodded sadly. "I knew that the day would come where I'd be having a conversation like this with someone, Marco. I didn't think it would be you, honestly, nor did I think you would do as much damage as you have. Can I ask you something?"

"Of course. Like I said, we're here to talk."

"Was all of this because of the girl? The one that I sent those men after?"

I shook my head, and opened the bag. Sal flinched as I reached inside, but relaxed when I pulled out two Double Whoppers with cheese and bacon. I offered both of them to Sal, who took one, then waited for me to unwrap the other and take a bite. "Don't worry Sal, it's clean," I said, chewing my lunch. "If I wanted to kill you, I wouldn't do it the same way I did Louis this morning."

Sal shook his head and took a bite of his Whopper. "I suspected it was you. The timing was too close to the time he died. Hey, how'd you pull of Petrokias? His shooting was too close to Han's for you to do it, and the clerk said you weren't there. Just a girl."

"I've had help, I'm sure you suspected."

Sal nodded and took another bite of his meal. "She really that good?"

"Better, even. She's a better person than I am, that's for sure."

We watched the ducks for a while, both of us finishing our burgers before I shared out Cokes and fries. Sal sighed, thinking. "I guess an apology is useless right now, isn't it?"

"A little late in coming."

"Marco, when I said 'was it all about this girl', you shook your head. What else?"

I took a sip of my soda and looked over at Sal. "I've always hated you, Sal. I respected you but I hated you, too. Not that I blame you, my father would have most likely ruined his life regardless of if it had been in your card games, or maybe Faoxin's father's gambling dens, or if he'd gone down to Atlantic City and done it legally. But he did it in your places, Sal. So as much as he screwed up, you get a good portion of my hate as well."

For the first time ever, I think I actually hurt Sal's feelings. Betrayal he could understand, even the killing of the other Confederation members. But to know that I hated him was somehow too much. The old man gaped, tears forming in his eyes, and he set the rest of his French fries aside. His throat worked, and he blinked a few times before looking out at the duck pond. "So what now, Marco?"

"You have a choice, Sal. The Feds might be kicking down your door any day now. Even I'm surprised at how fast this Fernandez guy is sweeping through down at DOJ. So, you can sit back and enjoy the last few hours with your family before they drag you off to prison."

"Or?"

"Sal, I said I hated you, and that was no lie. But I've met your family. Your granddaughters don't deserve the hell this could be. Your children neither. You did that part right at least."

I saw a tear trickle down Sal's face, and he nodded his thanks silently. "Look in the bag, Sal. Inside you'll find something you could use. Let's face it, if you're dead, the DOJ is going to let it go. They're going to be too busy dealing with the living to worry too much about the dead. I assume you've hidden at least some of your assets out of their sight?"

"Yes. Not all of it, but about three million in what they'll think are life insurances. Tell me Marco, will it hurt?"

I shook my head. "Not much. If the coroner doesn't look very carefully, he won't even suspect a thing."

Sal nodded, and looked over at me. "Thank you, Marco. And for what it's worth, I'm sorry. I'm sorry it came to all this."

"Me too, Sal." I handed him the bag, then dusted off my hands and got up. "Go easy, Sal."

"Have a good life, Marco."

I walked away, not turning back as I heard the brown paper sack open up. I walked to the end of the duck pond, before turning and taking some crackers out of my pocket, feeding the ducks while watching Sal. He saw me, and nodded once before putting the two white tablets into his mouth and taking a sip of his soda to wash them down. I finished my crackers and walked away, Sal still sitting on the bench.

"Good bye, Sal."

* * *

Sophie

As Mark had planned, the news that Tabby Williams was taking over as head of MJT was lost in the chaos that was the news that day. For the next week, about the only thing that got more attention on the local news was the NFL highlights on Sunday night. Still, within three weeks, enough other local news had happened that Owen Lynch's face wasn't on the news every night.

While all that was happening, Tabby had kept herself busy, modernizing and taking the bare bones second floor office that Mark and I had used to something that actually was worthy of a real company. She hired staff, and even had a secretary.

Her transition was admirable. The first time she was mentioned by herself in a news story, the reporter had even made the comment that Tabby was a perfect blend between Marcus and Sophie Warbird. "Beautiful and brainy, in this reporter's opinion, MJT is in good hands. Kudos to Marcus Smiley, wherever he is enjoying his retirement."

In many ways, we were. During the day, we would take care of Mount Zion, with Mark saying his favorite thing to do was mow the lawn on the large riding tractor that Tabby bought for him for just that purpose. When he "accidentally" got cut on his temple and leaving an impressive scar that sort of pulled the corner of his right eyebrow upward a few degrees, I calmly bandaged him up while he sat in the kitchen. Afterward, it was enough of a change that we both agreed he didn't need another.

In the evenings and at night, the three of us had our own little family. Tabby insisted on finding a doctor who made house calls, so that she could be there for at least some of my prenatal appointments, and in the afternoons and evenings when she came home the three of us got the real work for MJT done.

The only real surprise came about two months after the body of Salvatore Giordano, a grandfather and suspected head of the crime syndicate known as the Confederation, was found dead of an apparent stroke near the duck ponds in the park. I was washing up the dishes, and Mark was in the home office reviewing some of the paperwork Tabby had left for him when the doorbell rang. Being the middle of the day, Mark checked the door suspiciously. We hadn't expected any deliveries.

"Hello, can I help you?" Mark said, opening the door. The man standing outside was wearing what I could tell was a decent but still off the rack business suit, and was Latino, maybe about thirty five or forty years old.

"Hi, I'm Bernard Fernandez, of the Department of Justice," the man said, "tell me, is Miss Williams around?"

"No, she's at work right now," Mark replied. I set down the plate I was washing, wiped my hands, and joined them at the door. "Is there anything I can help you with, Mr. Fernandez?"

"I've been working a case recently, I'm sure you've seen it on the news. You mind if I ask you guys a few questions?"

"Not at all, please come on in," Mark said. It was safe. After all, the main part of the house was cleaned of anything involving our activities involving Mark's history. "Would you like a drink, Mr. Fernandez? And yes, my wife and I have seen you a lot on the television. How is your investigation going?"

"We'll see how it plays out," Fernandez replied, playing it cool. "By the way, can I have your names?"

"Sure, I'm Matt Bylur," Mark replied, "and this is my wife Joanna."

"Hi," I said, holding out my hand. Fernandez shook, then shook hands with Mark. "So would you like a drink? Sorry if I missed what you said."

"No, I only have a few minutes, I'm due at the federal courthouse in forty five minutes," he replied with an easy smile. "It was just, in the course of the investigation, Miss Williams' name came up. One of the businesses we got details on was an HVAC contractor. When we questioned the owner, well, there were some interesting things he had to say. Something about his son being brainwashed, and someone that he and a few of the others called the Snowman."

"The Snowman? Sounds like a nickname to me, I hope," Mark replied, his voice calm. I kept my own cool, even though on the inside my heart was trip-hammering in my chest. "What's this have to do with Miss Williams?"

"Well, when we questioned a Scott Pressman, the owner's son, he said that he was told by this Snowman that he worked with Miss Williams, and that she was under his protection. Tell me, how long have you worked for your boss?"

"Only just over six weeks now," I replied. "We came to the city just before this whole scandal broke. Let me tell you, it is not a good way to be introduced to the city where you want to raise your family, Mr. Fernandez. Corrupt politicians, dirty cops, and gangsters all over the place? Yeah, I was a little worried at first."

"I understand. I have a son myself, so I can understand your concerns. How far along are you, Mrs. Bylur?"

"Joanna, please. And I'm just about two months along."

"Ah. Hoping for a boy or girl?"

"We're split, really. I keep hoping for a little girl, I think Matt is secretly wishing for a boy, even though he says he's happy either way."

Fernandez chuckled and nodded. "I was the same way. Guess I got lucky. In any case, we just wondered if Miss Williams could help us with identifying this Snowman character. It's not a major issue if she can't, but I'd like to be ready in case the defense tries to pin all of this on some sort of gangland ghost."

"I see. Unfortunately we can't help you, but I'm sure if you call Miss Williams at MJT, she'll be happy to make an appointment for you two to chat," Mark said. "I have one of her business cards around here somewhere, she told us to give them to anyone who stops by."

"Oh, that'd be great," Fernandez said. Mark went and got one of the MJT cards from the magnet clip on the fridge, coming back a moment later. Handing it over, Fernandez took a look before tucking it into his suit inner pocket. "Thanks. You know, down at the office, we're kind of having a pool as to if this Snowman is real or not. Some of the guys think he was, some of them think he's just a figment of the Confederation's imagination, a boogeyman created to pin all their bad luck on. Me, I have no view either way. I will tell you one thing, though."

"What's that?" Mark said, still calm and collected.

Fernandez got up and buttoned his jacket. "If even half of what I hear is true, he did a lot to help me out. And if everything they say about him is true... well, I know there's some things in his past that have to be accounted for, but I'm not the man to do so. My office is concerned with making this a better city, not an urban legend. Hell, if I had the chance, I'd probably shake the man's hand, I don't think I'd have gotten a start on this investigation if it weren't for him. In any case, I'm due at the courthouse. Judge Carter might be a good judge, but she eats late attorneys for lunch, regardless of which side they're on. It was nice meeting you guys, I'll give Miss Williams a call later."

Fernandez walked to the door, and Mark opened it for him. He walked out, turning at the door to offer his hand to me again. We shook quickly, and then Mr. Fernandez held out his hand to Mark. "Thank you, Mr. Bylur," he said, a small smile on his face. "For everything."

Mark shook his hand, his own smile coming out. "Any time, Mr. Fernandez. It was good to meet you."

Fernandez nodded and turned around, leaving. After he got into his government Chevy and pulled away, I turned to Mark. "You think he knows?"

"He suspects," Mark said, "but he's not going to do anything. He knows that, at least in this city, sometimes justice takes indirect methods, sometimes."

I nodded, and we closed the door, going back inside. Mark got his phone and sent a text message to Tabby, telling her what had happened, then set it down. "So are you going to go on patrol tonight?" I asked as Mark headed back to the office. "It's been a few days."

"I might," Mark replied, stopping at the door. "After all, our baby's coming, and the city's not clean..... yet."

The End…

There is now a Book Two of Mr. Dark -- Ambition: Mr. Dark Book 2! Tabby and her new love interest, Patrick, are the main characters. However, Mark and Sophie of course are back and still kicking ass!

Also By Lauren Landish

Blitzed: A Secret Baby Romance
Relentless: A Bad Boy Romance
Off Limits: A Bad Boy Romance
Mr. Dark: An Alpha Billionaire Romance

See all my books at www.LaurenLandish.com

Manufactured by Amazon.ca
Bolton, ON